John Alexander Joyce

A Checkered Life

John Alexander Joyce

A Checkered Life

ISBN/EAN: 9783337055134

Printed in Europe, USA, Canada, Australia, Japan

Cover: Foto ©Raphael Reischuk / pixelio.de

More available books at **www.hansebooks.com**

A CHECKERED LIFE.

BY

COL. JOHN A. JOYCE.

—

"There's a divinity that shapes our ends, rough hew them how we may."
—*Shakespeare.*
"Variety is the very spice of life, that gives it all its flavor."
—*Cowper.*
"Homo sum et nil humanum a me alienum puto."
—*Terence.*

CHICAGO:
S. P. ROUNDS, JR., 175 Monroe Street.
1883.

INDEX.

CHAPTER XXIX.

CHAPTER XXX.

POETIC WAIFS.

PREFACE.

There is no human life without its lesson. Every bud that grows gives promise of leaf and fruit; every wind wafted over the ocean of life brings pleasure or pain to some heart.

Providence has visited me with a variety of misfortunes, yet like Job I have borne the trials without complaint, and with fortitude waited silently for redemption and peace.

This volume is true from beginning to end; and shows the milestones of a human life that may guide some pilgrim around the quicksands I encountered.

The world has misunderstood me in the past; and now, after eight years of silence, I give for my family, friends and generous hearts, the whole truth of a checkered life.

The detailed history of the 24th Kentucky Union Regiment, from Lexington, Shiloh, Perryville, Nashville, Knoxville, Kenesaw Mountain and Atlanta is given in full from daily memoranda made by a soldier who saw and felt the weariness of march and shock of battle.

Thousands of living mortals can testify to the veracity of my statements.

Seldom has a man of forty run the gauntlet of waif, scholar, lunatic, soldier, schoolmaster, poet, politician, orator, lawyer, prisoner and patriot.

He that runs may read, ponder, and beware.

J. A. J.

DEDICATION

I · dedicate · all · that · is · good · and · noble
in · this · book · to · my · wife, · who, · through
the · storms · of · misfortune · never · faltered
in · her · love · and · duty. · ✳ · In · peace · and
prosperity · she · was · genial · and · kind, · and
in · the · chilling · blasts · of · adversity · she
faced · trouble · with · heroic · calmness · and
fortitude.

CHECKERED LIFE.

A CHECKERED LIFE.

CHAPTER I.

BIRTH-PLACE AND ANCESTRY.

My father was the youngest of seven children. He was the favorite of his mother, and his nature was more generous than that of any other member of the family. At the early age of seventeen he became a husband, running away from school with my mother, who was only fourteen years old. They had known each other from childhood, separated only by a salmon stream that ran by the village of Shraugh, near Westport, on the western shore of Ireland.

The parents of my father were dead when the runaway match occurred, and as the old stone house in the village remained in charge of the youngest son and sister, the newly fledged couple immediately began the cares of married life in the old home. A small holding of land, a horse, cow, sheep, pigs and poultry constituted their worldly wealth; and with a heart as light as the mountain air my father tilled the soil, tended his flocks, and drew upon the river and sea for luxuries to supply his humble board. The village acknowledged him a leader in whatever he undertook, and although his youth and wayward nature aroused opposition, the old people would listen to his counsel and act upon his judgment. He had a good education for the time. What he lacked in the embellishment

of scholastic arts he made up in natural attainments culled
from the winding road of observation. When the labors of
the day were ended, he wandered into the mountain wilds to
enjoy a dash after salmon, in defiance of landlord laws that
put an embargo upon what God and nature intended for toil-
ing man. The beasts of the field, the birds of the air, and
the fishes of the sea were registered by English laws for the
benefit of a few petty tyrants, while the glorious sons of labor
were denied everything that improved and elevated their mental and physical condition. The dance and wake were attended to in proper form, while fights, foot-races and all feats of
strength never missed the presence of my father, who bore off
laurels in many hard contested struggles for village honors.
Thus the days and months went by until the 4th of July, 1842,
ushered into life your humble servant.

My mother was not quite fifteen years old when I was born.
She had fair hair, bright blue eyes, a rounded form, and could
dance and sing with the gayest girls in the village. Mother
and father have long since passed into eternity, where I soon
shall join them in the realms of the majority.

CHAPTER II.

SCHOOL-BOY DAYS.

In the year 1846 my father emigrated to America to seek amid the wilds of a new world that peace, prosperity and equality denied him in the land of his birth. Soon afterwards my mother, brother Thomas and myself picked up our worldly goods, bid a hearty good-bye to weeping relatives and friends, and embarked for the long voyage across the Atlantic to the port of New York. We joined my father near Saratoga, where he was engaged in the building of a railroad to Whitehall. Our cottage was very humble, situated on the skirt of a pine wood, overlooking a wild stream that roared incessantly to the sighing melody of tall trees that lined its banks. Winter soon set in. I remember the village of Gansvoort as enveloped in a winding sheet of snow, and the country roads choked with extensive contributions from the realm of Jack Frost. The old forked stumps that fenced the highways reared their blackened arms above the snow, and impressed the beholder with a sense of loneliness. My young heart shuddered at the forbidding scene, and longed for the spring-time, when I was promised initiation into the village school. The King of the North at last released his cold grasp upon Dame Nature. The sleigh-bells ceased jingling, the ice in the river broke into fragments, the snow on the hills melted in the sunshine, the tall trees shook off their frozen jackets, the snowbirds flew away to the land of frost, the bluebirds came tuning up the orchestra of love, fluttering in the highways, and building their nests in secret spots of the forest; the green grass, forget-me-nots, violets and trailing arbutus peeped out, and seeing that

Jack Frost had departed, nodded their beautiful heads in loving unity, and with perfumed breath called in the delights of genial Spring.

In the spring of 1850 my parents moved from New York to Kentucky. We settled for a short time in Maysville, on the Ohio River, sixty miles north of Cincinnati, where my uncle presided as priest over the Catholic church. We moved to Mayslick in a few months, where my father had charge of the repairs of the Lexington pike. I went to school in the town, and afterwards in the country.

We went to Wheeling, Virginia, in the year 1851. I again entered school, where professors and rude boys led me a miserable life. In the basement of the old Catholic cathedral I learned the rudiments of education. Lindley Murray and his rules I could repeat as fast as rain pattering on a roof, but I am conscious even to this day that nouns, verbs, adverbs and conjunctions were simply a string of words to be remembered.

I remained about two years at the cathedral school. It was the purpose of some of my friends to fit me for the priesthood, and to this end I was initiated into the good graces of the ruling spirits of the church. Professor Park took a particular fancy to me, as did Fathers Brazell and Durnin. I was also made known to good old Bishop Whalan, who honored me with his friendship.

Late in the year 1854 my parents moved from Wheeling to Moundsville, twelve miles below, where the Baltimore & Ohio Railroad first touched the beautiful Ohio. The village is situated in a triangular valley, backed by high rolling hills, dotted with rare Indian mounds, and watered on the south-east by a trout stream, where bones from Indian graves protrude from the banks of the crooked stream. One of the largest mounds in America can be seen in this town, where gnarled oaks of centuries have grown and now bedeck the mausoleum of some buried tribe that lived, perhaps, before the American Indian crossed from Asia to this continent. Who were the mound-builders? Where did they come from, and why is there no written record to tell the story of their rise and fall? These questions are easily asked, but not to be truthfully answered by men of to-day. We find household implements and agricultural machines buried in the same mounds that hide mouldering bones, and stone, iron and golden instruments fashioned into beautiful and useful shapes, but no history of the brain that invented or the hand that manufactured them.

I re-entered school in the old brick seminary under the shadow of the great mound. Mr. Chattuck was the principal, and had taught in the town for more than thirty years. Many of the prominent citizens had been his pupils, and he was respected and loved by all.

I continued in school at Moundsville until vacation, but in the fall, from some unknown freak, left home to seek my fortune and see the world. For more than a year I became a wandering waif, working in hotels, stores and printing offices, and going from steamboat to steamboat in various capacities. On first leaving home I boarded the magnificent steamer, City of Wheeling, on one of her regular trips to Cincinnati, with but three dollars in my pocket. The pilot took me under his care, and promised if I remained with him to make a young boy into a first-class pilot.

Night after night I turned into my bunk tired, and often heartsick and lonely, thinking of home and absent friends. How I shivered those dark, cold, windy mornings, rushing along over the hurricane deck or crouched in the pilot-house! The strokes of the great paddle-wheels and the hoarse sigh of the tall escape-pipes echoing among the silent hills sent a thrill of mournful music through every fiber of my frame, and even now awakens memories of the long ago. One morning, standing on the stern of the boat, with none in view save the form of the pilot seen through the thick shadows of early dawn, I looked fondly upon the ghostlike waves that rolled in the track of the steamer, and almost longed to bury my sad soul in the troubled waters. I had about determined to commit suicide and blot out forever my troubles. Some kind voice lured me back to reason, when sunbeams flashed across the river, the feeling of despondency was gone, and I ran into the pilot-house to hold down the wheel while the pilot drank a cup of black coffee.

We arrived in due time at Cincinnati, where the boat lay two days discharging and receiving freight and passengers.

The night before the boat started up the river, George Pepper and myself went to Wood's museum, where I saw all kinds of curious things and heard some unearthly sounds. After the performance, in going to the boat, I became separated from the pilot, and wandered for some time about the silent city. Under the shadow of the Spencer House I paused to rest and think. The hour was midnight; fitful gusts of wind swept over the stony streets, and made wierd sounds around the gas lamps, the lights of which rose and fell like tapers in a sick-room. The sound of distant footfalls broke upon my ears, and then was hushed into silence. The policeman's club sent its startling echoes down the deserted streets to some fellow watcher. The clock in the tower struck twelve, and the re-sounding tones echoed among the walnut hills and over the placid river like an invitation to prayer when the host bells sound in grand cathedral aisles. The city slumbered in repose; love, beauty and confidence were pillowed in the soft embrace of sleep, and dreaming perchance of yon blue realm where hope leads on to eternal life. The good, true and wise rested from the labors of the day, while the bad, false and poor wandered over the earth like uneasy spirits wafted by every breeze that filled the night with solemn cadence, knowing not where to lay their weary heads or quiet their troubled hearts.

In this solemn hour I beheld a poor female waif approach from a line of empty store boxes that skirted the pavement, while a lean, hungry dog followed at her heels—perhaps the only friend she had on earth. In her arms she held an infant. and in her eye glistened the tear of pain and sorrow. Her look was pitiful and innocent, her flowing hair straggling in wild confusion down her ragged shoulders, and tossed about

by the chilly night wind. She could not have been more than
sixteen years old, yet the melancholy lines that marked her
sweet face gave her the appearance of twenty. The babe cried
from cold and hunger, and the youthful mother begged me for
assistance. I emptied my pockets of all they contained—
thirty-five cents—took off my coat and threw it over the shivering mother and child. I then found my way to the boat,
for the night was crisp and cool, found my bunk in the Texas,
and pondered painfully upon the vicissitudes and misfortunes
of this unjust world. That whole night I lay awake thinking
of the poor child of poverty and disgrace, who wandered an
outcast in the streets of a rich city while her betrayer slept
in silken couches, drank champagne, and laughed the hours
away in company with beautiful belles who rivalled each other
for his hand. Ah, girls, beware lest the fate of the poor waif
be yours! Libertinism has no line to mark its bounds, no
standard to measure its audacity, and no law to limit its terri-
rible consequences; but is ever seeking, plotting and betraying
the holiest sanctuaries of affection. Avoid it as an asp that
stings and kills! Like the Upas tree, the crime of the gay,
luxurious villian blights everything it touches, leaving nothing
but ruin in his blistering track. The spruce, smiling fraud
who kneels at your feet is the viper that stings when your innocent love warms him into confidence, and while pleading at
the altar of love, he is plotting for the violation of chastity.
The strong battlements of your womanhood are despoiled and
desecrated when the angel of love sleeps on guard. You
awaken like one out of some terrible dream, gazing about in
wild frenzy for the form of your honorable (?) lover, and find
he has vanished forever, leaving a broken heart and ruined
character, dashed down like some stately structure in a storm.

For more than a year I was employed as a pilot, going up
and down the Ohio and Mississippi rivers; and in the solemn
midnight hour, when all were wrapped in slumber—when the
stars sparkled in the river, the harvest moon made a pathway
on the water, and the hills answered back the laboring voice

of the roaring steamer—my poetic heart would drink in the romantic scene and soar into illimitable realms of fancy. The good, the beautiful and true always found a lodgment in my heart, and even when the world pursued me with the howl of bloodhounds I could smile and forgive the sordid crowd who follow in the wake of any success, or pounce like hungry wolves upon the prostrate form of some devoted victim. I pity the ignorant, unthinking rabble, and regard their efforts to torture with contempt, knowing that the wrong of yesterday may be the right of to-day; and when oblivion shall have swallowed up the common herd, I may live in some good word spoken in life.

One night on my way up the Ohio river, while meditating in the pilot-house, I determined to leave the life of a river rover and plunge into the interior of Kentucky, for the purpose of continuing my education. I told the pilot my intention, and asked him to let me off and allow me to draw the few dollars due. Arriving at Maysville, I stepped ashore with twenty dollars in my pocket, and proceeded out on the Flemingsburg pike, in the spring of 1856, to seek my fortune afoot and alone in the midst of strangers. I had an uncle living in Montgomery county, near Mt. Sterling, and it was my intention to work my way in that direction.

CHAPTER III.

SCHOOL IN MONTGOMERY COUNTY.

I remained awhile in Flemingsburg, Tilton and Owingsville, working in stores and on farms, traveling the pike occasionally from Maysville to Mount Sterling with Dick Wood and his brother, who hauled merchandise in the old "prairie schooners" that rattled away behind six-horse teams. The wagons had regular stopping places for the night, where the landlord of the wayside inn and his guests made merry until the moon went down. Sometimes a band of serenading darkies would lend their sweet voices to the midnight revel, winding up with "juber," or a rattling "hoe-down," to punctuate the party. Early in the morning, Wood, the captain of the creaking schooner, and myself took breakfast, paid the bill of Boniface, and drove out into the broad pike heading for the hills of Montgomery. Seated on the stout saddle-horse, I imagined myself once more at the steamboat wheel. The long check-rein whacked up the leader, and sent the whole team on a brisk trot down the winding grade to the music of a black-snake whip, its sharp notes resounding among the hills and vales of the "blue-grass land." Those happy, harmless days are gone forever, and with them the lumbering old wagons, stages and drivers, who were very important in their time— the mercantile community depending on the promptness and honesty of these common carriers. The white canvas tops of the wagons and the swinging form of the high-topped stages have been puffed out of existence by the snort of the iron horse, and these useful vehicles of long ago have gone to the grave with the old fogy who put a stone in his meal-sack to balance his grist of corn.

My uncle was surprised to see me at his door in search of friends and education. Near the turbid waters of Slate and the chalybeate spring on Spencer Creek an old log school-house stood on a hill-top surrounded by forest trees. Opening vistas showed cleared corn-fields, where bleached bodies of dead trees reared their toppling heads and ghostly arms. The old school-house may have long since gone to decay, and the new generation that climbs the hill over the rugged country road may give no thought to the wayside hall of learning, or call up memories of the old play-ground; yet in the inmost precincts of my heart I still retain the image of many boys and girls who shared with me their hopes, homes and affection.

> "Some are in the churchyard laid,
> Some sleep beneath the sea."

My teacher at this school was "Doc." Orear, a sensible country gentleman, whose parents owned a neighboring farm. I see the old mill near the school even now, tottering on the brink of the creek like a drunken man at a banquet. The rumble and roar of the rusty wheels, the mill-race, the dash of the water over the dam, the shriek of the kingfisher, hawk and carrion crow—all come back to me now like the tones of vanished music; and as memory lifts the curtain, I see the players and actors of long ago troop across the stage of life, tripping away to the realm of shadows.

Have you ever been at a country mill waiting your turn for the grist? It is, to the romantic mind, a picture of fascinating life. There may be like yourself a score waiting their turn. Some are pitching quoits in the "big road," others racing horses, running and jumping on the sand, telling yarns and exchanging farm gossip, while in a quiet nook under the crumbling timbers you behold a party of mathematical rustics playing fox and geese, checkers, mumblety-peg or jack-stones.

> And still the old mill grinds away,
> And surely totters to decay;
> But the waters gone down to the plain
> Will never come back to grind again!

The following extract from a letter to the *Mt. Sterling Democrat*, of April 29th, 1881, from Mexico, Mo., in response to some reminiscences of mine, will show that "Doc." Orear still cherishes the memory of his old pupil through the varnish of twenty-six years :

"I distinctly remember young Joyce—a bright, precocious lad with black hair and sparkling eyes—with what alacrity he came forward to recitations ; his prompt and ready answers ; and another lovely trait, beautiful in a pupil and highly appreciated by the teacher—his perfect politeness of feeling and action on all occasions ; and then his readiness at declamation and composition.

"I take pride that I had for a short time the training of so bright and naturally so good a mind ; and, what is strange, the the lady I afterwards married was also his teacher at the academy in the Gatewood district. Dear old pupil ! May your aspirations and hopes, with mine, be anchored close to the throne of the Great Eternal in the heavens, where in time we may strike hands on the other shore. Hoping to hear again from that ready pen, I subscribe myself his 'teacher of the old log school house.' "

Leaving the country school, I attended the Highland Academy at Mt. Sterling, presided over by a benevolent gentleman named James B. Crane. I had my school trials and triumphs, and looking back over my career with a retrospective glance, I see again the boys and girls. Dave Chenault, Tom Hoffman, Howard Barnes, Billy Barnes, Bob Bean, Bill Thompson, Bill Hanley, Luther Wilson, Jim Anderson, George Everet, Joe Wilkerson, Marion Peters, Tom Metcalf, Jim Carter, Tom Grubbs, Wes. Chenault, Davis Reed, Tom Wilson, Joe Jordan, John Tucker, Henry Jones, Jim Gatewood, Colie Apperson, Jim Spradling, Joe Cool, Landon Chiles and Jim Lee, if alive, may call to mind my first trial for kissing the girls. It was very ludicrous and funny. I had only been in the seminary three days when the girls found out I could sing comic and love songs. At noon most of the scholars went home to dinner, but as I lived a few miles in the country, I brought lunch to school, and made a silent meal amid the broken benches up stairs in the general recitation room. One particular day a number of girls surrounded my desk and insisted that I should sing. Among the dear creatures I remember Laura Mitchell, plump and intelligent; Mary Wells, willowy and keen; Kizzie Wright, sedate and sterling; Luckett Anderson, sprightly and fascinating; Hawes Owen, modest and benevolent; Laura Lindsey, vivacious and loving; Fannie Ragland, musical and handsome; Nettie Prewett, beautiful and aristocratic; Nannie Chenault, slender and sympathetic; Emma Gatewood, stately and kind; Mary Chiles, sensible and honest; Mat. Hazelrigg, bouncing and beaming; Dolly and Mary Carter, bubbling over with fun and frolic; and a number of other "blue grass" beauties, whose faces and fascinating smiles still linger in my memory. I sang until I was tired for the knot of budding beauties, and they still insisted, like little Oliver Twist, for "more." To add to my anxiety and grief, they upset my ink-bottle on the piece of bread I had partially eaten, and caused a flush of passion to rise in my heart. I could stand the raid of the girls no longer, and "went for them then and there." As the bevy dispersed about the benches, I raced after them with impetuous strides, kissing each one that fell into my grasp, causing a general retreat among the fair daughters of Montgomery, and an upheaval of indignation for my so-called audacity. School was soon after "taken in," and Mr. Crane, the Principal, called up to the bar of justice all who had been concerned in the row. Tom Metcalf and Dave Chenault were the main witnesses, giving their evidence in an unvarnished manner, which was rather favorable to me in the causes that led to the raid on the girls, as a retaliation for their persistency. The girls begged off with tears in their eyes and humiliation in every movement. After a full investigation, Mr. Crane decided that the girls were to blame in forcing me to sing, and in destroying my books and bread, and that I was the chief sin-ner who had the audacious boldness to kiss any girl without the consent of her parents! Therefore all must be punished. At this announcement, the girls sobbed violently and I stood like "patience on a monument smiling at grief." Mr. Crane produced a hickory ruler, smiled upon me blandly and asked what I had to say. I simply extended my hand, and with laconic indignation exclaimed: "Pitch in!" With a stern face he complied with my order, and at every stroke of the ruler insisted that I should be sorry for what I had done. But with that peverseness that characterized my conduct in later years I was not to be moved against my sense of justice, believing that I did right in dispersing the beautiful girls. I was finally sent to my seat, while the girls were left to their tears and prayers. The teacher did not have the heart to enforce his verdict, but as he had promised punishment all around, appealed to me in the premises. The girls looked towards my corner with anxious longing. As my punishment had been administered, theirs would not add to my pleasure, and I therefore said: "Let them go," which was done with great satisfaction to the parties interested in my funny school experience.

Perhaps many of the actors in the foregoing scenes will recall them with pleasure; and although long years cover up the plane of memory, some loving heart will go back with me to the old play-ground and live again amid the haunts that blessed our childhood.

Ah, the friends that we make in later years cannot be compared to the loved ones of sunny childhood, when the heart was light and pure, unbiased by the glitter of the mighty dollar! Even this moment I am walking in my day-dreams out Winchester pike, with the beautiful niece of Newton Congleton. By-paths, through blue grass woods intervene, spring birds sing sweeter than ever, scampering squirrels run up the great arms of red oaks and ash trees, casting sly glances, chirping and chattering a defiance, seeming to say, "Catch me if you can." Wild flowers bloom in every nook, trailing vines clamber up the trees, the morning sunshine bathes the woods in golden glory, and the white clouds floating on the bosom of the upper blue come and go like angel messengers.

I finished school at Mt. Sterling in June, 1859. In preparing for the examination and exhibition held at the old court-house, I studied so hard, night and day, that my mental and physical condition became deranged. The following chapter gives the strangest and most eventful period of my life—the insane milestone.

CHAPTER IV.

A DESCRIPTION OF LUNATIC FANCIES.

EASTERN KENTUCKY LUNATIC ASYLUM,
Lexington, Ky., June 12th, 1881.

COL. JOHN A. JOYCE, Washington, D. C.:

DEAR SIR:—The records of this Asylum show the following, to-wit:

No. 2423, John A. Joyce, Montgomery County, Ky.; native of Ireland; 18 years of age; single; occupation, farmer; Catholic; habits; temperate and industrious; original disposition and intellect good, excellent; cause, hereditary form; mania, hallucination, perpetual motion. Admitted June 26, 1860. Discharged September 1st, 1860. Recovered.

Respectfully,
W. A. BULLOCK, M. D.
Med. Sup't E. Ky. L. A.

It is a rare thing for a recovered lunatic to write the history of his own derangement. The foregoing letter, received recently, is the evidence of truth and identity. Science and skill in every age have struggled to master the manipulated brain of the maniac, and ascertain the cure for a diseased mind. The body, the tangible part of man, can be easily nursed back from a dying skeleton form to robust health, but the intangible, wild, spectral mind has no chains to bind its rushing pinions, and no cure to quiet the crumbling fabric of imagination.

The mind or soul of man is unfathomable, and no plummet has ever yet been found to touch the bottom of this universal ocean. A very large majority of lunatics emerge from hereditary mouldings. The father or mother are the source of lunatic beings, and actual begetting is the fountain-head of the long train of fearful troubles that follow in the wake of the insane mind. The action of a moment ushers millions of human beings into "this breathing world scarce half made up, and that so rude and unfashioned" that long years and the lonely grave can only obliterate the terrible torture that reigns forever in the memory of the maniac.

When I look over vanished years and count the milestones along my rugged road of life, I approach with fear the fiery pillar that lit up the glowing realms of my lost mind. I should not speak now upon this phase of my checkered career were it not that a sense of duty impels me to give my experience to the friends and relatives of lunatics, as well as to impress attendants and doctors having charge of the insane with a proper sense of their responsibility.

I say it without fear of medical contradiction, that a full-fledged lunatic was never cured by brutal force or unreasonable restraint. All human beings have minds as varied as their features, and meat for one is poison for another.

In the days of Galileo, Tasso and the Prisoner of Chillon, it was considered the correct thing to put the insane in a deep dungeon, chained to a stone pillar, shut out from the sunlight, with no music to cheer the weary hours of day or lonely moments of night save the clanking of their chains or the wild echoes of their melancholy moans.

> "His bread was such as captives' tears
> Have moistened many a thousand years,
> Since man first pent his fellow men
> Like brutes within an iron den."[1]

Things have changed but little since those cruel ancient days. In Europe, Asia, Africa and America, at this very hour, thousands of poor human creatures, lost to friends and memory, are languishing in madhouses and almshouses, tortured by ignorant attendants, encased in straight-jackets, pent up in padded rooms, doused in shivering baths and shower-chairs, strapped to iron cots, or tortured by the lash of some petty tyrant who imagines that brutal blows can subdue the

mind. Ah, friends, how very little doctors and their assist-
ants know about the cure for insanity! All the medical plat-
itudes ever written by so-called scientific gentlemen have not
touched the outer edge of the insane land. It is a *terra incog-
nita* to all save those who inhabit the realm.

The leaves that tremble in the forest, the sands that glisten
on the sea-shore, and the stars that twinkle in the blue vault
of heaven, multiplied by incalculable millions, cannot com-
pare with the various ideas that bubble up in the mind of the
maniac. Every human being with a grain of common sense
is liable to become crazy. A fool or an idiot cannot pene-
trate into the sacred land of the insane. The ancients wor-
shiped madmen, and they were held sacred by the enlightened
people of antiquity. They said, let no one dare abuse what
God has touched with his magic wand. The brightest minds
that have been ushered into life were touched by the spell
of insanity; and I might say that every great undertaking in
this world has been invented, discovered or conjured up by
the brain of a person who had the insanity of deep, unusual
thought, and the unfaltering mania of desperate perseverance.

From the foregoing general principles, I shall proceed directly to the specific facts, as intensely and distinctly remembered in my own case.

In the spring of 1860 a vivid flash of imagination shot
across my brain like zigzag lightning from a blue sky. I told
my father and uncle, who were then living near Mt. Sterling,
that I wished to take a course in bookkeeping at Duff's commercial college in Pittsburg, and to this end induced them to
give me a hundred dollars to start for the "smoky city." I
went to Cincinnati, and thence by boat to Pittsburg. On my
way up the river I had the wildest and strangest feelings about
life and the small, creeping human things that crawled over
the earth. The idea of running the world and the wheels of
traffic by *perpetual motion* sprang into my mind. I felt sure
that the real problem of life was solved—a force superior to
the attraction of gravitation! Newton and his falling apple

were but atoms in the great discovery of running things by
perpetually acting balances suspended like a see-saw plank on
a middle pivot throwing out living oil into the fibers of the
great machine, which was to run on the principle of the cir-
culation of the blood—one continuous round of circulating
force and fluid, beginning at the end and ending at the beginning !

Even now I believe the day is near at hand when the indus-
trial machinery of the world will be run perpetually by elec-
tricity extracted from the air we breathe, and that we shall
navigate the upper atmosphere with greater velocity and cer-
tainty than has ever been attained by man on land or sea.
The flight of the condor, eagle or wild pigeon cannot equal
the height and swiftness that man, in his wisdom, will yet
achieve.

It was midnight when I arrived at Pittsburg.   Instead of
remaining on the boat, I wandered out upon the levee, amid
piles of freight, coal and iron, that covered the banks of the
river.   About daylight I found myself in a modest hotel not
far from Duff's college.   After breakfast, with no sleep the
previous night, I saw Mr. Duff at his school.   If I remember
rightly, he used an ear-trumpet to assist his defective hearing.
I entered my name on the school-roll, purchased some preliminary books, and spent a few hours in writing up a common
day journal.   That night, on my return to the hotel, I felt
my mission to be the lecture-field or theatrical boards ; and as
a large number of mediocre people succeeded in these voca-
tions, there was no reason why a man of my imagined greatness should not at once " hire a hall," " surprise the natives,"
and scoop in a fortune in a night.

The very next day I went to a printing office, had some
bills struck off advertising an intellectual variety show at Lafayette Hall.   I even went to the trouble to have a tin box
made, wherein the doorkeeper might put the cash and tickets
received by him in the rush of the natives to hear the most
wonderful prodigy of the age ! That night I appeared on the

stage at Lafayette Hall, and with song, dance, poetry, oratory, and flights of lunatic fancy surprised the few stragglers who paid their money to see a living lunatic on the mimic stage of life.

Poor King Lear, with the dead Cordelia in his arms, crying for the vault of heaven to crack, was not more mad than I, instructing and amusing an audience in a public hall of a great city. The curtain was finally rung down, the lights turned out, and the bill-poster met me at the door to receive compensation for services rendered. I, like all great men, referred the plebian to my agent, the fellow who kept the tin box and its contents. To this day I have never learned the fate of the bill poster or the agent. There may be some citizens in the Pittsburg theatrical world who can call to mind the foregoing facts, and wonder and laugh at how they were taken in by a lunatic; yet I have no doubt that often since they have been the victims of men not half as honest and sincere as I was at that time.

I next turned up in Wheeling, wandering about the streets, and through the homes of former friends. From Wheeling I went to Moundsville, thence to Marietta, Ohio. While in Marietta I was taken up by some humane person, and placed in the county lunatic asylum. They put me in a small room with bars across the windows and strong bolts bracing the door. For the first time I was depvived of liberty; and my royal spirit realized the shock, and outraged nature turned with a bound and smashed everything intervening between it and freedom. Before being locked up, I was kind and harmless; but the loss of liberty worked my mind into a perfect frenzy, and aroused the very devil in my tortured brain. I would have smashed or killed anything coming between me and freedon, and well it was for the keeper that I was not allowed access to those whom I imagined were the authors of my incarceration. In fact, I was pent up in a small, hot room, like a wild beast, and outraged nature revolted at the cruel treatment.

In some way, my father found me. His good old face and soothing voice broke in upon my imprisoned spirit like a flash of sunshine. A calm came over my mind, and the murky clouds of despair vanished. In a short time I was dressed, out in the open fields, and on the road to Kentucky. I confidentially told my father, as we moved along, that I had discovered perpetual motion; and, what was more, that I had found the philosopher's stone, or the secret of turning pebbles of earth into gold! As an evidence of my wild fancy, I picked up a dark pebble, scratched it with a pin, when—lo! and behold— it turned to yellow gold!

Even at this day I can see the smile on the lip and the tear in the eye of my dear old father, who seemingly assented to my hallucination, and even flattered my vanity. It took no harsh treatment—no bolts, bars or straight-jackets—to hold my body. I followed the directions of my father like a sportive lamb, and every terror was banished from my heart by his kind words and consoling actions. Liberty, even in my insane mind, was fostered by love, and although the balance-wheel of understanding flew around without a governor, the soul yet lingered in its sphere, but could not control the insane impulses of the infinitessimal fibers of the volcanic brain.

In due time, we arrived at my home near Mt. Sterling. For a few days, I seemed to be recovering from the mania that pursued me, and when thrown among schoolmates and friends, gleams of sanity would come and go like wavelets on a summer sea. I wandered about town for some time; visited the old seminary—the former theatre of my intellectual triumphs, —and mingled with my old schoolmates. It soon became plain to all my friends that the lunatic asylum was the proper place for one of my deranged mind. With deep sorrow and mournful regrets, a jury was impanneled, an investigation took place, and I was in due form pronounced *non compos mentis.* and ordered sent to the Eastern Lunatic Asylum at Lexington. The next morning I mounted the stage-box with a keeper and friend, and rode over the Winchester pike, singing on the way with a heart as light as the mist on the mountains. I imagined that I had been elected to the legislature of Kentucky, and was on my way to Frankfort to make laws for a lot of crazy people in Montgomery county. When we arrived in Lexington, I was taken out to see what was pictured to me as the capitol of Kentucky, where I would, of course, shine as an orator and statesman of extraordinary ability.

The long red brick building, four stories high, with regular rows of windows, broke full upon my view as I entered the enclosure of the asylum. I immediately mounted the steps leading into the front hall, and strode the long corridors like a king familiar with his ancestral palace. The doctor and his attendants seemed very obsequious, and took me through various doors, halls and apartments, until at last I was snugly placed in one of the upper wards, where an iron cot, bare walls and barred windows convinced me in a momentary return to sanity that I was anything but a king. All the terrors of my Ohio den came back like a flash. I hammered at the door, yelled through the window at quiet lunatics on the lawn, upset my iron cot, tore the sheets into strips and made them into a rope, that I might escape imprisonment and descend to the grass, flowers and sunshine that covered the fields and gardens below.

My mind was so wild, and muscles so strong for a boy of eighteen, that it took half a dozen attendants to overpower and strap me down to an iron cot. In fact, I smashed things fearfully and tore off every garment from my body, in an imagined desperate fight for liberty, the sweetest and dearest thing on earth to the human heart, and especially to the insane mind. Of course, a lot of rough and brutal attendants overpowered my body, but they did not convince my mind nor quiet my voice against their terrible tyranny. No! the soul within was more defiant than ever, and no physical punishment could subdue the God-given mind or curb its flights.

I was finally taken out of the regular wards and put in a place called Botany Bay, at the end of the lawn, where the

maddest maniacs were consigned to straight-jackets, dungeons.
chains and the tortures of a living hell! Wild, horrible, unearthly shrieks sounded in my ears night and day, and all the
imps of pandemonium martialed in a fairy battalion could not
have made more clangor, to my mind. All was "like sweet
bells jangled out of tune." I was turned into an open vault-
room to parade with the rest of the animals, but soon the doctors and attendants learned that I was a royal Bengal tiger,
and would not herd with common beasts. I immediately put
to flight the biggest and wildest of the drove, and made them
cower before my imagined superiority. A big, burly attendant slipped up behind me, felled me to the floor, and dragged
me to a dark room, where I was chained to the wall, strapped
to a bare iron cot, punished and rebuked for a poor distorted
mind that God in His wisdom endowed me with.

I, myself, was not myself; but what was left of my independent self revolted at the ignorant and cruel treatment of
men who knew not that soul and liberty cannot be mastered,
curbed or confined. You may stripe and torture this frail
tenement of clay, but no cruel ingenuity of man has yet devised the means to harness the immortal mind.

The blow of the attendant rankled more in my heart than
on my body. I determined to be even with the ignorant
brute, and to this end cunningly prevailed on him to allow me
more freedom in the little cellar-room, and also implored the
doctors, when they visited me, to grant more liberty. Dr.
Chipley, the superintendent of the asylum, was an intelligent,
though rough-looking, gray-haired man. I imagined that he
was an uncle of the devil, and that the patients were all his
children. The Doctor, although curt, was innately kind; and
I am convinced now that many rude acts were done by the
attendants that did not come to his knowledge, else the man
who struck me would have been dismissed at once.

Dr. Dudley was the assistant—a man whose gentle words
and graceful action stole upon my affections like sunshine amid
opening flowers. I put him down as my friend, and would

take medicine from his hands when the proffered cup from attendants was considered rank poison. For weeks I was confined in a small basement room, with an upper grated window to admit light and air. My door was bolted, and food was poked through an aperture, as wild beasts are fed at a circus.

All was lonely and sad until I made friends of two little mice and a family of gray spiders that sought my cell for safety. Part of my daily food was set apart for the mice. At first they were very shy at my impulsive movements and shrieking voice, and would dart into their hole in the wall like a flash. But, finally, kindness begot confidence, confidence banished fear, and in a short time they ate from my hand, played on the cot, or danced around the room to a low musical trill that I whistled for their amusement. The big dark spiders would come out of their thick web and eat the flies I caught for their meal. Sometimes they would fight for their food; but like a metropolitan policeman, I came to the rescue when both were exhausted, and easily captured the combatants and separated them with a straw. Like a well-regulated housekeeper, the wife would soon go to work weaving a fine, brown garb around the innumerable eggs she laid, while the "old man" would spin long yarns up and down the wall, scampering over his growing web with the mathematical precision of a scientific surveyor. He was perfect in all his gossamer lines; and the octagonal shapes that seemingly grew out of his mouth and feet filled me with a nameless surprise. When the mice or the spiders heard footsteps at my door, they would immediately stop play or work and run into their holes, seeming to know that sane man was on his round of ignorance to minister to the insane. But what cared I for the cruelty of man?

> "With spiders I had friendship made,
> And watched them in their sullen trade;
> Had seen the mice by moonlight play,
> And why should I feel less than they?
> We were all inmates of one place,
> And I the monarch of each race."

I gradually gained the liberty of locomotion in my small room, and the attendant that knocked me down, instead, of poking my food through the hole in the door, would open it wide, and pass in the victuals with a look of mingled shame and fear. I was nursing my wrath to keep it warm, and cunningly smiled upon the brute, who no doubt imagined that I had forgotten his cruel treatment. There was nothing in the room that I could strike him with, but with the quick device of a lunatic I pulled off one of my iron heel-tap boots, and as he one day approached the door without caution, I swung my boot by the leg and planted the iron heel on his head. He fell like a struck steer, and although he was a powerful man, lay like one dead until companion attendants carried him away. Of course the doctors and attendants bound me up as usual, and upbraided me for nearly killing my keeper. I was perfectly happy, however, in thinking that the punishment he received at my hands was only a just recompense for the secret knocks and blows inflicted upon my fellow lunatics.

Days and weeks wore away, and still my mind rambled in the briers and flowers of imagination. The morning sun rose like a ball of fire, and I followed his track across the heavens until the evening shadows settled down upon the earth, and night flung out her jeweled curtains to flutter in the winds and brighten in the silver light of the moon. How I watched that full, round, harvest moon, as it rose in the month of July, 1860. Luna, my beautiful midnight companion, sent her soft rays through my barred window, and its glorious beams played hide and seek upon the floor, or danced to the music of the zephyrs as they tripped through the leaves and branches of a fine old tree that shaded my lonely cell. I would talk by the hour to imagined spirits, and in the rapture of· my soul spin poetry faster than my spiders spun their web. I dashed into flights of eloquence that would have put to blush the ravings of Demosthenes, Mirabeau or Patrick Henry.

Strange to say, while I praised in poetry and lunatic eloquence the greatness of "Harry of the West," his son Theodore was a chattering lunatic by my side, and cheered the flights of fancy that bubbled up in my troubled brain. Theodore Clay had been an inmate of the asylum for thirty years, and was considered in his youth the brightest child of the old statesman. It was said that love and disappointment provoked his lunacy. A beautiful Lexington girl pledged him her hand and heart, but when the nuptial night came round, the groom appeared in all the glow of matrimonial expectations, while the fair bride had eloped with a hated rival. This blow cut the highly wrought strings of intellect, and left but a poor, broken instrument to tune out his mournful days in a lunatic asylum.

It would take a volume to describe the different kinds of lunatics and the various forms that the mind takes on in its ravings. There is the chattering type, as he walks the wards and taps the bars like a caged beast; there is the moody, low-browed man, sitting alone, counting over and over his finger-tips or watching the flies and spiders as they buzz and weave in the sunshine. There comes the General, as he strides the halls, commanding large armies and fighting great battles at Pharsalia and Waterloo, who imagines himself Cæsar or Napoleon. There is the King in all his royal glory, carrying a broom for a sceptre and a torn sheet for a purple robe. In the next ward can be seen his royal consort, imitating the strut of Queen Victoria, straws and chicken-feathers in her hair for a royal crown, and a simpering smile for the poor sub-jects who gaze upon her pretended rank. Now comes the confidential, wise inventor, who will tell you of the great things he has done, of the millions he controls, and the in-numerable ships that plough the ocean for his advantage and profit. There is the self-styled Jesus Christ, who preaches forgiveness and salvation, ending with a blessing and general absolution from sin, and asking in return only a bit of tobacco! In fact, the very earth blossoms at his will, and the sun, moon and stars give light at his command. It is only a generous charity that keeps him from shutting up this universal world and retiring into chaos. There is the beautiful, delicate girl, like a withered lily, humming a low love-song to her darling, who is personated by the pillow in her arms, but who may never again give back the warm kisses that come and go like celestial messengers. See another fair Ophelia, posturing before a looking-glass with comb in hand, and tangled hair, sighing or weeping for a lover or father snatched from her warm embrace. She speaks: "They say the owl was a baker's daughter—Lord, we know what we are, but know not what we may be." Look at the despair of the weeping mother as she bends over the imaginary body of her babe, sleeping in the shape of a sweet little doll on the broken rocking-chair by her side, impelled backward and forward with the wail of a lost spirit. Gaze on the sailor from the salt sea, swinging to the right and left, heaving the anchor or hauling away hand over hand the never-ending round of imaginary ropes. He strides the ship like a royal Viking, and looks aloft at the whirr of the tackle, sails and ropes, with all the pride of a jolly Jack Tar out on the ocean blue. No blackened bars or brutal attendants hedge in his soul or clip the power of his insane pinions. Like a sea gull, or one of Mother Carey's chickens, he rocks upon the crested wave of freedom, and with a piercing eye scans the horizon or lingers for the night winds to lull him to repose in the cradle of the deep.

The occasional dance and theatrical performance in the hall of a lunatic asylum are events of rare interest to the student of human nature. I have attended these amusements both as an insane and sane spectator, and must say that in the former I felt more joy than in the latter situation. I once took part in the play of the Lady of Lyons, personating the enthusiastic Melnotte, pouring out a flood of wild eloquence at the feet of a fair but unfortunate Pauline. There, indeed, was "a palace lifting to eternal summer—perfumed lights stealing through the midst of alabaster lamps—music from sweet lutes, and murmurs of low fountains that gush forth in the midst of roses." All the warm glow of lunatic fancy was heaped in my acting, and while Booth, Montagne and Mc-Cullough may have rendered the role with more harmony and felicity, they never could approach my earnestness, or touch the lightning flashes of love that shot across my fevered brain.

For a month after my arrival at the asylum I did not sleep an hour. Exhausted nature would now and then doze off into a few moments of delicious delirium, and again the devil of insanity would call up his myriad of royal imps and hold the usual banquet in my brain. I was gradually growing weaker, and the doctors saw that something must be done to force sleep. Doctor Dudley came to my room one morning, talked to me with the kindness of a lover, humored my hallucination, and said that he had a nice cup of coffee for me to drink. From the hands of Dudley everything was taken with confidence and relished with avidity. I drank the so-called coffee given by the doctor, and for the space of seventy-two hours I slept in a semi-conscious state. The *laudanum* did its perfect work ; and out of a terrible, awful dream, the piston-rod of lunacy flew back into the cylinder of reason, beginning to move in its accustomed groove. My hot fever had gone, the nerves had relaxed, my voice assumed its natural tone, and tired nature lay like a drooping plant in the mid-day sun.

I soon began to complain of the fearful noise made by the insane, day and night, and craved the privilege of the grounds and a place to sleep far away from the howl of the maniacs. Mr. Littlefield, the genial gardener and farm superintendent, took a particular fancy to me, gave his word to the doctor that I would be quiet outside the walls, and that he would have me help in the garden and among the flowers. I went forth from a close room to the walks, flowers and trees in the beautiful grounds, and in a small brick house, occupied by the gardener, I slept in confidence and peace until the first of September, 1860, when I was pronounced recovered and discharged from the asylum, after a stay of two months and four days!

Twenty-three years have passed since the terrible scenes of my insanity, and yet

> ' Remembrance wakes, with all her busy train,
> Swells at my breast, and turns the past to pain.
> In all my wanderings round this world of care,
> In all my griefs, and God has given my share,"—

I still have hopes that life has not been in vain, and that out of my trouble and insane experience may grow the sweet fruits of charity and love, to strengthen and cure the poor, oppressed and unfortunate lunatics who chatter, sing and howl to-day in mad-house miseries.

The feelings of a lunatic are almost indescribable. In my own case, ideas would spring up in my brain with the heat and force of a red-hot shot, sending my body on to some desperate action entirely beyond my power to restrain or subdue. There seemed to be some whispering devil at the threshold of my mind, urging me on to deeds that I knew were wrong, but for my life, had not the power to prevent. I knew what I was doing all the time, and felt inwardly before the act a sense of moral shame at the thing to be committed, and yet could not resist the impulse and seductive advice of the unknown power that rushed me on to spurts of desperation.

Reason waged war against insanity, but some inexplicable, unknown force propelled me into the very jaws of death, at which I smiled with disgust and contempt. My supreme egotism was only equaled by my indifference to life; and while having at times the outward semblance of sanity, the inward fires burned like a furnace, and hurried me on to commit any deed that chanced to pop into my shattered soul.

The rushing swoop of the eagle, the fearful whiz of a north-west blizzard, or the bolt of lightning, are not more fatal in their destination than the spirit pulsations of a lunatic brain. The world whirls around like a circular saw, the rivers run like molten silver, the sun burns a hole in the earth, the moon is filled with crumbling mountains, the stars are sparkling diamonds in some far-off ocean, and mankind but puppets that appear for a moment and are gone forever to the realm of shadows!

Abolish forever private lunatic asylums, established in fear and cupidity, conducted in fraud on human nature, festering all over with the sores of financial iniquity. Wipe out the county mad-houses, only kept up for the use of some local doctors and petty politicians, who get their bread at the expense of shrieking lunatics. Let the state and the nation take full charge of the insane, establishing spacious buildings and extended grounds, where the most perfect freedom can be given to the body, and where even the mind will not be convinced that it is cut off from the world like an imprisoned felon. Tear out the black bolts that bar the windows, paint in bright, cheerful colors, let clambering vines, blooming flowers, running waters and the song of birds entrance the weary mind, and let the soft sunshine into the black holes and damp dungeons that man has made for man.

Classification, separation and kindness, will tend to cure the insane if there is but a gleam of reason to light up the soul. Force will compel the body, but cannot touch the mind, and the medical fraternity might as well try to dam up the Amazon with green grass as to attempt the cure of the insane with physical terrors. Humor and love, cleanliness, good food, fresh air, and above all, freedom for the body, will make the mind of the madman calm and serene, and bring him back to reason, home and friends.

CHAPTER V.

The election of Abraham Lincoln, in November, 1860, and the firing upon Fort Sumpter, in April, 1861, sent a thrill of indignation through every heart, and aroused the nation from center to circumference. In Owingsville, Bath County, a beautiful town on a hill-top, where I was employed as deputy clerk of the circuit court, party lines began to be drawn, and home guards and state guards began to drill. Every breeze from South Carolina brought to our ears the tramp of resounding battalions, and every mail was loaded down with parting words and patriotic envelopes expressing the sentiments of the writers. I remember a prominent citizen who showed me an envelope he had received from South Carolina, upon which was poorly printed a picture of a palmetto flag, and I was solicited to join the state guard company, commanded by one of my friends. Most of my intimates were preparing to embark their fortunes with the Sunny South. All my social surroundings conspired to drive me into rebellion against the old flag. Pea Ridge, Bull Run and Wilson's Creek followed in rapid succession, driving into the vortex of war all that had the courage of their convictions and bravery to fight and die for what each warrior deemed right.

A large portion of the people of Bath county were at first inclined to stand by the armed neutrality proclamation that Gov. Magoffin issued for their consideration. The radical few, however, saw in the action of the state government but a subterfuge to lull the people to repose until the Confederate leaders could put their clamps on Kentucky and chain her to the chariot wheels of Rebellion.

In the summer of 1861, a peculiar and fortunate circumstance took place in the town of Owingsville, which perhaps precipitated the citizens to action. A certain photographer had his gallery on the main street. Military companies were in the habit of parading once a week, and a rebel flag was flung from the window of the photographer, attached to a long staff. A group of Union men saw the act, and somebody said the flag was a rebel one. The eye of Smith Hurt flashed like a torch, and remembering that he fought under the stars and stripes in the Mexican War, he bluntly said: "By blood ! let's tear down the infernal rag ; " and making a rush for the street, we gathered a lot of stones and threw them at the obnoxious flag. The very first stone thrown by Hurt, with his left hand, brought down the emblem of treason, and another heaved by Clarke Bascom broke the staff, the whole thing coming to the ground, where it was torn to pieces by the infuriated knot of daring patriots.

The photographer threatened to shoot the man who tore the flag down, but as Hurt did not cringe or apologize, and talked and acted defiantly to the last, there was no blood spilled. The whole town was in an uproar at the occurrence, and the city fathers were called out to keep the peace and smooth down the ruffled feathers of the belligerents.

During the summer of 1861, a great number of picnics and barbecues were held in the central counties of Kentucky, ostensibly for the purpose of social enjoyment, but in fact to recruit soldiers for the Southern army and crush out the growing spirit of Unionism in the state. I attended some of these meetings, and listened intently to the fiery oratory of Southern leaders.

Gen. John C. Breckenridge had come home from Washington to cast his lot with the Rebellion. Col. Roger Hanson was stumping the state, urging the people to stand up for the South, and General John S. Williams—scenting the smoke of battle—had already established a recruiting camp at Prestonsburg, in Eastern Kentucky, with Humphrey Marshall in command of the district.

Squads and companies of chivalric Kentuckians were daily marching through and near Owingsville, to join their comrades in the mountain camps. The home of " Cy." Boyd. near the mouth of the Slate, was a rendezvous for Southern recruits, they making his house a resting-place for food, drink and shelter. Ewing, Connor, Stoner, Cluke, Everet and a number of other local Southern men concluded that it was getting too hot to remain longer inactive, and in the month of September they cut loose from the moorings of the Union, and drifted into the wild breakers of Rebellion.

Suspicion lurked in every eye, and death held high carnival at every cross-road. I determined for myself that, come what might, I would never desert the flag under which I had been reared and protected—a flag which sheltered my exiled father from the heartless and cruel laws of British tyranny.

I did not believe in the doctrine of secession, and could not see the justice of Southern states going outside the Union to fight for their rights under a strange flag. While I believed the states to be supreme in their powers regarding local laws, I knew and felt that this must be a Union inseparable from the dictation of any of its members; and as the whole of a thing is greater than any of its parts, I was sure that the Nation had the right and power to force its rebellious children into submission.

In September I went to Olympian Springs with Capt. Davidson's company, and stood guard as a private many nights with other raw recruits from the surrounding precincts, who had there assembled to the number of five hundred, as the nucleus of the 24th Regiment Kentucky Volunteers. Major Hurt took charge of the troops, who volunteered, on their own hook, to fight for the Union, and for weeks we supported ourselves as best we could, standing as a wall against the surging waters of Secession. An isolated battalion, in a remote part of a Southern state, standing alone for the old flag and the Union ! A braver or better part was not played at Thermopylæ. The charge of the Light Brigade and the heroic dash of Arnold Winkleried in making a pass for the liberty of his country through the spears of the hated Austrians, were not inspired by more noble daring and fortitude than the loyal hearts of the 24th Kentucky, who first held the pass at Olympian Springs.

Northern people will never know how much Southern Union men suffered for their principles. It is easy enough to be brave and outspoken when the cheering crowd are unanimous and there is no danger of losing your life in the expression of an opinion. The people of the Northern States stood by the Union from self-interest. The loyal people of Maryland, Missouri and Kentucky owned slaves in many instances, and had fathers, brothers and sons who went out to fight and die for Southern rights. Yet, with all these material inducements to make them falter, they stood like a rock in mid-ocean against the roaring breakers of rebellion. The government owes everlasting gratitude for their fortitude and faith ; yet I fear, in many instances, the obligation has not been equal to the duty performed by the loyal citizens of the Border States.

CHAPTER VI.

HISTORY OF THE TWENTY-FOURTH KENTUCKY REGIMENT.

As a fitting introduction to this chapter, I present a letter from General Sherman, expressing gratification at the proposed publication of the history of my regiment :

Washington, D. C., June 30th, 1881.

Col. John A. Joyce,
            Georgetown, D. C.

Dear Colonel : I have received yours of June 30th, and the newspaper, which I have not had time to read. Am glad you are engaged on the history of your regiment—the 24th of Kentucky—and beg you will not spare the Old Man; only don't change results, so as to compel us to fight the war over again.   Yours truly,

W. T. Sherman.

The following letter from the late commanding officer of the 24th Kentucky gives the early history of the regiment :

Owingsville, Bath Co., Ky, }
June 15th, 1881. }

Dear Adjutant :

Yours of the 4th of May duly received, and I have deferred answering because of the hope that I should be able to furnish you an account of the earliest transactions of the 24th Kentucky Infantry. But, in consequence of extreme nervous prostration, produced by a recent attack of fever, I am at present entirely incompetent to the task, being now scarcely able to write. I have, however, every confidence that should you undertake to give a history of the regiment's operations during the war, you will, by reason of your intimate connection and acquaintance with it, and your ability and inclination, be able to do it ample justice.

Should my health improve, and I can procure the data, I will with pleasure furnish you the information desired. Nothing is dearer to me than the deeds of the gallant 24th; and I cherish a fond recollection of the brave and gallant officers and men who composed it, and feel it a great honor to have been its chief commanding officer. I can say truly that I was always ably seconded by my gallant Adjutant.

Though the deeds of other regiments of Kentucky deserve the highest encomium, yet when we take into consideration the perilous condition of this section of the state when the organization of the regiment was commenced, and the check it gave the secession movement in this isolated region, and its subsequent deeds during the War of the Rebellion, it is quite doubtful whether any of the Kentucky regiments should take a more honorable place in the history of that conflict.

I remember that on the 29th day of September, 1861, three of the companies—Davidson's, (the Owingsville company), North's and Barber's companies—concentrated at Olympian Springs, and I was selected to take command of them, and did so. We were armed partly with *Lincoln muskets*, and partly with others obtained from the Military Board of Kentucky. For more than a week we had only such rations as were furnished by the loyal citizens, neither the State or Federal governments having during that time taken charge of the troops. Or, as I can more readily express it, we were acting "on our own hook." These three companies numbered about two hundred men, armed as before stated. At the end of this time about three hundred unarmed recruits had joined us, making five hundred men, and it was this nucleus that the 2d Ohio Infantry—the advance of Gen. Wm. Nelson's command—joined in the first part of October.

You can, therefore, readily see that but for the action of those three companies, in seizing the Olympian Springs as a strategetic point, the rebel recruits from north-eastern Kentucky, instead of concentrating at Prestonsburg, as they did, would in all probability have concentrated at the Olympian Springs, near the center of the state, and that Gen. Nelson's small force would have had to operate against the rebel troops at this place instead of Prestonsburg, Ivy Mountain and Piketon; and Col. JAS. A. GARFIELD, of the 42d Ohio Infantry, (now our President), instead of defeating Gen. Humphrey Marshall at Middle Creek, on Sunday, as the Union forces did, would have had to seek him at or near the Olympian Springs.

I have always believed that the three companies seizing Olympian Springs on their own responsibility at the time they did, (though in the light of subsequent events a small matter) went far towards saving Kentucky to the Union.

A day or two after the arrival of Colonel Harris, 2d Ohio Regiment, L. B. Grigsby, of Winchester, arrived at Olympian Springs, with a commission as Colonel, and took chief command of the companies and recruits before mentioned, and three other companies, viz: Cary's, Hedges' and

Blue's, that were organizing from the recruits, and were armed by the state, making six companies in all; and on the 8th of October, 1881, they were mustered into the military service of Kentucky for one year. My rank was that of Major. The state, from that time until we were mustered into the military service of the United States, furnished rations and other supplies, with the exception of the time we were with Gen. Nelson on his expedition to Prestonsburg and Piketon.

Soon after we were mustered in, Gen. Nelson arrived at the Olympian Springs, and also Cols. Sill, Phyfe and Norton's regiments, of Ohio; Col. T. A. Marshall, 16th Ky. Infantry; a battery of artillery—twelve-pounders; a company of regular cavalry; a fragment of Col. Leonidas Metcalf's 7th Ky. Cavalry;—and this force included the six companies of the 24th Kentucky.

Gen. Nelson assumed command, and made his comparatively bloodless campaign on the Sandy, driving the rebel force, under command of Gen. John S. Williams, (now senator), into Virginia. At the beginning of the expedition, Gen. Nelson detailed Davidson's company of the 24th, one company each from Cols. Marshall, Sill, Phyfe and Harris's regiments, forming what he termed the Light Brigade, which he placed under my charge, and which I commanded until the campaign ended with the affair at Piketon, resulting in the rebel forces being driven into Virginia.

After the expedition started, the other five companies of the 24th, under Col. Grigsby, were left at Hazel Green to guard our communications and the depot of supplies at that place.

When the campaign was over, the 24th was ordered by Gen. Nelson to take station again at the Olympian Springs, to complete its regimental organization, and guard that region of country. It remained there until December, 1861, when it was ordered to Lexington, Ky., and was joined by Capt. Smith's company, from Montgomery; Capt. Scovill's company, from Laurel; Capt. Hall's company, from Powell, and Capt. Potter's company, from Knox—making the regiment complete, with ten companies—about a thousand men, rank and file.

The regiment then elected regimental officers, resulting in the choice of Grigsby as Colonel, myself Lieut-Colonel, and Smith, Major. James Turner was made Adjutant, David Trumbo Quartermaster, and James Sympson, Surgeon of the regiment.

On the 31st day of December, 1861, the 24th regiment was mustered into the military service of the U. S. by Capt. Bankhead, for the term of three years, or during the war.

You were with us at that time, and are too familiar with the history of the regiment to need any suggestions from me up to the 27th of June, 1864, when you were so severely wounded at the desperate charge on Kenesaw Mountain.

I will only add that the regiment participated in the battles around Atlanta, resulting in its fall, and also that, under my direction, it performed that perilous task of burning and destroying the rebel pontoon timber bridge on the Augusta road, under the siege-guns of Atlanta.

When Gen. Sherman made his movement to capture the Macon road, on the 1st of September, 1864,—a movement that forced Gen. Hood to evacuate Atlanta—I was in command of the leading regiment, the 24th Ky., of Gen. J. D. Cox's division, with skirmishers deployed under command of Lieut.-Col. Lafayette North; and these were the first Federal troops that struck the Macon road near Rough and Ready, and came near capturing a train of cars. We instantly cut the telegraph wires, thus severing quick communication between Hood at Atlanta, and Hardee's corps at Jonesboro. This was the evening before the battle of Jonesboro, in which Hardee was defeated, and Hood was compelled to evacuate Atlanta.

After the fall of Atlanta, the 24th regiment's term of service having expired, it was sent to Covington, where it was mustered out on the 31st day of January, 1865, having served the State and Nation three years, four months and two days.　　　Truly yours,

J. S. HURT.

The following were the various company officers of the 24th Kentucky, from its organization to its close. There were several promotions among these officers to higher grades, but some of them were not mustered into the United States service.

Company A.

Hector H. Scoville, . . . Captain.
Wiley Jones, ... 1st Lieut.
Wm. B. Johnson, ... "
Daniel O. Morin, . . . 2d Lieut.
George W. Freeman, . . "

Company B.

James Carey, ... Captain.
Washington J. McIntyre, 1st Lieut.
John Henry, ... 2d Lieut.
Daniel F. Winchester, . . "

Company C.

Green V. Hall, ... Captain.
Joseph L. Judy, 1st Lieut.
John Kinney, ... "
Thomas J. Bush, ... "
Stephen G. Lewis, . . . "
James McChristy, . . . 2d Lieut.

Company F.

James A. Hawkins, . . . Captain.
James Blue, ... "
Thomas J. Bush, ... "
John N. McIntyre, . . . "
Wm. H. Norris, . . . 1st Lieut.
Thomas N. Likes . . . "
Cornelius E. Mastin, . . "
Dillon White, ... 2d Lieut.

Company G.

Peter T. Hedges, ... Captain.
John J. Sewell, ... 1st Lieut.
John C. Padgett, . . . 2d Lieut.

Company H.

Edmund Jones, ... Captain.
Robert G. Potter, ... "
Reuben Langford . . . . "
James H. Wilson, . . . 1st Lieut.
Richard L. Ewell, . . 2d Lieut.

Company D.

George R. Barber, . . . Captain.
Mathias T. S. Lee, . . 1st Lieut.
Lander Barber, ... 2d Lieut.

Company E.

Lafayette North, ... Captain.
John M. Gill, ... 1st Lieut.
Wilkins Warner, . . . 2d Lieut.
Jessee P. Nelson, ...   "

Company I.

Roy D. Davidson, . . . Captain.
Fountain Goodpaster, . .   "
Wm G. Howard, . . . 1st Lieut.
John A. Joyce, ...   "
Daniel Wilson, ... 2d Lieut.
Julius C. Miller, ...   "
Benjamin P. Desilve, . .   "

Company K.

John J. Evans, ... Captain.
James M. Anderson, . .   "
James Caughlin, . . . 1st Lieut.
T. D. Moss, ... 2d Lieut.
David G. Howell, . . .   "

The number of enlisted men at the organization of the regiment was 664, addition soon after by recruits 400, making the total number of enlisted men 1,064. The loss by battle, disease, missing, transferred and discharged, was 694, leaving only 370 to be mustered out at the expiration of the regiment's term of service.

I joined Company I, 24th Ky., as a private, doing guard duty many a frosty night, and meditating on my future of "three years or during the war." In the lonely midnight hours, pacing my measured beat around the old fair-grounds, I determined to become an officer, and give up the musket for the sword, believing that I could be of more service to the Union in the latter capacity than in the humble though honorable station of a private soldier.

The 24th remained in Lexington some weeks, completing its regimental organization, and the raw recruits went through squad and company drill each day. Dress-parade was held at the fair-grounds each morning, where many citizens attended. It was a difficult thing to keep the men in camp.

The captain of my company, Roy D. Davidson, recognized my education. The first opportunity presented, I was promoted from the ranks to the position of orderly sergeant, becoming the practical man of the company, and the confidential soldier of the captain.

After a few weeks' drill, and when the regiment was completely equipped with all the requirements necessary to the prosecution of active duties in the field, we were ordered to Louisville, Ky., by General D. C. Buell, the Department Commander.

On the 12th of January, 1862, we marched through the streets of Lexington, drums beating and banners flying, and took the cars for Louisville, where we arrived on the following day, camping at the Oaklands, near the city. The regiment remained here until the 19th, when it proceeded to Bardstown, Ky., where we were properly brigaded, Colonel Wm. Lyttle commanding, and assigned to the division of General Thomas J. Wood, a West Point graduate. We remained at Camp Morton until the 7th of March, when we took our line of travel to the town of Lebanon. The battle of Mill Springs had been fought by General Thomas about this time, and many of the wounded on both sides were being cared for in the hospitals of the town. The rebel General Zollicoffer, of Nashville, was killed in the fight by Col. Speed S. Frey, who commanded the 4th Kentucky Infantry. The body of the heroic son of the South fell inside the Union lines, and was forwarded to his friends in Nashville, where he had but recently departed with all the hopes that inspire valor.

The regiment marched to Springfield and New Market, and countermarched to Lebanon, and thence to Mumfordsville, on to Cave City and Bowling Green, reaching camp on the 1st of March.

On the line of the Louisville and Nashville Railroad, the rebel General Hindman had torn up the track in a number of places, causing Buell's army to proceed slowly, repairing the road as it moved along. Various tunnels were blown up to give the forces of the enemy, stationed at Bowling Green, ample time to fall back on Nashville. On the 5th of March, Wood's division moved out on the pike from Bowling Green,

and by easy marches arrived in Nashville on the 13th, camping near the city, which had recently been evacuated by the
enemy.   I had just received a commission as second lieutenant, and emerged from the role of an enlisted man to the
exalted station of a United States officer.

The armies of Grant and Buell were making simultaneous
movements on the rebel forces supposed to be concentrating
on the Tennessee River, near Pittsburg Landing.   Grant was
moving up the Tennessee on transports to the town of Savannah, while Buell was marching across the plains and iron hills
of middle Tennessee to the same place.

The battles of Mill Springs, Fort Donelson and Fort
Henry had given a new impetus to the Union forces, and
General Halleck, from his headquarters at St. Louis, directed
a grand movement on the railroad communications between
Corinth, Meridian and Chattanooga.   To secure these railroads would greatly intercept communication between the
armies of Lee in the east, and Johnson and Beauregard in the
south-west, and give to the Union armies a strong hold of the
backbone of the South.

On the 29th of March my regiment moved out on the
Franklin pike with Wood's division, by quick marches, to
Savannah, Tennessee.   We passed through Spring Hill, crossing the Duck River at Columbia, and marching on through
the beautiful valley, dotted with highly cultivated farms and
stately mansions of the slave aristocrats of Tennessee.   The
Pillows, Polks and Jacksons had settled in this smiling valley
years before, and by their intelligence and wealth made it
blossom like the rose.   Great, tall, ancestral oaks, black walnut
and white ash, covered the rolling hills and blooming vales,
and all nature wore the green garb of prosperity.   The proprietors, however, had gone to fight for their rights, leaving
behind their women, children and slaves, to weather the
storms of war as best they might.

The line of war kept winding towards the Tennessee River
like a huge black snake, passing Mount Pleasant and Waynes-

boro, across a long sterile ridge covered with tall pines, iron furnaces and charcoal pits. Swollen mountain streams and muddy roads intercepted our progress, the wagons sinking to the hubs, the poor mules to their knees, and the soldiers often drenched to the skin with slush and rain.

On Sunday, April 6th, 1862, when thirty miles from Savannah, we heard the long roar of heavy artillery, sounding over the rugged hills of Tennessee like periodical thunder claps from a distance.

Orders were passed all along the lines to quit wagons, baggage, tents and all extra accoutrements, and with light haversacks, sixty rounds of cartridges and our Springfield rifles, we dashed off in the evening for a thirty-mile march to the terrible battle of Shiloh.

CHAPTER VII.

THE BATTLE OF SHILOH.

The roar of the wicked gun-boats, Tyler and Lexington, and the rumble of field-pieces broke upon our ears like a sad requiem over the graves of buried heroes. Bomb, bomb, thrumb, thrumb, sounded the music of our march, and through that long Sunday night the incessant song of the murderous gun-boats was the death-knell of many a son of the South. The flood-gates of heaven seemed open that fearful night, and the rain came down on the wearied trudging soldiers like hail-stones.

The roads were worked into sticky slush by the artillery wagons, and the weary warriors wound along amid peals of thunder and flashes of lightning, looking like gnomes from some infernal region. It was a hitch and a halt, a push and a run, a rest and a route, until the straggling shanties of Savannah came into view on the swollen waters of the Tennessee, just as the gray of morning dissipated the black shadows of night and brought another day of battle and blood.

In passing through the streets of Savannah down to the transport steamer that was to take us to the battle-field, six miles above, I saw for the first time wounded soldiers borne on stretchers from the bloody work at the front. An hour before, the proud form of the soldier had been rushing on the enemy with the spirit of a lion; but now his mangled manhood lay prostrate, carried to the rear by sorrowing comrades, never again, perhaps, to mingle his voice with the roar of battle, sing love-songs around the nightly bivouac, or greet the loved ones at home.

The 24th Kentucky was immediately pushed aboard the transport steamer *Evansville,* and at once proceeded to the battle-field, arriving on the scene of slaughter and demoralization at noon. The 57th Indiana and 24th Kentucky were immediately placed in line of battle by Col. G. D. Wagner, commanding the 21st Brigade, while the 15th and 40th Indiana supported the advancing column.

The battle was raging, and the enemy was making a last stand on the rough hills behind a clump of water oaks and thick hickory underbrush, when amid shot, shell, and deadly buck and ball, Colonel Lewis B. Grigsby, the commander of the 24th, made the following impromptu speech as the regiment rushed to battle :

"Fellow-soldiers, the field of honor is before you. The foe is over the hill waiting your salute. Kentucky looks to her soldiers to carry the flag of the Union to victory. Remember that you are sons of the heroic men who fell at the River Raisin, New Orleans, and on the bloody plains of Buena Vista. Stand by your colors to the last, preferring death to defeat. Now at the enemy! Forward, guide right, charge!"

The 57th Indiana had dashed off to the front by this time, touching on the left of Rosseau's Brigade of Kentuckians, of McCook's Division; while the 24th aligned on the left of the gallant Indianians, all charging right into the retreating forces of Van Dorn and Breckenridge, who moved with a sullen tread from their victorious ground of the previous day.

About a quarter of a mile to the left of Shiloh church, and near the Corinth road, the 24th, in one of its charges, captured about forty prisoners and sent them to the rear. Among the prisoners were a field officer, a chaplain, and a surgeon named Redwood, of an Alabama Regiment.

During the afternoon the closing battle-scenes shifted with alternate success and defeat, the enemy contesting every inch of ground. But the army of General Buell, commanded by Nelson, McCook, Crittenden and Wood, was too much for the heroic warriors of Johnston and Beauregard. About 4 o'clock the enemy was in full retreat, on the road and through the interminable forests leading to Corinth. Wood's division followed the retreating army about five miles out on the Corinth road, and successfully repelled several cavalry dashes made by General Forrest; although in one instance the Confederate General dashed right through the 77th Ohio Infantry as if it had been but so much chaff, scattering the blue-coats through the underbrush and tall timber.

The darkness of night put an end to the bloody battle; and after throwing out pickets on the various roads, Wood's division marched back to the main body of the army.

The armies of Grant and Buell slept upon the battle-field that soaking Monday night. No real effort was made to follow the retreating foe. We were only too glad to rest after the terrible two days of blood, and gather up the remnant of our broken forces.

> "Our bugles sang truce, for the night-clouds had lowered,
> And the sentinel stars set their watch in the sky;
> And thousands had sunk on the ground overpowered—
> The weary to sleep, and the wounded to die."

Such a scene of havoc and desolation as the field of Shiloh presented, I never witnessed in the marches and fights of after years. Around the old Shiloh meeting-house could be seen clumps of dead soldiers, scores of dead horses, broken artillery caissons, smashed wagons, tents riddled with bullets, trees torn to splinters, underbrush cut down by the murderous Minnies, great giant oaks blown up by the roots, and prostrate like the swollen human forms that festered below; while a look above presented the broken arms of the forest as they moved in the chilling night winds against the gloomy outline of a leaden sky!

The rain came down in torrents, the mud and forest slush being almost knee-deep. During the night I was detailed to take charge of the prisoners that we had captured in the afternoon. They were collected in a group under the dripping leaves and branches of a spreading oak. The night was chilly, the soldiers thinly clad, and the demon of hunger threatened the weary warriors. In the race of Buell to the battle-field, commissary and regimental wagons had been left behind, and thousands of human beings were without shelter, save such temporary covering as could be obtained by broken branches, swamp grass, and long slabs of bark peeled from surrounding trees.

About 12 o'clock Monday night I was taken with a congestive chill and relieved from duty by Goodpaster, my companion Lieutenant of Company "I." In searching for shelter from the drenching rain and cutting winds, I stumbled into a tent that had been riddled by bullets, and feeling about in the midnight darkness, found some sleeping soldiers. In my wild hunt for rest I sank down between the sleepers, pulling their rough blankets over my shivering frame. Weary, cold and hungry, I soon fell into a deep slumber, and on the airy wings of blissful dreams was wafted away over hill, river and plain to my home in Kentucky. I sat again by the fireside of those I loved, and basked in the sunshine of bright eyes. How my wild, delirious fancy painted happiness in the beautiful land of slumber and imagination. Angel voices lulled me to repose, rare viands and rich food haunted my hungry eyes, and sweet music cheered my sinking soul. The chill and pain of the midnight hour vanished away, the cold gray shadows of morning brightened the dark woods, and some straggling comrade roused me from the fantastic flowers and melody of dreamland. The heart would fain slumber and the chill of the body beat back the sweet voices that implored me to linger in the realm of fancy.

> " 'Stay, stay with us; rest; thou art weary and worn;'
> And fain was their war-broken soldier to stay;
> But sorrow returned with the dawning of morn, -
> And the voice in my dreaming ear melted away."

Sorrow indeed returned; for, in rousing from sleep, I discovered that my blanket companions were dead, having been shot, no doubt, that terrible Sunday morning, when Sidney

Johnston and his dashing heroes rolled over the Union troops like mad waves on the sea-shore. At the door of the Sibley tent I saw dead soldiers scattered about like huge cord-wood sticks. In each of the company streets tattered tents, camp-kettles, pans, broken guns, torn blankets, empty canteens, haversacks and knapsacks, lined the bloody battle-ground. The "Blue" and "Gray" rested side by side in eternal sleep. Many I saw were grappled in death, and the bright bayonet that did the desperate work was clenched in the hand that dealt the murderous blow.

No mind can conceive or pen portray the startling horrors of Shiloh. It was, for the number engaged, the bloodiest battle of the war, and the very pivot of the victorious Union. Had Grant, Buell and Sherman been defeated at Shiloh, the Federal forces could not have been re-formed for battle south of the Ohio River ; and Kentucky and Tennessee, in all human probability, would have been lost to the Union.

At seven o'clock on the morning of the 6th of April, 1862, the division of Gen. Sherman occupied the advanced position of the Union army, his right resting on the Purdy road, near Owl Creek, and his left stretching in front and beyond Shiloh church on the Corinth road.

The division of Prentiss was on the left of Sherman, and McClernand occupied the line in rear of Sherman, while Hurlbut and Stuart were farther to the left rear, near the Tennessee River, leaving Lew. Wallace, with his lost division, in the swamps of Snake Creek.

Gen. Sherman's division stood the brunt of the first day's battle, the desperate onslaught of Johnston bearing down on his left, and on the right of Prentiss, with the weight of a roaring flood, compelling the first line to fall back on McClernand for support, which was given promptly. General Prentiss and quite a large number of his division were taken prisoners in the morning, and during the subsequent fighting his command was but a shattered body staggering about on the bloody field.

Night found the Union forces badly demoralized, their left resting on the Tennessee River, having been driven from three battle-lines during the day. McClernand's and Sherman's divisions still occupied the ragged front of battle, while the victorious Confederates feasted on the provender of the Federal troops.

During Sunday night, the gun-boats Tyler and Lexington kept up a periodical fire on the enemy, throwing shells into the ranks of the victors. Grant and Buell had a consultation with their subordinates on Sunday night, wherein it was determined to take the offensive on Monday, and retrieve our lost ground, if possible.

Lew. Wallace occupied the extreme right of the Union forces, with Sherman, McClernand, Hurlbut, McCook, Wood, Crittenden and Nelson extending for two miles to the left, making a cordon of determined bayonets ready to pierce the enemy. They moved against the Confederate forces in unexpected strength early Monday morning; and, while varying success characterized the contending armies during the second day of the great battle, four o'clock in the afternoon found the rebel warriors in full retreat, and the Union army completely victorious.

I am satisfied that the Army of the Ohio, commanded by Gen. Buell, turned defeat into victory, and were it not for the timely arrival of six divisions, the brave soldiers of Grant and Sherman would have been driven into the Tennessee River, or captured by the daring soldiers of Johnston and Beauregard.

Gen. Sherman, in his Shiloh report, says that Rousseau's brigade of McCook's division advanced beautifully, deployed, and entered the dreaded wood where a few moments before Willich suffered defeat. He says: "*I saw for the first time the well-ordered and compact columns of Gen. Buell's Kentucky forces, whose soldierly movements at once gave confidence to our newer and less disciplined men.*"

Whole Union regiments from Ohio, Indiana, Illinois, Michigan, Missouri and Kentucky, were literally used up, and it was days and weeks after the battle before some Ohio regiments could be found, to form a nucleus for re-organization.

May be it has never occurred to the peaceful citizen of to-day how much he is indebted to Grant, Sherman, Meade, Sheridan, Thomas, McPherson, Hancock and other gallant commanders, for the blessings that came with the salvation of the Union and the starry flag. We think of these men, little realizing that to their brain, nerve, dash and valor is largely due the establishment of a Union without a slave, and a nation without a peer. They will only be entirely appreciated after their death, when their scurrilous detractors are rotting in un-remembered graves. Their statues, in marble and bronze, will decorate the parks or the National Capital, telling to genera-tions yet unborn the glowing history of their heroic actions at Donelson, Shiloh, Gettysburg, Winchester, Atlanta and Ap-pomatox.

Our forces held the field of Shiloh, but that was all; and while the enemy leisurely retreated to Corinth, the victorious army showed no disposition to follow, but wallowed along like a huge anaconda for seven weeks, through the swamps and forests of Tishimingo county, before reaching Corinth, only thirty miles away! Gen. Halleck was preparing for a great battle with his hundred thousand fresh soldiers, and when he actually got ready to strike the blow against Beauregard on the 30th of May, 1862, found that the heroic Confederate had evacuated Corinth with his entire army, two days before, leav-ing nothing to our grand parade General but long lines of empty breastworks, broken camp-kettles, and a few ragged prisoners!

It was laughable to see the preparations Gen. Halleck made for the great impending battle which was to come off at Cor-inth. Rows of large hospital tents, to accommodate a thou-sand men, were erected along the Purdy, Farmington and Cor-inth roads; nice, new cots, furnished with clean linen sheets; rose blankets; variegated quilts, and pillows with frilled cases, had been sent from the North to comfort would-be wounded warriors.

When long rifle-pits were dug every mile or so through the
woods, the "boys" would say that they were all owing to the
great forethought of Gen. Halleck, who not only fixed up beds
and shelter for the living, but provided new-made graves for
the dead! The old General did everything in tip-top style,
according to his "elements of war," except—fighting! This
necessary element of war seemed to be a secondary consideration with the great tactician. Yet, at that time the war was
young, and the Generals had to grow to the idea that the enemy had to be conquered, not by kindness, but by killing.

The following extracts from official reports will show, in successive form, the place and conduct of various regiments, brigades and divisions of the army at Shiloh:

General D. C. Buell says:

Headquarters Army of the Ohio,
Field of Shiloh, April 15th, 1862.

"Two brigades of Gen. Wood's division arrived just at the
close of the battle, but only one of them (Col. G. D. Wagner's) in time to participate actively in the pursuit, which it
continued for about a mile, and until halted by my order.
Its skirmishers became engaged for a few minutes with the
skirmishers (cavalry and infantry) of the enemy's rear guard,
which made a momentary stand. It was also fired upon by the
enemy's artillery on its right flank, but without effect. It was
well conducted by its commander, and showed great steadi-
ness."

General Thomas J. Wood says:

Headquarters 6th Division, Army of the Ohio,
Battle-field near Pittsburg Landing, April 10th, 1862.

"Savannah was reached early on the morning of the 7th,
and as soon as possible the embarkation for the battle-field
commenced. Wagner's brigade, (the 21st), consisting of the
15th, 40th and 57th Indiana, and 24th Kentucky Volunteers,
was first embarked. In order to hasten, by my personal supervision, the embarkation of the remainder of the troops, I remained in Savannah till the 20th brigade (Garfield's) embarked,
and ordered one of my Aides-de-camp (Capt. Leonard) to ac-

company the 21st brigade to the battle-field and report it to
the Commanding General. The brigade had fully debarked
at 12 M., and for its operations from that hour to my own arrival at 1 P. M., I refer you to Col. Wagner's report, herewith
submitted, with the simple remark that it did good service in
driving the enemy from his last strong stand, and compelling
him, by a vigorous pursuit, to a rapid retreat."

Colonel G. D. Wagner says :

Headquarters 21st Brigade, }
Camp near Pittsburg Landing, April 9th, 1862. }

"I have the honor to inform you that this brigade arrived
upon the battle-field on Monday, April 7th, in time to participate in the winding up of the great battle of that date. We
disembarked and were immediately ordered by General Grant
to reinforce the left wing of the army, which was then being
hotly pressed by the enemy. The 57th Indiana Volunteers
were first engaged, being thrown out to the right of the brigade, and on the left of Gen. McCook, where they did good
service, advancing upon the enemy under a heavy fire, with
the coolness of veterans, until the enemy were driven from the
field. I was ordered by Gen. Buell to take up a position on
the Corinth road with the remaining portion of my brigade,
to-wit : the 15th and 40th Indiana and 24th Kentucky. We
advanced in line of battle, driving the enemy before us, with
infantry, cavalry and artillery. The cavalry were soon dispersed by a few volleys from our advanced line, with considerable loss to themselves, the infantry retreating at the same time.
We captured some forty prisoners, among whom was a field
officer, a chaplain and a surgeon ; and retook some of our men
who had been captured. The enemy at the same time retreated beyond the range of our guns. I was then ordered by
Gen. Buell to retain that position, which I did until your arrival. I must be allowed to commend the coolness of both
officers and men of my entire command."

The following letter, written after a lapse of twenty years
from the battle of Shiloh, gives the opinion of a great General
concerning war matters, and the controversies of to-day, indulged in by little people at the rear, who were always complaining and talking when officers and soldiers at the front
were fighting and dying for the salvation of the flag :

Headquarters Army of the United States, }
Washington, D. C., May 18th, 1882. }

JOHN A. JOYCE, Esq.,
        Washington, D. C.

        Dear Sir: I beg to acknowledge receipt of your letter of
May 17th, asking me to give you in writing, for publication, a statement
" epigrammatically of the philosophy and bravery that impelled my division
to resist the bloody encounter of Johnston at Shiloh, and the desperate ma-
neuvres of Hood at Atlanta."

This is no easy task; and as I have hitherto—in reports, publications,
letters and speeches—given to the public my version of the facts in both
these cases, I prefer not to condense any further.

In war, success ends all reasonable controversies.

At Shiloh the Union armies were eminently successful—as also at Atlanta
—and there the controversy should end.

Historians may dispute the details, and account for results; but I would
not ask any man to see with my eyes without having all the witnesses.

The printed proceedings of the Army of the Tennessee contain much
valuable testimony about both .these events, and I advise you to consult
them before completing your work.

I wish you all possible success in your undertaking.

                With respect,
                        Yours truly,
                                W. T. SHERMAN.

CHAPTER VIII.

On the 1st of June, 1862, General Halleck had a hundred thousand soldiers in front of Corinth, ready for battle at a moment's warning. Beauregard had retreated to the south, leaving the Memphis & Charleston Railroad in possession of the Union forces, who commanded a great portion of the Mobile & Ohio Railroad communications.

The armies of Pope, Buell and Grant, commanded by Halleck, could have marched at that time through the Confederacy, and whipped any army that the enemy could have assembled. The colors of the victorious heroes of Shiloh could have been planted over the tall steeples of Vicksburg or Mobile. By cutting loose from our base of supply and subsisting off the country, we could have marched and fought through Mississippi, Alabama and South Carolina, unfurling our flag over Charleston.

A hundred thousand men can whip in detail twice its number. Courage, discipline, intelligence and superior arms are the pivots upon which great battles are won. Miltiades, at the battle of Marathon, near Athens, more than twenty-three hundred years ago, whipped a hundred thousand Persians with eleven thousand valiant Greeks. The Persians lost six thousand four hundred men, while the Athenian loss was only one hundred and ninety-two.

The disparity in the losses of the contending armies is accounted for by the superior spears, breast-plates, helmets and arrows of the Greeks, combined with their great daring and renowned intelligence. The Persians were only equipped with wicker breast-plates and short spears, and inspired only by the ignoble spirit of cupidity.

The army of the Union at Corinth was inspired with the lofty idea of human liberty and the salvation of the Republic, while the enemy could only boast of fighting for their local rights and the liberty to hold four million human beings in abject slavery. God and nature denied them success ; for he who attempts to enslave his fellow man is forging shackles for himself.

What Halleck did not do in June, 1862, with a hundred thousand men, Sherman with sixty-two thousand soldiers successfully performed in November and December, 1864, two years and a half afterwards. He marched to the sea, smashing right through the Confederacy, never resting by river, forest or swamp, until he planted the old flag over Savannah, on the morning of December 21st, 1864.

> "Oh, proud was our army that morning,
>   That stood where the pine darkly towers,
> When Sherman said : ' Boys, you are weary,
>   But to-day fair Savannah is ours.'
>
> Then sang we a song of our Chieftain,
>   That echoed o'er river and lea,
> And the stars in our banners shone brighter
>   When Sherman camped down by the sea."

The grand army of Halleck broke up in front of Corinth. Pope, with his command, went east ; Grant and Sherman went to the south-west, on the Mississippi line of action; while Buell and Thomas went north-east, towards Chattanooga and the upper Tennessee.

The division of Gen. Wood marched out on the Farmington road on the 2d of June, keeping along the line of the Chattanooga Railroad. My regiment proceeded with the command, over bad roads and through pelting rain-storms, passing through Iuka, a pretty mountain town, on the 4th, and on to Bear River, where the railroad bridge had been previously destroyed. Lieut.-Colonel James N. Kirpatrick, of the 40th Indiana, was drowned while performing his duty in rebuilding the bridge. He was a gallant officer, and his unfortunate death cast a shadow of gloom over our whole brigade.

The 24th assisted in rebuilding the bridge, which was finished in a few days, making uninterrupted communication for cars back to Corinth and forward to Tuscumbia, where another bridge had been destroyed. My regiment was again called into requisition in getting out timbers for the new structure. We remained about Tuscumbia from the 14th of June to the 25th, when the regiment took up its line of march for Decatur, on the Tennessee.

The town of Tuscumbia is situated in a delightful location, the surrounding hills and lovely valleys, stretching away to the distant horizon, filling the eye and heart with peace and beauty. The largest spring in the United States bubbles up from an abrupt hill adjacent to the town. It is wide and deep enough to float a steamboat to the Tennessee, some eight miles away. The water is clear and pure, being used by the citizens for drinking purposes.

The march from Tuscumbia to Decatur led through peaceful valleys and fertile fields, where corn and wheat grew in luxuriant profusion, nature presenting at every turn abundant harvests and smiling plains, leaving war and its desolating track to man and his vaulting ambition.

On the 27th of June we crossed the Tennessee River on a gun-boat, and marched east some six miles, where the division camped for rest and drill, remaining about two weeks. The location of the camp was all that soldiers could wish. A fine old forest stretched away to the Tennessee River in primitive beauty, and a large number of crystal springs bubbled up from the ground, cool and refreshing as the dews of morning.

On the 4th of July a large number of Wood's division assembled at the headquarters of Garfield's brigade, to hear its eloquent commander discourse upon the Declaration of Independence, the Revolutionary War, and the heroic sons of

Revolutionary sires who still battled for the perpetuity of the Republic. The speech of Gen. Garfield revived memories of home and friends; and as the soldier went back on the wings of imagination to his northern fireside, a thrill of patriotic inspiration for his country and flag found continual echo in the hearty cheers that greeted the orator.

The army of Gen. Buell was watching the movements of the enemy under Gen. Braxton Bragg, and as that officer began to move into Tennessee, the Union forces broke up camp, passed through Huntsville, Alabama, on the 13th and 14th of July, and on the 16th camped near Shelbyville. From there the 24th passed through Wartrace, camping near by for a few days, and thence to Tullahoma, marching out occasionally to reconnoiter for the enemy or procure forage for the horses and provisions for the men.

While in camp at Wartrace, on the 28th of July, I was sent for and appeared at the tent of Col. Grigsby, the regimental Commander. He informed me that I had been recommended for Adjutant of the 24th, and ordered me to take charge of the reports, books and papers, at once. This was a pleasant surprise, as I had not sought or expected the distinction and promotion when so many other officers of home influence aspired to fill the important post.

The regiment remained at Tullahoma about two weeks, when it struck tents for Manchester, thence to McMinnville and Vervilla, where it drilled, foraged and performed picket duty in hunting the imagined warriors of Bragg, who were reported to be moving about the brush like fire-flies in the Dismal Swamp. The regiment was called into line at all hours of the night. Col. Wagner, the brigade Commander, would dash off with his men as if the Confederacy was on the eve of dissolution, and our warriors were invited to handle the corpse and set a stone over the Great Defunct. It was nothing for us to march twenty miles in a night, climb the heights of Altamont, ford deep streams, skirmish through dense cedar thickets, and be back the next morning at McMinnville.

CHAPTER IX.

It soon became known that Bragg, with thirty thousand men, had stolen a march on Buell, and was going full tilt for Kentucky and the Ohio River. The Union forces picked up their military accoutrements, and hurried after the Confederates. The army of Buell crossed at Nashville, while that of Bragg passed through Lebanon, and crossed the Cumberland at Gallatin. Then it was a race for Louisville and the blue-grass fields of Kentucky.

At Mumfordsville there was a fight, where the marching armies struck together and bounced off to the right and left, like bumping steamers in a river race. Bragg evaded a general engagement, and Buell seemed anxious to reach Louisville and save the capital city of Kentucky from Confederate occupation, rather than push the enemy and force him to battle.

The 24th camped near Louisville on the 25th of September, and for nearly a week the whole army rested without following Bragg into the interior of the state. On the 1st of October, after a reorganization of the army into corps, we marched out on the Bardstown road towards Springfield and Perryville, where the enemy made a desperate stand and suffered a bloody defeat.

The troops of McCook and Thomas suffered considerable loss in the fierce attack of Bragg. He had been compelled to make a stand at Perryville, in order to gain time to escape through the hills of Rockcastle River and the mountain passes of the Cumberland. Crittenden's corps did not do much in deciding the day at Perryville, as for some reason the soldiers were kept waiting on the roads and in the woods to the extreme right. Gen. Wood's division got on the field about three o'clock. My regiment wheeled into line on a ridge overlooking the battle, and for a considerable time we stood the cannon shot and shrieking shells of the enemy as they retreated from the field. Wagner's brigade advanced in the evening, but it only stumbled over the killed and wounded. Night put an end to the contest. We rested on the outer line of picket-posts, ready for pursuit and battle on the morning of the 9th of October. When we advanced, it was found that Bragg had crossed Dix River, leaving his dead and wounded in our hands, and was moving in full flight to the mountains of south-eastern Kentucky.

Some of the most gallant soldiers of Kentucky were killed in the battle of Perryville, and none fell with more heroic grandeur than General James Jackson, of Louisville. He was a noble character, generous as a prince and brave as a lion. His death cast a gloom over the blood-purchased victory, and dimmed the luster of success.

> He fell in the heat of the fight,
> While charging the stubborn foe;
> He died for the Flag and the Right,
> In the years of the long ago.

Buell followed Bragg to Danville, Stanford, Mount Vernon, and on to Rockcastle River—thence to Wild Cat, London, and to the ford of Cumberland River. In many places Bragg cut down tall trees, throwing them across the mountain roads. Our progress was thus interrupted, and as the enemy were moving out of Kentucky, the Union troops were recalled from the chase, and leisurely retraced their steps to Tennessee.

While the troops were moving among the Rockcastle hills, it was difficult to get a square meal, as our commissary stores had been left behind in the race after Bragg. The whole army had been chucked into a mountain gorge, as it were—a rugged region where farmers were scarce, and provisions almost exhausted.   What the enemy did not consume on the route, the Union soldiers devoured in their hungry raids.

I remember one morning at Rockcastle Ford, giving a soldier a two-dollar and a half pocket-knife for a single hardtack cracker, and then dividing it with one of my comrades.

· The 24th returned to Mt. Vernon, Crab Orchard Springs and Stanford—thence to Danville, Columbia and Glasgow—where it camped for a time to straighten up and discipline the men, who were becoming very restless at leaving Kentucky again before seeing their families.

On the 29th of October, 1862, Colonel L. B. Grigsby was placed in command of the 21st Brigade, by Gen. Thomas J. Wood, leaving Hurt in command of the regiment.   Great dissatisfaction existed among the men.   A number of soldiers deserted while the regiment was at Glasgow, and for some unknown reason Col. Hurt was temporarily displaced by General Wood, leaving the command of the 24th to Capt. Hector H. Scoville, a solid mountain patriot.   From Glasgow the regiment proceeded to Scottsville and Gallatin, crossing the Cumberland River to Lebanon and Silver Springs, on the road to Stone River and Nashville.

After commanding the brigade for three weeks, Col. Grigsby returned to the regiment, and at once proceeded to strengthen its shattered ranks.   He went to Nashville and secured an order from Gen. Rosecrans to proceed with his command to Kentucky and report to the commander of that department.   The regiment went by rail from Nashville to Louisville, on the 27th of November, and arrived at Lexington on the 1st of December.   Through the months of December, '62, and January, '63, the 24th recruited its depleted ranks, camping a great portion of the time on the high hills overlooking the Kentucky River at Frankfort.

Gen. Gilbert, of Ohio, commanded the district of Frankfort, and regimental reports were made to him.   Col. Grigsby was placed in immediate command of the city post, and for a time his headquarters were at the Governor's mansion.   He had married the beautiful daughter of Gov. J. F. Robinson, and an invitation was extended to the gallant Colonel to make his headquarters, personally and officially, at the residence of the patriotic Governor.

I acted as regimental and post Adjutant, doing double duty, and put in a good portion of my time in social communion with the beautiful girls that cluster about the hospitable homes of Frankfort. Evening dress-parade was an occasion when all the pomp of military glory presented itself to the heart and eyes of buoyant boys and glorious girls. The Adjutant, with his trim military cut, bright buttons, golden shoulder-straps and flashing sword, presents a picture of dash and elegance to the hearts of susceptible sweethearts.

About the latter part of January, 1863, many of those who had been absent, with and without leave, returned to the regiment and took their places in the ranks of honorable soldiers. I dislike very much to make excuses for soldiers who desert their post of duty; but a statement in connection with the men who took French leave would seem to be just, under the peculiar circumstances surrounding the case in point.

In the fall of '62 and winter of '63, the proclamation of President Lincoln freeing all the slaves was talked up and promulgated. Many of the men of my regiment were directly or indirectly interested in slave property; and thus, while they had arms in their hands, fighting for the integrity of the Union, one scratch of the President's pen took away forever their property, placing them in the same category with the men who rebelled against the Government. This fact made many of the people of Kentucky lukewarm in their support of the Union, and was the cause of bitter abuse against Northern politicians who could be so cruel as to take, without any compensation, the property of loyal men who were bleeding on the field of battle for the perpetuity of the old flag.

In addition to this source of dissatisfaction, the majority of my regiment were raised in north-eastern Kentucky, where rebel guerrillas overran their homes in the winter of '63, while they were at the front. Houses were burned down, corn-fields laid waste, fences destroyed, relatives outraged and murdered, while wives and children were driven out in the woods and fields, to die of exposure and starvation. These cruelties were communicated by letter, day after day, to sons, brothers and husbands, who were unable to succor the loved ones at home; and, as the Government did not protect the families of the men who were fighting its battles, the natural love of home prevailed, and under the pressure of self-preservation, a number of the men scattered to their homes in the mountains, left some money with their families, re-established worldly matters, and then returned to the ranks. If there ever was an excuse for desertion, the loyal men of Kentucky—whose houses were destroyed and property taken, not only by the Government but by the enemy—could lay claim to every mitigating circumstance.

After remaining more than a month at Frankfort, the regiment went to Louisville on the 28th of January, with increased numbers, and camped on the Oaklands, awaiting orders to reinforce Gen. Rosecrans on the Cumberland. Gen. Gordon Granger was in command at Louisville, dispatching all available troops to the front. While waiting transportation by boat, the men of the regiment again became demoralized at the thought of leaving the state, and the camp-scenes were more in keeping with the acts of a mob than that of well disciplined troops. Col. Hurt became disgusted, and resigned, but was prevailed upon to withdraw his resignation. We remained a week in the metropolitan city of Kentucky.

CHAPTER X.

LOUISVILLE EXPERIENCES.

Many funny and curious scenes transpired about the camp, and in the homes of the rushing city. I became acquainted with a very beautiful Southern belle, whose family was of the best blood in the state. She had two brothers in the army: one with Morgan, fighting for the "stars and bars," and the other with Rosecrans, fighting for the "stars and stripes." The father was old, and bowed down with grief at the terrible scenes transpiring around him, while the mother's mild manner sent a glow of love and peace through the household.

A social party was given at the mansion one evening, and I was invited to attend. On my arrival, I found a large number of well-dressed guests, gray colors predominating, I being the only blue-uniformed individual present. Dancing, song and feasting were indulged in until midnight, when, to cap the climax, Miss Ella asked the privilege of singing and playing the "Bonnie Blue Flag." As the tune had been filched from Yankeeland, and as I had heard "Dixie," another Yankee air, played in the heat of battle—and more particularly as I was not fighting against women and children—I interposed no objection.

The beautiful young lady threw all her soul in the so-called rebel air, and out in the midnight silence it sounded as if the belles of Richmond were in chorus with the whole Confederacy. Great applause greeted the performance, but the cheers had not died away when a provost-marshal with a squad of soldiers broke in upon the festivities, and arrested the whole party for treasonable conduct. Everybody became alarmed at the predicament, the proprietor of the house seeing nothing but Camp Chase or Fort Lafayette, with their ponderous jaws ready to receive him.

In this emergency, I replied to the arrest and taunts of the bluff captain, saying that I alone was responsible for the singing of the treasonable song, having requested the young lady to render the air for the social pleasure of the guests. He replied that if that was the case, I should go with him at once to headquarters, where my conduct would be reported; and as I took the responsibility of the song, I should suffer whatever penalty might be inflicted by the Government.

I bade the host and hostess good night, leaving them to their liberty and social cheer, thus sacrificing myself for the good of other mortals. When I reached the commanding officer, who had authority and common sense, I explained that it was all a piece of fun and pleasantry, and a magnanimous thought on my part, to gratify an enthusiastic girl who desired to sing a few notes in honor of the Southern cause. The Confederacy always received my blows on the field of battle, but in the gloom of defeat I extended my hand and the generous words of a soldier to a fallen foe. I was not in favor of a parlor war, only striking those with arms in their hands.

The next day I called at the mansion and relieved the anxiety of the household by informing them that the commanding officer of Louisville had released me from arrest, while the superserviceable officer received no encomiums for his great energy and intense loyalty in breaking into a private house to disturb innocent festivities.

A few nights after this occurrence, I stumbled on one still more ridiculous. Capt. Gill, Lieut. McIntyre and myself had been at the Louisville Theater, to see Maggie Mitchell in her charming play of "Fanchon." Before returning to camp, after the close of the performance, I proposed that we go to Walker's restaurant for refreshments. This proposition was readily agreed to, and without delay we repaired to the festive resort and ordered a fine bird supper. The small rooms, fitted for four persons, were well patronized that night, and the thin sheeting partitions could not shut out the voices or words of the respective occupants. During the supper, a friend of McIntyre joined him,—a citizen from the "blue-grass" region—who got into an argument with "Mac," on the proprieties of the war.

Champagne went down, and loud words quickly came up, until at last McIntyre made a lunge at the friend of his youth, knocked him against the panels of the small room, and down with a crash went the whole side on the elaborate supper of Major-General Gordon Granger and his staff officers. Excitement ran high, and Granger's face looked like a thunder-cloud that had been split up by lightning. He knew me, but did not know my companions. The suppers were destroyed; McIntyre and the citizen were finally separated, the lights turned out, and we were ordered to our camps under arrest, to report at the Galt House the next morning at ten o'clock.

Granger and his officers were very jolly that night before we threw down the side of the stall on their supper, and I am convinced that our superiors were as much influenced by fumes from Bacchus as we were.

It was about two o'clock when we got into the street; and while we had been peremptorily ordered to camp, three miles away, and in a keen, frosty night, I proposed that as we had to report to Granger at ten o'clock in the morning, we go to the hotel, take a good rest and breakfast, and face the military music like men, which proposition was adopted.

Promptly at the appointed hour we put in an appearance at the Galt House. Granger was not yet out of bed. We told his orderly our mission, and asked him to inform the General. While waiting, it was agreed that I should do the talking and pleading, and that "the boys" should assent to every excuse I made for our conduct of the previous night. We were soon admitted, and found Granger sitting up in bed with his legs dangling over the side. We saluted, as became good respectful officers, and he said: "Young men, you were drunk last

night.   I am ashamed and astonished to see officers of the
army conduct themselves in such a disgraceful manner.''

I replied that we never drank, and before we left home we
had each made a solemn pledge to our sweethearts that for the
period of three years, or during the war, we would not taste,
smell or handle ardent spirits.

Granger looked astonished, and asked Gill and McIntyre
if my statement was true.   They held up their hands in earnest asseveration, and testified firmly to the truth of what I
had uttered.   The General arose immediately from the bed,
proceeded to the mantel-piece, took therefrom a half-filled
bottle of Bourbon whiskey and glasses, and said : '' Gentlemen, you are the most magnificent liars it has ever been my
lot to behold.   Your coolness and audacity deserve a reward,
and I shall take it as a great favor if you will condescend to
join me in a glass of old Bourbon.''

I replied that his request was equal to an order ; and, as we
had sworn to obey all orders of our superior officers, the pledge
we gave our sweethearts must give way to the rules of war ;
and however reluctant we might be to violate the obligations
of love, we could not, with self-respect, decline to comply
with the promptings of patriotism and duty.

We parted with mutual respect for each other.   I believe
that the General who takes a social glass with his staff is no
worse than the soldier who empties a canteen with his comrade
on the hot and dusty march.   I shall never forget the Pick-
wickian look and quizzical smile of Granger on that occasion.
He was certainly a generous character, and had the philosophy
and common sense not to rebuke too severely the conduct in
another which characterized himself.

> '' The hand and heart will show the noble mind ;
> A fellow feeling makes us wondrous kind.''

On the 3d of February, 1863, the regiment embarked for
Nashville, on the steamer Woodside, leaving Kentucky very
reluctantly.   Capt. Gill and myself remained behind, and

followed by rail a few days later, to the City of Rocks. From there we proceeded in search of the regiment down the Cumberland River, on the steamer Hazel Dell, landing at Clarksville, and riding through the enemy's country to Bowling Green, where we took the railroad for Nashville, arriving at the regiment's camp on the Franklin Pike, near the suburbs of the city, on the 17th of the month.

An expedition under Gen. Crook was projected to the upper waters of the Cumberland, where he could watch the movements of Bragg, and protect Kentucky from sudden invasion. On the 22d day of February my regiment, with other troops, moved out of camp and embarked on steamers ready to transport us up the river. We went on the steamers Belfast and Delaware, several boats being in the flotilla. Winding our way slowly among the bluffy banks of the mountain river, we arrived at Carthage, some fifty miles or more from Nashville. The regiment disembarked on the 27th, and pitched tents on a fine bluff overlooking the river. We remained about a month around Carthage, foraging, skirmishing, marching and reconnoitering toward the camps of the enemy. Several fights occurred between our advanced posts and the raiding troops of the Confederates, and many prisoners were taken on both sides, while several soldiers were killed and wounded.

Col. Grigsby had been quietly working to procure the transfer of the regiment to the Department of Kentucky, in order that he might put forth another effort to recruit its broken ranks. An order finally came from Gen. Crook, directing us to report to Gen. Gilmore, at Lexington, Ky.; and on the 21st of March we embarked on the Fanny Miller, and proceeded down the river with light hearts, ariving at Nashville the next day, where we made preparations to transfer the men to the steamer Sultana, bound for Louisville.

On the 24th, the Sultana got under way, passing Clarksville, Fort Donelson, and out into the beautiful Ohio, passed Smithland and Evansville, arriving in Louisville at five o'clock on the morning of the 27th.

The ill-fated Sultana was afterwards destroyed by an explosion on the Mississippi River, while carrying two thousand soldiers, a large number of whom were burned and drowned by the fearful catastrophe. The loss of life was the greatest recorded in steamboating annals.

The regiment proceeded at once to Frankfort and Lexington, reporting to Gen. Gilmore, who ordered us to Mt. Sterling on a raid after the enemy. We got into Mt. Sterling on Sunday, the 29th, but Col. Cluke, the Confederate commander, had scampered away towards the mountains. We followed the daring raider as far as Owingsville, killing and wounding a few of his men, and taking a number of prisoners.

When the regiment marched through the streets of Owingsville and stacked arms in front of the old court-house, the measure of my ambition was full. A little more than a year before, I had left the town a private soldier, and now returned to the haunts and scenes of my boyhood as an Adjutant. And what gave poetic zest to my heart and soul, was the fact that the beautiful girl I loved most stood at her father's gate as the regiment marched by.

A detachment of the command pursued Cluke to Licking River, where the chase was given up. Loyal citizens entertained the regiment in fine style, feasting the boys in blue with all the good things at command.

What a medley of contradictions war produces! The day before our arrival in Owingsville, Cluke, Stoner, Ewing, Everet and their men, who wore the gray, were entertained with as much love and patriotism as the most gallant defender of the old flag. It certainly was a cruel war, founded in slavery and begun in the heat of party spirit. While fighting against my schoolmates and friends, I could not but regret the deplorable situation that made it necessary to cast aside all personal considerations in the larger element of National preservation. The greater always includes the less; and, while I had the utmost respect for the local rights of the states, I could not quietly stand by and see the stars and stripes torn down from

the battlements of Fort Sumpter without lifting my arm in its
defense.

The regiment retraced its steps to Mt. Sterling through a
driving snow-storm, and on the 1st of April camped in a locust
grove adjacent to the town.   Col. Grigsby was in command
of all the troops in the place.   For a week, drilling and scout-
ing parties made things lively among the hills of Montgomery.

I visited many old friends that I knew in school-boy days,
and although some of them sympathized with the Southern
cause, they betrayed no enmity to me, but opened their hearts
and homes for my reception.   A number of prisoners were
captured and brought into camp during our rendezvous at Mt.
Sterling.   I remember the case of Capt. Alf. Bascom, of Bath
county, who belonged to Cluke's command, and had been
captured by Lieut. Julius Miller, while on a raid on Slate
Creek.   Bascom was very much alarmed at his prospect of being sent to Camp Chase, and were it not for my intercession,
combined with the former friendship of Col. Hurt, he would
certainly have gone.   Clarke Bascom, his brother, was a Union
man, and to show our regard for his good faith in sticking to
the government when his relatives went into the rebellion we
released the Confederate captain on his parole of honor.

I took dinner one evening at the house of Mrs. Emily Barnes,
in company with her talented daughter Julia, and a number
of her loyal sons were also present.   Howard Barnes was my
favorite among all the boys who went to school at the old
Highland Seminary.   He was generous to a fault, manly in
his actions, musical and witty, and had the rare faculty of
making and keeping friends.   "Billy," another brother, was
more impulsive, but true to his word, and brave under all circumstances.   Mrs. Barnes had been my friend when I was a
poor boy hunting for education, and her lovely daughter often
taught me music.   Emily Barnes was a splendid woman.   Her
hand and heart went out to the poor and needy, and when the
downcast and weary were turned from the doors of the opulent, they could always rely on her benevolence and support.

The grass of many long years has grown upon her grave, and the flowers of spring have come and gone with the changing seasons, since last I beheld her charitable face; yet, in the choicest nooks of memory she is venerated by thousands for her noble acts performed in the interests of humanity. The motto of her life can be summed up in the following beautiful stanza from the Universal Prayer of Pope:

> " Teach me to feel another's woe,
>   To hide the fault I see;
> That mercy I to others show,
>   That mercy show to me."

On the 7th of April, the regiment struck tents and moved out on the pike towards Winchester; thence marched to Richmond, to Crab Orchard, and on to Mt. Vernon, where the brigade of Gen. Gilbert was encamped. We remained here a few days, and then moved up into the Wild Cat hills as an outpost for the brigade, which continued to camp at Mt. Vernon.

A number of raiding parties from the Cumberland River dashed about London and Barboursville, giving us a great deal of trouble. Capt. Stough with a command of mounted men caught up with some of these daring raiders on the 23d of April, near Williamsburg, and killed and captured quite a number. The 24th was ordered to his support, and by a hurried march we dashed over the rolling Wild Cat hills and entered the town of London early the next morning, moving out on the mountain road leading to Williamsburg. We chased the enemy across the Cumberland River to Seven Mills, where they were lost and scattered in the mountains. The whole command returned to London, where we camped and scouted for about two weeks.

From this place we were ordered to fall back on the impregnable hills of Wild Cat, overlooking the brawling waters of Rockcastle River. From the 15th of May to the 15th of July, 1863, the regiment encamped on the very topmost height of the bold ridge where, in the fall of 1861, Col. Garred made

such a gallant stand against the enemy. Raiding and foraging
parties were continually sent out by Col. Grigsby, who reported
the movements of the Confederate forces to Gen. Gilbert, at
Mt. Vernon.

About this time, I was detailed to proceed to Somerset and
report for duty on a court-martial convened for the purpose of
trying Lieut. Lee, of the 24th, for drunkenness, and also such
other officers as might come before the court. I finished my
duty in a few days, and returned to Mt. Vernon.

The regiment broke up camp from the Wild Cat Pass on the
5th of July, and marched to Mt. Vernon, joining the brigade,
which proceeded to Crab Orchard, Stanford, Camp Nelson,
Camp Dick Robinson, and thence to Danville, where General
Burnside was massing an army of ten thousand men to pene-
trate into East Tennessee, capture the railroad communication
of the enemy, and thus wrench the backbone of the crumbling
rebellion.

A more perfect organization of the various regiments took
place at Danville. Drilling and dress-parade came off every
day, and a large number of ladies and gentlemen visited the
parade-grounds every evening and witnessed the "pomp and
circumstance of glorious war." I received a leave of absence
for five days, and went to Frankfort to engage Capt. Denny
Healy as the leader of our regimental band. A number of men
were employed and mustered in for the band, and some fine
silver instruments were bought in New York by the officers of
the regiment. Capt. Healy, the leader, was a young Irishman, who devoted his life and talents to music. He could
compose and play almost any kind of music, and was what
might be called a musical prodigy. He remained in the regiment nearly two years, and did a great deal to inspire its discipline and minister to the pleasure of the command. After
the war he settled in Louisville, organized a city band, and
was very successful in his chosen profession.

CHAPTER XI.

Before leaving for the East Tennessee expedition, Col. L. B. Grigsby resigned his commission, (July 16th, 1863,) on account of business and bad health. Col. J. S. Hurt then took command of the regiment, remaining to the close of the war.

On the 17th of August, the regiment moved to Stanford and Crab Orchard, and thence to Somerset, where our brigade (the 2d, commanded by Gen. Daniel Cameron, in Haskell's Division,) crossed the Cumberland River on the 23d. We were now fairly pointed for East Tennessee, with hot, dusty days, rugged mountain roads and brawling streams before us. The passage of the Cumberland, at Smith's ferry, was a very difficult undertaking by the assembled army of Gen. Burnside. On the south side of the rapid stream we were compelled to haul up the wagons and artillery by ropes grasped in the hands of a thousand men.

When all was ready, we began a weary march through an unknown country that had been occupied by the enemy since the beginning of hostilities. A trail of twelve days in the mountains lay before us ere we could tap the railroad near Knoxville, and sever Confederate communication from Richmond to the south-west. Our wagon trains did not get up on the night of the 23d until twelve o'clock, and the soldiers had to camp out on the bare, rocky earth, with nothing to cover them save overhanging branches. The air was chilly, and the starlight shone down on the sleeping camp with a cold gleam. Bright and early in the morning twilight we proceeded on the rough march to Jacksburg, traveling over narrow, rocky roads that almost defied the passage of wagons and mules. We began to ascend the spurs of the Cumberland Mountains, winding our way over a back-bone ridge, until we crossed the rapid waters of New River. In many instances, over the mountain plateau, we passed fifteen and twenty miles without a sign of human habitation. One vast wilderness stretched away to the horizon, only broken by lowering clouds that settled on the bosom of that upland sea of emerald beauty.

On the 29th and 30th of August we passed over the topmost peaks of the mountains, and camped some ten miles from the town of Montgomery, situated near the southern base of the mountain range. The sight from the tops of the Cumberland Mountains was grand and inspiring. Bold, bare rocks shot out against the sky like huge ships upon a raging sea. Deep, dark chasms yawned in majestic horror upon the eye of the traveler, and the thundering roar of some far-off falls broke upon the ear like the rush of a mighty wind sweeping over a primeval forest. The Cumberland looked magnificent.

> " Its uplands sloping decked the mountain side,
>   Woods over woods, in gay theatric pride."

But to the romantic soul filled with unutterable admiration, the gloaming, the starlight and the moonlight must intermingle to bring out in bold relief the beauty and grandeur of mountain scenery. One moonlight night I stood upon one of the wildest and highest peaks of the Cumberland, the sighing pines singing to the stars, the crickets chirping at my feet, and the sound of dashing cascades carried on the wings of the night, while the "bright and burning blazonry of God" glittered in their eternal depths, and lit up the green mountain tops with a glow of celestial light.

At such a moment the soul communes with its Creator; and while we may, perhaps, doubt the reason of prayers, creeds and churches, the most unreasoning man cannot deny the existence of a God, in the vast and mysterious realm spread out before him in air, water, earth and sky! Those majestic mountain tops were not called into being and clothed with a rich eternal verdure by chance. Those crystal springs and flowing rivers did not rise and meander to the sea without some grand design. The blue heavens above were not spread out in illimitable magnificence, and dotted all over with shining worlds, without a plan. No! God lives in every breeze that wafts over the earth; shines in every star that glitters in the blue vault of heaven; sings with every warbler that flutters in the forest; breathes in every fragrant flower; and when the mortals of this transient life have lived out their little span, they mingle again, for some mysterious end, with the component parts of earth, and sink back into some grand omnipotence, great and eternal!

* *
*

The troops passed through Montgomery on the last day of August, to the undulating plains of East Tennessee, the "promised land" of loyalty. Montgomery at that time might well be compared to the Deserted Village of Goldsmith. Its inhabitants lived in rural comfort before the rebellion, surrounded by smiling fields and productive vineyards, that decked the upland sunny slopes. These mountain people were loyal to the flag, and when the tocsin of war sounded, they fled to the North as refugees, in search of peace and protection against the plantation "chivalry," who made it too hot for Union men to live in the atmosphere of slavery and Confederate conscription.

In going through the village, I did not see a single living mortal; but the torn roofs, broken fences, rotten doors, creaking sign-boards, straggling hedges, tall weeds, blowing thistles, hanging cobwebs, and "swallows twittering from their straw-built shed," betokened decay, desolation and death.

> "Sweet, smiling village, loveliest of the lawn,
> Thy sports are fled, and all thy charms withdrawn;
> Amidst thy bowers the tyrant's hand is seen,
> And desolation saddens all thy green.

> Sunk are thy bowers in shapeless ruin all,
> And the long grass o'ertops the mouldering wall;
> And trembling, shrinking from the spoiler's hand,
> Far, far away thy children leave the land."

I left Montgomery, and looked back with a sigh upon the straggling village, as the setting sun shone on the dilapidated homes of those loyal hearts who forfeited all but truth and honor in their devotion to the old flag.

For four days the army toiled over rough roads and rapid streams, towards Kingston and Knoxville. Reports came in that the enemy had evacuated these places, and withdrawn into Georgia and Virginia. About four o'clock on the afternoon of the 4th of September, my regiment struck the East Tennessee Railroad at Lenoir, a small station south of Knoxville. The Holston and Little Tennessee Rivers form the main arm of the Tennessee, which wanders away for more than five hundred miles in its course to the sea. A thrill of satisfaction and triumph pervaded the ranks of the army when the shrill blast of the iron horse came echoing down the road from Knoxville. We felt that our long, weary march through the mountains had not been in vain, and that the "stars and stripes," though often torn down and insulted, would yet wave in glory and peace over a united land.

The possession of Tennessee by the Union army compelled the Confederate commanders to shift their base of operations farther south, and thus shorten the space that intervened between them and the Atlantic Ocean. I could see, even at that time, that fate and fortune frowned upon the Confederacy, and while many battles remained to be fought, every Union soldier was confident of ultimate success.

Lingering at Lenoir for a couple of days to rest, the regiment took up its line of march for Concord, a village fifteen miles south of Knoxville, where we pitched tents in a pleasant grove, and enjoyed the ease of camp life for a week, making friends of the loyal people, who flocked in from the surrounding country to behold their Union deliverers.

Gen. Burnside projected an expedition towards the Virginia line, in search of the enemy, who fled at his approach. Marching orders were received, and on the 15th of September, for the first time, we passed through Knoxville, the capital city of East Tennessee, the home of Parson Brownlow and Horace Maynard, both of whom have since mingled their loyal dust with that of the state they saved to the Union.

The regiment marched through the town with banners flying, drums beating, horns blowing, and hearts throbbing to the music of freedom. We reached Strawberry Plains in due time, and camped at Panther Springs; from there proceeded to Morristown, on the railroad, where Gen. Burnside came up and made a cheering speech to the citizens, who assembled at the depot to hear his patriotic words. The command moved on to Greenville, the home of Vice President Andrew Johnson. This beautiful village is situated amid a circle of rolling hills, the huge forms of the Smoky Mountains looming up in the distance, separating Tennessee from North Carolina.

Over these rugged mountains a few years before, crossing the French Broad and the rapid Holston, wandered a poor, penniless boy in search of work and fortune. He met kind friends in the mountain town of Greenville, who cared for his immediate wants, and secured for him a place on the bench of a tailor-shop, where he could master the trade and support himself by honest labor. The boy was very apt, and soon ingratiated himself into the affections of all who knew him. He had never gone to school, and felt the want of education. A kind and loving friend, who afterwards became his wife, undertook the task of instructing the young tradesman in the rudiments of education. His advance in knowledge was rapid, for God had stamped the rustic mountaineer with an extraordinary brain, which was backed by indomitable pluck, and never-failing energy. He had the ambition of Alexander and tenacity of General Jackson. No clouds or storms could obscure the sunbeams of his heart, or twist him from a purpose he had once formed. The people trusted him, and believed in his manly honesty. From the lap-board and iron of the tailor, he rose·to the position of Alderman, Member of the Legislature, Governor, Congressman, Senator, Vice President, and finally, through the horrible death of our noble and beloved LINCOLN, put on the Presidential robes and became the Chief Magistrate of the Republic.

I went into the small brick tailor shop where "Andy Johnson" once made trowsers for the people of Greenville; and I thought deeply on the startling changes of this mysterious life. We rise and fall like bubbles on a stormy sea. The last become first, and the first become last.

***

The enemy was reported in force at Center Station, near the Wataga River, and early Sunday morning our command moved off for Jonesboro and Johnson Station. Some slight skirmishing occurred, three of our men being killed and wounded by the cavalry of the enemy that lay in ambush near the road. Near the banks of the Wataga the enemy had erected a fort. Gen. Burnside came to the front in person, and a reconnoitering party was thrown out, when considerable firing occurred. A flag of truce was sent in by the commanding General for the capitulation of the place, and as there was no response to it, my regiment was ordered to charge the redoubt. We went towards the ridge with a yell; but, to our chagrin, the enemy had fled, leaving nothing but two dismantled cannon. We followed up the retreating force towards Bristol, on the Virginia line, but shortly began a retrograde movement towards Knoxville, abandoning all the towns and posts we had previously occupied.

It was said that the Confederate General Crittenden, of Kentucky, and the gallant Cerro Gordo Williams were in command of the troops that fled towards Virginia; but, be this as it may, our expedition proved fruitless, and we finally returned, to be pent up in Knoxville, besieged by Gen. Longstreet.

CHAPTER XII.

THE SIEGE OF KNOXVILLE.

On Sunday, the 27th of September, the 24th encamped on our old ground at Concord, one of the outposts of Knoxville. We remained at this delightful post until the 30th of October, when we were ordered to Knoxville, and encamped on the south side of Holston River, on a circle of quite abrupt hills, which we proceeded to fortify. The right of my regiment lay on the bluff hills of the Marysville road. The prospect seemed to be that we might have to remain all winter among these hills; and with this end in view, orders were given to erect snug log houses in company rows, leaving sufficient space between each cabin and company for sanitary purposes and company formations.

When the cabins were completed, the ten rows with their uniform construction had all the appearance of regular barracks. The field officers had hospital tents erected on the apex of the hill, commanding a view of all that transpired in camp, and at the same time securing a fine sight of the valley looking south.

I was detailed by Gen. Hascall, the Division Commander, in conjunction with Capts. Kennedy and Runkle, of the 65th Illinois, to meet at headquarters and proceed as a " board of survey," to condemn the various transportation material and quartermaster stores submitted to us by Capt. T. W. Fry. We finished our labors in a few days, condemning property to the amount of over a million dollars. I wrote the report, which we all signed, after which we returned to our respective regiments.

Fortifications were being rapidly thrown up on each side of the Holston River, and Fort Sanders, a strong field-work on the north side, was looming up into impregnable proportions. Longstreet was reported at Loudon, making his way towards the Tennessee, at Kingston, with an army of twenty-five thousand men devoted to the defeat or capture of Burnside's sixteen thousand isolated soldiers. The outposts of Burnside were soon driven inside the earthworks that had hastily been thrown up around Knoxville. Longstreet surrounded the town on the 17th of November, with a cordon of confident warriors who had often known success on many hard-fought fields on the Potomac.

Instead of stopping to skirmish and throw buncomb shells after the boys in blue, and hesitating at a large brick house on the hill-top to the south-west of the city, the Confederate commander should have formed his advancing columns into the shape of a wedge and hurled the mass, at all hazard, against the wavering army that occupied the newly made breastworks. Had he done this, the entire army of Burnside would have been dispersed, captured, or killed; and the loyal city could have been left a mass of smouldering ruins and ashes.

But Longstreet let the opportune moment pass, and every hour afterward his chances for success became less, while the besieged troops became stronger and more confident to resist until succor came from Grant and Sherman, whose daring soldiers had recently defeated and routed the veterans of Bragg on the bold heights of Missionary Ridge and above the clouds at Lookout Mountain.

A succession of daily skirmishes took place while the enemy worked up to our breastworks, by rifle-pits, parallels and batteries, coming at last within a hundred yards of our strongest redoubts. On the south side of the river Generals Law and Robertson had posted their brigades, along a bold ridge, their left resting on a rocky bluff abutting on the river, while the right extended towards the Marysville road, where Wheeler's cavalry had driven in our mounted men. General Hascall's

division confronted the Confederates, our right resting on a
parallel ridge.   The brigade of Gen. Daniel Cameron occupied the right of the division, and the 24th Kentucky stood
behind rifle-pits in the woods on the extreme right of the
brigade, having the place of danger and honor.

The Confederate lines were being tightened from day to
day around Knoxville, like a huge boa-constrictor about its
prey.   On the 24th of November, the enemy kept up a sharp
fire on our advanced line. Sidney Gobbart, of Company "A,"
was killed by a sharp-shooter.   The regiment remained in the
trenches all day, and made occasional sorties.   Capts. Barber
and Hall, with their respective companies, advanced on the
skirmish-line of the enemy, driving it back on the main column, occupying the ridge a thousand yards across a ravine to
our front.   These companies were in turn forced to retreat to
their original position by the superior force of the enemy.
A number of advanced sharpshooters kept up a galling fire
during the day, and it was worth a man's life to expose his
body.   Several of our men had been wounded by a gray-
headed Georgian who had burrowed himself at the roots of an
old tree, and I was anxious to get a shot at him.   To this end
I crawled out to our front vidette, who had been exchanging
fruitless shots with the Confederate.   I took a Springfield rifle
from the soldier, and laid my plans to get a good shot at the
defiant game who had killed and wounded our men without
exposing himself.   I could see the spot from whence came the
death-dealing missiles; and crawling up to the point of a jutting rock, I took off my cap, placed it on a stick, and slowly
moved it into an exposed position, when, quick as a flash, a
bullet went through it, and I let it fall to the earth as if the
head of a soldier went down to death.   The Confederate, believing that he had killed the man in his immediate front, did
not exercise his usual caution in reloading his gun, but exposed
two-thirds of his shoulder and breast in the operation.   I took
a dead aim from the rock where I lay, and pulled the trigger.
A flash—a groan—a lurch, throwing up the hands—and one

of our most dangerous foes had passed over the River of Time. Our main line was advanced during the day, and as a matter of curiosity I went to the roots of the gnarled oak and found the sharpshooter with a bullet through his right breast, calm and peaceful in the sleep of death. I had some of my men bury the old warrior at the foot of the oak, which served for a monument. He had lived his allotted span, and I have no doubt that his last breath was offered up on what he deemed the altar of patriotism.

On Wednesday, Nov. 25th, 1863, we noticed a great commotion among the Confederate troops occupying the heights. Early in the morning the artillery opened fire on our earthworks in the woods, shells bursting over our heads in rapid succession, smashing tree-tops that fell into our wavering ranks, while solid shot shrieked over the ridge, tearing up trees and earth as if a cyclone had started on its mission of death. We knew the terrible artillery fire was the precursor of a charge by the enemy, and while our guns feebly replied, we kept a keen watch across an old field that lay between us and the foe.

Suddenly there emerged from the opposite ridge a gray line of battle, two columns deep, with flags flying, bayonets glistening, and coming right across the field with that confidence born of assured success, while the artillery from the heights poured a stream of shot and shell into our ranks.

We were ordered to reserve our fire until the enemy showed the whites of their eyes, and then to blaze away and charge down the hill upon the ranks of the advancing troops. When within fifty yards of our earthworks, coming in gallant style, a death-dealing volley was given the enemy, as a morning salute, which caused them to stagger about like drunken men. Yet still they came ; and when within a few feet of an old worm fence on the margin of our woods, we dealt them another fire, and at the same time Gen. Cameron, riding on his excited steed, ordered a charge along the whole line. There was some hesitancy in obeying the order on the left of our line, and a seeming unwillingness to take the open field, thereby exposing the whole command to the murderous artillery that poured their missiles down upon us with remarkably sure aim. To start the charge, I ordered some of the men to throw down part of the fence in our right front, and putting spurs to my horse, jumped the barrier at a bound, calling upon the men to dash forward to the charge, and meet the enemy in the open field.

All was now in motion, and with fixed bayonets the men rushed on to the foe, who broke and fled down the hill faster than they came up. Col. Hurt led the left wing of the regiment, which joined on the 65th Illinois, with the 103d Ohio supporting our advancing column. I was put in charge of the right wing of the regiment, abutting on the rugged rocks of the Holston River. In a narrow gorge, our men endeavored to scale the heights and turn the left of the enemy ; but they perceived the movement, and depressed their cannon on our struggling ranks, pouring into us a shower of shot and shell. In one spot the regiment got into a tangle among the rocks, and wavered backward and forward in the effort to advance and also at the same time escape the fury of the fire from the heights. Our color-bearer, James Jackson, was shot down and dropped the flag, which was taken up by another soldier, who soon met the same fate. For a time it looked as if we would be compelled to retreat; but just as everything seemed giving away, Col. Hurt rushed up and grasped the prostrate flag, when our broken ranks rallied to his support and established a line so close under the enemy's guns that they could not depress them enough to make fatal shots, the shells and balls shrieking over our heads as if a myriad of demons were treating us to an infernal serenade.

Gens. Shackleford and Woolford, with their mounted corps, came to our aid in this trying ordeal, Col. Charles D. Pennybacker, of the 27th Kentucky, who commanded a brigade in Woolford's division, bringing his gallant Kentuckians to the front and strengthening our broken lines. The fight went on with alternate success and defeat during the day, and even the artillery of heaven joined in the roar below. Clouds, rain, thunder and lightning accompanied the roaring fray. The evening sun at last shot forth its parting beams, piercing the dense woods with arrows of golden light. A final charge was ordered. With five companies of the 24th Kentucky, I began to climb the heights, and touching, as I thought, the column on my left, we made our way through underbrush and dark timber to the cannon that had been firing on us during the day. All was seemingly still; the guns were there, but the soldiers had fled down the hill towards their pontoon bridge that connected the north side of the Holston with the main column of Longstreet. I went to my left, and found, instead of support by the brigade, nothing but an interminable forest. The whole command, it seems, had fallen back to our original base in the woods, and left me with the five companies isolated but victorious on the enemy's ground. I knew it was useless for me to attempt to hold the captured position without support, and as I saw through the timbers a line of soldiers advancing to reoccupy the ground they had so suddenly vacated, I determined that in this particular instance discretion was the better part of valor, and withdrew my men down the hill and through a large open field, back to the works we had occupied in the morning. It was reported to Gen. Burnside, at Knoxville, that I had been captured with all my men; and many of my own regiment, including Col. Hurt, thought I had been taken in as fresh food for Andersonville and Libby prison.

I believe it was acknowledged by all that if the brigade and division had been actuated by my enthusiasm, the Union forces on the south side of the Holston would have camped on the ground of the enemy that bleak November night, and the two Confederate brigades would have been compelled to recross the river.

It is a ludicrous thing to behold brave soldiers fighting each other and each moment increasing the distance between battle-lines—each party fearing the other, and both retreating when . no one pursues. This may be on the principle that

> " He who fights and runs away
> May live to fight another day;
> But he who in the battle 's slain
> Will never live to fight again."

From the 25th to Sunday, the 29th, my regiment was constantly engaged in skirmishing with the enemy. It seems that Gen. Longstreet determined to make one desperate effort to break our lines and capture Fort Sanders before Gen. Grant could send troops to our relief from his successful army at Chattanooga. An assaulting column of two thousand veteran soldiers, commanded by Gen. McLaws, was selected to dash against Fort Sanders early Sunday morning, while the balance of Longstreet's command were to stand in readiness to support any lodgment the forlorn hope might secure. Brave hearts beating high with hope stood ready to charge to the death, in the first dawn of that fatal Sunday morning.

During the night, information was brought to Gen. Burnside of the contemplated attack. Action was immediately taken; additional troops were silently sent to the support of the fort, and the breastworks to the right and left of it were filled with men, who rested on their arms in anticipation of assault.

Mr. Hoxie, superintendent of the railroad, in this emergency thought of a Yankee trick, and suggested to Capt. Poe, chief engineer, that a lot of loose telegraph wire be utilized to trip up the charging enemy in their dash on the fort. The ditch in front of the bastioned work was eight feet deep and twelve feet wide. Jutting angles with close embrasures contained heavy guns loaded with grape and cannister, shot and shell. The wire was trailed zigzag around the stumps and through the grass that margined the pits in front of the fort. Lieut. Benjamin commanded the artillery in the fort, and did splendid work. About two thousand men dashed on the earthworks with all the confidence of victory; but just as they neared the deep, broad ditch, they began to stumble, and many were pitched headlong into the jaws of death; the double-shotted guns were touched off, and a perfect pandemonium prevailed in the bloody, torn ranks of the gallant besiegers, who climbed over the forms of their dying comrades up the steep sides of the fort, which still belched forth certain death to the struggling mass of devoted heroes.

Blood and bone, combined with noble daring, was not sufficient to overcome the heroic conduct of our soldiers, the unforeseen wire entanglement, and the terrible cannon and musketry fire that poured a blaze of death into the very face of the assaulting column. A short half hour found the Confederate heroes dead and dying in the ditch, which ran with human blood. Out of the assaulting brigade, one thousand had been killed, wounded or captured, while the Union loss was only four killed and eleven wounded. A Colonel of a Georgia regiment was in command of the forlorn hope, and, strange to say, he succeeded in climbing the steep side of the fort, and planting the " stars and bars" in the very teeth of our men. An artillery sergeant lifted his heavy cutlass to strike down the daring officer, but a more generous and magnanimous soldier struck aside the blade, and saved the life of the brave and reckless Georgian.

Thus the death of our young and gallant General Sanders, of Kentucky, was desperately avenged in the assault on the fort named in his honor.

While the assault on the fort was in progress, Law and Robertson, on the south side of the river, made several attacks on our works, and succeded in driving us out of our front lines. The division of Gen. Haskell was reinforced by the command of Gen. Shackleford, when we moved on the enemy and reoccupied our lines. My regiment suffered severely ; the flag was shot down, but through the staying qualities of Col. Hurt and his men, we more than held our ground until night put an end to the carnage. In the several engagements about Armstrong's Heights, on the south side, my regiment lost fifty-six men in killed and wounded. With our superior mountain marksmen, we were constantly in demand at the front, and thus suffered more severely than other regiments in the brigade.

In one of the charges of the regiment through the woods, Will Cortmell, Company "I," a Bath county boy whom I knew at home, was shot through the head, just at my side. Lieut. Lewis, Company "K," of Montgomery, was severely wounded, as also was Lieut. Desilve. About this time I was struck down by a Minie' bullet, which shocked my whole frame. I felt at once for the hole in my left breast, but on close examination, discovered that the ball had passed through my overcoat, dress coat and vest, and imbedded itself in a thick memorandum book that I kept in my inside vest pocket, the bullet being flattened out by the resistance. And, strange to say, the bullet cut the leaves of the book from the first date of the year to the 25th of November, the very date of the battle. I am writing now with the same torn memorandum book of twenty-one years ago before me, and I am sure that were it not for those thin, compact leaves, I should have been pierced through the heart. Some are thus fated to escape death in battle and otherwise by a hair's breadth—

> "To grasp the skirts of happy chance,
> And breast the blows of circumstance."

Longstreet was very confident, when he drew his lines about Knoxville, that Burnside and his "boys in blue" were fated to surrender. He sent in a flag of truce demanding the unconditional surrender of Burnside and his men ; but "Old Burny," as the boys fondly called him, replied in these curt words: " I have a few rounds of ammunition and a few soldiers ; and if you want them, come and take them ! " I will give Longstreet credit for trying to accommodate Burnside, for in the charge upon Fort Sanders there was no nonsense in design nor halting in execution.

During the last week of the siege, provisions were very scarce with the men and officers of the various regiments, whatever may have been the supply at headquarters. Brown bran bread, baked in brick ovens at Knoxville, was issued, and corn and fat bacon from the Holston and French Broad were distributed in sparing quantities. I divided my supply of corn on the cob with my sorrel horse, who found his sustenance on the twigs, roots and branches of the woods, while six ears of corn per day were given him as a luxury. I shelled my corn in hot ashes, and filled my pockets with the roasted kernels. In the constant call for our services in the trenches there were no stated times for meals, but when the gnawings of hunger attacked our patriotism, we resorted to parched corn and water from the babbling brook. The brook did not babble as sweetly as in the love-lit long ago, but it was very filling under the circumstances, and after a banquet of corn and water we might have been taken for the warriors of Falstaff or a lot of Dutch aldermen.

On the night of the 4th of December, 1863, Burnside was advised of the advanced command of Gen. Sherman, that had hastened to our relief by the way of Kingston and Marysville. Longstreet became very uneasy and pulled up stakes, leaving leisurely for East Tennessee and Virginia.

The relieving command of General Sherman must have numbered thirty thousand men, including the troops of Howard, Granger, Blair and Long, who first marched into our camp on the south side of the Holston, bringing new hope and strength to our depleted, hungry columns.

On the morning of the 6th of December, General Sherman, Granger, Blair and staff officers, rode by our camp with ten thousand men of Granger's command. We looked down upon our supporting comrades from our strong fortifications on the Marysville road with a feeling of security, knowing that sure deliverance was at hand, and that the enemy was in full retreat to the Virginia line.

On the 7th of December, my regiment left their line of log huts that skirted the Marysville road, and crossed the Holston in pursuit of Longstreet. That night we camped near the railroad bridge at Strawberry Plains. The enemy was reported in force at Blain's Cross-Roads. We moved out the next morning on the road to Rodgersville and Rutlidge, and for several days camped, skirmished and foraged among the spurs of the Clinch mountains. Several prisoners were taken from the straggling soldiers of Longstreet, and many of his men deserted, coming into our camp for food, raiment and protection.   They were cold and hungry.

I was greatly astonished to see some of the prisoners barefooted, in the snows of winter, among the sterile hills of Tennesse, starving and in rags, fighting for what they deemed the right.   Their bravery and misfortune commanded my respect and admiration, and I never failed to divide with them my last cracker or corn-dodger.   I thought of the rebels at Valley Forge, under the immortal Washington, when fighting in the snows of winter, hungry and naked, against the English tyrant, and compared the Revolution patriots of '76 with the Confederate soldiers of '61.   I saw this difference, however—the first fought for the liberty of *all* men, while the latter fought for the liberty of some men!   One fought a government of fraud and force, while the other fought the government of their own making, and that, too, in the interest of slavery, which gave to the purse-proud few the right to enslave millions of human beings.

Our command now camped, and marched about Strawberry Plains until the 16th of January, when we were ordered to move on Dandridge, where a heavy column of the enemy camped on the French Broad.   General Foster had taken command in East Tennessee, and General Parke had charge of the forces in active service in the field.   We went up to Dandridge in brave style—met the enemy, and returned a great deal faster than we went.   On the night of the 17th, our army moved back to Strawberry Plains, continually harrassed by cavalry.   Such a night march is seldom seen. Wagons blocked the road, which in many places scemed to have no bottom.   Longstreet captured our beef cattle and considerable commissary stores. Rain came down in torrents. The next day my regiment was left as a rear-guard to the army.   We had to make several stands and fire into the pursuing cavalry, in order to allow the tired mules and lumbering wagons to escape capture.   During the night our road of retreat was lit up with burning wagons. We camped on a mountain slope near Strawberry Plains, about twelve o'clock in the night, and sank down to rest after forty-eight hours of foolish marches in search of an enemy that our commander in the field dare not fight when found. The snow came down thick and fast during the night, and when the morning sunlight ushered in the day, we arose from our cold slumber, weary, hungry and dejected.

The enemy followed us to the Holston River, and the railroad bridge that we had but recently rebuilt was burned to prevent the Confederate cavalry from crossing. We continued our retreat to Knoxville, while the enemy followed us nearly to the outworks of the town in great force. The idea of twenty-five thousand veteran soldiers retreating from a few thousand ragged and starving Confederates was disgraceful. There was not even a private in the army at Dandridge that did not want to fight. We went there for that purpose, and our generals flunked. Why our army of twenty-five thousand men, including the command of Foster, cavalry of Sturgis and corps of Granger, did not stand and fight was commented upon freely, at the time, by men and officers.

I venture to say if "Uncle Billy" Sherman had remained in immediate command, instead of returning to Chattanooga, the broken army of Longstreet would have been accommodated with a first-class fight ; and the strong probabilities are that the Confederate forces would have been thrashed in the open field. I don't say this in any spirit of boasting, but as a simple evidence of the faith soldiers have in a commander who finds the enemy, and fights him then and there. This thing of drill and dress parade in front of the enemy is all flummery and bosh ; and the only generals who have ever succeeded in battle, down the centuries, are those determined, lunatic characters who say :

> " I have set my life upon a cast,
> And will stand the hazard of the die."

CHAPTER XIII.

In the spring 1864, great preparations were being made to move against the Confederate army entrenched upon the strong hills of Dalton on the railroad south of Chattanooga. General Joseph E. Johnston, an accomplished commander, concentrated about fifty thousand men to check the further progress of the Union army.

Generals Grant and Sherman finally concentrated an army of a hundred thousand men about Chattanooga. The army of the Cumberland was commanded by the old Roman, George H. Thomas. The army of the Tennessee was commanded by the chivalric and dashing McPherson, while the army of the Ohio was commanded by the calm and imperturbable Schofield.

General W. T. Sherman, the best field-fighter of our war, took immediate command of the combined armies, and by masterly movements never stopped his onward triumph until he planted his victorious colors down by the sea.

The 24th Kentucky moved away from Knoxville in the early days of 1864, passed on to Loudon, Charleston and Cleveland, where it rested awhile to recruit and organize its broken ranks. General J. D. Cox commanded our Division ; Daniel Cameron, 65th Ill., was put in command of the brigade, while Gen. Riley, 104th Ohio, occasionally commanded.

About the 6th of May, 1864, we moved off towards Rocky Face and Buzzard Roost, the 23rd Army Corps joining on the left of General Thomas in the movement against Tunnel Hill and Dalton. The movements of Sherman's army pressed strongly about the entrenched lines of Johnston on Dalton

Heights, and while Thomas and Schofield made it hot for the advanced Confederates about Rocky Face, McPherson was moving through Snake Creek Gap, a long, deep, narrow valley, to the left rear of Johnson, leading to the town of Resaca.

It was intended that McPherson, with his twenty thousand veteran soldiers, should strike the railroad at Resaca in rear of the Confederates, and thus dislodge them by a bloodless flank movement. While the General was not at once successful in causing the enemy to let go their strong hold on Dalton, two days after, on the 11th of May, they vacated their works and fell back to an entrenched position at Resaca.

The whole army soon marched through Snake Creek Gap, and followed quickly in the wake of the Confederates. The rugged heights and country roads were as rough as breastworks, fallen trees, rifle-pits, dense underbrush, mud and rain could make them.

On the 14th of May the army drew its bayonet-lines about Resaca, and at once proceeded to business. The Oostenaula River was a protecting line to Johnston, and in the event of defeat it would cover his "advance to the rear;" but Sherman threw a couple of pontoon bridges across the river below the town, where he could quickly dispatch troops towards Calhoun and Kingston. McPherson occupied the right, Thomas the center, and Schofield the left.

The division of General Cox moved on the enemy's strong works about noon, the 24th Kentucky occupying the extreme right front of the command. We charged across an open field interspersed with dead trees that flung out their ghostly arms to welcome us to the shadows of death. A roaring fire of artillery burst from the enemy's works on the margin of the woods on our front; shot and shell fell among the dead tree-tops and crashed down upon the moving columns like a shower of meteoric stones. An incessant musketry fire lent its music to the roar of battle, and the charging ranks forgot the danger of the moment in the excitement of action.

Scaling a ridge in the immediate front of the enemy's breast-works, the 24th Ky. and 65th Illinois, supported by the 103d and 104th Ohio, dashed off on a bayonet charge, and before the Confederates could realize the situation, we had captured their first line of works and driven them back upon stronger fortifications. At this point in the battle, a young hero from Mount Sterling was shot through the head, and died with a smile on his face. Colie Apperson was a favorite with every one in the regiment, and had formerly enlisted in Company "K," as a private. His youth, spirit and education attracted the attention of Col. Grigsby and Quartermaster Trumbo, who made the eighteen-year old boy Quartermaster-Sergeant, which position he held on the morning of the Resaca fight.

When the charge across the field was being made, I noticed him as a file-closer, in the company of Captain Anderson, and knowing that he should be in the rear with the wagons, ordered him back out of danger, saying that it was not his duty to be with a gun fighting in the ranks. He begged me to allow him to fight in one battle any way, as he had enlisted for that purpose. I spoke to Col. Hurt in regard to him, and as everything was under way, all that could be done was to allow matters to work themselves out as fate dictated.

Peaceful and calm the young soldier lay in the trench, never again to hear the roar of battle or join in the cheers of his comrades. When night put an end to the carnage, Will L. Vischer, the standard-bearer, and Sam Nelson, the commissary sergeant, fashioned a rude coffin and buried him in a temporary grave near a farm-house, marking the spot. At the close of the war his remains were removed to Mt. Sterling by Vischer, and buried among the friends who loved him in life. Peace to the ashes of a noble young soldier who stepped even beyond his duty to strike a blow for the old flag.

The 24th suffered severely at Resaca. Capt. Cary, Company "B;" Capt. Hedges, Company "G;" Lieut. McIntyre, Company "B," and Lieut. Nelson, Company "E," were wounded; four enlisted men were killed, fifty-four wounded, and nineteen

were missing—making a total loss in the battle, of eighty-one
men. The 24th had only about three hundred men for immediate duty after the fight, being crippled more than any other
regiment in the brigade.

Gen. M. D. Manson commanded our brigade in the Resaca
fight, and exposed himself like the rest of the men in the advance upon the earthworks. Just before the close of the battle
he received a painful wound, and was compelled to retire from
the field. Col. Hurt then took command of the brigade, and
Lieut.-Col. North assumed command of the regiment. The
latter had a fine horse shot under him, but continued to lead
the men on foot as if nothing had occurred to disturb his equanimity. North was a man without the varnish of education,
but he had that sterling loyalty, determination and good common sense, that made him superior to the general run of college
graduates.

Johnston was compelled to loose his hold on Resaca and the
Oostenaula River, falling back upon the hills of Cassville and
Cartersville, on the Etowah. Schofield's command followed
on the left wing of the army, passing through Adairsville, and
on the morning of the 20th of May advanced to battle against
the supposed strongholds of the enemy ; but instead of fighting
at Cassville, the Confederate commander retreated across the
Etowah, leaving behind long lines of fresh breastworks, rifle-
pits, field-forts, and that desolation which marks the track of a
retreating army.

We camped for a few days in the vicinity of Cassville and
Cartersville. General Cox's division was kept busy reconnoitering along the upper waters of the Etowah, in conjunction with our cavalry. About fifteen miles from the railroad
bridge over the Etowah, to the north-east, iron works and
foundries had been established, where the Confederates manufactured munitions of war. Schofield desired the destruction
of these works, and Gen. Cox was selected to devise means for
destroying them. Our brigade was appointed to perform the
task, and a part of the 24th Kentucky, with a detail of men

from the 65th Illinois and 103d and 104th Ohio, composed the raiding party. Fifty picked men were selected, and placed under the command of Lieut. James Caughlan, of Company "K," 24th Kentucky, who was at the time serving as aid-de-camp on the staff of Gen. Cox. He was empowered to select some other officer to assist in the undertaking, and as a number had volunteered to enter the enemy's lines on this perilous duty, he finally resolved upon my aid, believing that I had the determination to take the consequences of a forlorn hope.

The fifty men who volunteered knew, through a loyal citizen-guide, that the works were guarded by a regiment of cavalry. When all was in readiness, we marched off through the mountains, in by-paths, with our guns and forty rounds, and hard-tack. After going nearly fifteen miles without meeting anybody, we were suddenly brought to a halt by our guide on a hill-top overlooking the smoking foundry and the winding waters of the Etowah. It was after six o'clock, and the mill-hands had quit work for the day, while the cavalry guarding the bridge, ford and works, were preparing their evening meal in fancied security on the bank of the river.

A quick reconnaissance showed us a gulch leading down to the rear of the mill. We prepared torches of pine splinters to throw among the combustibles of the factory. Part of the men were left in a clump of bushes commanding the bridge, over which the cavalry might dash. Caughlan and I led the other men down the secret gulch, into the mill, which we left in smoke and flames quicker than it takes to tell it. We also fired the bridge, and before ten minutes had elapsed the object of our raid was accomplished, and we were in full retreat to our supporting base at Cartersville. The cavalry followed us for several miles, but by taking advantage of lanes, short cuts and mountain paths, the "horse marines" could not compete with "Sherman's bummers." We destroyed the Confederate arsenal and returned to camp without the loss of a man, receiving the encomiums of our comrades and the thanks of General Cox.

Lieutenant Caughlan was the leading spirit and determined genius of the raid. He coincided with my desperate suggestions, believing, as all true soldiers believe, that the bold and unexpected thing results in success. In war, if it becomes necessary to burn, wound and kill, do it at once, and sentimentalize when the enemy is dead. No man ever made a successful general unless he believed in his own power to win the battle before it began. The soldier who enters a fight with a doubt is half whipped before the action commences; but he who has no doubt of his own heart and strength will almost invariably meet with the success his bravery engenders.

Caughlan was a natural soldier, young and enthusiastic. He was of Irish blood, imbued with the firmness and patriotism of General Lyon, and the religious solemnity of Stonewall Jackson. While serving on the staff of General Cox, at the battle of Franklin, he was shot through the body in rallying broken Union forces, fronting the charging lines of Gen. Pat Cleburne, the Confederate warrior. Both of these gallant Irishmen fell on the field of Franklin, one fighting for the "stars and bars," and the other for the "stars and stripes."

The grass has long since grown above their heroic graves, and the blooming wild flowers have come and gone in the circling years; but in the halls of memory they are enshrined by those who loved them in the long ago.

> " So with an equal splendor
>   The morning sun-rays fall,
>   With a touch impartially tender
>   On the blossoms blooming for all
>   Under the sod and the dew,
>   Waiting the judgment day;
>   Bordering with gold, the Blue,
>   Mellowing with gold, the Gray !"

Johnston was unwilling to risk a general battle at Cassville, on account of the cold support received from General Hood, one of his corps commanders. Hood was a fiery officer, and wanted his own way in attacking the enemy. He had the courage of a lion, but lacked that calm judgment necessary to success in great emergencies. When a boy at school, in Mt. Sterling, Ky., and previous to his designation to West Point, he would frequently get into quarrels with his schoolmates, and while he always fought bravely, he generally got the worst of the encounter. So, again, we have the truth of the old adage: "The child is father to the man." Peace to the ashes of a brave soldier and a warm-hearted friend.

Between the 23d and 25th of May, Sherman's army had passed over the Etowah, and had started a flank movement through the Allatoona Mountains in search of the retreating enemy. It was necessary for us to keep up our railroad communications with Chattanooga, and while Johnston and his men destroyed all the bridges in their flight towards Atlanta, they were rebuilt as if by magic, by the intelligent engineer corps of the army. No more important work was performed by any part of the army than the rapid reconstruction of railroad bridges, upon which depended the supplies for our troops, who were fighting in front on short rations.

Schofield, with the army of the Ohio and Stoneman's cavalry, kept on the left of our advance, near the railroad, through the Allatoona range. We passed near the village of Burnt Hickory in making our way towards Dallas. Our march through the rugged roads of Allatoona was the weariest and worst I ever experienced. We passed gulches formerly worked for gold, toppling rocks and splintered crags, narrow ridges scarcely broad enough for wagons, swamps and ravines covered with thick underbrush, and tall pines and scrubby oaks, whose dripping boughs pattered a funeral requiem to the dying groans of company officers and advanced pickets, who constantly went down to death.

The Confederate army had stopped among the abrupt hills of Allatoona at a place called New Hope, named in honor of a Methodist church established there some years before. It now seemed that a general engagement was imminent, and that the long-sought battle was at hand. The broken ground and field fortifications were all in favor of the enemy, and although General Sherman had superior numbers, he was offset by the splendid position of Johnston. There was no time lost by us in moving to the front, quick as muddy roads and rolling hills would admit. Each day we advanced through rain, mud and brush, throwing up breastworks with head-logs as we steadily drew a cordon of bayonets about the enemy. Firing was constant, and I could almost swear that during the month of May, the rain, roar of artillery and rattle of musketry never ceased, night or day.

The 24th went to rest in the woods about New Hope church, wet, hungry and desperate. When the blessed angel of sleep seemed to hover over us, the sound of small arms broke our repose, and the bullets kept plugging our earthworks and head-logs, while many of them found a lodgment in the breasts of the boys in blue. McPherson, Hooker and Thomas kept pushing the enemy, and a number of engagements that rose to the dignity of battles were fought by the contending armies.

About the 1st of June, Johnston began to relax his hold on the foot-hills of Allatoona, and by the 4th he was retreating to the heights of Kenesaw Mountain, where fortifications were erected that defied assault. Schofield's command swung around on the railroad, passed through Ackworth to Big Shanty and began at once to move upon the bold peaks of Kenesaw that stood out in grand relief against the evening sky.

Kenesaw, Pine Mountain and Lost Mountain had to be taken before we could march in triumph to Atlanta; and the contract was not easy to accomplish. But, as we worked our way through fearful obstacles among the passes of Allatoona and New Hope, we felt confident of success in the almost insurmountable job before us; and on the 10th of June drew up against frowning mountains that lay in our pathway.

The bridges and railroad behind us had been quickly repaired, and the snort of the iron horse was soon heard echoing among the gorges of Big Shanty, in sight of the enemy on the mountain tops. They must have thought Yankee railroad workers possessed the lamp of Aladdin, having only to wish and rub for the accomplishment of every desire. I, myself, was amazed at the rapidity with which we were supplied with beef, crackers, pork and the materials of war, coming through Kentucky, Tennessee and Georgia to the front of the rebellion. The generality of soldiers have no conception of the thought and trouble taken by the commander of an army to supply his troops in passing through an enemy's country, where every vestige of forage and food has been swept away by retreating soldiers.

The battle of Kenesaw Mountain, and encounters leading up to that fatal June day, were the stepping-stones to Atlanta, and the threshold to the back door of the Confederate temple.

McPherson worked around to the left on the railroad, Thomas supported his right, and Schofield changed base to right in rear, and swung around Lost Mountain to the foot-hills of Kenesaw. Hooker, as usual, fought at every turn in the road, and like his fellowtype, Hood, never calculated the chances while there was any body to hit. The real object of " Fighting Joe" was to fight somebody and reap unexpected glory for himself, irrespective of his comrade's renown. The old soldier was a little vain ; yet, considering his aristocratic education at West Point and his experience in three wars, no particular blame should be attached to the bold hero who fought above the clouds at Lookout Mountain, and never refused a fight while he had a man to command. The " boys" had confidence in the valor and brilliancy of " Fighting Joe," and in the coming years his name will be sung and told in story. The old warrior had his failings, but halting and hesitating were not in the list, and while the enemy was in front he never asked a better post than that of danger.

CHAPTER XIV.

From the 10th of June to the 27th, the fighting about Kenesaw was almost continuous. The rain came down in torrents, superinduced, no doubt, by the concussion of roaring artillery and the rattle of musketry. Roads, fields and woods were resolved into quagmires, and the small creeks leading from the frowning battlements of Kenesaw were swollen to the magnitude of rivers, and spread over the bottom land in all directions.

On the 14th, while General Johnston was surveying the advancing columns of Sherman from the heights of Pine Mountain, in company with Hardee and Polk, a solid shot from our artillery hit the latter in the breast, causing instant death, throwing a cloud of sorrow over the ranks of the Confederates.

Leonidas Polk gave up the peaceful canons of the Episcopal church for the cannon of bloody war, and like his namesake at Thermopylæ, died with his harness on. No nobler monument than Pine Mountain could mark the spot where the fighting preacher fell, and as the coming ages roll away, the tall pines on the bold mountain peak will sing a requiem to his memory, and the waters of Chattahoochee will mingle with his fame forever.

On the 22d of June, Schofield had swung around to the right of Hooker, commanding the 20th Army Corps. We were on the road leading from Powder Springs to Marietta, the rear base of Johnston.

113

8

In the afternoon, when no particular fight seemed at hand, the enemy made a fierce and determined attack on Hooker, which was returned by the divisions of Geary and Ward with double vigor, and just as the right of the 20th Corps was being turned, Schofield, who watched the attack, threw in the division of General Hascall, supported by General Cox and his command, routing the audacious soldiers of Johnston and Hood. The killed and wounded of the enemy were left on the field of battle, and afterwards buried by our men. The 14th Ky., of Hascall's command, acted very gallantly as advanced fighters, and while the loss in killed and wounded was severe, the survivors were glorified in the action, and maintained the renown of Old Kentucky.

Rain continued to pour down as if emptied from a sky-tank with the plug out, while Schofield wiggled along to the right and front, his men drenched to the skin, with only an occasional smudgy fire improvised to cook their coffee and bacon. The men of the 24th often wished that they could be led directly against the enemy and die on the field of battle, rather than shake out their lives in the dripping woods and underbrush that waved in the chilling winds.

Our division was headed down the Sandtown road, across Olley's Creek, swollen to the extent of a river, and the country bridges over tributary streams had been swept away by the flood, or torn up by the enemy. On the 25th and 26th, we endeavored to cross a bridge over a big creek on the Sandtown road. Generals Sherman and Schofield were anxious to make our alignment with Hooker and Thomas, and thus close in on the fortified base of Kenesaw. The bridge just mentioned was guarded by cavalry and mountain howitzers on the extreme left of Johnston, protecting the roads leading to Marietta. The 103d Ohio had endeavored to dislodge the enemy from the high road on the opposite banks of the stream, but whenever they emerged from the timbers leading down to the bridge, a fearful rattle of howitzer missiles assailed them, driving them back.

The General commanding rode up in the woods, near a church, with his staff officers flying about like blackbirds in a corn-field. Orders were given to cross the stream at all hazards. General Cox came to Colonel Hurt and asked him to move the 24th to the front, reconnoiter, and if possible, charge across the bridge, and make a lodgment on the south side, so that the troops of Schofield and Stoneman could pass over and complete the advancing line. The General assured Colonel Hurt that our desperate charge would be supported by a battery that had just unlimbered in the margin of the woods, and we should receive the assistance of the whole division if necessary, while General Riley would be in immediate support with his brigade.

The 24th was drawn up along the Sandtown road in double file, heading towards the bridge a hundred yards in front, looking down a steep decline. Col. Hurt and myself consulted, and examined with a glass the status of the bridge. We found that the flooring had been torn up, and nothing but a few sleepers, hand-rails and long stringers were left to cross upon. The flood had almost reached the stringers, and was running rapidly through the woods. It was concluded to dash down to the bridge and let the men scramble over as best they could, and those who succeeded in getting over first, were to charge up the hill right in the face of "Jackass battery." I went to the captains of the ten companies in person, and ordered them to instruct their men regarding the perilous charge before us, and as I returned to the head of the line, gave the men encouragement, assuring them that while other regiments had tried to cross the creek, the "Old 24th" was equal to the task, and would certainly meet with success.

Hurt and myself took the head of the regiment—he the right file and I the left. When all was in readiness the artillery opened, and we dashed off at a rapid run for the bridge, scrambling across like squirrels. One murderous fire was all the battery could pour into us, for before they could reload we cut down the gunners, killed a number of horses, captured two pieces, and sent their cavalry support in rapid flight down the road to Marietta.   Our loss was only seven men.

In half an hour the corps of Schofield had crossed over the bridge, the divisions had made alignment with Hooker, and the cavalry of General Stoneman was pressing the enemy to the very parapets of Kenesaw.   The 24th received the thanks of Schofield and Cox, and the privilege of resting for coffee and "hard tack" on the night of the 25th, advancing next morning in fine condition for the coming battle of the 27th of June, 1864.

The morning sun rose bright and warm on the frowning heights of Kenesaw.   The enemy lay behind strong fortifications, with fifty thousand men ready and willing to receive our charging columns.   Sherman, McPherson, Thomas and Schofield determined to make a direct assault on the mountain barriers.   A hundred thousand victorious soldiers were thought strong enough to capture any place; and as Johnston had made his boldest stand at Kenesaw, Sherman concluded to give him direct battle and risk the consequences.

About nine o'clock on the morning of the 27th, the charging columns of McPherson and Thomas were moving in full force against the parapets at the base of the mountains, while Schofield continued to tighten his grip on the Confederate left, threatening the railroad at Marietta.   Artillery and musketry kept up a constant fire.   My regiment moved to the right of Hooker's command, and as we made our way through the dense brush, dark woods and fallen trees cut to intercept our progress, I could see, far to the left, long dark lines as they swayed backward and forward in the rising smoke of battle. Loud and long came the thundering noise of shot and shell from the mountain top on our advancing troops.   Heaven's artillery seemed working in Titanic grandeur, to destroy our wavering lines.   McPherson and his men, at one period of the battle, scaled Little Kenesaw, and the right flank of Johnston seemed in imminent danger; but when the smoke had cleared away, they were seen to be backing down the mountain under a galling fire. Old " Pap " Thomas sent his army against the tangled abatis and earthworks with the power of a centre wedge, driving his men into the very jaws of death, but the stubborn heroes of Johnston would not give way, sending a constant stream of lead and iron into the vitals of the Union army. Schofield endeavored to swing into the rear of the Confederates, pressing right up to their fortifications, and crouching down in front of the fallen trees and rifle-pits he could not surmount.

Human blood and bravery have seldom done more in three hours than Sherman's men did at Kenesaw; and while this is true, I must candidly acknowledge that the defiant heroes of Johnston did more, for they repelled to the last our repeated assaults, and prevented our army from taking their fortified mountain.

About 11 o'clock in the morning I was struck by a conical ball in the upper part of the right thigh; the missile passing between the femoral artery and thigh bone. The wound was painful and dangerous. I had dismounted from my horse, and was on the left of the regiment moving to the front, ahead of the men.

The 24th hesitated somewhat in the margin of a wood before entering an open field that lay in our immediate front, and directly in view of the enemy's works at the base of the mountain. In order to encourage the men to the charge, I dashed into the open field, sword in hand, raised a cheer, threw up my hands, and fell to the earth pierced through and through with a Confederate bullet. The shot almost paralyzed my whole frame, and it seemed as if some strong woodsman had struck me with a maul.

General Riley and his surgeon were among the first to salute me after I fell, my regiment having passed to the front in a charge upon the rifle-pits of the enemy. My long cavalry boots soon filled with blood, and it seemed as if I had been shot through the foot; but when the doctor, pulled off my boot and ripped up my clothing, the wound was soon discovered. A silk handkerchief was tightly twisted above the bullet-hole, stopping in some measure the flow of blood.

The battle was still raging, dry leaves caught fire, and sputtering bullets kept plugging the underbrush and trees that surrounded my prostrate form. General Riley remarked, no doubt for my encouragement, that he would give five thousand dollars for my wound, in order to get an honorable leave of absence, and retire from the ragged edge of battle to the languishing, love-lit eyes of his Buckeye belle. The old General was a wag, and between himself, Jack Casement, Daniel Cameron, Smith Hurt, John Gill, Wash. McIntyre and myself, there existed a cordial friendship outside of official rank, which never refused the fried chicken of the farmer, or the more exhilarating enthusiasm that gurgled from the mouth of the old canteen.

> Let us drink to our friends who fell;
> Be their memory fresh and green;
> For they served their country well,
> Like the glorious old canteen!

Captain Goodpaster, of Co. "I," was wounded in the face during the battle, and several men of the regiment were hit. Night set in with the Union lines defeated in their designs against the enemy, but there was a general confidence that our desperate onslaught was the stepping-stone to early victory, as was shown in the course of a few days, by Johnston relinquishing his grasp on the mountain barrier, and retreating to his strong field-works on the Chattahoochee river, and soon after to the fortified environments of Atlanta.

The only mistake made by Sherman from Chattanooga to Atlanta was his direct charge and assault on Kenesaw. We lost about three thousand men in three hours, who might have been saved by one of those flank movements so successful in previous advances; but soldiers are paid to fight and be killed. I think the incessant skirmishing, bad roads, tearing underbrush, constant rains and daily retreats of the enemy so worked upon the mind of the General commanding, that when he saw a real chance of engaging the Confederates in actual battle, he bluntly determined to fight them at any cost, and moved at once upon their ramparts. It can readily be seen how natural is the impulse to strike a retreating foe, particularly when he stands to fight every few miles, only to cover his crumbling lines to a farther base of operations. It is very aggravating to know and feel that you can whip an enemy, but cannot catch him, and his show and bluster for battle adds recklessness to ambition.

During the months of May and June, 1864, General Sherman lost about seventeen thousand men. When the nature of the ground is taken into consideration, and daily advances against a stubborn enemy behind strong field-works, contemplated in a military light, the aggregate loss is not large, and the wonder is that twice the number were not lost.

I laid in a field-hospital the night after the battle, covered by the spreading branches of an oak, and by my side were many other soldiers who received their death-wound that fatal day. The stars shone brighter than I ever saw them before, and while pain tortured my body, my soul was wafted away into the realms of fancy and patriotic contemplation that made me feel, in the event of death, I would die, at least, the heroic death of a soldier, among comrades who had fought and fell in battle. I left my friends in front with regret, to suffer in hospital wards for months, and hobble around on crutches, receiving the attention of doctors and the sympathy of "home-guard" humanity.

CHAPTER XV.

BATTLES ABOUT ATLANTA.

The gallant 24th Kentucky went on towards Atlanta, from victory to victory, participating in the engagements that secured that stronghold of rebellion.

McPherson, Thomas and Schofield kept hammering away at the brazen front of the Confederacy, and day by day the portals of their strength and ambition became weaker.

General John B. Hood, the fighting school-boy, had been placed in command of the Confederate forces, superseding one of the most cautions, and at the same time the most daring, commanders in the South.

The Union generals knew that placing Hood in command meant fight. Like Joe Hooker, he would fight ten times a day, and go back the eleventh time to show the foe that he was not afraid to kill his last man. We admire the pluck of such characters, but their judgment is held at a discount.

On the 22d of July, at Peach Tree Creek, Hood marched out in force, and made a desperate attempt to turn the left of McPherson's army. In fact, he got in the rear of the Union lines, and doubled divisions and brigades upon each other, as if they had been so many reeds in a cane-brake. Seven successive assaults were made upon the Union lines, and seven times repulse came to the foe. Dead and wounded lay in piles in the fields and woods, and thousands of prisoners were taken on each side.

The first bold and desperate battle of Hood did not meet the expectations of his friends or government. He was compelled to crouch back to the narrow precincts of Atlanta,

bleeding and dying in his first attempt to retrieve what Johnston had lost. It is true, he made Union ribs crack and loyal
hearts shiver at his terrible audacity, convincing every man at
the front that a regular Swarrow held the flashing sword of
desperate war.

Gloom and sincere sorrow settled down on the Union camps
that July night, and when the evening stars lit up the " boundless blue,'' every soldier knew that General McPherson, commander of the Army of the Tennessee, was dead. Victory
was dearly purchased by payment of such a price. He was
the beau ideal of a soldier. Murat, Ney or Kellerman never
inspired their men with more sublime daring than the heroic
McPherson. His clean-cut form, handsome face and flashing
eye can never be forgotten ; and as the years roll away, his
memory will grow greener and brighter, and be sung by the
descendants of the Army of the Tennessee while that historic
river runs down to the ocean.

*
* *

On the 28th, a general movement was made to the rear of
Atlanta. Schofield swung around toward East Point to the
Macon Railroad near Rough-and-Ready, with Thomas on his
right, while General Howard threatened Jonesboro'. On the
31st, the whole army began to tighten its grip about Jonesboro', where Hardee held his corps in stubborn defense.
Schofield was the first to strike the railroad, when a general tearing up of rails, ties and bridges began.

The 24th Ky., the advanced skirmishers of Gen. Cox's Division, 23d Army Corps, was the first regiment of Federal
troops to strike the railroad near Rough-and-Ready, the blow
resulting in the immediate evacuation of Atlanta, and the occupation by the Union army of that most important stronghold of the rebellion.

The whole North saw in the victories culminating in the
capture of Atlanta, the beginning of the end, and that a few
short months would close forever the dying eyes of the Confederacy.

General W. T. Sherman was the head and front of the Atlanta campaign. To his great genius, indomitable energy and military knowledge, can be traced the untiring advancement of the army, constant fighting, and the glorious success that finally rewarded his heroic achievements. The stream cannot rise higher than its source, neither can an army go beyond the genius of its general. A brave and intelligent commander in the open field with fifty thousand men can whip a hundred thousand good soldiers commanded by a theoretical, hesitating, namby-pamby character. Show me the general, and I'll show you the army. Show me bravery without ripe judgment, and I'll point to defeat; but the general possessing both has half won the victory before he fights.

Compliments poured in thick and fast upon General Sherman and his gallant men after the fall of Atlanta.

President Abraham Lincoln said:

"The marches, battles, sieges and other military operations that have signalized the campaign must render it famous in the annals of war, and entitle those who participated therein to the hearty applause and thanks of the nation."

General H. W. Halleck said to Sherman:

"I do not hesitate to say that your campaign has been the most brilliant of the war."

General Grant, commanding the armies of the United States, said to the hero of Atlanta:

"I feel that you have accomplished the most gigantic undertaking given to any General in this war, and with a skill and ability that will be acknowledged in history."

Encomiums such as these are rarely given by high authority to subordinate valor, and I am very sure that every officer and soldier in Sherman's command appreciated the justice of the compliments.

" Pap" Thomas shared in the glory of "Uncle Billy," and Schofield, Howard, Logan, Dodge, Blair, Davis and Cox were delighted in the crowning victory that broke the back-bone of the rebellion, and finally crushed in its ribs, when Sherman marched down to the sea. Gen. Logan was conspicuous in push and dash after the fall of McPherson, and made a record that will live in the golden page of heroes.

The day after the battle of Kenesaw Mountain I was placed in an ambulance, and taken over a rough road to Big Shanty, on the railroad, where I was put in a freight car, and sent to Chattanooga with a number of wounded comrades.

Arriving at Chattanooga, the wounded were taken to the hospital located on Lookout Mountain. I remained on the mountain but two days, during which time my wound became very painful, and mortification began. I was placed again in an ambulance, and taken down to Chattanooga and Nashville.

As the ambulance driver was turning a prominent point on Lookout Mountain I got a splendid view of Chattanooga, Missionary Ridge, and the serpentine waters of the Tennessee, meandering through foot-hills and plains below. My heart and imagination went back to that raw November day when Sherman, Hooker, Thomas and Grant moved in massive columns upon the stubborn lines of Bragg, strongly fortified upon these bold heights, with the rugged peaks of Lookout on the right, frowning dark and terrible upon the "boys in blue" as they charged up the rocky face of the mountain, with "Fighting Joe Hooker," who planted the stars and stripes, carried by heroes from the 8th Kentucky regiment, above the lowering clouds.

The flag was baptised anew in the storm of battle, and when its broad stripes and bright stars caught the evening sunshine breaking through the clouds of Lookout Mountain, a wild patriotic cheer went up from the hearts of a hundred thousand men, that echoed and re-echoed among the hills, and floated away in defiance above the roar of battle.

When I arrived in Nashville my wound was in a very bad condition, the thigh swollen with a dark greenish hue. The surgeons of the old stone college hospital examined the wound minutely, and concluded that it was necessary for my leg to be cut off in order to save my life. When I heard their conclusion I protested, and stated to the old German surgeon in charge that I preferred death to being a permanent cripple, and if he could not cut and burn out the gangrene matter without taking off my leg, he might allow nature and death full swing.

I was finally placed on a dissecting table, with half a dozen doctors around the board, ready and willing to carve me up with neatness and dispatch. I would not take the chloroform until promised by a young surgeon, named Walker, that my leg should not be cut off. They finally cut into the wound, and found the bone had only been splintered, and the nerves and muscles but lacerated. After two hours I woke up, and found myself lying on a cot in ward "A," among a number of wounded officers, and strange to say, out of ten in the room, eight belonged to the staff of the army. For about a month I suffered great pain. I was then transported to Louisville, and admitted to the officers' hospital, superintended by Doctor Brady, a gentleman of fine ability and great kindness of heart.

During the entire month of September, 1864, I remained in the hospital, and towards the early days of October, I began to recuperate my strength, feeling well enough to walk about the hall and wards on crutches.

About the last of October I was discharged from the hospital, and went to Lexington, Kentucky, to perform convalescent duty on the staff of General N. C. McLean, to enable me to receive further treatment for my gun-shot wound. I remained but a short time in this position, assisting Adjutant-General J. S. Butler in the performance of his official duty.

I was recovering my strength very fast, and as I had been absent from the 24th more than four months, I began to think of leaving the service to give some ambitious officer of any regiment a chance for promotion. While in this state of uncertainty, the following order was received from the War Department, which resolved my doubts and promptly settled my anxieties:

War Department, Adjutant General's Office, }
Washington, D. C., Nov. 4th, 1864. }

SPECIAL ORDER, }
    No. 383. }   " Extract."

The following officers are hereby honorably discharged from the service of the United States, on account of physical disability from wounds received in action, with condition that they shall receive no final payment until they have satisfied the Pay Department that they are not indebted to the Government.   *   *   *   *   *   *   *

1st Lieut. John A. Joyce, Adjutant 24th Kentucky Infantry Volunteers.
By order of the Secretary of War.
E. D. TOWNSEND,

Assistant Adjutant General.

I had no financial complications or indebtedness with the Government, and Paymaster A. Diven, at Louisville, paid my back dues on the 25th of November, 1864, when I left the service of the United States with an honorable record.

While in Louisville I became personally acquainted with Gov. Thomas E. Bramblette, who was organizing some new regiments to take the field, and wished to commission me. I had previously secured some recommendations for the position of Colonel of one of these new regiments, and as an evidence of the opinion of my superior officers and kind friends, submit the following extracts.

Gen. Daniel Cameron, commanding the 3d Division, 23d Army Corps, says to Gov. Bramblette :

" I beg respectfully to address you in relation to Lieut. Joyce, Adjutant 24th Ky. Infantry. He has been for some months past under my command, and I have had many opportunities of observing his efficiency as an officer. I consider him a young officer of great merit, well worthy of promotion. He is brave, energetic and capable, has had much experience, and on all occasions has acquitted himself to the entire satisfaction of his superiors.

In bringing his claims before your Excellency, I feel that I am but doing justice to Lieut. Joyce, while I am at the same time promoting the interests of one who is an honor to his state and to the service."

Gen. Milo S. Hascall, commanding the 2d Division 23d Army Corps, says to the Governor :

" It affords me great pleasure to recommend to your favorable consideration, for promotion, 1st Lieut. and Adjutant John A. Joyce, 24th Reg't Ky.

V. I. He has been in my command for some time, and I have had opportunities on several occasions to notice his great bravery and efficiency as an
officer. He is now absent from his regiment, suffering from a severe wound.
The term of service of his regiment has about expired. Anything you can
do for him will be considered a great favor."

Gen. J. D. Cox, commanding the 23d Army Corps, says in
his endorsement :

"I take pleasure in adding to the within testimonial the statement that
Lieut. Joyce distinguished himself in the early part of the Atlanta campaign,
at Kenesaw Mountain, where he was wounded, and has since been off duty
in consequence. I cordially endorse the statement of General Cameron as
to his efficiency and good qualities as an officer, and recommend that Lieut.
Joyce's services be recognized by the state of Kentucky in some fitting
manner."

Major-Gen. S. G. Burbridge, commanding the district of
Kentucky, says :

"It gives me pleasure to endorse Lieut. Joyce, Adjutant 24th Ky., for
any position in the gift of the Governor. He is anxious to enter the service
again, as Colonel of one of the new regiments, and if you can accommodate him, it will be a favor conferred upon a young man who has nobly
served his country, and bears the wounds of battle upon his person."

The Board of Military Enrollment for the Fifth Congressional District of Kentucky, composed of Murch, Hervey and
Dr. T. S. Bell, say :

"We cordially urge the strong claims of Adjutant Joyce as a faithful so.-
dier and excellent and worthy officer, who has been crippled in the military
service, and is a young man of fine capacity. He is worthy of any favor
that can be conferred upon him."

Dr. J. Gardner, Assistant Surgeon of the Board, says :

"I have personally served with Adjutant Joyce, and do not know any
person who deserves more favor than he does."

Hon. James Speed, the most distinguished lawyer in Kentucky, and Attorney-General under President Lincoln, says :

"I trust that the place desired will be given to Mr. Joyce."

Col Hurt, of the 24th, gave me a very complimentary letter
to Governor Bramblette, wherein he praised my capacity and
bravery, and remarked that I was well fitted for the position
of a Field Officer.

The term of the 24th was so nearly completed that I hesitated about going back to the regiment, but had an ambition to continue in the military service, where daring action might throw about me " the perfume of heroic deeds."

When the goal of my ambition was about to be reached, I discovered that my wound was too tender to allow me to take the field on horseback, and therefore was compelled to relinquish the fond hopes I had cherished, and bid farewell to the fascinations of military life.

About the last of December, 1864, I visited the 24th Ky., camped at Covington, awaiting final muster out. The regiment had come up from Atlanta, spent a few days at Mt. Sterling, proceeding from there to Covington, where final disposition could be made of men and material. The old regiment had been greatly depleted, and many of the boys who enlisted with me in the early days of war were sleeping their last sleep on the sunny slopes of Tennessee, Alabama and Georgia, or limping their weary way to the tomb amid the hills and vales of their mountain homes.

I remained at the Burnet House about a week, being cheered in the evening by Hurt, North, Nelson, Gill and McIntyre, who came from the regiment to pass a few hours of pleasure among the delicious allurements of the Queen City.

CHAPTER XVI.

LEAVING THE ARMY.—EXPERIENCE AS A SCHOOL-TEACHER.

On the 1st of January I bid good-bye to the old 24th, never again to mingle with it in the rush of battle, or join in its cheer of victory. Mountain, valley, stream, camp and battle-field were left behind to my comrades who fell in the roaring fray; and while the birds sang as sweetly, the rivers ran as freely, and the flowers bloomed as brightly, they would never again awaken heroic melodies in the hearts of those daring warriors who went down in the shock and crash of battle.

To comrades who have survived the pangs of hospital treatment and the shock of war, I send forth greeting, and say that while life lingers we cannot forget the glory and renown of the old 24th, whose flag rose triumphant on many a battle-field, and whose record for daring deeds may be equaled but cannot be surpassed by any regiment that served the government.

The 24th Kentucky was organized in the very face of treason. It defied relatives and friends for the sake of the Union, fought in front when loved ones at home were being destroyed by the enemy, skirmished on the advanced dead-lines of brigades, divisions and corps as an entering wedge to victory, marched by road, rail and boat more miles than any other regiment in the service, and at last furled forever the torn and blood-stained flag to rest with the archives of a state saved to the Union by its valor.

To every soldier in every land, and in every good cause, I extend a heart and hand, whether or not we kneel at the same altar or worship the same God.

Fame, like the soul, is immortal.

> " The stars shall fade away, the sun himself
> Grow dim with age, and nature sink in years ;
> But thou shalt flourish in immortal youth,
> Unhurt amidst the war of elements,
> The wreck of matter, and the crash of worlds."

The unsettled state of society in my old Kentucky home induced me to accept an invitation to visit an uncle who lived in Allamakee county, Iowa.

The winter of 1865 was very severe in the North-west. A few quite frigid days among the rugged, snow-capped hills of Allamakee made me wish for the warm rays of the sunny South, and the genial smiles of those dear army-friends I left behind. I was about to leave the Hawkeye State in disgust at the cold reception nature extended, when my uncle and family suggested that I should procure a country school, and turn my mind away from brooding over the past.

SCHOOL-TEACHER.

I concluded to make application for a school located at Paint-Rock Church, overlooking the waters of the Mississippi River, and within a mile of Harper's Ferry, a small town in the southeastern part of the county.

The trustee of the school, Barry, was willing that I should enter upon the duties of teacher at once, but a certificate must first be procured from the county superintendent, whose office was located at Waukon, the county seat, fifteen miles away. I easily procured the needed certificate.

Being now armed with official authority, I presented myself at the new stone school-house one blue Monday morning in January, 1865, and began the role of a country pedagogue.

Arriving early in the morning from Harper's Ferry, I unlocked the establishment, and found nothing but cheerless walls, damp and musty. A few benches were scattered about the room, and a pine desk was stuck in one corner to accommodate the presiding autocrat. An old Franklin stove, that might have warmed its namesake in the Revolutionary War, opened its broad jaws for the reception of fuel. The wood-pile outside was unchopped. As some of the "big boys" gathered in, I advised them to procure an axe from one of the neighbors, and split enough wood to dispel the cold and frost that had settled on the stone wall, and even fringed the "Old Franklin" with fantastic embellishments. After digging about in three feet of snow that surronnded the wood-pile and school-house, we finally fished out enough to make a roaring fire, and warm the shivering children that vied with each other in scorching their clothes in an effort to straddle the stove.

When nine o'clock arrived I rang the bell with the air of a sucessful auctioneer; keeping a stern face, that would have done great credit to a philosopher of sixty, much more to a youth of twenty-two, who had just launched out as an educator.

When silence prevailed I rose at the desk, and addressed the seventy-five scholars who came from the snow-clad farms of Allamakee.

I merely said that I had been employed by the trustees to teach the school for a period of six months, and hoped that the boys would behave like gentlemen, and the girls act like ladies. In conclusion, I had only to lay down the simple rule that when they did right I should reward them, and when they did wrong I should certainly punish them.

These remarks were taken by the younger children with humility, but a few of the larger boys winked at each other, as much as to say, "That's an old gag, that can't frighten scholars who have ducked bigger teachers than you are. It might be well to give that speech to the 'marines,' but for the stalwart sons of Erin living among the grubs of Allamakee it will not do; the colors of your eloquence will not wash!" Notwithstanding this imagined reply to my first and last effort as a teacher, I proceeded at once to bring order out of chaos, and class the school.

The third day of my mission brought about a free fight among the scholars during my absence at dinner. When school

was called, I proceeded to ascertain the cause of the row.
It seems that a son of Erin and a waif from the Fatherland
disputed about the honor and bravery of their respective ancestors, and the other scholars joined in the fight, with a clannish
spirit that would have been an honor to the bogs of Ireland
or the upland slopes of Scotland. After due investigation, I
implicated only seventeen boys and girls in the fight, sending
the residue of my institution to their seats and books. When
all was ready, I went to business with a fine hickory ruler that
had been provided in anticipation of just such troubles. The
smaller scholars took their light punishment with suppressed
sobs, and went to their benches with sulks. The leader of the
riot was the only one who attempted to resist, and treat my
proposal to whip him with contempt. I reasoned with the
stalwart Hibernian, impressing upon him his violation of school
rules, and my intention to have equality of punishment. He
finally squared off, swore with the swagger of a prize-fighter, but
ere he could execute his threat I hit him with the rule just under the ear, and sent him to the floor in a shiver of pain. A
dipper of water brought him to, in tears, when I finished his
punishment by additional blows on his hands, sending him to
his seat as if nothing had occurred to disturb the equanimity
of the school.

From that day to the close of my term in June I was boss
of the institution, and had no further occasion to punish any
of the scholars. When the examination and exhibition closed
on the last day, scholars, parents and friends left me with
thanks, praise and tears; and many of my dear old pupils will
remember to this day the pleasant hours and loving chats we
had under the noon-day shade of Paint-Rock Church, and the
delightful strolls we took among those rugged hills and blooming vales.

My experience as a village schoolmaster will long be remembered; and the beautiful site of the school, church and
graveyard was all that the most romantic heart could require.
Situated on a high hill, overlooking the rolling plains to the

west, and commanding a view to the south and east, with the waters of the Mississippi sweeping along to the sea, it was no wonder that my young heart swelled with emotion when contemplating the beauty of the landscape. How often have I lingered in the tangled walks of the old church-yard, under a spreading oak, and gazed in rapture at the golden glory of the setting sun, as the storm-clouds in the west swept across the cardinal colors of the day. My pathway through woods and fields was made radiant with boys and girls. Sleigh-rides, parties and occasional balls at Harper's Ferry, intervened to banish the monotony of country life, and while I kept the face of a stern philosopher in the school-room, I acted with all the vanity and freedom of a drum-major in the ball-room.

Spelling-matches at the country schools were occasions for fun, and opportunities for the belles and beaux to indulge in the never-ceasing eccentricities of Cupid, who shoots his arrows where least expected, inflicting wounds that never heal, and romantic pangs that never die.

My patrons and scholars insisted that I should give a spelling-match at the old school-house, and as I was always ready and willing to indulge the love **of** sociability, I readily consented to the proposition. The **evening** arrived, and with it came more than a hundred of the neighbors and their children, anxious to battle for the mastery in spelling ; after which, dancing was indulged in to the great satisfaction of all present.

A match was soon arranged by two rural beauties, who tossed up for the first choice of spellers. I was chosen by one of the contestants, and so it went on to the end of the programme, when two lines of warlike intellects stood facing each other for battle. The person who missed stepped down and out, and the one that remained on the floor to the last carried off the prize, and became the noted champion of the evening. After the first round, a simple word was given to me by the umpire, and ludicrous to relate, I went down by the first shot, retiring to one of the benches amid the laughter of the **whole** audience.

A beautiful young girl of fifteen carried off the prize, receiving the encomiums of the whole house for her remarkable memory and precise information. I know it is inexcusable for a man of education to be a bad speller; but, even to this day, I am liable to insult the memory of Noah Webster, and even rattle the bones of Lindley Murray in violating his rule that a verb must agree with its nominative in number, person and case.

The schoolmaster is a wonderful man among yeomanry, and the greatness of Goldsmith's pedagogue may well illustrate his rural renown :

> " The village all declared how much he knew,
>   'Twas certain he could write and cipher too;
>   Lands he could measure, terms and tides presage,
>   And even the story ran that he could gauge;
>   In arguing, too, the parson owned his skill,
>   For e'en though vanquished, he could argue still;
>   While words of learned length and thundering sound
>   Amazed the gazing rustics ranged around;
>   And still they gazed, and still the wonder grew
>   That one small head should carry all he knew."

CHAPTER XVII.

TAX-COLLECTOR AND CANDIDATE FOR LEGISLATURE.

At the conclusion of my school I went to Lansing, and through the instrumentality of the county treasurer, a shrewd and pleasant gentleman, was employed to collect delinquent taxes, long due by the rustic citizens of Franklin and Linton townships. With the necessary books and a commission as deputy collector, I took up my headquarters at the village of Volney, and advertised that I was ready and willing to collect delinquent taxes. I waited for my pronunciamento to take effect, but as the good people did not rush frantically from the hills and valleys in response to my call, I concluded to go to the mountain, since the mountain would not come to me.

The life of a delinquent tax-collector is not a happy one—particularly where the ground has been worked over for ten years by ambitious deputies. The doctor is looked upon with fear and anxiety by his patient; the lawyer is tolerated with hope and suspicion by his client; the undertaker comes with a melancholy face to perform the last sad duty for mankind; but the delinquent tax collector is looked upon in his official capacity as a combination of all the horrors—a pest to be avoided and a nuisance to be abated.

I spent the month of July, 1865, among the hills of Yellow River, coaxing and threatening the good people with penalties unless they paid the real and personal taxes demanded in the name of the Hawk-eye State, and was unusually successful in securing the payment of taxes that had slumbered for many years. I shall never forget the bold move I made on an old

Irish bachelor who lived like an anchorite on a forty-acre farm perched on a rugged height overlooking Yellow River. He owed the state of Iowa about fifty dollars, but had for more than ten years evaded every tax-collector who came to the neighborhood. They could never find him at home when endeavoring to give the notice of levy, and although the deputies often climbed the bluffs in pursuit of the delinquent, they never succeeded in getting the taxes.

Duly armed with my legal documents and an army " pepper-box," I started away one bright morning through the crooked defiles leading out from Volney, and began to climb the heights reaching to the lands of the fierce old bachelor. I imagined myself for awhile in the highlands of Scotland or among the heather mountains of Ireland, in search of some bold outlaws who worked the secrets of the still. While thus musing, in contemplation wild, I beheld a curl of smoke rising out of a clump of trees. and saw a yoke of oxen grazing near a corn-field in the vicinity of the old bachelor's cabin. I let down a pair of bars, turned the cattle into the corn-field, and awaited developments. The joy of the cattle was great while crunching the young corn, and all went merry as a marriage-bell until the old bachelor rushed from his cabin, bare headed and yelling like a trooper at the oxen. The thought of saving his crop made him oblivious of my presence. As he rushed by me in his flight after the cattle, I cried, " Halt ! " He looked at me with a gaze of astonishment, showing all the rage of a trapped lion. I at once made known my business, and with the legal documents in one hand and a revolver in the other, served due notice on the delinquent, levied on his yoke of oxen to satisfy the debt, and thus, with the air of a victorious general, maintained the majesty of the law and sustained the honor of Iowa, while threatening to blow off the head-piece of the citizen if he dared to decline my demand or interfere with me in the execution of my office.

When he realized the trap he had fallen into, and saw me drive off his cattle, he immediately sued for quarter ; and be-

fore I got back to Volney he had caught up with me and ten-
tered the taxes with all penalties and costs attached. I gave
the old fellow his receipt in full, released the oxen, shook his
hand, bade him be virtuous and consequently happy; and I
have no doubt but that the lesson he received gave him greater
respect for human laws, and a wise discrimination to know that
a legal document, backed up by a pistol, is not to be ignored.

My duties as a tax-gatherer soon ceased, and after deducting
my per cent., I turned in the balance to the treasurer of Allamakee county.

* *
* * *

I had often heard that it was sweet to die for one's country;
and as my soul was filled with hope and poetry, I concluded
to cast my drag-net into the Republican county convention
that assembled at Waukon on the 19th of August, 1865.

After a laborious campaign among the primary caucuses,
making all the promises incident to the canvass of a congressman, assuring the honest voters that they were the salt of the
earth, and I but the humble instrument to wait for and record
their will, the convention met, and I received a unanimous
vote as candidate for the legislature. As this high honor came
unsought (?) to a young man of twenty-two who had lived in
the county scarcely a year, I could do nothing else but accept
in a modest (?) speech, expressing the usual surprise, and informing the convention of my unworthiness; then soaring aloft in
the realms of native eloquence, I pledged undying love to the
principles of the Republican party, and proposed to bear onward
the standard of freedom until the election sunset of October
shone pure and bright upon the victorious folds of the star-
spangled banner planted upon the crumbling ramparts of democracy!

I made a joint canvass with the democratic nominee, who
was more than fifty years of age—an old stager who could
change his political opinions with as much ease and facility as
a diver changes his suit. I talked to the county statesmen
with the air of a Bolingbroke or Pitt, and imagined, until the

votes were counted, that Jefferson, Lincoln and Douglas were poor sticks in comparison with my growing greatness and the glorious renown that awaited me in the halls of legislation at Des Moines. I made a speech in every township in Allamakee county, and had bills posted up at stores and cross-roads, in advance of my coming.

It was during the campaign of 1865, at Waukon, that I first met Hon. William B. Allison on his congressional tour through the third district of Iowa. A joint discussion was in progress at the court-house, when we consented to divide time with the Congressman, and give him a chance to enlighten the citizens of Iowa regarding the propriety of striking the word "white" out of its constitution, thereby admitting to the ballot-box all male citizens twenty-one years of age, irrespective of color or previous condition of servitude. Mr. Allison consumed about an hour in the delivery of his speech, which was logical and sound.

My opponent, Paulk, followed the congressman in a very good speech from his stand-point. The old gentleman ignored my presence altogether. I arose to close the debate, and launched in with the fire and audacity of youth, belaboring the stay-at-home, peace-at-any-price crowd.

The day after the vote was announced, having lost all my enthusiasm in the election, I embarked on the fine steamer Gray Eagle at Lansing, and proceeded to the city of Dubuque. Standing on the hurricane deck of the steamer as she swept away from the wharf, and rounded toward the bald bluff of South Lansing, I breathed a sigh of regret at leaving relatives, pupils and friends, where youth and love had mingled in the scene, and confidence and ambition cast a glow of supreme happiness through the halls of memory. Some very dear friends are yet living in Iowa, who may call to mind the scenes I have depicted; and, perhaps, in the evening twilight, when the walking shadows of night climb the river bluffs, they may recount to their children and friends the romantic career of a country pedagogue and would-be legislator.

CHAPTER XVIII.

Arriving in Dubuque, I called at the law office of Mr. Allison, the Congressman I met in the late canvass. I told him of my desire to continue the study of law, which had been interrupted by the war. He at once secured me a clerkship in the office of Hon. Henry A. Wiltz, the United States surveyor-general for Iowa and Wisconsin, at the same time tendering the use of his books and office.

I spent the winter of 1866 and the summer and fall of the same year in diligent study of the law, pondering on the wisdom of Blackstone, Chitty, Kent, Parsons and Greenleaf, with all the enthusiasm of youth and ambition ; receiving my license to practice as an attorney in the courts of Iowa, on the 11th of November.

The memories that cluster about Dubuque can never be forgotten, and the friends that assisted me in the old Julian building in the study of law present themselves to-day in the form and appearance of yesterday.

Mr. George Crane and Captain T. Palmer Rood were the law partners of Mr. Allison, and while he was mostly engrossed in political calculations, they attended strictly to the details and work of an important law firm. Mr. Crane was a man of fine judgment, and had the entire confidence of his clients, and the respect of the bar, which numbered some of the best lawyers in Iowa, such as Bissell, Shiras, Adams, Mulkern, Samuels, Knight, Wilson, Cram, Henderson, Cooley, O'Donnell and a rare genius named Charles McKenzie.

Captain T. Palmer Rood, the junior member of the firm, was my daily and nightly companion ; and often in the lonely midnight hours, when lessons had been recited, he would talk of love and friends in the Empire State, and wind up our mutual joy by throwing his soul into his magic flute, in a symphony from Beethoven, a trill from the mocking bird or a warbling note from the matchless air of " Home, Sweet Home," while I joined in the sweet words of John Howard Payne :

> " An exile from home, splendor dazzles in vain,
>   Oh, give me my lowly thatched cottage again."

These sentiments would often take possession of Rood's mind, and on the airy wings of fancy he wandered back to the home of his childhood, and lived again in the love of his first conquest. Philosophic conversations were frequently indulged in—birth, life and death claiming our consideration. I remember well a conversation we had upon the reason and justice of suicide ; he taking the ground that a man had the right to destroy himself because God gave him the power to do it. It was hard to combat this logic, but I appealed to his honor and bravery, arguing that it was nobler to live and battle with a frowning world than take a leap in the dark and blot out the ills that flesh is heir to. I insisted that no man in his sane mind could commit suicide, for the inherent principle of self-preservation revolted at the thought ; while he felt satisfied that a troubled, but sound, mind could take nature by the throat, and end the horrid phantoms that came like brooding shadows.

Rood was of a rather melancholy and sensitive nature, and the very soul of honor in his dealings with the world. He was neat in dress, choice in his associates, and bore some secret sorrow that I could not fathom. I introduced him to a beautiful and accomplished young lady, who afterwards became his wife, and bore him a fine son.

I left Dubuque in November, 1866, for Washington city, and although our lines were cast in different places, we kept up a friendly correspondence until he committed suicide on the closing night of December, 1879, when his sensitive and poetic spirit took flight into the new year.

The night of his suicide he left his home for a festival among his friends, kissed his wife and boy a last good-bye, departed with seeming gladness for the halls of revelry, dressed in fault-less style, without a known cause to ruffle the equanimity of his soul; and in the morning sunshine anxious friends found him dead in his law-office, propped back in an arm-chair, the victim of chloroform administered by his own hand.

On the outside of his locked door the searchers found a card bearing this laconic announcement: " Gone—Rood !" On the desk, near his chair, the following pathetic note to his wife and boy were found as testimony of the tortured brain that could act no longer, or battle with the disappointments and rude tempests the world inflicted :

ANGIE AND WILLIE.

DUBUQUE, IOWA, Dec. 31, 1879.

Dear Angie, Dear Willie:

Oh ! how I have suffered in my head.   I am going to rest to-morrow !

Your affectionate husband and father.

Who can ever know the pangs of melancholy, regret, re-morse and desperation that welled up in the troubled soul that penned these dying lines? Who can appreciate the sleepless nights and lingering, lonely hours that poor Rood battled with in fighting the temptations of suicide, or the demon of insanity !

About a year before his death I received a long letter, from which I extract the following asseverations of friendship :

" I am right glad to hear from you and yours; for the years, though many, and vicissitudes, though rough and various, have greatly separated 1866 and 1878 in the toils, cares and interests of life, still an ever vivid recollection of the days that will never return, and pleasures that have no duplicates, furnish an impetus and desire for the continuance of our friend-ship. Colonel Henderson pictures your surroundings as pleas-ant and delightful. I would like to make proof of it, by stepping in upon you, and chatting about old friends and sweet memories, that may be varnished over by departed years, but cannot be eradicated from the heart that feels, and the soul that communes with truth, love and ambition ! Angie sends her kindest regards to you and Mrs. Joyce, as also Willie, who remembers you with pleasure ; and often in the twilight I take up the beautiful flute you gave me, and play some of the airs we loved so well in the long ago. Now, John, write me a long letter in reply to this, and throw into your words and ideas the beauty and romance that cheered my melancholy hours in the old Julian building, when we

> ' Dipt into the future
> Far as human eye could see.' "

Poor fellow ! I wonder if he could see the sad termination of his earthly career when we talked to empty benches in the Julian Theatre, preparatory to taking the stump in a Congressional canvass.

I could linger for days in calling up reminiscences of my career in Dubuque, floating on the river, exploring among the lead mines, strolling over the rugged bluffs in search of wild flowers, rattling away to the five-mile house in moonlight hours, or making my first New Year calls to the homes of hospitable citizens, whose pretty houses were perched on the steep hillsides like swallows' nests in overhanging cliffs. Many of those I knew and loved in 1866 have passed into the dark shadows of eternity, and slumber forever on the upland slopes of the Hawkeye State.

> Yet memory, with her magic fingers,
> Will turn with hope where joy still lingers,
> And bless the friends beneath the sod,
> Who loved us here, then went to God.

After receiving license to practice law, I felt like the humble Oriental who had been presented with a white elephant ; and whether to " go West" or go East with my license and ambition, was a problem more intricate than the solution of one in Euclid.

CHAPTER XIX.

One cool, bright morning in November, 1866, I knocked at the door of Hon. Wm. B. Allison, located in the historic chambers of Willard's Hotel. The congressman bade me enter, and while a look of surprise shot across his face, he greeted me with the old smile, and from his large gray eyes beamed that magnetic fire that never failed to beget confidence, or secure the friendship of the man he trusted. I told him I came East for the purpose of spending a few winter months in Washington, and while here would be pleased to secure a clerkship; and that when spring with its sun and flowers decorated the earth I should go to the boundless West, and grow up with the country!

He laughed at my proposal, shook his head in seeming sorrow, making the remark that if he had a son, he "would rather see him a blacksmith, farmer, or hod-carrier in the West, than have him bury his independence and manhood in the red tape pigeon-holes of Washington." He said no more, but the next morning went with me to the office of Hon. A. E. Rollins, Commissioner of Internal Revenue. I was introduced in a meaning way. There were "no vacancies," of course, but I was examined by a civil service board, with Wm. E. Chandler, Assistant Secretary of the Treasury, as chief, and ere I knew what had occurred, I received the appointment of a first-class clerkship.

I was duly assigned to the "law division" of the Internal Revenue Office, presided over by a sensitive and elegant gentleman from the hills of New England. The division contained about a dozen men, each one having such work as his presumed capacity commanded. All frauds against the revenue were sent to our room for settlement. Compromise cases were chief subjects for consideration, and the letters of agents, assessors, collectors and district attorneys touching this branch of business consumed the time of the clerks, in their important duty of solving the innocence or guilt of a taxpayer who had failed to return the legacy and succession tax of his grandmother, cancel the check-stamp of his uncle, the cigar and beer-stamp of his neighbor, and the terrible whiskey-stamps of rectifier and distiller.

When I entered the division, the chief and subordinates looked upon me with dignity and suspicion ; dignity, because of their unapproachable learning and information ; and suspicion, because I might come in the way of the next promotion. My capacity was at once gauged with unerring judgment; and, in company with another clerk, I was instructed in detail in briefing the contents of letters received, and ruling straight, red, parallel lines under the names of country officials. I continued in this business for more than three weeks, until a slight attack of brain fever set in, superinduced by the herculean duty performed in the realms of red tape and red lines ! I spoke to the chief one evening after office hours, and asked him if he could not find another assistant to relieve my excruciating labor.

A clerk in a government office is perfectly happy if he can find some other clerk to boss, but the poor devil stretched out as the mudsill of the official bridge is indeed a miserable creature, unless he can occasionally get a kick at a messenger, or scrub-woman. Of all the petty tyrants I ever knew, the domineering, egotistical, clerical jackass who happens to be " clothed with a little brief authority," exceeds the whole tribe of reprobates.

The chief gave me a bundle of papers every morning to digest and write an opinion upon, no doubt to test my qualifications as a reasoner, lawyer and philosopher. I ripped into the official pile like a crosscut saw through a five-foot log, extricating from the debris of straddle revenue, opinions, recommendations and conclusions in the premises.   When completed, I laid the letter, with my initials at the bottom, before the head of my section, who pondered over it with the air of a sage, cut out about half, and returned it for correction.   I put the original letter aside, wrote as the great man of the section dictated, and placed it on his desk, receiving his initials on the left hand upper corner, then with the pride of an American Polyglot shot the letter under the eyeglass of the division chief, who read it carefully, crossed out two-thirds, and ordered me to write out in shape what was left.   I put that letter in my desk, wrote a new one, and in due course presented a non-committal letter to the section and division chiefs for signature, and carried the precious document down stairs to the commissioner.   He gazed in an absent kind of way at the letter, and then, as if a magical thought struck him between the diaphragm and the brain, he slashed out three-fourths of it, and ordered me to correct, and bring it to him instantly.   I did this with an injured air.   By the time all the initials and signature of the commissioner were attached to the document, there was scarcely a word of my original composition remaining.   I felt like a subdued sheep, and was willing to be slaughtered ever after by any official butcher that came along.   I immediately fell into the rut of official imbecility, and never afterwards indulged in an idea that had not been patented at least a hundred years.   I sneezed when the section-head took snuff, laughed when the division-head told an ancient story, and fairly split my sides when the commissioner bade me good-day.

I soon found that promotion did not always go by merit, and that a polished, daring clerk, with live political backing, was sure to be advanced, while his desk companion of genius and learning would die unnoticed upon the stem of virgin modesty.

The chief clerk of an office is a great man, in his own estimation, and struts about with the air of a Spanish hidalgo, waiving off his subordinates with a curt reply, or with an imperial sweep of his strong right arm. He would not exchange place with the king of Siam, or deign to compete in dignity with the sultan of Turkey. The Secretary of the Department and Head of the Bureau may occasionally unbend from austere official labor, but the importance and dignity of the chief clerk remain stern and unalterable as the laws of the Medes and Persians. While his personal and political influence lasts, he is lord of the official realm; but when the lightning of dismissal strikes his devoted head, you behold him, after many years of service and tyranny, walking Pennsylvania Avenue as a second-class tramp, eking out a precarious existence among the holes and by-lanes of the city.

Clerks average twenty or thirty years in the tread-mill of Department life, starting in with bright faces, cheerful hearts, and a laudable ambition to perform faithful work, save some money for a rainy day, marry the girl of their choice and move to the boundless West, where strong hands and brave hearts never fail to carve out a name, fortune and place. But, alas for human calculations, they are stuck in a seven by nine pigeon-hole, tramp the daily tread-mill with their fellows, join the Masons or the Johnidab lodge, live at one of the numerous boarding houses of the city, meet some beautiful and innocent female clerk, cream her, wine her, theatre her, boat her down the Potomac by moonlight, and then in due course procure a ten-dollar preacher, and marry.

The die is cast. Sinbad, the sailor, might get out of the diamond valley on a roc's back, but a twelve-hundred-dollar clerk with a wife and four or more children astride his official shoulders may never again hope for the peace and prosperity of youth, or shake off the fetters he has entwined about him. Age comes, obligations increase, political influence dies, and the dreaded "yellow envelope" reaches him at last, clipping off his official head with the withering coldness of a killing frost. The poor fellow—worn, wrinkled and gray—mopes about the streets and hotels, the very ghost of a man, seeking some senator, representative or other official, to assist him in getting back to the prison cells of the Department. But another new-made grave in some lone cemetery—perhaps in the Potter's Field—will be all that is left to mark the spot where crumbles the clerk and his early hopes.

By careful manipulation I was promoted every few months, to the amazement of my fellow clerks, and soon arrived at the summit of a "fourth-class" station, receiving eighteen hundred dollars per annum for laboring, with my tongue mostly, four hours a day; spending the other twenty in reading, feasting, strolling, courting, and political wire-working.

A year after my arrival in Washington, Cupid shot one of his fatal darts at my susceptible heart, and before I hardly realized it, I was married to a vivacious and intelligent young lady from the Highlands of the Hudson.

The bright side of clerical life is found in the home circle when holiday rest and pay-day intervenes to break the monotony of official labor. Parties, balls, picnics and excursions down the Potomac, are never failing sources of pleasure, and the clerk who cannot procure a sweetheart to accompany him must be in a bad way—unworthy of notice or social friendship.

Honesty, sobriety and thrift are cardinal virtues; and while some frivolous clerks sport away their butterfly existence in running after the gauze and glitter of official receptions, the majority of the ladies and gentlemen in the various Departments toil faithfully to support the woman, man or child they love. Very few in the outside world, when they behold the human stream pour in at nine o'clock in the morning and come out again at four o'clock in the afternoon, appreciate the troubles and responsibilities of the weary hearts and tired brains of the faithful workers who run along with box or basket containing their frugal lunch, and hasten back when the day's work is done to some modest house in the suburbs, where rents are cheap and fashion has not invaded.

Washington society is cosmopolitan in the main; there are four distinct classes, that never mix for any length of time, viz: citizen, diplomatic, congressional and clerical. The old citizen, who lives on the money and reputation of his ancestors, holds at arm's length the flitting families of to-day, and boasts of the "good old days before the war," when Jackson, Polk and Pierce dignified the White House, and every gentleman had a thousand dollar "nigger" to sell as a stake for a horse race or a forfeit at a poker table. In the march of progress these old barnacles of a bygone age are passing away like morning mist, and the generations now sweeping over the earth will find them in the future with a monument and a faded memory, under the cool, romantic shadows of Oak Hill.

The Diplomatic Corps is clannish, proud, and often presumptious. They laugh at the rude manners of our young Republic in comparison with those of their ancient kingdoms, where millions toil in slavery to support the royal few in their silken sloth and hereditary idleness. You find them occasionally out in force, when some public demonstration gives them a chance to display their sleek forms clad in royal style, with elaborate gold braid and tinsel sparkling here and there, not thinking that their rich garbs are wrung from the tears, sweat and blood of poor toilers who labor from the cradle to the grave as mud-sills for monarchy.

I have seen congressional society come and go for twenty years—one crowd of official accidents wiping out the other, like waves upon a sea—when perchance an occasional breaker dashes over some Senator, Representative or Cabinet Minister, and lays him forever in the tomb of official oblivion. Wives, sons, daughters and friends float around the surface of their noted chief, in apparently everlasting power; but the silent ballot of the country plowman sends these creatures of a day to join the innumerable caravan of politicians who have passed to the pale realms of shade.

The clerical class of society is the largest in number, and for general intelligence and good behavior compares favorably with the other three. They can be found at church entertainments, raffle-fairs, masonic festivals, listening to band music at the Capitol or White House, and in summer they crowd the steamers that ply to and from the historic milestones along the lapping waters of the Potomac.

Groups of the "boys" may be found after office hours in the halls of the National, Metropolitan, Arlington, Ebbitt, Riggs and Willard's, discussing matters of state over a blooming "cocktail," a bottle of Cliquot, or a quart of Imperial from the vine-clad slopes of Missouri. They are jolly, good natured mortals, who treat while a cent remains, and never refuse an invitation to "smile," for fear of insulting the gentleman who extended the invitation. I have known many splendid characters among clerks; and some who have passed over the River of Time would share their last nickel with a friend, although they knew that the contribution-hat would be passed around among their comrades to procure funds for their own burial.

There is another class of people in the District of Columbia who do not particularly depend on Government for their support, and who do not court any society that lives but a day and then vanishes into the night of forgetfulness. I mean the rich merchant, the wealthy farmer, the noted lawyer, the real estate owner, the prosperous banker, the scientific physician, and the retired millionaire. They are independent citizens, caring no more for the "May-flies" of official renown than the rustle of a passing breeze. They live in quiet, conscious of their worth, knowing the latent power of their character, treating the world with politeness and decorum, and pass to the tomb in the evening glow of a just and happy life.

Washington is the Paris of America. "Boss" Shepard took it from the mud of Slavery, and placed it in the concrete of Freedom. He had the genius, the soul and the bravery to secure large appropriations for improving and beautifying the Capital, and by his primary surveys actually forced Congress at succeeding sessions to continue the grand work he inaugurated. Money was, no doubt, spent with a lavish hand, and while a very few contractors became rich, the majority, with

Shepard himself, received but abuse, kicks and poverty. The pirates of the press assailed the Governor as a national robber; but with the-nerve and fortitude that never forsakes the honest man, he kept right on in his grand enterprise, and to-day has lived down the unjust and villainous abuse of jealous mediocrity. The day is near at hand when his statue in marble and bronze shall decorate the beautiful parks he fashioned and improved; and in future years of national glory his memory will be revered in story, and eulogized by pen and eloquent tongue when his traducers are lost in forgotten graves.

A laboring plumber, a great contractor, a daring and patriotic governor, a successful miner and a social prince, are the practical points of Shepard's career, and his children's children will look back with pride upon the illustrious example of their ancestor, who never struck below the belt, or cowered before a cyclone of vituperation and malediction.

CHAPTER XX.

Washington City and its surroundings hold more natural, artistic and historic interest for the tourist than any other city in the United States. Rome, Paris, London and Pekin have the frost of two thousand years to glorify their hoary heads, while the capital of the Great Republic has but a century of deeds to match the illustrious capitals of antiquity.

And yet, when art, science, progress and human liberty are considered, our Western giant strides over those ancient cities with the pride and strength of a Colossus. The steamer, telegraph, sewing machine, cotton gin, spinning jenny, telephone, locomotive, Hoe printing press, elevated railways, cable street cars, elevators, mowers, reapers and binders, electric lights and an endless variety of other great and useful inventions are of American hand and brain.

While the nations of Europe and Asia boast of great writers, architects, painters, sculptors and warriors, and trace their history along the widening centuries, in the battles of their kings, czars and emperors for beauty, booty and power, the land of Washington is content with its record in behalf of freedom, education and equal rights.

When summer with its fruits, flowers and foliage bedecks the undulating slopes and rolling hills of the national capital, the traveler from domestic and foreign lands may spend a profitable hour under the bronze statue of General Winfield Scott on the romantic heights of the Soldiers' Home Park, as the evening sun sinks behind the hills of the Old Dominion.

Far to the left, looking south, you behold abrupt mountain spurs fading into Maryland landscapes, with the silver waters of the Anacosta sparkling in the view. White and bold, the round dome of the capitol looms up into the blue sky like a snowy cloud in the glimmering distance ; and as the eye peers along the green banks of the Potomac to Alexandria, Fort Washington and Mount Vernon, twenty miles away, sweeping back to the right, where Fairfax Seminary, Arlington Heights and Georgetown University lift their classic crests—the soul imbibes the glorious scene, and views Washington with poetic rapture, as she sparkles in her setting of emerald hills, like a variegated jewel shining in the purple twilight.

Before turning away from the beautiful walks, drives, trees, flowers and Arcadian slopes of the Soldiers' Home, let the thoughtful traveler look down the historic vista of a hundred years, where human valor shone bright and brave at Lexington, Bunker Hill, Trenton, Saratoga, Yorktown, New Orleans, Lake Erie, Mexico, Chapultepec, Buena Vista, Bull Run, Fort Donelson, Shiloh, Chancellorville, Lookout Mountain, Atlanta, Gettysburg and Appomattox ; and taking a long, lingering look at the capitol, he beholds the last rays of golden sunset shining on the starry flag and Goddess of Liberty, and may justly exclaim : Blessèd be the name and fame of an American citizen !

BOAT CLUBS.

The boat clubs of the National Capital are great sources of health and pleasure. When leafy June clothes the rolling hills and blooming vales of the placid Potomac with an emerald garb, hundreds of happy mortals in artistic row-boats, may be seen darting along the beautiful river like swallows, as the golden sunbeams in the west melt into the silvery light of the rising moon.

The Capitol, Long Bridge, Washington Monument, Arlington, Aqueduct Bridge, Catholic University and the romantic heights of Georgetown can be seen in the glimmering twilight ; and as day departs into mellow moonlight, the hum of busy ·

insects, tinkling bells, and merry serenaders in boats can be heard for miles along the river, rocks and gorges, that echo back rhythmic melody to hope, love and beauty. Then it is that the heart of man and woman, boy and girl, casts aside dull care, and allows nature to assume its own realm, in ramble, song and dance; crowning shell, out-rigger, picnic and barge party, with a halo of happiness.

The Analosta, Potomac and Columbia Clubs may be respectfully denominated as aristocratic, autocratic and democratic; yet all ministering to health and pleasure, vieing with other clubs in annual regattas for golden cups, medals and banners. I have often been a delighted guest of these clubs, and in an humble way have lent my grist of nonsense and song to cheer the pleasant hours, scattering a few wild flowers along the by-paths of the classic Potomac.

As the years roll away, pleasure-boating on the river will increase, until every well regulated family in the District of Columbia, will have a representative in the clubs, where each lady and gentleman may secure a closer friendship that shall ripen into lasting felicity.

The Grand Canal of Venice, with its interesting water-ways, beautiful gondolas, royal barges and marble palaces has made the "Queen of the Adriatic," noted in song and story along the lapse of ages; and although the "Bridge of Sighs" spans her silvery spray, the music and loves of boating beauties and gallant knights have kept alive her glory, and shall, while the snowy peaks of Alpine ranges continue to shine in the soft sunlight of an Italian sky. So shall Washington and the Potomac gather for us some unfading laurels, and glorify our aquatic triumphs in marble, poetry, love and song, even when the searching storms of decay shall have swept over the crumbling monuments of Columbia!

> "I heed not if my ripppling skiff
> Floats swift or slow from cliff to cliff;
> With dreamful eyes my spirit lies
> Under the gates of Paradise."

FAMOUS CHARACTERS.

The pen of Dickens and the brush of Reynolds would be needed to describe the noted and peculiar characters that cluster about the Capital. For twenty years I have seen them come and go, like swallows in season, or like the foliage that blooms in spring, brightens in summer, fades in autumn, and dies in the withering blasts of winter. The winding corridors of the capitol and the halls of hotels and restaurants have sheltered the motley group.

There is SAM COX, the brightest and best-informed man in Congress; and while his "sunset" of life glows with a mellow light, his sparkling wit shines like drops of diamond dew at sunrise.

Look at GEN. SHERMAN, striding towards the war office—quick and nervous as a mountain deer, with military cloak and broad-brimmed hat—the very picture of a dashing soldier. He knows and loves everybody, and receives a double grist of admiration for his heroic virtues. Like a gray eagle from some splintered crag, his bright, flashing eye spans the vale below, and although rare birds of variegated plumage fill the forest with dulcet notes, he sweeps into the boundless blue of intellectual grandeur, and leads the chorus of the mountains.

See General GRANT, short, solid, imperturbable—the child of destiny, and sure as Fate. He believes in himself, and never doubts the field of fortune, but sweeps on with the assurance of calculated audacity !

Behold PHIL SHERIDAN, a born soldier, an epigram in war, an exclamation point of success; inflexible against despair, snatching victory out of the iron jaws of defeat. Wailing Winchester still echoes his name.

> "He dashed down the line, 'mid a storm of huzzas,
> And the wave of retreat checked its course there, because
> The sight of the *master* compelled it to pause !"

WADE HAMPTON moves about the capitol with the supreme confidence of a soldier, and the elegance of a gentleman. Bold and patriotic for his cause, and generous to a fallen foe, heroic and sincere in life, his memory will be cherished by the brave and true who fight for home and fatherland.

There comes GEORGE B. CORKHILL, a round and perfect gentleman, who sprung at one bound into notoriety by launching *Guiteau* into " the pale realms of shade," in justice to the martyr GARFIELD.

Who does not know beaming BOB INGERSOLL, who dares the world with his curious infidel convictions? He says, " Life is a narrow vale between the barren peaks of two eternities," yet his heart and soul can hear the " rustle of a wing," and see the bright stars of hope sparkle in the realms of God. He may write, lecture and argue to the tomb, but he knows and feels in his inmost heart, that God and nature sing the song of everlasting life !

GEORGE ALFRED TOWNSEND is the most graceful reminiscence writer in the country. He has a looking-glass mind that can reflect all objects received. He writes beautiful, poetic lines ; and had the Adriatic instead of the Chesapeake sang at his birth, the classic tones of Tasso might have inspired his lute.

Gaze upon LUCIAN YOUNG, a gay Viking of the salt sea. Kentucky never produced a braver man, and the navy has no better sailor. While Cape Hatteras roars over the wreck of the ill-fated *Huron*, the glory of Young will be sung in storms, and the lives he saved in breasting the billows of fate will place his name in the proud roster of naval heroes.

Classic JOHN DANENHOWER has the cool, quiet bravery of his companion Young ; and while the icebergs of the Arctic sea glitter in the cold sunlight of Siberian solitude, *Danenhower*, *Melville* and *De Long* will be seen in the noble procession of naval heroes who have suffered for science and country.

There is a conundrum of a character leaning against Willard's antique portals—TOM OCHILTREE—he with that Titan top-knot, a lover of truth, and as modest as a maiden. He came as a blizzard from Texas, and lingers like sunshine mid open flowers.

Proctor Knott is a walking compilation of wit and magnetic humanity. While he is not as quick in repartee as Congressman Cox or Senator Vest, he has better staying qualities in the field of fun, and a faculty of making the most out of the world that laughs. —

His satirical description of the tropical clime and rosy surroundings of Duluth made him governor of Kentucky! . Few men have prospered so long and well on one funny speech. Yet he might have been a rival of Douglas Jerrold and Dean Swift, and sat with Beau Nash among the beauties of Bath. His gray hair, fine brow, bright eye and florid face, are golden sign-boards to his genial heart. Love and confidence follow in his train, and the clouds of misfortune have never dimmed the luster of his polished humor.

As lawyer, congressman and governor, he has been the pride of Kentucky; and while curmudgeons may not like the ease and freedom of his manner, the heart of the people beats responsive to his own.

> Long may he live to cheer the festive board,
> And spread his bounty like a royal lord.

And there is **James G. Blaine**, sauntering down Pennsylvania avenue to the capitol with one of his senatorial chums. He talks and gesticulates incessantly, not only for his side partner, but for the world at large. He might have been a rival of the actor Garrick.

> "On the stage, he was natural, simple, affecting,
> 'Twas only that when he was off he was acting."

As school-teacher, editor, representative, speaker, senator and secretary, Blaine has filled a rich nook in our Republic for thirty years; and while not endowed with the profound knowledge of Aaron Burr or Henry Clay, he possesses the scheming elegance of the former, and the audacious independence of the latter statesman. He belongs to the irrepressible race of Celts, whose hand and brain can be seen on the milestones of human history, through the valleys and across the rugged mountains of antiquity.

Look at royal ROSCOE CONKLING as he strides the senatorial chamber, posing for the gallery gods, and sneering at his senatorial compeers, who crouch beneath the satire and lightning flashes of this modern Ajax. He possesses the wisdom of Burke, the eloquent flights of Mirabeau and the imperial philosophy of Cæsar, who believed that the people were created for his imperial use.

> " Why man he doth bestride the narrow world like a Colossus."
> *   *   *   *   *   *   *   *
> " Now in the name of all the gods at once,
> Upon what meat doth this our Cæsar feed—
> That he lords it over all ?"

Glance for a moment at that tall, straight, classic figure as he walks to his senatorial desk, and dashes off letters and bills with the rapidity of a stenographer. That is CHARLES SUMNER, the Massachusetts statesman. His hair is bushy and gray, his face clean-cut and studious. The beauty of Alcibiades must have shone in his youth ; while the eloquence of Pericles, the Athenian, moulded his manhood. Like his Athenian prototype, he was the uncompromising patron of the people, and lovers of art, letters and science found a friend in the noted abolitionist. Although the bludgeon of slavery struck him down in the senate, he was the first statesman in America who dared to blot out from the victorious flag of freedom the battle-scars of civil war. Aspasia in her most noble days, might have chosen him instead of Pericles, and as he possessed the intelligence of the Grecian, he had the unalterable fortitude of Cato, the illustrious Roman.

Look at JAMES B. BELFORD, a curious compound from the cloud-capped peaks of Colorado. He swaggers along with the air of a Rocky Mountain stage-driver, or the buck-skin boldness of a miner. While receiving the sneering shots of his more genteel companions in Congress, he gives them an occasional broadside that strips their surface-plates to the water's edge, exposing the worm-eaten wood of mediocrity. Belford, like Sumner, is a man of the people. He has a thorough knowledge of letters, law, and constitutions. Labor finds in him a champion of strict integrity ; and while capital mocks at his opposition, the day may come when its votaries will kneel at his feet as the Danton of another revolution.

Capital and labor will be at war while God stamps men with unequal body and brain. All that the legislators of the earth can do is to *regulate* the never-ending jealousy that arises out of the eternal laws of self-preservation.

The ground-swell of labor may rise every century, and throw off for a time the cruel crust of poverty and tyranny; but like volcanic upheavals, the earth and sea settle back into their wonted depths, and the coral insects of honest labor build again over the desolation they have wrought !

Behold the *Bacchus boquet* of bar-room beauties as they meander off to " smile" away the lingering hours. Generals, colonels, clerks, doctors and irrepressible judges have passed before my vision for many years, and to-day they seem as "willin' " as Bacchus to take "suthin," and as fresh as morning zephyrs in cheeking down adversity. *Ponce de Leon* might have discovered the fountain of youth had he known how faded gentility lives at the Capital without any visible means of support. *Esto Perpetua.*

CHAPTER XXI.

IMPEACHMENT OF PRESIDENT JOHNSON.—LEAVING THE INTER-
NAL REVENUE OFFICE.

The Impeachment of President Andrew Johnson was rife
with interest, excitement and ambition.   Washington society
was stirred from center to circumference ; and while the Department officials leaned to the side of their immediate " bread
and butter," there were thousands who acted secretly with
congressional influences, and held a sail to windward to catch
the radical breeze of success.

If there is any one thing that a Washington Department
official can do with great neatness and dispatch, it is the acro-
batic performance of turning his politics with each succeeding
administration.   It is related of old "Joe" Wilson, who was
Commissioner of the General Land Office for nearly thirty
years, that at a social reception he was taunted by a senator of
promptly changing his politics to accommodate every new administration.

Joe, not the least embarassed, replied : " Mr. Senator, I pro-
fess to be a man of genius, and a walking encyclopædia of varied information, and I thank God that I never yet saw an administration that could turn faster than I can !"

I was in the House gallery the day Articles of Impeachment
were passed against President Johnson.   The Radical members, led by Thaddeus Stevens, the greatest man in Congress,
determined to push the articles through under whip and spur.
Butler, Boutwell, Bingham, Schenck, Washburne, Poland and
Allison, belabored the Administration with trip-hammer blows.
Wood, Brooks, Cox and Eldredge, endeavored to stem the tide

of Radical progress, and break the storm that roared about the devoted head of their chief.

Hon. Charles A. Eldredge, of Wisconsin, was the leader of the forlorn hope of Democracy, and for many years stood in the way of the Radical reconstruction laws of Congress. He was taunting and badgering in his attacks, and delighted in stirring up the congressional menagerie with a long, logical pole. As a satirist and wit, he had few superiors ; and as a man of generous judgment and a lawyer of fine ability, he had few equals. The "Old Commoner," of Pennsylvania, acknowledged the ability of Eldredge ; and while he fired his ponderous oratory at the political heresies of the Wisconsin statesman, he never broke that rare personal friendship that lasted until the luster of life faded forever from those great gray eyes of the Pennsylvania radical.

In the passage of the Impeachment articles, the "previous question" was finally secured by the unalterable determination of Thaddeus Stevens, who arose in his seat like a bold mountain crag lifting itself above the gurgling waters, rolling plains and hill-tops around. He sent forth satire at the Reconstruction vetoes of Johnson, accusing him of high crimes and misdemeanors, with as much power and eloquence as Burke spent upon the doomed head of Warren Hastings. His bold flights of logic and accusing wrath reminded me of the sweep of the mountain eagle, or the condor of the Andes, that soars away into illimitable space to "bathe his plumage in the thunder's home."

But how vain are all the calculations and battles of man ! The impeachment of Andrew Johnson is now but a memory in the march of the Great Republic, and the principal actors have long since mingled their dust with that of the hills and valleys they loved in life. Johnson rests on the mountain slopes of East Tennessee, where the morning sunbeams, darting over the Smoky Range, may linger for a moment on the rugged character who was unconquerable in life and honored by all in death.

The last look I had of Thaddeus Stevens was in the rotunda of the capitol when his body lay in state. That great angular head, crowned with a broad, high forehead like a beetling cliff, breaks upon my memory now, and takes me back to the scenes of his forensic triumphs, when he lashed the halting and hesitating into the Radical lines, as if each word that issued from his pale lips struck in like a whip of scorpions. But the great heart and broad intellect that gave free schools to Pennsylvania, and universal suffrage to the nation, sleeps in modest glory at Lancaster. Some day the people of Pennsylvania will erect a grand monument to his memory, and the teachers and school-children of the Keystone State, will contribute a marble statue of the great man holding a book, and writing with a golden pen : Equality and freedom for all mankind !

****

In the fall of 1869, I left the Internal Revenue Office. Through the instrumentality of Hon. Columbus Delano, Commissioner of Internal Revenue, I was sent West to take charge of the official papers of the supervisor's office for Arkansas and the Indian Territory, and perform the duties incident to that responsible position. Headquarters were located at Little Rock, the capital and most beautiful city of Arkansas. The supervisor's office, when not carried in a hat, was located at the old Anthony House.

I left Washington City one starlight night, leaving behind family and friends, and with high hopes and poetic expectations rattled away over hill, mountain, river and plain until I reached the city of Memphis, situated on a bold cliff, overlooking the turbid waters of the Mississippi. Resting at the Overton House for a day, and becoming acquainted with a number of citizens bound to their homes in Little Rock and Duvall's Bluffs, we secured passage on the old side-wheel steamer *Commercial.*

The Commercial was loaded to the guards with freight and passengers, and as the evening shadows lengthened, she slipped her cable, and with the rhythmic song of darkey deck-hands sounding a farewell chorus, we steamed down the river toward Fort Pillow, and into the mouth of White River.

In due course we landed at Duvall's Bluffs, and took a ram-shackle railroad for Little Rock. The train lurched forward and sideways as if each puff of the engine would land us on the wild prairies, or among the burr-oaks and black-jacks of the swampy woods. My heart was in my mouth, and even the assurance of Colonel Price that the road was smooth and safe, did not quiet my day-dreams of death, until the iron horse whistled his shrill notes for the shanty depot opposite the town of Rocks. We crossed the Arkansas River on a ferry, and climbed the steep streets leading to the center of the city, put-ting up at the Anthony House, where a good supper and soft bed banished dull care.

I remained in Little Rock about two months, visiting, riding and manipulating in the walks of pleasure, when not engaged in the stale rut of official work. The U. S. Arsenal was a re-sort of fun and jolly entertainments, where officers and soldiers joined in contributing to the enjoyment of citizens, irrespective of party. Many private houses threw open their hospitable doors, and entertained with a lavish hand those citizens who had left home and friends in the North to battle with prejudice and unknown fields, in a land of strangers. Many of the "old families," however, would not mingle with the new-fledged birds of passage that had tried their "carpet-bag" wings in the capital of the state. Nor is this to be wondered at. A great, desolating war had just swept over the land; the deep scars of defeat and death could be still seen on the fertile bottoms and broken hill-sides of Arkansas. Fathers, brothers and sons had gone down in the shock of battle, and their green graves punctuated resentment.

"A Fool's Errand" and "Bricks Without Straw," with the harrowing details may not be overdrawn, but if the brilliant author will turn the tables and reverse the glass for a few mo-ments, he might recite and contemplate with more horror the picture of a triumphant South playing the adventurer and

"carpet-bagger" over the North !   I am candid to acknowledge that if fate had doomed me to defeat I should never,
while life remained, have acknowledged the slave oligarchy, or
bent my knee and neck to the yoke of the conqueror ; and I
believe the free spirit of the North would have committed a
million more crimes, in the interest of their defeated manhood,
than have ever been laid at the door of the White League or
Kuklux Klan.

Little Rock is beautifully situated on a high bluff, overlooking the Arkansas.   On the hilly margin of the stream a large
number of fine mansions have been erected since the war.
The Pike mansion in olden times often rang to the music of
the piano, violin, guitar and banjo, and young hearts and old
heads tripped away in the merry dance to the tune of "Monnie
Musk," "Fishers' Hornpipe," or "The Arkansas Traveler."
Bright-haired Apollo and beautiful Venus vied in the boundless
pleasure of the hour, where

> " Joy leaps on faster with a louder laugh,
>   And *Sorrow* tosses to the sea his staff,
>   And pushes back the hair from his dim eyes,
>   To look again upon forgotten skies !"

Albert Pike, the good, gray poet, who penned these classic
lines, was the presiding sage that gave to the Pike mansion its
glory, and made it the Mecca of literary pilgrims from home
and foreign lands.   But the glory of those ancient halls has departed ; the cobwebs of time interlace the crumbling lattice ;
the bat and the owl flit in the grove in twilight hours ; the
sound of revelry only comes back through the magic memory
of vanished years, and the old poet, like a relic of bygone
days, moves among the throng of the National Capitol, peering through the gloaming of the past into clouded, but not
" forgotten skies !"   A kind thought and sad tear shall fill the
measure of the old man's ambition, and when our greatest masonic light goes out forever, his modest hopes shall not be disappointed, and his own pathetic lines will be a prophecy to
his mystic brethren in every land and clime :

> " Perhaps when I have passed away,
> Like the sad echo of a dream,
> There may be some one found to say
> A *word* that might like *sorrow* seem!"

I knew several remarkable men at Little Rock, who congregated to the city from the North after the close of the war, and organized the state government in " carpet-bag" days.

Powell Clayton, Alex. McDonald, Tom Bowen, Jack McClure, Steve Dorsey, Jim Hodges, Bill Oliver, Joe Brooks and Charles W. Tankersby were the ruling conclave.

Tankersby was the most remarkable man of the party. I saw him on one occasion, at the assembling of the Legislature, take the Speaker's chair in a factional fight, and hold it like Napoleon did in the days of the French triumvirate. " Tank," as he was familiarly called, was a born leader, and had he been schooled in war would have made a great general.

In the course of my official career, it became necessary to proceed to Fort Smith, where temporary headquarters were established, and alleged frauds on the revenue were being perpetrated by manufacturers of tobacco, who had erected their factories along the line of Arkansas and the Indian Territory.

District Attorney Huckleberry, Marshal Britton, Deputy Collector Arthur Gunther and Deputy Collector R. C. Kerens were consulted in regard to the alleged frauds. It was conceded by all that tobacco was being manufactured and shipped into the states without payment of the prescribed tax, under the impression of treaty stipulations empowering Indians to do under the revenue laws what white manufacturers could not do.

The Indian manufacturers always insisted that they had the sanction of the Internal Revenue Office in the establishment of their factories, and that no fraud was intended ; while the officers believed that the Indians were simple figure-heads for the brain and capital of cunning white men, who escaped taxation, and thereby unjustly competed with honest manufacturers in the states. Be this as it may, some of the parties allege their entire ruin, and now present an equitable claim for loss incurred through the government prosecution.

CHAPTER XXII.

In the summer of 1870, the states of Missouri, Kansas, Texas and New Mexico were added to the supervisory district of Arkansas and the Indian Territory, with headquarters at St. Louis. I took charge of the St. Louis office, located on the corner of Fifth and Pine streets, as chief clerk of the establishment. Soon after, I was promoted to the position of a general revenue agent, but continued to perform the legal duties of the office in conjunction with Thomas Walsh, a gentleman of fine clerical ability, and an honorable man.

I made periodical trips through the District, investigating the offices of collectors and assessors, and examining into the general enforcement of the revenue laws, reporting my conclusions and recommendations to the Commissioner of Internal Revenue at Washington. When not engaged with official duties in Missouri, I took part in politics, and became a worker, writer and speaker for the Republican party. I was what might be termed a natural politician, and took to the eccentricities of the trade with vivacity and pleasure. Ward, city, county, state and National Conventions found me as a delegate.

The Presidential campaign of 1872 was a remarkable one. Grant had been in office about four years, and had failed to put a million chronic office-seekers into a hundred thousand places. This was sad, but true. The patriotic men in the Republican party, who carried torchlights in 1868, and grew hoarse in praise of the hero of Appomattox and the historic apple tree, and who failed to get office, were hungry and rampant four years later.

On the 22d of February, 1872, the Republicans of Missouri held a state convention in Jefferson City, for the purpose of nominating thirty delegates to attend the National Convention to be held in June at Philadelphia. The convention was composed of about seven hundred delegates, every county in the state being represented. The Liberal wing, led by Henderson, Stanard, Dyer and Grosvenor, and the Radical wing, commanded by Blow, Filley, McKee, Burdett, Van Horn, Newcomb and Krum, endeavored to lay down their old differences on the altar of harmony, and retrieve what they had lost in the "sell-out" of Gratz Brown to the Democracy. The factions approached each other very gingerly, and while talking of harmony, worked secretly to nominate their own men.

I was elected as a delegate from the ninth ward, and went into the convention "red hot" for the Administration. There was no trouble in my going to any convention as a delegate from the ninth ward after I learned the ropes of city politics.

The night before the convention at Jefferson City, a great crowd assembled at the Madison House. "Slates" were fixed up, ciphered upon, rubbed out, and smashed. Knots of delegates assembled in rooms, halls, and on the pavement, discussing the prospects of the next day, and predicting that such and such parties would be put in nomination.

I walked over to the state house on the morning of the convention, with Chauncey I. Filley, my room-mate of the previous night. We had fixed up a slate for President of the convention, but through some unforeseen circumstances, our man was not presented. After Henry T. Blow, chairman of the State Central Committee, called the meeting to order in a patriotic, harmonious speech, the name of George H. Shields, a law partner of John B. Henderson, was put in nomination for President of the convention, and his election was secured without opposition. Committees were duly announced, credentials examined, and everything put in working order. I was appointed on the committee to draft resolutions; and being a sentimentalist, prepared a set before I left St. Louis, that embodied my idea of Republican principles. The endorsement of Grant's administration and a firm assertion of hard-money principles were the main features in my "cut and dried" material, outside the usual buncomb promises in the interests of truth, virtue, honesty, economy and liberty.

Gen. John B. Henderson saw at once that I was pitching about like a young colt in a wasp's nest, or like the Hibernian at Donnybrook Fair, hunting for some one to tread on the tail of his coat. He quietly caught me under the shadow of one of the pillars that supported the porch of the capitol, and with a peculiar twinkle in his eye, said : " Joyce, my dear fellow, let me give you a little advice. Go to the drug store, get a pint of red pepper, put it in your boots, and draw the heat out of your head ! " Before I conld reply, he shot off with a laugh, and left me to muse on his good natured cut.

My real object in attending the State Convention was for the purpose of becoming a delegate to the National Convention, and thus pave the way for Congressional preferment in the 3d District. I consulted with Mr. Filley, with whom I held the closest personal and political relations, and who never, when he was in power, failed to advise with me on current political matters.

I was often at his residence, and dined with himself and his charming and intellectual wife. Knowing that he made a regular business of politics, I often gave way to his expert talent in running "the machine." He suggested that I had better not run directly as a delegate to the National Convention, but turn in and pull the wires for his election ; and as he only wanted the glory and power that being a National delegate would afford in the new Administration, I could, when the proper time came, take his proxy and be, to all intents and purposes, an actual voting delegate.

I assented to the arrangement, and in due time the following certificate and letters were placed in my hands, making me a voting delegate at the Philadelphia Academy of Music in the National Republican Convention of 1872 :

City of Jefferson, State of Missouri, }
February 22d, 1872.　　　　}

This certifies that at a Republican State Convention, held in the city of Jefferson, in pursuance to a call issued by the Republican State Executive Committee, for the purpose of choosing delegates to the Republican National Convention, to be held in the city of Philadelphia, State of Pennsylvania, June 5th, 1872, Hon. Chauncey I. Filley was chosen as delegate for the First Congressional District of the State of Missouri, to attend said National Convention.　　　　Geo. H. Shields, President.

Theodore Brown, Secretary.

Col. JOHN A. JOYCE,　　　　(*)　　　　St. Louis, June 30, 1872.
　　Philadelphia, Pa.

　　　　Dear Sir: I hand you my credential and request to Delegation to make you my proxy.　　　　Yours, etc.,

Chauncey I. Filley.

I had gone to Philadelphia among the first of the Republicans who departed from St. Louis, and took rooms at the Continental Hotel which Filley had previously engaged. I was afraid for awhile that he would not send me as his proxy. The following letter shows something of his anxiety:

St. Louis, June 2d, 1872.
Col. JOYCE:

　　　　The chances are against my coming. So you can take the whole of my room and put in whom you choose. If I should come, I can go to a friend's house and stay nights.

I am looking upon you as my friend, and the friend of Republican success. Henderson will not leave until to-morrow, Monday, night. I may come with him, but don't keep the room for me.

Yours, truly,　　　　Chauncey I. Filley.

Mr. Filley did not come to the Convention; his obligations to me, and his shrewd instinct of not antagonizing any of the elements he relied on to put him in the St. Louis post-office, prevented his voting as a delegate. I was duly elected by the delegation on the proxy given me, and acted as Mr. Filley's "friend" and the "friend of Republican success" from the beginning of the Grant and Wilson campaign until its triamphant close. Gen. Henderson arrived at the Continental

* This letter in Filley's writing (fac simile) appears near the end of the book.

the day of the Convention, and as all the rooms were crowded, I shared my bed with him.

Immediately after the National Convention, Republican decks were cleared for action, the sinews of war were collected and applied, and every means taken to defeat the Dolly Varden Brindle Pup Liberal - Republican - Democratic ticket, led by Greeley and Brown. Of course, every sensible man knew that this ticket was a fraud from the beginning, and as such could have but one ending—ignominious defeat. In Missouri, and particularly in St. Louis, there was a very bitter feeling against Grant's administration. Brown, Blair, Schurz and their followers were rampant, and constantly seeking for every straw to lay in the way of Republican success.

A meeting of the State Central Committee was called, and means suggested and devised for raising funds. · I was a member of the committee for three years, representing the Third Congressional District. Hon. Henry T. Blow, the chairman of the committee, and the particular friend of Gen. Grant; Wm. McKee, the editor and proprietor of the *Democrat;* Hon. Charles W. Ford, an intimate friend of the President, the Supervisor and myself, put our heads and hands together, and raised what was known in the campaign as " the silk stocking fund "—a sum of money amounting to thirty thousand dollars.

This was to be expended by Grant's personal friends in their own way, and while the State Committee, through the importunity of Mr. Filley, endeavored to control the fund, Mr. Blow would not allow it to use any of the money.

The " silk stocking" fund was raised by "voluntary contributions" from collectors, assessors, deputy collectors, assistant assessors, agents, storekeepers, gaugers, distillers, rectifiers, liquor dealers, tobacco and cigar manufacturers, merchants, brewers, lawyers, doctors, preachers, and from any citizen who felt an interest in the election of Gen. Grant. I drew up the subscription-paper, procured the bulk of the contributions, and turned the money over to Hon. Henry T. Blow, who doubtless put it where it did the most good. I was simply a bold, executive broad-ax in the hands of my many personal and political friends, and never failed when running "the machine" to hew to the line, let the chips fall where they might.

Mr. Filley was not satisfied with the manner in which the Central Committee ran the campaign, and after consulting with Gen. Isaac F. Shepard, E. O. Stanard, E. W. Fox, C. A. Newcomb, George Bain and myself, it was determined to organize the " Missouri Club," an institution that did practical yeoman service during the Presidential campaign of 1872.

George Bain, a shrewd politician, an active business man, and a gentleman of undoubted integrity and ability, was chosen President of the Club, and James B. Nicholson was made the Recording Secretary. An Executive Committee of seven was also appointed.

I was selected as *Corresponding Secretary*, and received and sent out all the campaign literature. Headquarters were located at Temple Hall, corner of Fifth and Walnut streets. A Vice-President of the club was selected from each of the congressional districts, from the most prominent men in the state.

During the campaign I made several speeches, wrote numerous editorials for the *Democrat*, St. Joseph *Herald* and Kansas City *Journal*, and sent telegraphic political messages to the New York *Times*, doing every legitimate thing in my power to secure the success of the Republican party.

The November battle resulted, as all know, in the almost unanimous election of Grant and Wilson, burying poor Greeley beneath an avalanche of misfortune, from which the great editor and kind heart never recovered, but went to his grave the victim of Liberal hypocrites and his own vaulting ambition !

CHAPTER XXIII.

DECORATION-DAY AT JEFFERSON BARRACKS.

In the spring of 1873, great preparations were being made to celebrate Decoration Day at Jefferson Barracks. A soldiers' meeting was held at the court-house, with Hon. Thomas C. Fletcher as chairman. I had often thought there was no reason, in good morals or law, that prevented the Federal and Confederate soldiers from going with their friends to the last sad resting-place of their heroic dead, and there strewing the brightest and sweetest flowers.

With this end in view, I offered a resolution in the soldiers' meeting to invite ex-Confederates to join us in celebrating Decoration Day at the Barracks, where slept about ten thousand heroes, "blue," "gray" and "black." A number in the meeting were opposed to the proposition, but after a warm discussion it was carried, two to one. Then it was a question whether any of the ex-Confederates should be invited to speak from the platform with the regular orator of the day. I insisted that it would not be right and just to invite them to participate without extending every privilege we claimed ourselves, and that in fact, such men as Marmaduke, Frost and Slayback would spurn our invitation with contempt unless it was given with the broadest spirit of liberality and common brotherhood. The committee and speaker finally selected General John B. Gray as president of the decoration ceremonies ; Gustave Hienrich as the German speaker; Col. A. W. Slayback, an intellectual and gallant ex-Confederate, for an address, and I was selected to deliver the regular oration.

Decoration Day with its May blossoms and fragrant memories arrived, and to the National Soldiers' Cemetery at Jefferson Barracks there went forth from St. Louis ten thousand beating hearts to do honor to the heroic dead that slumber forever by the murmuring waters of the Mississippi.

The sun shone bright, the air was cool and clear, the shadows of the woods came and went over the modest graves like messengers of celestial wing, the birds sent forth their sweetest songs, the grasshopper, cricket and bee joined in the melancholy hum of decoration, and all nature was clothed in a dark emerald mantle in honor of the immortal dead.

In the presence of ten thousand sympathetic, beating hearts from the ranks of the "blue" and the "gray" I delivered the following oration :

Ladies and Gentlemen :

Twelve years have passed since the old flag fell at Sumter. Eight years have winged their flight to realms of eternity since our glorious banner rose triumphant at Appomattox. Four years of terrible war desolated the land, blackened the homes and crushed the hearts of millions to place that darling symbol on the highest pinnacle of Freedom's temple, and perpetuate its meaning to the last syllable of recorded time. Brave men fought and died to preserve us a nation. This day we assemble to commemorate the event, strew upon their green graves the earliest flowers of spring, and water these hillocks of patriotism with the tears of affection. This day we devote to the memory of the loved and lost, who offered up their lives as pledges for the perpetuation of liberty. Let us, the survivors of "grim-visaged war," renew our devotion to the great Republic, and swear by the blood of our dear old comrades that the "red, white and blue," under which they fought and died, shall symbolize forever. All freedom for all men !

Can we ever forget the first drum-beat of rebellion, the muster, the drill, the march, the bivouac, the charge, the bloody battle, the groans of the dying, and the pale faces of the dead ? From the Manassas to Mission Ridge, from Gettysburg to Vicksburg, from Donaldson to Shiloh and Atlanta, through brake and brier, flood and field, swamp and forest, the boys in blue, led by the greatest warrior of modern times, kept right on in the path of duty, and at last planted their colors over the graves of the boys in gray, who fell bravely—victims to the Moloch of slavery.

No word of mine shall ever impeach the bravery and sincerity of those who fought and fell for the sunny South. Like men they met us on the field of battle, and foot to foot and hilt to hilt they acted the noble part of soldiers. We were brothers of the same maternal line, and God grant that hereafter we may kneel at the same shrine and worship at one common altar of law and liberty. Here let us dedicate an everlasting temple to heroism. This green sward shall be the mausoleum of heroic hearts, its dome the bending heavens, and its altar-candles the watching stars of God. Year after year let us assemble at this Mecca, and, kneeling by the graves of brave men, let the living clasp hands in fervency of friendship, and strew sweet flowers upon the moldering remains of the blue and the gray.

> "From the silence of sorrowful hours,
> Let desolate mourners go,
> Lovingly laden with flowers
> Alike for the friend and the foe,
> Under the sod and the dew,
> Waiting the judgment day;
> Under the roses the Blue—
> Under the lilies the Gray."

In the fight for Union and freedom the waters of the Potomac were crimsoned with the life-blood of our Eastern brothers, and the majestic river flowing at the foot of these graves will murmur forever the battle glory of the West as it wends its way through the land of sun and flowers to the surging waters of the Gulf. Upon its bosom commercial palaces float, unimpeded by war, from the Falls of St. Anthony to the Delta, taking the cereals, minerals and wares of the North in exchange for the cotton, spices and fruits of the South. Blessed be the patriots, now sleeping beneath the sod, that gave us by their blood, at Island No. 10, Fort Pillow, Vicksburg, Port Hudson and New Orleans, a free river to the bounding billows of the ocean. Each succeeding year will add new laurels to their fame; and as the Grecians loved to ponder upon the valor of those who fell at Thermopylæ, so shall we, by chisel, brush, harp and eloquent tongue, commemorate the glorious deeds of the boys in blue, and transmit their names to generations yet unborn.

The surviving soldiers of Missouri, and those who loved the Union, can never forget Wilson Creek and the bravery of Lyon, Lexington and glorious Mulligan, nor the daring march of Sigel to Rolla. Patriots from the blue waters of the Rhine and the green banks of the Shannon stood side by side with the native sons of America in the conflict for freedom and law; and wherever the battle was fierce and deadly, there could be seen the flashing sabre of Germania reflecting back the bristling bayonets of Erin and Columbia.

The emancipation proclamation of the martyr Lincoln gave to our arms the black warriors of the South, and on a hundred battle-fields they won, by the price of their blood, the right to perfect manhood. Let us not forget that the bondsman of yesterday is the freeman of to-day; and while we strew roses on the last resting-place of the blue and the gray, let us generously drop flowers on the grave of the black soldier who fell for freedom and his native land.

While we decorate the graves of the soldier dead, let us not forget their widows and orphans who gave all they held dear to propitiate the demon of war. We must minister to the support of the one and the education of the other, and prove by good works to the living that it is truly sweet to die for one's country.

A scene during the late struggle I shall ever remember—an epitome of the whole war. It was in June, 1864, in front of Kenesaw Mountain, Georgia. During the long, weary day Sherman battled with Johnston, and step by step drove him from the field. My regiment was on the skirmish line, and just as the sun bid good-bye to the tree-tops on the distant mountain, a desperate fight ensued—the winking stars and the silvery moonlight lighting up the last encounter. Silence and night soon hung around us. A few chosen comrades and myself went to the front to reconnoitre. Between the contending armies, in the dense underbrush of the forest, we discovered two soldiers grappled in death, the struggling light of the moon dancing upon the uniforms of the gray and the blue. A hasty search could only discover that they were each about twenty years of age, and nothing on their persons to tell the story of their lives. We quickly and quietly fashioned a rude grave, and, side by side, laid them to sleep until the trump of the Archangel sounds the resurrection morn, when the blue and the gray shall be crystalized into celestial white and dwell together in blissful immortality.

> " Slowly and sadly we laid them down,
>   From the field of their fame fresh and gory;
>   We carved not a line, we raised not a stone,
>   But left them alone in their glory."

Who will care for these loved mounds when we are gone? Who will then strew roses and plant bright flowers? Other patriotic hands of brave men and fair women will take up the roll of duty; and even when all but liberty has perished from the earth, the robin and the blue-bird, the jay and the mocking-bird will warble at sunrise a reveille over the green sod that wraps this sacred clay. Nature herself will deck the graves of our fallen comrades, and the winds of heaven will chant a requiem to their memory and kiss the loved spot where valor sleeps.

Thousands of our dearly loved comrades rest in unknown graves far away from the loved ones at home. They slumber in a land of strangers, where the tears of love cannot moisten the green shroud that mantles their ashes. But if no kind hand is there to strew flowers, or loved eye to shed the tear of sorrow, there is One that reigns among the eternal stars that daily floods the unknown grave with sunshine, and nightly waters the budding wild flowers with dews from heaven.

To-day, thank God, we are all Americans, protected by the same flag, representing one country and one destiny. We have no North, no South, no East, no West; naught but the priceless heritage of Liberty and Union. Let our friendships and interests be as lasting as the eternal hills, so that peace and material prosperity shall crown our labor and spread the cement of brotherly love and union from the surf-beaten shores of the Carolinas to the golden boulders of California, and from the lazy lagoons of Louisiana to the rock-bound coast of Massachusetts.

> " Let Summer send her golden sunbeams down,
>   In graceful salutations for the dead,
> And Autumn's moving host of leaflets brown
>   Break ranks above the fallen soldier's head.
>
> And we, survivors of the fearful strife,
>   While gathered here around this hallowed clay,
> Let us anew pledge honor, fortune, life,
>   That from our flag no star shall pass away.
>
> We reverently swear by all we love,
>   By all we are, and all we hope to be,
> Yon starry flag man's steadfast friend shall prove,
>   And wave forever o'er the brave and free."

General John S. Marmaduke, of St. Louis, an ex-Confederate officer, wrote me a letter on the philosophy and propriety of keeping alive the memory of our dead heroes, who fought for what each deemed right; and as there is wisdom and patriotism in what the gallant General says, I present the following extracts:

"This joint memorial ceremony—Federal and ex-Confederate—for the purpose of decorating the graves of the brave who gave up their lives for what they deemed right, is to my mind a wise, patriotic and beautiful act; and that those who fought under the blue, the victors, should invite those who fought under the gray, the vanquished, to unite, and make this ceremony a joint one for the dead of both armies, is as it should be, and reflects a patriotic purpose creditable alike to their head and heart, which I believe every man and woman who were genuine Federals and Confederates will respond to with their whole hearts.

Both sides should recognize that the Confederates surrendered because they were overpowered, and did not have men or money enough to whip in the fight, and for no other reason. That now and henceforth the men who worthily wore the " gray" are ready and willing to march side by side with the victors of the " blue," in bearing the bayonets and banners of the *United States* to other victories !

It is a dangerous folly for us to quarrel over the past ; let that be buried, and let us go forward with our new-born nation. Those who were nobly in earnest should feel a personal pride in the army heroism of either side.   It was *American pluck*, to which each side contributed to an extent that challenged the admiration of the world, and which the United States should claim and hold as valued property.

Let these decoration ceremonies be free from all partisan significations.   Let them be the Nation's worship—her floral tribute to her brave dead !''

The sentiments engrafted in the foregoing paragraphs by General Marmaduke are worthy of the brave and honest soul that inspired them ; and if we are to live a thousand years as one Republic, each integral part of the Nation must act for the equality and liberty of the whole, leaving no scar of discrimination to irritate the body, or rankle in the soul.

CHAPTER XXIV.

I MAKE AN EFFORT TO OBTAIN A FOREIGN MISSION.—ORATION
AT AN EMANCIPATION CELEBRATION.

In the spring and summer of 1873, I conceived the idea that
I wanted a better place than the post of Revenue Agent. In
fact, like all great (?) men, I wished a foreign mission, where
the work would be light and the pay large. As I had performed
yeoman service during the Grant campaign, I applied to the
men who controlled political matters in Missouri, and received
the most cordial letters and recommendations to President
Grant, from which I select the following extracts.

Hon. William Patrick, United States District Attorney, said:

"I desire to bear testimony to Joyce's public and private services. In
the last campaign, he, as a member of the Republican Central Committee
of the State, as Corresponding Secretary of the Missouri Club, as a public
speaker and writer, rendered very valuable assistance to the Republican
ticket. Col. Joyce has made a faithful officer, and has always been prompt
and willing to give any information or perform any duty required by the
office. I have every confidence that the duties of any position in which he
may be placed will be performed by him with ability, integrity, and credit
to the administration."

George W. Fishbeck, one of the editors and proprietors of
the St. Louis *Democrat*, said:

"Please let me add my word in commendation of the eminent services
performed by Col. Joyce in this city and state during the canvass of last
year; and permit me to say that any promotion you may see fit to give him
will be most heartily approved by your friends in this city."

Gen. Isaac F. Shepard, the Appraiser of Customs for the
port of St. Louis, said:

"I have known Col. John A. Joyce personally for two years or more,
and have been associated with him in political matters quite intimately.

During the last campaign, he was for a portion of the time a member of the State Central Committee, and also Corresponding Secretary of the Missouri Club. In his private as well as public capacity he has been an unwavering friend of Republican principles and an unflinching devotee to your administration. He has more than a common culture, with many fine gifts, and I cordially commend him to your favorable consideration in any contingency that may occur to your Excellency to the advancement of his interests."

Hon. E. W. Fox, Surveyor and Collector of Customs for St. Louis, and former Chairman of the Republican State Central Committee, a gentleman of fine culture and ripe experience, said:

"I take great pleasure in presenting to your most favorable consideration, Col. John A. Joyce, who, in addition to discharging with signal ability his duties as Chief Clerk and Revenue Agent in the Supervisor's office, has been one of the most active, intelligent and sagacious workers for the Republican cause in Missouri.

As member of the State Central Committee, as Corresponding Secretary of the Missouri Club, and as a constant contributor to the party press of the state, he has well earned the confidence and best wishes of the true Republicans of the Western States.

I heartily recommend him to advancement in the country's service, and am sure that his talents and integrity eminently fit him to represent the Nation at foreign posts. I feel assured that whatever position you may bestow upon him, he will discharge his duty with credit to himself and honor to his country."

Col. A. R. Easton, Assessor of Internal Revenue, said:

"During the recent campaign, Col. Joyce rendered valuable service to your administration by his energy and sound judgment as a member of the Republican State Central Committee, Secretary of the Missouri Club, and writer for the press of this and other states. He is a young man of superior ability, a good speaker and fine writer, and I am sure he will serve the Government faithfully in any position for which he may be selected."

Col. C. A. Newcomb, United States Marshal, said:

"I have known Col. Joyce for four years, and have been associated with him personally and officially, and take great pleasure in bearing witness to his efficiency as an officer and merit as a man.

No person connected with the Civil Service of the Government here has been more watchful of its honor than he; always quick to discover a wrong or irregularity in the service, and equally prompt to apply the remedy.

Col. Joyce is a man of fine culture and large business capacity. It would be a great satisfaction to himself and his friends if he could be employed in a more lucrative position than the one he now fills."

Hon. Chester H. Krum, ex-United States District Attorney, and Judge of the Circuit Court of St. Louis, said :

" Republicans in this state have substantial reasons for feeling under obligations to Col. Joyce for his industry, energy and zeal in harmonizing opposing elements, and thus presenting a united front to the political enemy. I have yet to learn that a single act of omission can truthfully be charged to Col. Joyce during the campaign of 1872.

During my own experience as United States Attorney for this Judicial District, I had many occasions to remark the faithful discharge of Colonel Joyce's duties as a revenue offier. Although he came here quite a stranger, he soon gained a large acquaintance. Having had large experience in bureau duties, he was well qualified to give, and freely gave, valuable assistance to efforts made for the detection of crime and the enforcement of the revenue laws. He was quick in expedients, and prompt in their execution. To these qualities he added fearlessness and substantial business habits.

As I have left a field of service which I shall always look back upon with pleasure as having been opened to me through your indulgence and confidence, I beg leave to add my testimony to the well-deserved assurances of Col. Joyce's fidelity, competency and zeal as an officer of the Revenue Department, which he has won and received during his residence in this state."

Hon. Chauncey I. Filley, ex-Postmaster of St. Louis, and a noted political wire-worker, said :

" My acquaintance with Col. Joyce justifies me in saying that he has abilities of more than an ordinary character, which fit him for a better position than he is now holding. He has been an active and judicious participator in events here to promote the interests of the service and of the party, and has always been ready in action and work, and otherwise; and since the campaign has not allowed the grass to grow under his feet in matters which eventuated in advancing the interests of the cause.

Col. Joyce rendered valuable service as Secretary of the Missouri Club, as well as a member of the State Central Committee, and his work has come under my personal observation. He is a ready and apt writer, and has not been idle in that way; and I commend him to your best consideration."

In August, 1873, a change in the revenue laws made it necessary for the collectors throughout the country to assume the duties previously performed by assessors, thereby imposing additional work upon them. Collector C. W. Ford, of St. Louis, an intimate personal friend of Gen. Grant, was much annoyed because the Department would not allow him proper and just compensation in the premises. After his efforts had failed, he applied to me, and in due time I convinced the revenue office that Ford's application for extra compensation was just. The following extract from a long letter shows his anxiety:

"I shall be under many obligations to you if you will put this letter among your papers, and when you get to Washington bring the facts before Commissioner Douglas, and get the proper allowance made.

Col. Easton, the late Assessor, says he received no pay for March, and would be greatly obliged if you will look after it for him.

I get away from here Monday night, for Monroe, Mich., and will drop you a line from there, to let you know when I go to Long Branch."

On the 2d of September, 1873, while Collector Ford was receiving the hospitality of President Grant at his Long Branch cottage, I received another letter, from which I extract the following:

"I wrote you three letters to Boonville, N. Y., and the day before I left Sackett's Harbor I telegraphed to Boonville to find your whereabouts, and learned you were at the Fifth Avenue Hotel; but when I applied there you were *non est.* I was sure I'd get you here, but nix. You had gone to Washington, and are now on your way to St. Louis, so I give up the chase.

I hope you have been successful in getting the Commissioner to make me proper allowances. I don't know how long I may remain here, but two or three days, I reckon, will find me on my way to New York."

I have several other letters from the late Captain Ford, but as they refer mainly to matters of no interest to the public, I omit them. In the latter part of October, 1873, Capt. Ford visited Toledo to attend a meeting of the Army of the Tennessee, and consult with Gen. Grant relative to his entering the Cabinet as Secretary of the Interior. But fate broke the last link in his life-chain on the 24th of October, 1873, and he died in Chicago, from a severe cold contracted on his trip to Toledo.

Ford was a man of kind impulses. He had been for many years agent of the United States Express Company, and performed the duties of that important post with energy, capacity and honesty; and when President Grant called him to the post of Collector of Internal Revenue, he brought the same business principles to bear, making the best Collector that St. Louis ever had.

I knew Ford intimately; and while he would do any legitimate political thing to advance the cause of his old friend, President Grant, I am absolutely convinced that he never, either directly or indirectly, winked at or had knowledge of any whiskey frauds on the revenue, although his confidence may have been abused by his chief clerk and subordinates.

*_**

In August, 1873, I delivered the following oration before five thousand colored people at St. Louis, on the occasion of their emancipation celebration:

Fellow Citizens :

The emancipation of an enslaved race is a theme fit to be couched in noble eloquence, monumented in bronze, and sent to the latest posterity in poetry and song. From the earliest dawn of creation, when the morning stars sang together, human thoughts and human action lingered at the shrine of freedom; and even in the night of Egyptian darkness and bondage, the sweet pæans of liberty sounded in the soul of man and found a responsive echo in the celestial realms of the angels.

God, in his infinite wisdom, created all men free, and it was only tyrants who could forge the chains of slavery and find consolation in the sharp music of the lash. Ignorance, selfishness and fear make a man a tyrant, while intelligence, benevolence and love fit him for the priceless blessings of freedom in this world, and open a way to his eternal home beyond the sun and stars.

The celebration of this day will bring vividly to your mind the trials and tribulations and victories achieved by your race in the West India Islands, where the genius of Toussaint

L'Ouverture held at bay the cruelties of the proud Spaniard, and even foiled the expectations of the great Napoleon. The pen and voice of L'Ouverture exposed the flimsy pretense of slavery, and his flashing sword cut in twain the Gordian knot of despotism and initiated the first successful emancipation movement. To-day, in the mountain cabins of Hayti and San Domingo, the name of this apostle of liberty is sounded with love and veneration, and as the circling years go by, the fame of Toussaint L'Ouverture will grow brighter until every human heart pulsates with the sublime sentiments that actuated him in life, and made him a conqueror even in the torturing hours of death in the dungeon of the tyrant. The clanking chains of Napoleon and the excruciating pangs of cold, thirst and hunger could not subdue the proud spirit of the black warrior and statesman. His free soul and glorious nature triumphed over the grave; and long after you and I are consigned to the dust from whence we sprung, this hero of San Domingo will live in monumental greatness, and inspire the world with his example.

L'Ouverture laid broad and deep the foundation of the Republic of San Domingo, and the day is near when the stars and stripes shall float over the land he died to save. God will work in his mysterious way, until the continent of Africa shall be disenthralled from the darkness of ignorance and slavery, when one universal republic shall bless the world and realize the fondest hopes of the human heart. The wail of oppressed humanity comes sounding down the centuries; the cry for liberty and light is wafted to us in every breeze that blows from ocean's boundless shores.

> "Hark! our brothers call,
> From Greenland's icy mountains,
> From India's coral strand;
> Where Afric's sunny fountains
> Roll down their golden sand.
> From many an ancient river;
> From many a palmy plain;
> They call us to deliver
> Their land from error's chain."

In the year 1620, two hundred and fifty-three years ago, *forty-five* slaves were landed on the James River in Virginia, forced from the coast of Africa and sold into bondage to cultivate the plantations of the Old Dominion. From this "direful spring" Columbia has suffered more unnumbered woes than Achilles' wrath brought to Greece. I can see now in the jungles of Africa the fierce spirit of Caucasian cupidity hunting down the first load of human freight. The simple life of the black man in his native wilds knew no master but his God, pictured in the rising sun, and smiling in the blue waters of the Nile and Ganges.

I see that fatal ship stealing quietly out from the golden sands of Africa, speeding on its way to America freighted with human misery and terrible grief. Would to God that she had sunk to the bottom of the ocean, and buried forever even the just and the unjust, ere her prow touched the shores of Virginia, and began that reign of slavery that cursed our country and culminated in the great conflict of 1861.

Great crimes deserve great punishment, and fearful has been our retribution. Two millions of human lives were sacrificed to purchase the emancipation of American slavery, and to-day the tears of the widows and orphans flow at the mention of those loved hearts that went down into the dark valley of death in the musical whiz of the Minie rifle, or the roar of the Rodman gun!

The colored people of this nation have great cause to boast of the deeds of their heroes. The first blood shed in the American revolution was that of the slave Crispus Attucks, of Boston, Massachusetts. In the massacre of March 5, 1770, in an assault upon the British soldiers he fell for freedom and his native land. The blood of the slave has nourished the tree of liberty, and under its wide-spreading branches you sit to-day basking in the sunshine of equal rights, proud of your citizenship and ready at all times to strike for

> "The land of the free
> And the home of the brave!"

The freedom of American slavery required long years of education and toil.   Adams, Jefferson, Clay, Garrison and Phil-
lips dug from the mountains the crude ore of liberty ; but it
was left to Lincoln, Seward and Grant to put it through the
furnace-heat of the rebellion and forge out the trip-hammer
that knocked forever the rusty shackles from four millions of
slaves.   The emancipation proclamation of Abraham Lincoln
broke the back of the rebellion.   Its thunder-tones will go
sounding down the ages, and the lightning flash of each sentence will irradiate the rugged road of the human race and
light up the darkest nooks of imperial government.   The memory of Lincoln will live as long as human hearts pulsate with
love of liberty.

Rooted firmly and deeply in the rifted rocks of time shall be
his temple of everlasting glory.   The mountains of Columbia
lifting their heads into the boundless blue, and the murmuring
rivers of the continent, shall mingle forever with his fame ; but
the noblest monument to his memory are the four million
shackles struck from the galling limbs of the bondsman.   Already the lesson of the proclamation has found its way to the
plains of the Amazon and the bleak regions of the Ural mountains, where twenty million Russian serfs breathe at last the
pure air of freedom.   So shall the example of the immortal
Lincoln continue to bless the human race, until, crowned with
the diadem of liberty, we shall acknowledge the image of God
in all men, and pluck from the calendar of our hearts the demon of caste and persecution.

From my earliest years I hated the very name of slavery.
The word burned upon my tongue and blistered in my heart.
Even as a boy, in the land of Clay, I sighed for the hour to
strike at the hell-born iniquity ; and when the clash of arms
came I went out to battle for the perpetuation of the Union
and the freedom of the slave.   The first shot at Sumter sounded
the death-knell of slavery, and it will echo in the hearts of
generations yet unborn, until every land and clime hears the
sweet songs of liberty, and joins in the chorus of equality.

Your own stout arms and valiant hearts struggled in the cause of freedom. Port Hudson and Fort Wagner will long be remembered as the bloodiest battles of the war, where the First Louisiana and Fifty-fourth Massachusetts colored regiments fought with terrible desperation, and made a page in American history that will transmit the glory of the black warrior to the last symbol of recorded time.

Since the close of the war the behavior of the black man has been truly remarkable, for never in the history of the world did men come up so quick out of the dark forests of ignorance and bondage, and show such capacity for civil life and constitutional freedom. Lift up your eyes and hearts to God, and never despair. Seven centuries ago the Caucasian race was wandering half naked in the black forests of Germany, and th Scots and Picts of proud Albion were little above the wild animals that furnished their food and raiment.

In the Senate of the United States and lower house of Congress, representatives of your race have sat side by side with white men, and have maintained their independence and manhood. To-day you, stand upon the same political platform with the greatest and best of your white fellow citizens, and even those who once held you in bondage have become reconciled to the logic of events. Forget, if you can, the cruelties of slavery in the gratitude you owe the nation for clothing you with the inestimable power of the ballot—

> "A weapon that comes down as still
> As snow-flakes falling on the sod,
> And executes a freeman's will
> As lightning does the will of God!"

In conclusion, let me impress upon you the great importance of temperance, economy, education and peaceful conduct toward your neighbors. Whether as laborers, mechanics, merchants or professionals, you must rely upon yourselves, and by untiring perseverance and honesty procure a home, where the blessings of peace and prosperity shall crown the evening of life, and give you a taste of that immortal happiness found only in the beautiful land around the white throne of Jehovah, where the angels always sing and the light of heaven shines eternal.

CHAPTER XXV.

In the spring of 1874, I received orders from Hon. J. W.
Douglas, Commissioner of Internal Revenue, to proceed to
San Francisco and make a thorough investigation of the operation and enforcement of the revenue laws on the Pacific Coast.
Frequent complaints came from San Francisco that the distillers and rectifiers of that locality were defrauding the Government out of taxes on spirits, and that some of the revenue
officers were in collusion with the whiskey men.

Several revenue agents had been sent to the Pacific Coast,
from time to time, but their efforts to bring the violators of
law to justice proved abortive, because, they alleged, nearly
all of the United States officers in San Francisco were more or
less in collusion with the rich distillers and whiskey-traders,
who put up their money in political campaigns to make and
unmake congressmen, governors and senators. Be this as it
may, the so-called Pacific Coast Whiskey-Ring were "too
smart" for the "minions" of Uncle Sam, and they only went
in the front door of the United States Court with a wink and
a laugh at the prosecution, to come out at the back door with
their satirical tongues wagging defiance at the foiled revenue
agents.

I made a careful investigation of the working of the revenue
laws on the Pacific Coast, embracing the collection districts
of California, Oregon and Washington Territory. For nearly
three months I traveled through the country towns and cities
of the Coast, taking memoranda of my investigations; and

from the orange groves of Los Angeles to the falls of the Columbia River beyond Portland, and on to the solemn waters
of Puget Sound, through the pine lumber region of Tacoma,
Seattle and Port Townsend. I left no subject of revenue un-
touched, examining offices and business houses wherever I went.
Supervisor L. M. Foulke accompanied me in my tour, and
rendered every assistance I desired. He was a man of very
few words, but with a fine vein of humor.

After a full investigation in Oregon and Washington Territory, instead of taking an ocean steamer at Portland for San
Francisco, I took the cars for Roseburg, and thence overland
by stage—a distance of three hundred miles—through the Pitt
and Snake River valleys to the golden gulches of California.

The ride was one of the most romantic I ever had. Winding around the crest of some rugged crag toppling far above
Snake River, as the morning sun bathes the world in glory,
you may gaze away for a hundred miles through the transpar-
ent atmosphere, and see the blue peaks of the tallest mountains capped with eternal snow above the floating clouds, like
Titanic ghosts of buried centuries. Then shorten the vision
to hill, crag, valley, tree, water-fall, blooming wild flowers,
and warbling birds, together with the downward rush of the
break-neck stage, and you have a sensation of life and romance
that spurns danger, and sweeps away like a mountain eagle
among the peaks of his native home.

I arrived in due time at San Francisco, and wrote up my
investigations, making a voluminous report in detail of the
violations of law discovered during my examination. If the
Commissioner of Internal Revenue ever succeeded in bringing
them to justice and punishment, I never heard of it; and perhaps, after all, the prophecy of De Young, of the *Chronicle,*
was fulfilled—that my official report would not amount to anything, but would be ignored and pigeon-holed in the interests
of powerful politicians. However, I performed my duty, and
left the balance to the consideration of superior officers in the
Treasury Department.

A breakfast at the Cliff House is one of the memorable milestones of a trip to the Pacific Coast. I took the reins of a double team, and accompanied by a beautiful and intelligent lady from the East, who was stopping at the Grand Hotel, proceeded to the celebrated resort. Out Market Street, by the old Mission, through the park, over a succession of rolling hills, up winding roads, and along precipitous crags to the top of mountain spurs that overlooked the Ocean House and the golden sand-hills that sparkled down the coast as far as the eye could reach, we rode in the exhilarating air. On the crest of the highest hill of those that margin San Francisco with an emerald frame, I looked back in amazement at the silent city rising from its silver couch in the sparkling waters of the beautiful bay.

On we went, by winding road, sandy foot-hills, and yellow beach, until the tumbling waters of the Pacific dashed in musical spray against the rocky base of the Cliff House.

After a refreshing breakfast, we turned our faces towards the city, over a broad gravel road as smooth as a floor, rising and falling with undulating swells like the broad-backed billows of the ocean. Toward the right is the Catholic cemetery, nestled among the foot-hills, and on the left Lone Mountain Cemetery, overlooking San Francisco, with a glimpse of bay and ocean in the shining distance.

Lone Mountain shadows the graves of Senator Broderick and General Baker; one the victim of Duke Guinn, Terry and slavery, while the other lost his noble life at Ball's Bluff fighting for Freedom and the Union. They rest almost side by side. Many pilgrims from home and foreign lands will love to dwell upon the memory of these brave patriots who fell for Liberty; and as long as the rivers and mountains of Oregon embrace the golden streams of California, Baker and Broderick will live in the hearts of the good and true, shining as beacon lights to irradiate the pathway of progress.

"Not in vain the distant beacons; forward, forward, let us range!
Let the great world spin forever down the ringing grooves of change."

Previous to leaving St. Louis for the Pacific coast, I promised the editor to write a series of descriptive letters for the *Globe-Democrat;* and, as they dropped fresh from my pen, I engraft them in this volume just as they were written, believing that the reader will be better pleased than if I revamped them now from the encrusted fields of memory.

SCENES AND INCIDENTS OF A TRIP TO THE PACIFIC.

Correspondence St. Louis Globe-Democrat.

San Francisco, Cal., March 25, 1864.

The readers of the *Globe* have no doubt often wished themselves on the golden sands of the Pacific; and to those who have never made the overland trip, I hereby extend an invitation, insisting only that their imagination and good will shall follow me through the serpentine windings of the Union and Central Pacific Railroads over plains, hills, mountains and dashing streams, where nature plays its grandest part.

Remember now, gentle reader, before starting, that " touch and go'' is our programme, and pleasure and profit our motive power. With ticket and trunk-check in our pocket we step into one of Pullman's fine palace coaches at St. Louis, on a Sabbath evening, and soon we are wending our way toward Kansas City, arriving Monday morning, connecting with the Missouri Valley and Council Bluffs Railroad, which deposits us safely that night in Omaha, where, at the Grand Central Hotel, we feast and rest until the morning sun warns us that the Union Pacific train waits not for laggards. Our experience in the late unpleasantness prompts the necessity of "three days' rations in haversack,'' ready to march or starve (?) at a moment's warning. At 11 o'clock in the morning, promptly, the overland train moves out of the depot and heads off for the West, and, as we turn over the bluffs of Omaha, bid good-bye and give a last fond look at the " Big Muddy'' as it wends its way to the Gulf. Onward we move over the rich prairie lands of Nebraska, stopping occasionally at way stations for mails and passengers. Near Grand Island, one hundred and fifty-four miles from Omaha, where the train stops for supper, we behold a splendid prairie fire, just as the sun sinks behind the western hills. No one who has not witnessed it can appreciate the grandeur and fearful sublimity of a general prairie fire. Far as the eye can reach, long waves of flame, like molten metal, crackle and skip at the sport of the wild winds, filling the air with dense clouds of smoke, rushing on like the wild breakers of the ocean until dashed to pieces and extinguished against some bare bluff or barren crag.

A good night's rest brings us to Sidney, Neb., for breakfast, and after a splendid run over undulating plains, we reach Cheyenne, Wyoming Territory, a central distributing point for Colorado and New Mexico. Dinner is served up in good style here, and the overland argonauts continue their journey with light hearts and full stomachs. About 3 o'clock in the afternoon we arrived at Sherman, named in honor of our dashing general who cracked the shell of the rebellion and marched his "bummers" in triumph to the sea. This is the highest point on the road, attaining an altitude of eight thousand two hundred and forty-two feet above the level of the ocean. To the south, one hundred and sixty-five miles, is Pike's Peak; and to the southwest, seventy-five miles is Long's Peak, both visible.

From Sherman we dashed away over rough hills, narrow cañons and high bridges spanning terrible gorges, until Laramie City is gained, where supper is in waiting. This is the town where the first woman jury in the United States was impaneled to try one of the opposite sex for theft, murder, or some other mild form of crime, and to their credit be it said the "Lord of Creation" was convicted on every count! Who will say that woman acts from sympathy and not from a spirit of justice, after this showing?

Rushing out of Laramie, with tne stars and stripes fluttering over Fort Sanders in the distance, we enter the Laramie plains, extending sixty miles towards the west, and twenty miles toward the foot-hills of the Rocky Mountains. This valley is one of the finest grazing sections in the country, and a hundred thousand head of cattle can easily find food and water along the tortuous windings of the Laramie River.   For ten miles we struggle on towards Sheep Mountain, twelve thousand feet above the level of the sea.   Here the Laramie River takes its rise among the gloomy gorges of dense forest, overhanging rocks, and eternal springs.   Deer, bear, mountain lions and wild sheep range the rugged sides of the Black Hills and mountain peaks.

The traveler will notice, from Laramie on, that the sons of the Celestial empire work the railroad, and cut up old mother earth for the benefit of the Yankee nation.   See one John Chinaman and you see them all.   Dark, almond eyes, round expressionless face, shaved head, blouse, boxed shoes, and the eternal pig-tail, make up the sum and substance of this patient, untiring child of Confucius.   While they are not of us or with us in make and education, let us consider that they are human, and long before our double-storied Caucasian head learned its letters the Chinese wrote and taught the eternal justice of doing to others as you would they should do to you.

Night has passed, and we draw up in the early morning at Green River Station, where a good breakfast greets the wanderer.   We continue on the Green River, which takes its rise in the Wind River Mountains and empties into the Colorado, one hundred and fifty miles from the station.   On we go towards Fort Bridger, which was established in 1858, by General A. S. Johnston, who suffered so much with his little army in the "scrimmage" with Brigham Young.   The fort was named after Jim Bridger, an old hunter and trapper who lived in this region for thirty years, and who, I am informed, now resides in St. Louis.   The iron horse is dashing away towards Evanston, where dinner makes glad the heart of the traveler.   Deer, elk and antelope abound in this region, and from the car window I behold a large drove of the latter, more than fifty in number, quietly ranging and grazing within gun-shot of the train.   (Rodman gun.)   We now come to the wilds of Echo Cañon, where the shrill whistle of the locomotive finds

tongue in rocky crags that answer back the defiant shriek.
We clatter and dash through tunnels, over break-neck trestle
bridges, until the wilds of Weber River usher us into the renowned Weber Cañon, one of the grandest sights on the road.
For more than thirty miles the river rushes foaming and boiling between two mountain walls, which shut in the landscape
on either side.   Frequently the torrent leaps over some huge
rock that has fallen into the deep, dark chasm from the tower-
ing cliff.   For over six miles the fettered stream dashes down
through the narrows where the road-bed is cut out of the solid
rock, and at one point, where the old emigrant road crossed
the gorge, is so narrow that the torrent has worn its bed into
the form of a crooked S or Z where you would naturally imagine that its rush must cease or sink altogether into the bowels
of the earth ; but a few miles further on it passes out into the
plains as placid and clear as if no struggle had taken place.
As we emerge from the' cañon, the celebrated Thousand-mile
Tree is passed, marking the distance from Omaha.   This is a
grand old pine, that has long weathered the storm, and sheltered by its wide-spreading branches the red rover of the plains
and the lonely emigrant on his toilsome way to the land of
gold.   Here the Mormon settlements began to appear, and
the followers of Brigham utilized every foot of valley land, rear-
ing thereon their household gods with remarkable thrift

At dusk we reach Ogden, the terminus of the Union Pacific
Railroad, where we change cars for the Central Pacific, and
those who desire can run up thirty-eight miles to Salt Lake,
and pay homage to B. Young & Co., which is a strong firm in
this region.   "All aboard for San Francisco," 882 miles distant, prompts the tourist to take his place in the silver palace
sleeping cars.   On we go now past Corinne, through the Great
American Desert, sixty miles square, where the eye fails to see
a green shrub, and only alkali wastes of gray sandstone meet
the vision.   There are many evidences that this tract of country was once the bed of an inland sea.   In the early morning
Pilot Peak, an old emigrant landmark, meets the view, and

passing on to Toano, where we lay snow-bound for six hours, we strike down upon the head waters of the Humboldt River through Osino Cañon, a wild, rocky region, where bunches of sage grass and stunted shrubs grapple with the mountain sides.

Elko, Nevada, is reached for breakfast. It is the center of a vast silver mining country, including the White Pine region. Humboldt Cañon is in sight a few miles from Carlin, and standing on the platform, we wonder how the train can ever get through the mountains. The Humboldt River rolls at our feet, tossed and churned in its rocky road. On we glide towards Humboldt, where good meals are furnished, then to Hot Springs, down Truckee River to Verdi, over the line to California. Seven and fourteen miles from Truckee City are Donner and Tahoe Lakes. I would like to linger here, and tell you all about the Donner party and the matchless suffering they endured in the winter of 1864, on the borders of this renowned lake.

They were sixteen in number, bound from Illinois to the land of gold. A long and extremely heavy snow-storm overtook them. Mr. Donner, his wife and a German proposed to remain on the lake and let his children and the other emigrants endeavor to cross the mountains, expecting, when the storm subsided, to meet them in the Sacramento Valley. The main party crossed the mountain safely, but poor Donner and his wife, the bold pioneers, died of their sufferings.

From Truckee City we journeyed on to the summit of the Sierra Nevada Mountains, and such another serpentine climb there is not on the continent. The road for thirty miles is covered with snow-sheds, through which the train pushes. Just . think of a continuous tunnel of that length, with now and then a ray of light blinding the eyes, and you have some idea of snow-sheds. At Summit Station we breakfasted on delicious trout, caught in the lakes and streams of the surrounding mountaims; this, too, in an eating - house covered by sheds and twenty-five feet o snow !

Down the mountains we dash at break-neck speed, through Emigrant Gap, Dutch Flat and Gold Run, when, soon after, Cape Horn looms up in sight, and the gold mines of California meet the view wherever we turn. Chinese cabins and miners' huts peep out from every nook and gorge. On the 19th of January, 1848, near Placerville, El Dorado County, the first gold was discovered by one J. W. Marshall, in the mill-race of the noted General Sutter. From this discovery has grown the greatness and wealth of the Pacific coast, which has given our country a leading position among the nations. The gold-hunters from every state in the Union have been here to try their luck, and while hundreds have grown rich and settled in the beautiful valleys of this state, thousands and tens of thousands gave up the ghost in their overland tramp, or died alone and neglected in their unprofitable search among the crags and foot-hills of the coast range and Sierras.

Rounding Cape Horn, a bold, sharp peak, we look perpendicularly 3,000 feet below to the golden stream that flows at the base of the crag, like a variegated ribbon in a green field. In the distance is the thriving town of Colfax, named after our ex-Vice-President, and far away to the north-west is Mount Shasta, overlooking the waters of the Pacific Ocean. A short run brings us into the Sacramento valley, and right ahead can be seen the city of Sacramento. The sudden change from the region of ice and snow to the balmy breezes of the tropics, where violets and buttercups gladden the eye, and lilies grow in the open air, can be felt, but not described. Stopping but ten minutes at Sacramento, we move on toward San Francisco and the Golden Gate. Now we dash down the Sacramento valley, with Oakland and San Francisco before us, and the Sierra Nevada behind us.

Out into the bay, over the extended wharf, the train heads towards Goat Island, and the engine blows its last whistle for "down brakes" at San Francisco, where the long rows of gas-lights across the water wink a kind invitation to the weary pilgrim, who slumbers his first night in the city of seventy-seven hills. A large and commodious ferry-boat lies in waiting to carry us over the bonnie blue bay, and having escaped with our lives and our pocket-books from the infernal importunities of hotel runners and hackmen, we are snugly located at the Grand Hotel, six days' ride from home.

SOMETHING ABOUT THE EARLY HISTORY OF SAN FRANCISCO.
Special Correspondence of the St. Louis Globe.

San Francisco, Cal., April 25th, 1874.

Twenty-five years ago this city was but a straggling village, containing only a few miners and their huts and tents scattered along the bay, among the sand hills. The Indian, Mexican and Spaniard had long ranged the coast mountains and the waters of San Francisco Bay, and the Golden Gate had re-sounded to the music of the mission bells of the Castillian race nearly a hundred years before the Yankee nation poured out its dashing warriors and gold-hunters amid the Sierra Nevada Mountains. To-day San Francisco boasts of its two hundred thousand population, assembled from every clime on earth, embracing the most daring spirits of every race, and dashing forward with that indomitable perseverance and manly pluck that has made the Golden State the brightest gem in the coro-net of Columbia. Ships of every nation load and unload their rich freights here at the back door of the Union; and while New York is *the* metropolitan city of the nation, and St. Louis looms up as the Future Great City of the World, San Francisco, the representative of California, puts in a claim for the finest harbor, the richest mines, minerals and mountains, the biggest grain-fields—forty miles by twelve—the grandest scenery, the fastest women, and the largest and smartest men on top of dirt! If you don't believe what I say, ask any one of the "Forty-Niners" who cross your pathway on Montgomery or California streets. They will tell more than I can imagine of the won-derful past and grand future in store for all good Californians. I am inclined to encourage the pride of these whole-souled people; for, seeming blessed, "they grow to what they seem."

Everything here is on the broad gauge. The smallest boot-black bores with a big auger, and gimlets are never used except by us wandering, benighted Arabs east of the mountains. Go along any of the thoroughfares of this rushing city, and you will see such portentous signs as "The Oriental Boot-black," the "Pacific Peanut Peddler," the "Celestial Wash-stand," the "Empire Laundry," and the "Occidental Oyster Depot." When such big-sounding names are used by the small fry, you can imagine how the bankers, brokers and merchants inflate their business, although financial inflation here is tabooed by every man of sense.

California street is the Wall street of this coast. There you daily see the maddening rush for gold—young and old, rich and poor, struggling for the shining dust. There on the corner stands a shrewd man who made a million out of "Belcher," and his friend across the street lost a million on the same silver mine. Here is the sharper who induced the rich banker to invest in the diamond mine of Arizona, and there goes the banker that was taken in. There is the man who buys up all the wheat on the Pacific coast and bulls the Liverpool market, while his friend against the lamp-post manufactures and sells all the Pioneer wine and brandy of California. You would not think that the little red-faced, red-nosed, gray-haired man biting his finger nails, on the curbstone, made a half a million last week on "Crown Point." No, he lost all he invested, and like a shark waits for some gudgeon to get even on.

There comes Ralston, the president of the Bank of California, a man of extraordinary pluck and off-hand venture. He is about forty years old, I believe, has a good address, a constitution like an army mule, and an iron nerve. Ralston is one of the pushing spirits of the Pacific coast. His generosity is unbounded, and his hand and heart are ever open to the poor and unfortunate. Years ago he was clerk on a Mississippi steamboat, and many of the business men of your city remember him as a dashing young blood who was always ready to work, and never absent from roll-call.

A trip to "Belmont," the home of Mr. Ralston, situated among the coast foot-hills, is something to be remembered by tourists who are out in the world for pleasure and information.

It was no uncommon thing for Ralston, with his party of friends and his "four in hand," to drive to Belmont, twenty-five miles away, in two hours. Sometimes, when the train lagged for passengers, the financial king with his team would beat the locomotive, and enter the precincts of his fairy home as the engineer whistled " down brakes." Two hundred guests could be accommodated at his hospitable board, where fruits, flowers, flowing wine, singing birds and instrumental music made the heart and soul imagine that some bright enchantress with her magic wand had called into celestial life the tropical romance of Belmont.

Scattered to-day in every land and clime are the guests of Belmont, and as the mind of the traveler turns back over the checkered road he has passed, his heart will often linger with pride and love upon the memory of the royal hand that dispensed romantic pleasures at that renowned home among the golden sands of California.

There are more than twenty millionaires in San Francisco, all having arrived on the coast poor and friendless, and many are the strange tales you hear about the great fortunes won and lost at the point of the pick, or the turn of the last trump—not Gabriel's.

The city is progressing rapidly, new buildings going up daily, like new wine injected into old bottles. Speaking of wine, this state will in time furnish all the pure wine and brandy consumed in the United States, always excepting Ike Cook and his " Imperial" fluid, which has become so entangled with the growth of Missouri that it is part and parcel of our natural existence.

San Francisco by gas-light " takes the rag off the bush." In company with the chief of police, T. G. Cockrill, this wandering Arab viewed the elephant and saw where the giraffe came in. Cockrill was formerly from Missouri, and claims relationship with Colonel Crisp, who, with the assistance of Hutchins, the good, preserves the virtue of the *Evening Dispatch,* and purifies the political atmosphere of St. Louis. But Cockrill is not responsible for his relations, and I can afford to accompany him through the dark haunts of this city. Down Montgomery to California, up Kearney and Dupont to Jackson street, and into the Chinese theater we go, where the painted Celestial, with his Dolly Varden stage costume, squeals out an unearthly noise in his operatic contortions, and causes the stranger to wonder whether he is in a lunatic asylum, being entertained by the maudlin mimicry of maniacs. After looking about for a few moments upon the numerous pig-tails hanging to dilapidated pumpkin-heads gazing with a look of inanity upon the stage stock, we withdrew to a dark alley near by, and being reinforced by Officer Schimp, proceeded to inspect the lower depths of Chinese infamy. Down two flights of stairs, through the sinuosities of inferno equaling that of Dante, we were ushered into a small room, with six bunks against the walls, where "John" was inhaling the aromatic perfumery of opium with a zest that made my Christian stomach weaken and long for the pure air of the upper world. In this den were reclining six Celestials, puffing and blowing away their poor existence. I asked the policeman regarding the occupation of these beautiful dreamers, and with a knowing twinkle in his eye, he replied that they were very careful, industrious men, who could not see anything go to waste, and in the lonely hours of midnight sallied out to take care of such property as their neighbors had left unlocked. We immediately saw that the "dark ways" of the Heathen Chinee bore a strong resemblance to the illustrious customs of the Caucasian, and, having but a small purse, we "passed out" into the street. We had often heard of the almond-eyed daughters of Confucius, and could not resist the importunities of the "Chief" to gaze upon the beauties of a harem that would have made Mrs. Lalla Rookh, Hinda and old Mr. Moore look sick. The new woman's movement being now all the rage, we lingered a moment in search of information, that we might contrast the beauties of the far East with the bouncing belles of the West. The "Chief" aided us in examining the peculiarities of the Celestial sisters, but I must confess, with a feeling of sadness, that what I saw did not come up to my expectations, and I retired from the scene in favor of anything that will make women better and men truer and more generous to the weaker sex. We traveled along to "Barbary Coast," where the "hoodlums," or rowdies, make night hideous with their drunken brawls. Into the cellar dance-house we peeped, and saw men and women swearing, talking, dancing, drinking, and fighting their way through those desperate dens. Scarcely a night passes but some poor drunken sot is robbed or murdered in these vile haunts, which are in collusion with the twenty-five cent lodging houses that skirt the dark alleys of murder row.

While I thus show the dark side of San Francisco, there are, thank God, pure and happy homes looming up all round, where virtue and intelligence reign supreme, and the hearthstone blazes with a hospitable light for the worthy stranger.

Chief Cockrill pointed out to me some of the finest mansions on the coast, surrounded with evergreens and sitting upon terraced hills overlooking the shining waters of the bay. Well it is for the people of the city that they are blessed with a chief of police who is in every respect a natural gentleman, and who guards their slumbers in the silent watches of the night by a force that is not excelled in the United States for efficiency and intelligence.

Having just returned from Los Angeles, the orange grove of Southern California, I will digress from the main track and give you a brief resume' of my trip. Ten days ago I was invited to accompany an examining railroad commission upon a tour of inspection, and as my business called me in that direction I availed myself of the hospitable offer. Taking the cars at Oakland, across the Bay, we proceeded to Delano, in the San Joaquin Valley, and from thence by stage to the mission of San Francisco, where the cars were waiting to hurry us through to Los Angeles, distant from here about four hundred and fifty miles. My companions were L. M. Foulk, Supervisor of Internal Revenue ; Eugene Sullivan and Calvin Brown, composing the railroad commission, and Colonel Gray, Redning, Madden and Brown, of the South Pacific Company. The party were ever on the *qui vive* for fun, and the stage ride over the Sierra Nevada Mountains was enjoyed by your correspondent with a zest that will not soon be forgotten. After our arrival in Los Angeles, a trip to the San Gabriel Mission was planned and executed with alacrity, where the party had an opportunity to view the beauties of the orange groves, the prevalence of the grape vine, and the grandeur of the distant mountains reflected in the deep blue sea. It was noon when we neared the orange groves, dashing away over rolling hills, seven of us behind six spanking bays. All was seemingly serene, when we heard that the noted highway robber, Vasquez, had just robbed an old ranchero, and was on our track. We at first laughed at the report, but it was soon confirmed by two men who were just ahead of us, and were relieved of their money and watches by the bold bandits. Each man of our party grew to the size of a first-class Alexander when it was known that the robbers missed us ten minutes, and a cooling draught of wine at the vineyard of Messrs. Wilson & Shorb appeased the wrath of the railroad warriors. There is a reward of twenty thousand dollars upon the head of Vasquez, but up to the present time he has defied the whole state of California, and from his mountain wilds dictates terms to the people like the Italian bandits calling for ransom in compensation for blood. He is an educated Spaniard, and has the sympathy of his race to aid him in his daring exploits.

We first visited the orange and grape ranch of Gen. George Stoneman, the bold Union raider of the late war. On his place can be seen the orange in all its golden beauty. Upon the same tree I saw the bud, blossom, green and ripe orange, which to me was phenomenal. The trees bear nine years from the seed, and two thousand oranges to a tree is frequently gathered, and sold at from two to five dollars a hundred. The orchards of Wilson, Cuen and Rose are the finest in the valley—thousands of tropical fruit trees and millions of grape vines in bloom, and bearing the whole year round. Here I actually saw growing oranges, lemons, limes, figs, English walnuts, almonds, pomegranates, plums, cherries, peaches, olives, pears, quinces, apricots, citrons, apples, medlar and nectarines. The soil is of a dark, dry, gravelly formation, and for three months in the year, during the dry season, irrigation is absolutely necessary to prevent trees from dying. Land is no object in this beautiful valley, although held in large bodies; but water is the main thing for farming purposes. The water is sold and distributed carefully, and the land is thrown in for a hundred dollars an acre. Modest people, arcn't they? Standing upon General Stoneman's place, looking south-east, the traveler beholds the peaks of Mount San Bernardino covered with snow, the ocean to the south-west, and the golden fruit of the tropics blushing at you from beneath their dark-browed branches. Oh! if I were a poet, wouldn't I stay here and go it!

The church or mission of San Gabriel is one of the oldest Spanish buildings on this coast, having just celebrated its one hundred and third anniversary. I went all through the old ruin, now going fast to decay, but still a resort for the faithful few that daily assemble at the sound of the old bells in the tower.

How the memory of other days crowds upon the traveler as he views crumbling piles of masonry erected by the hands of those faithful natives that made the Jesuit fathers rich and arrogant, until their wealth excited the envy and rapacity of the Mexican Government, which sequestrated the great land-grants and property of these religious families. A few more years and the missions of California will be chronicled in the musty archives of the past; the bells that now peal forth an hourly invitation to prayer will sound the funeral march of the natives, and the wild waves of the Pacific will chant an eternal requiem over their lonely graves on the mountain side.

The city of Los Angeles is beautifully situated in a grove of orange trees, twenty miles from the ocean by rail. The grape grows in the wildest profusion all around the city, and thousands of gallons of the purest wine are made annually. Kohler & Frolina have one of the largest cellars in this region, and, combined with their vineyard in Sonora county, do the largest business on the coast. Mr. Kohler is the pioneer wine man on the Pacific. He is progressive and intelligent, possessing those noble characteristics that make the Teutonic race respected in this land, where energy and thrift find recognition. Mr. Kelley, his Hibernian neighbor, has a very fine orange and lemon orchard, thousands of grape vines, and cellars well stocked with the choicest wines and brandies.

From Los Angeles I proceeded by stage to Santa Barbara, on the Pacific coast, with the Santa Cruz Islands in sight, thirty miles distant. This is one of the most thriving towns in Southern California, and is fast settling up with an Eastern population, in search of health and fortune. I visited the Old Mission, and the celebrated grape vine, fifty-five years old, eighteen inches in diameter, the trunk five feet high and the branches trained over an arbor fifty by sixty feet, where the town folks assemble during the summer months, and floating away in tropical joy, to the music of the Spanish fandango, perform the intricate steps of the "grape-vine twist!"

From Santa Barbara I took an ocean steamer, the Constantine, to San Francisco. On the way I saw four whales—the genuine article—blowing, spouting and riding the wild waves of Monterey Bay. In the distance they looked like floating islands heaved up by volcanic action. I was forcibly struck with nature and its destructive elements. The wild sea-gull went for the little fish; the seal went for the gulls as they floated in fancied security on the waves; the shark went for the seal and the salmon ; the whale went for the shark and the seal, and the Yankee went for the whale, (and got him, too,) and that's what became of the whale because of his natural inclination to spout. Let all politicians take warning from the fate of the whale !

Last evening, just as the sun sank behind the western waves, our staunch steamer pushed through the Golden Gate, dashing a heavy sea from its prow as it passed the rocks that guard the entrance to San Francisco. On the right sits the celebrated Cliff House with the seal-rocks covered by a moving mass of seals. One of the largest and ugliest is named in honor of Ben Butler, and the natives say that he is eternally barking for something. The biggest seal is named General Grant. He sits on the topmost crag, surveying those below him with a conscious dignity; but occasionally, when he is riled by the barking of Benjamin and the others, he drives them off the rocks. On the left of the Gate is the light-house, and ahead is Fort Alcatraz and Goat Island in the distance, with the City of the Hills margined by a forest of masts.

A TOUR IN OREGON AND WASHINGTON TERRITORY.

Special Correspondence of the Globe-Democrat.

San Francisco, Cal., May 29th, 1874.

In my last letter I gave you an idea of Southern California and its resources, and struck at some of the peculiarities of this city. Since that time I have visited Oregon and Washington Territory, where the great Yankee nation whittles out timber for a living.

Taking the steamer Ajax on the 5th of the present month, your correspondent, in company with a jolly crew and cabin companions, pushed out through the Golden Gate, beyond the light-house, and steered away up the North Pacific to Portland, Oregon, where the inhabitants enjoy their annual shower, and with the assistance of their web feet and patent life-preservers, manage to keep their heads out of the gentle inundation which visits that state only once a year.

As the evening sun of the fourth day out bathed its last blushes in the briny bosom of the Pacific, we came in sight of the land-jaws that lock up the mouth of the Columbia River, with a rough, chopping sea beating over the sand-bar at the front door of Oregon. It was so rough that we had to anchor outside the bar until five o'clock in the morning, when the high tide swept us over the breakers and into the placid bosom of the Columbia. Astoria soon came in view, and the pine-clad mountains rose up abruptly on either side, hemming in John Jacob Astor's town with a weird-like stillness that would have suited the taste of Rip Van Winkle.

Years ago the great Germanic-American fur monarch established this as a trading-post with Indians and trappers. Then every little stream that emptied into the Columbia was alive with fur-bearing animals, and every gorge in the mountain was tracked with the wild beasts of the forest. The red rover of the hills and the pioneer Caucasian basked in the sunshine of prosperity while hunting in the mountains, or fishing for salmon in the Columbia. The fur-bearing animals of this region have almost entirely disappeared, and the great havoc by voracious fishermen will soon destroy the grandest salmon fisheries on the continent. A law should be enacted to protect the fish of this stream from the wholesale slaughter that now goes on, in and out of season.

Our good steamer moved gracefully up the river, passing beautiful islands overshadowed by rocky crags that have stood the pelting storms of ages. All along the fishermen were engaged in spreading and hauling their nets, and each boat we passed was filled with the shining beauties of the Columbia. In the past two or three years some thirteen canning establishments have been erected along the banks, from the mouth of the stream to the Willamette River.

The running season of the salmon commences in May and ends in July. They are taken from one to ten thousand daily. By the labor of Chinamen they are cut up into pieces, canned in tin boxes, steamed, soldered, labeled, packed, and shipped direct to the London market by vessels, some of which were loading as we passed. A hundred men or more are employed at each house, and the *modus operandi* of preserving the salmon fresh for the markets of the world is a sight to the traveler. You may know that the business is profitable, when I tell you that last season one firm made a profit of $60,000. The fish-ermen sell the salmon for twenty-five cents each, large and small, and considering that they weigh from twenty to seventy-five pounds, you can imagine the great profit to the capitalist.

About five o'clock in the afternoon we entered the Willa-mette River, and within an hour afterward we beheld Portland, the metropolitan city of Oregon, situated on the first river-bench of level land from the mouth of the Columbia. In the background the hills rise abruptly, and great pine forests sigh to the music of the wild winds, sunshine and shadow forever flecking the scene below. Twenty years ago Portland was but a name, and the beautiful waters of the Willamette were only ruffled by the paddle of the Indian with his canoe, the splash of the salmon, or the dash of the wild duck. Now, ships of every nation load at its harbor with grain and lumber. The whistle of the iron horse and the hoarse shriek of steamboats awaken the slumbering echoes of the mountain, and fifteen thousand inhabitants, including Ben. Holliday, bask in the wild glare of nature, wondering whether God ever made a finer country than that skirted by the Columbia and Willamette.

Spending but a few days in Portland, your correspondent invaded the soil of Washington Territory by way of the North Pacific Railroad, to Kalama, Tacoma and Olympia, the capital of the territory. This city is situated at the head of Puget Sound, and has about five thousand inhabitants, mostly en-gaged in lumbering and political expectations. Every other man here thinks he would make a first-class governor, and the balance think themselves fitted for Congress—or a saw-mill. I might say, without exaggeration, that all the people of the Pacific coast feel that they were made to govern the country, and no good Californian, at least, can be found who would not, at a moment's notice, assume the helm of State and un-dertake to pilot the ship through the roughest breakers.

Taking a steamer at Olympia one charming morning, this Arabian knight paddled down Puget Sound, the most magnifi-cent sheet of water in America. On we went over the sparkling waters, passing green islands, dashing through narrow necks into broad bays, and turning points—the Coast Range of mountains covered with snow on the left, and the Cascade Range on the right—and all at once we touched the town of Tacoma. Mount Rainier, the highest mountain on the continent, lifted its glorious form to view, and there, in grand proportions, sixty miles away, the old snow-clad monarch lifted his bold head into and beyond the highest clouds, piercing the very dome of heaven with his awful form

The evening was bright and clear, and, standing in the pilot-house, with marine glass in hand, I brought all the beauties of the mountain close to view, showing the deep gorges, rocky ribs and glaciers running to the very crest, where a dark bare spot shows volcanic heat and action.

In August, 1870, P. T. Van Trump and Hazard Stevens—two young men from Olympia—scaled the rugged heights of this mountain, being the only two human beings that have ever been known to go to the top. The trip took three days, the boys being compelled to camp on the crest of the volcano over night. They came near losing their lives, for while one side was almost burning up with heat, the other was freezing with cold. What is it that young Yankees won't dare and do?

Our steamer touched at Seattle, a thriving town, and on to Port Gambel, the great saw-mill point, where half a million feet of lumber is turned out daily by one mill company. The timber in Washington Territory, along the streams and bays, grows down to the water's edge; and the shrewd lumbermen of Maine, seeing this rich field twenty years ago, took advantage of it, and now supply this coast and South America with all the lumber required.

Continuing down through Admiralty Inlet, past Port Townsend, the last revenue port of entry on Uncle Sam's farm, we headed across towards Victoria, on Vancouver's Island, leaving the island of San Juan immediately to our right. These islands, as it will be remembered, came into our full possession by the decision of King William of Germany, who was the arbitrator upon the boundary line of 1846. Victoria is a conservative spot, established years ago as a post for the Hudson Bay Company. During the Frazer River gold excitement in 1858, the Yankee boys made the place lively, buckwheat cakes and molasses ruling the roost, but the denizens of the town have again settled down to quiet habits.

Returning to Portland by rail and river, I could not suppress my inclination to visit the cascades and dalles of the Columbia River. Taking the steamer Daisy Ainsworth, we pushed out from the wharf at 5 o'clock in the morning, down the Willamette, twelve miles distant, and headed up the Columbia, touching at Fort Vancouver, W. T., where Generals Grant and Sheridan passed their early military life. Many are the strange stories told about our President and Sheridan, by the oldest inhabitants. But while many are ridiculous, the people who tell them pride in the fame and prosperity of our Union warriors, pointing out the resorts that were once the glory of the young lieutenants. The view from Vancouver is remarkably grand; to the northwest is Mount St. Helen and Mount Adams, and to the northeast Mount Hood looms up one of the finest and sharpest peaks on the coast. Right ahead, as we steam up the river, bold mountain bluffs 5,000 feet high rise almost perpendicularly from the troubled waters as they fret and foam through the rocky cañon to find outlet to the ocean. Down these mountain-cracked gorges dash a hundred waterfalls at different points, spending their headlong fury in the rushing waters below, while the sun and the wind weave a picture in the spray more beautiful than the fantastic colorings of fairy land. Arriving at the cascades, a railroad portage of about six miles takes us to the head of the rapids, where another steamboat is in waiting to take us to the Dalles, six miles up the stream. The whole route up the river is one ever-changing picture of rocky islands, pointed peaks, columnar walls and bouncing billows, fretted into snowy spray by the rocks that lie in the channel. For two miles before reaching the town of the Dalles, the river is confined in a narrow rocky bed, cut out by the hand of nature with as much architectural skill as if man had labored for centuries to erect the wall. A night at the Dalles satisfied our curiosity. Here begins fifteen miles of rapids, where the river rushes over a broken bed of rocks flung from the surrounding mountains, or heaved up by some volcanic action. I was tempted to go to Walla Walla, two hundred miles farther north, but as I saw all that was beautiful and grand below, nature could only repeat herself farther up the stream, so I returned to Portland by the same route—seeing on my way back the Indians catching salmon off the rocks at the cascades as they endeavored to jump the rapids that intercepted their progress. Salmon have been seen to jump ten feet over rocky falls. The Indian lays in wait with his dip net and spear; when the fish jumps, the red man strikes, and, missing his aim, dips his net, when sooner or later the salmon is caught and bagged for market

From Portland I took the cars for California as far as Roseburg, Oregon, and then jolted over a gap of three hundred miles by stage to Redding, on to Sacramento and San Francisco. I was forcibly impressed on my overland trip with the Willamette Valley and the beautiful country that surrounds Salem, the capital of the state. It is the finest site for a city on the coast, and when the new state house is finished and the woolen factories are all under way, and the contemplated railroads built, Salem will be one of the most desirable places I have seen.

The Willamette Valley is two hundred miles long by fifty wide, embracing the best wheat lands in Oregon Land sells for from five to fifty dollars an acre, and so far as water is concerned, there is an unfailing fountain from above and below. Oakland, near the terminus of the railroad, is a beautiful place, snuggled into the top of the mountain. We took supper there, and you may not believe me when I say that strawberries and cream were furnished at this railroad eating station, and every other luxury that the hills and streams could afford. Did you ever sit up three nights and days on the top of a stage? Try it once, just to encourage the stage company, and experience the wild dash of six-in-hand, as they wheel around some mountain crag, with the head waters of some great river rushing three thousand feet below !   In the distance, you may discern the road before you, winding its zigzag way in the vicinity of Mount Shasta, like a black serpent crawling up the rugged gold gorges, near Yreka.   On, ever on, goes the wild stage-driver and his blooded beasts, caring not for the rush of the storm, the scream of the eagle, or the genii of the mountains.   Time and success has made him fearless, travel has made him rough, but kind, and nature has stamped upon his weather-beaten brow the nobility of manhood ; and when he jumps upon the box for *the last drive*, thinking alone of his passengers and team, he wails out from the depths of his breaking heart, " On the down grade, and can't reach the brakes !"   But although this pioneer of travel cannot reach the brakes on this stage of action, his foot rests firmly on the threshold of eternal life, and on the golden grade of Paradise he can drive the chariot of Apollo with angels for passengers and Jehovah for superintendent !

THE YOSEMITE VALLEY.

Special Correspondence of the St. Louis Globe-Democrat.

Yosemite Valley, California, June 10, 1874.

In company with Ike Cook, wife and daughter, of St. Louis, I started from San Francisco and proceeded to Merced, in the San Joaquin Valley, and from thence took stage to Clark's and the Big Trees.   At Merced, our company was increased by a bridal party, composed of Mr. Briggs and wife, of Clyde, N. Y., and Mr. Baker and wife, of Columbus, Ohio.   Starting at 6 o'clock in the morning, we arrived at Clark's for supper, seventy miles away over hills, streams, and the rugged roads of the Sierra Nevada Mountains.   During the day we passed through the celebrated Mariposa gold mine region made famous by Fremont and his financiering.   The mine is now unworked, and the region that once yielded millions to the placer diggers is almost deserted, save here and there a Mexican or Chinaman ekeing out a scanty share of the precious dust, by the panning and rocking process of the " forty-niners." There is as much gold, no doubt, in the ribs and gorges of this mountain region as ever, but some company owns the claim, and will not work it, leaving the future development of the quartz to time and interest.

The morning after our arrival at Clark's we prepared to visit the celebrated big trees. The stage company furnished us with animals, and Thomas H. Tremmed, one of the oldest and most reliable guides in the mountains, was detailed to show the party to the spot where grow the largest trees on earth. The sun had just risen over the distant mountain when the horses, saddled and packed for the day, were brought up, and soon we mounted and dashed after the guide with the wild freedom of Comanche Indians. I rode a menagerie mule, striped like a zebra, that trotted before, paced in the middle, and galloped and kicked behind. The trail wound up through the foot-hills of the mountains, and gradually ascended for several miles. On the route, and near the mountain top, we were struck with the beauty and singular situation of the blood-red snow flowers peeping out from the margin of the snow belt that capped the pointed peaks. The Fallen Monarch was the first big tree we saw, twenty feet in diameter and three hundred feet long. Its body is large enough to drive a St. Louis omnibus upon. The sides of the old monarch are scarred all over with the names of the great from every land and clime.

The Grizzly Giant, the largest tree in the world, was the next wonderful object we beheld. With the assistance of the ladies, I measured the circumference of the tree, and found it to be a hundred and eight feet—thirty-six feet in diameter. A hundred feet from the base it has a limb six feet in diameter, fit for the largest saw-log. We continued through the grove until we came to the Hollow Tree, two of us riding upright and abreast through its fallen body. We passed the " Faithful Couple," twin monarchs having one great body and two tall heads that lift into the sunshine and the storm. We took lunch near " Ohio" and " Illinois," at a bubbling spring, right under the shadow of " General Grant," a magnificent tree, three hundred and fifty feet high and twenty-five feet in diameter. Most of the trees are named in honor of some celebrated character. There was one tree right across the little rivulet, twenty feet in diameter, and three hundred and twenty-five feet high.

On our return to Clark's ranch we were taken by the guide upon the highest peak of the mountain, where, looking down into the valley, we beheld a grand scene stretching away as far as the eye could reach. The wondering delight at the big trees must be seen to be felt.

A good night's rest at Clark's and a good breakfast put us in trim for the twenty-six mile trip to the Yosemite. Over hills, streams, rocks and zigzag mountain roads, we walked, rode, galloped, shouted and sang. The perfume of wild flowers and the aroma of the pine forest, brought to us on the wings of the bracing breeze, lent vigor and hope to the scene, and prepared our minds for the first view of the Yosemite Valley, as it presented itself from Inspiration Point. Before us lay the winding beauty of the Merced River, meandering through a sheet of emerald, set in a framework of natural splendor, and across the valley dashed the Cascade Falls, the El Capitan Mountain, where the Virgin's Tear trickles down the bold cliff in a shower of diamond beauty, catching the rays of the evening sun in its satin spray.

Then comes a grand, bewildering succession of lofty peaks and mountains —the Three Brothers, Eagle's Nest, Grizzly Bear, the Yosemite Falls, Indian Cañon, Royal Arch, Washington Column, North Dome, Mount Watkins, Mount Hoffman, Cathedral Peaks and Clouds' Rest—ribbed with snow and sunshine far above them all. Then we see South Dome and Mirror Lake at the base ; Unicorn Group, Mount Missouri, covered with snow and pines ; Sentinel Dome, Sentinel Rock, the Three Graces, with the Bridal Veil, flowing over the rounded rocks in gauzy grandeur, shadowed by the Leaning Tower, and right in front of where I stand the bold sides of Palisade

Rock, its steps washed by Cataract Falls ; and here my vision and mind checks in mute admiration at the circling wonders of the deep valley.

Taking shelter for the night at one of the so-called hotels, I proceed in company with the guide to view the beauty of Vernal Falls, 350 feet, Nevada Falls, 700 feet, and Glacier Point. Passing up the brawling stream to the falls, great jagged rocks that have fallen from the crags intercept the way, and fearful mountain walls and jutting cliffs shadow the traveler. Vernal Falls, as seen from above, looks like a huge sheet of fretted lace, with a dash of bright green through its folds—the margin pines reflected in the troubled waters. Leaning over the balustered rock at the edge of the falls, you gaze down into the gorge below, spanned by the rainbow of promise, the spurting spray dashing from the rocks in clouds of beauty. A hundred yards above Vernal Falls is Silver Chute, running over an inclined bed of granite, with more than the rapidity of a race-horse. A large rock thrown into the stream by the guide was swept over like a chip. Wild Cat Chute, just above Silver Chute and under the shadow of Liberty Cap, is one of the most interesting spots in the valley. Leaning over the rustic bridge that spans the rocky gorge leading to Snow's Hotel,—Vernal Falls and Glacier Point, to the front, and Nevada Falls to the rear—the traveler gazes in silent astonishment at the wild plunges of the cataract as it escapes from the rocky jaws, set with granite teeth that have tested tide and time. Look for a moment at the milk-white spray leaping into coral trees, chasing each other with the rapidity of lightning as they dash through the rocks, and the sunlit rainbow circling the wild rush of the stream. Let loose suddenly the Compton Hill Reservoir, through a metal tube, three feet in diameter, the nozzle at the *Globe* office, and you can conceive the desperate dash of the Wild Cat Chute. Take this point, all in all, with the cracked mountain, falls, trees, sunshine, pine shadows and cloudless dome of heaven, it is, without exception, the wildest, grandest spot in the Yosemite.

Leaving Snow's Hotel, the guide led me up a narrow gorge at the base of Liberty Cap, and on to the left of Nevada Falls, where the crooked road angles every fifty feet in reaching the table rock. Arriving at the top, I scampered over the drift-wood and rocks until I sat upon the rocking boulder that juts out over the fearful fall, where the boiling, steaming waters dash in eternal fury down to the mad stream below, where the tall pines reflect their green branches and dark shadows in the churned stream. Liberty Cap looms up on my right, its splin-tered sides flecked with passing clouds and scorched by the sun of centuries. Far to the north-west is Eagle Point, Glacier Mountain, and away over the brow of El Capitan the clamber-ing clouds pile upon each other, showing the bright blue of the horizon through their fleecy folds, where the rays of the warm sunshine dance to the music of the wild winds.

Winding around the rocky ribs of Piney Point, I passed over a bridge that led up the steep sides of Glacier Mountain, and looking back to the east saw the grand gorge of Vernal and Nevada Falls, hemmed in by the monarchs of the mountains, margined by the graceful branches of the pines, and singing the song of the universe. From the top rock of Glacier Point, inspired with fearful awe, the traveler gazes upon the immediate beauty and grandeur of the Yosemite Valley. Four thousand feet below, the hotels sit like bird cages on the margin of the Merced River, as it meanders on its brawling way to the sea. The Yosemite Falls is immediately in front, across the valley, while to the right you see the bold form of South Dome re-flected in Mirror Lake, with the inverted forms of pines pho-tographed in its glassy bosom, stirred by the gentle breeze that fitfully lingers in doubtful repose in this emerald gem of the Yosemite. In the early pre-Adamite days, when the mountains battled for the mastery, and volcanic fires and earthquakes shook the world, Clouds' Rest and South Dome fought long and fierce; but when the temper of the mountains cooled, there stood Clouds' Rest above them all, while South Dome stood near by and defiant, but conquered in the contest.

Descending from Glacier Point, you pass Union Point, and turning the angles of the zigzag road, an ever-changing scene is presented. The rocks that but a moment ago looked like rugged crags, now assume the shape of cathedral spires, pointed peaks or bald boulders; and the little fall seen in the distance, like a silver ribbon fretted by the wind, changes to the Bridal Veil, Yosemite or Nevada; and that still small voice, hushed by the sighing pines, breaks upon the ear at the turn of yon mountain point with the complaining roar of the cataract.

In closing up my wild wanderings in the valley, I induced Mr. Cook, wife and daughter, to accompany me to the top of Clouds' Rest, the highest point, twelve thousand feet above the level of the sea. We were among the first of this season to undertake the hazardous journey. Mounting my zebra mule, I dashed away over three miles of snow, from five to fifty feet deep, our animals sinking at every step. There was no trail after we struck the snow-line, but keeping my eye on the mountain top, and leaving the guide to aid the ladies, I pushed onward and upward, through pine forests, throwing their dark branches on the bright snow, with occasional murmurs at my audacity in disturbing their sleep. When near the mountain top a fearful storm came up, skipping through the tree tops, causing a panther to jump across my path, and disappear down the gorges. Being anxious to take my mule on the granite back-bone of the Sierra Nevadas, I rode far ahead of the party, getting along boldly on the crest of snow that divided and showed the rough rocks on either side far down into the dark valley, when all at once, and within fifty feet of the top, the mule sank into the snow and threw this wandering Arab over his head. Then you might see a solitary mule, "as it were," lunging about and sinking until nothing could be seen but his ears and tail wagging in the breeze of freedom, and the rider, "so to speak," holding on to the bridle like grim death to one of our ebony fellow-citizens!

The view from Clouds' Rest is simply magnificent. Far below where I sat, the clouds whirled and broke into banks of fog, ripped up by the winds and painted by the darting rays of the sun.   Looking to the far west and into the green valley, I saw before and around me Mt. Hoffman, Mt. Watkins, North Dome, the spray of the Yosemite Falls, Eagle Point, El Capitan, Inspiration Point; at the foot of the valley, the Three Graces, Sentinel Rock, Sentinel Dome, Glacier Point, South Dome, Piney Point, Liberty Cap, Mt. Broderick, Mt. Starr King, Cloud Peak, Unicorn Group, Mt. Washington and Mt. Clark, the snow melting and dashing down the mountain sides, the fleecy clouds flying to the north, and far below I beheld the glory of the far-off peaks as they jut up and beyond the rim of the blue horizon.

CHAPTER XXVI.

On my return trip from California I stopped off for two days at Salt Lake City to examine the collector's office, and take in the "malaria" of Mormonism. I put up at the Townsend House, visited the Mount Zion combination stores, the Bee-Hive and the Temple, rode out to Camp Douglas, and gazed in wonder upon the blooming fields that a fanatical religion had grasped out of the desert wastes of Utah. To cap the climax of my curiosity, I talked and dined with Brigham Young and two of his wives. He reminded me of a gnarled oak that had withstood the storms of centuries, and with his large head, thick neck and deep-set eyes, impressed me as a man of wonderful firmness, tenacity and indomitable perseverance, combined with cunning, hope and tyranny. We talked freely of the prospects of Mormonism in the march of civilization, and he strongly insisted that the constitution of the United States guaranteed freedom of religion to every man and woman in the nation; and that every human being was privileged to worship God according to the dictates of his conscience.

I could not well combat this logic, and replied that it was not the mere ritual or creed of the Mormon religion that the people of the United States so objected to, but to the blistering doctrine of polygamy, where one man was accorded the right to take a hundred or a thousand women to satisfy his lust. He quickly replied: " Even in this we have the precedent of the old patriarchs, David and Solomon; and if they were wrong, why do you preach their lives from your pulpits every day? Throw away your Bible; let your city men be honest and true to one wife, and not in midnight hours give loose to their passions over the wine-cup and at the silken couches of illicit love. Mormonism tolerates no hypocrites. We practice what we preach, and preach what we practice in the sight of God and man; and from a handful of devoted worshippers who followed in the footsteps of our chief prophet, Joseph Smith, and who revere his memory with undying affection, we plucked from the wilds of nature this rich territory, through the very religion you Gentiles ignorantly condemn! No, sir, it is the cupidity and robbing propensity of the Christian that turns his hand in this direction, and his professed horror at polygamy is only a subterfuge for his grasping avarice; and since he has "might" on his side, readily makes it "right" to prowl like a bold bandit amid these gold and silver mountains, rich valleys and fertile fields, in search of wealth, booty and empire!"

I leave legislators and ministers to reply to these arguments, contenting myself with the remembrance that I dined with one of the religion manufacturers of the world.

I returned to St. Louis, and immediately visited Washington. The Commissioner of Internal Revenue was so well pleased with my work that he gave me an order to proceed to New York and New England to examine the collectors' and supervisors' offices in that region.

It was the month of July, and while I did not go on my eastern tour for any special investigation, my orders would permit me to combine pleasure with business, just as presidents, senators, representatives, cabinet ministers and generals do in their tours of investigation and inspection, when the so-called "malaria" of Washington, drives them to Newport, Cape May, Coney Island, Long Branch, Saratoga and the Rocky Mountains. This is certainly a great country!

I returned to St. Louis in due course, and put on official harness with the same ease I had discarded it in my eastern tour. Politics and official business went hand in hand with me.

During the five years I lived in St. Louis I became acquainted with a number of representative gentlemen.

Among the most prominent of my associates were Col. J. C. Normile, William Patrick, Chester H. Krum, Thomas C. Fletcher and Nat Claiborne, of the law profession.

Among journalists I held social relations with Stilson Hutchins, of the *Times;* Joseph Putlizer, of the *Westlich Post;* William M. Grosvenor, of the *Democrat;* William Hyde, of the *Republican,* and Joseph B. McCullagh, of the *Globe-Democrat.*

The stable and influential citizens who gave me their friendship were David Armstrong, Isaac Cook, E. O. Stanard, A. W. Slayback and James B. Eads.

As each of these fifteen self-made men bore a prominent part in the make-up of the community who trusted and honored them, a pen-picture of each may not be uninteresting to the reader.

*_**

Col. J. C. Normile was born in Ireland, on the banks of the Shannon, and emigrated with his parents at an early age to America.

He went to school and graduated at the Georgetown Jesuit University in the District of Columbia, and afterwards studied law in the office of Hon. Thomas Ewing, ot Ohio. Secretary Browning, of Illinois, took great interest in Normile, and keenly appreciated the fund of literary information possessed by his young friend. While he was Secretary of the Interior, under President Johnson, Browning made Normile Librarian of the Interior Department, and was so well pleased with him that the young lawyer was a constant companion of the Secretary, sharing his home and hospitable board on the heights of Georgetown.

When a change in the political complexion of the Departments took place, on the advent of General Grant to the Executive Chair, Col. Normile determined to resign his lucrative office, and cast his lot with the progressive citizens of the teeming West. He appeared in St. Louis a stranger, with no friend but his talents, and no fortune but that courage and in-domitable perseverance that never fails ultimately to secure success.

It was soon discovered that Normile had unusual ability as a writer and orator, and when he first shone as a forensic debator and pleader in the celebrated Fore–Beech murder case, the whole bar as well as the press acknowledged him a master of magnetic eloquence, whose lacerating logic and classic periods went to the heart and soul of the vulnerable jury, securing an acquittal of a cold-blooded murderer, on the technical plea of insanity.

The Democratic party, soon after the acquittal of Fore, nom-inated Col. Normile on their ticket for the position of Com-monwealth Attorney, and while some of the ticket was defeated, Normile was triumphantly elected, and served four years as district attorney, doing great credit to himself as a criminal prosecutor, and conferring honor upon his adopted state.

What was very strange, and seemingly providential, the very man, Joe Fore, who was defended and acquitted through the instrumentality of Normile in the murder case, was afterwards prosecuted, convicted and sentenced to ten years' imprisonment for an assault, with intent to kill, upon his wife. Thus, as a defender and prosecutor, one man rises into fame upon the pivot of a criminal action, while the other unfortunate lan-guishes in lunatic desperation in a felon's cell, and finally dies by the knife of a fellow-prisoner.

> " God moves in a mysterious way
>   His wonders to perform ;
>   He plants his footsteps in the sea
>   And rides upon the storm."

The declamations, speeches and orations of Normile are va-rious, and his services were in continuous demand at every so-ciety and club entertainment, where Attic wit and poetic elo-quence struggled for the mastery. His oration appealing for the acquittal of Fore in the Beech murder case was a classic pro-duction, and worthy the oratorical flights of Wirt, Prentice or

Brady.   His oration before the Knights of Saint Patrick, at a Southern Hotel banquet, might rank with the flowing periods of Sheridan, Meagher or O'Gorman; and wherever the Celtic race rises into the realms of mellifluous eloquence, the orations of Normile should be placed in the front rank of the impassioned productions.

It was my privilege to be the intimate companion of Normile for nearly five years; and while we differed in many characteristics, there was no break in our mutual confidence, and no frost-work to chill the warmth of our friendship.

*_**

WILLIAM PATRICK was Assistant United States District Attorney, under Chester Krum, when I first made his acquaintance. He had been educated in Philadelphia, studied law, and moved to St. Louis, where he at once took rank as a gentleman of honor and a lawyer of unusual legal attainments.   His form was built in the nervous, willowy, classic mould, and his blue eye flashed love or defiance as the lightning darts from a thunder-cloud to waste itself in airy nothingness, or strike the fatal blow.   His keen perception of men and their motives made him a valuable acquisition to a client, and the same energy, ability and honesty that guaranteed success to his civil clients was doubly enhanced when he became United States District Attorney for the Eastern District of Missouri.

I was personally, politically and officially associated with Mr. Patrick for four years, and sounded the very secret springs of his enthusiastic nature.   If you approached him with sincerity and honesty, he met you squarely on the same basis; but if you attempted by innuendo and subterfuge to divine his will, he was as silent and mysterious as an Egyptian mummy.

He was the very soul of honor; would not conspire to betray, and would not conciliate for profit or immunity.   He performed his whole duty to the defendant and the Government; and when a man threw up his hands and asked mercy, he was the first officer of the court to find some palliating circumstance to relieve the victim of the law.

As an officer, I always found him honest and faithful; as a politician, he was reliable and unflinching; as a friend, he was generous and kind; and as a man, he was noble and sincere.

*_**

CHESTER H. KRUM was considered a learned young lawyer when he graduated from Harvard. His father, John M. Krum, had been practicing law in Missouri for more than forty years, and the detailed office knowledge imparted to the son made him at once a successful practitioner. When I first went to St. Louis, I found Judge Krum in the position of United States District Attorney, and was necessarily brought in contact with his office in the prosecution of revenue cases.

His form was large, round and dignified; and with his mild dark eye, matchless teeth and elevated forehead, he might have been taken for any of the double storied lawyers who have honored the bar and bench since the days of Lord Mansfield. When not officially engaged, we often met with a circle of choice spirits and whiled the hours away in hatching political plans, singing songs, or clinking glasses to the memory of our ancient friend Bacchus.

Judge Krum was not demonstrative to ordinary acquaintances, but when he found a truthful and trustful spirit, the icy margin of formality faded away before the sunshine of confidence and friendship.

*_**

THOMAS C. FLETCHER was born in De Soto, Missouri, studied law, moved to St. Louis, became a major-general during the late Rebellion, and about the close of the war was elected Governor of his native state. He was the only Governor of Missouri who had been born in the state; and although the commonwealth had been devoted to slavery in the old days, he never sanctioned or acknowledged the proposition that one man could rightfully own another as a chattel; and as a result of this philosophy was elected a Republican Governor.

Mr. Fletcher is a fine specimen of stalwart manhood, standing six feet two inches, and weighing over two hundred pounds.

His head is massive, and his mild, enchanting eye never fails
to secure confidence.   His worst fault is his excess of good
nature, that will not allow him to repel even those who may
have injured him.   Like the Vicar of Wakefield with his poor
congregation—

   "Careless their merits or their faults to scan,
   His pity gave ere charity began;
   Thus to relieve the wretched was his pride,
   And even his failings leaned to virtue's side."

Mr. Fletcher is a good lawyer, a renowned orator, and an
unchanging friend.   He is incapable of performing a mean act;
and while he may be slow in reaching a given point, he never
fails to reach it in the end.   His Masonic brethren have reason
to take pride in his truth, intelligence and nobility; for as an
Eminent Commander of Knight Templars he presided with
justice and dignity, leaving a memory that will blossom with a
sweet perfume when the last sprig of acacia decorates his grave.

His comrades who knew him in the army delight to honor
his genius and good heart, and so long as the Army of the
Tennessee or the loyal people for whom it fought shall celebrate the victories of freedom, their friend and orator will
not be forgotten.

As a friend and client I tested the truth and fealty of Mr.
Fletcher in the deepest vale of misfortune ; and while a con-
catenation of unforeseen circumstances twined themselves about
me like a group of deadly serpents, he never failed to strike
their twisting grip or paralyze their efforts for my destruction.
And when time and the sunshine of redemption brought peace
and victory to my heart and home, he delighted to break bread
at my board, and praise me for the fortitude I displayed when
injustice and so-called reform sought my ruin.

*_**

NAT. CLAIBORNE was born in the Old Dominion, in the region of its earliest settlement, and imbibed from his surroundings the miasma of slavery.   Yet, in his inmost heart he never
consented to the right of property in man, because his native

generosity, charity and love of liberty made him the natural enemy of oppression and wrong.

Leaving Virginia at an early day, he came to St. Louis and began the practice of law. For the daily rut and routine of a law office he had little taste; but when the Democratic party wanted an orator, or a special gathering needed a flowery and magnetic speaker, Claiborne was always in demand. I have seen him on the hustings electrify even the opposition, and with his broad provincial pronunciation, magnetize the crowd into continuous applause, or sadden their hearts with his tales of woe. I met him often under the gas-lights when his generous nature found relief in the wine-cup, and his heart and tongue bounded away in song and story, as light as the mist on the mountain.

I shall long remember the night at the Pacific Hotel in St. Joseph, when the state commissioners determined to locate the lunatic asylum in that flourishing city. John L. Bittenger, Zach. Mitchell, Mr. Hax, Joe Rickey, Tom Walsh, Mr. Koch, Col. Parker, Mr. Toole, Col. Wilkinson and a number of other jolly spirits, assembled in the double parlors of the hotel to celebrate in fluid form the decision of the commissioners, and particularly to expatiate upon the natural distribution of the fifteen thousand dollars that the citizens of St. Joseph contributed as a practical argument in their favor, as against the other cities of Missouri.

"Uncle Johnny" Able, as he was fondly called by "the boys," did the heavy part as host. Champagne flowed like water from a town pump, and as soon as one basket of Mumm was empty, another was opened with neatness and dispatch. About midnight a band of three darkey minstrels was ushered into the parlors. One played a banjo, the other a double mouth-organ, and a small specimen from Congo performed on the triangle.

Doors were locked, and none were admitted without the royal countersign—"Mumm." The occasion and philosophy of the meeting made this kind of a pass-word appropriate and

invaluable.   The boys were hot, and threw their garments right
and left as a relief to their volcanic condition.

Nat Claiborne proposed a dance to the classic tune of " Shoo-
fly," and the Congo minstrels struck up the air in their most
inimitable style, while a circle of ghosted mortals swung through
the mazy dance with their under garments floating in the
breeze of freedom, and their hair standing on end like a collection of serpents on the heads of the Furies.   Nature was finally
exhausted, the band departed, the lights were turned low, Mor-
pheus usurped his magical reign, and the " good and true"
citizens of Missouri slept the sleep of the innocent and just !

I hope the boys will forgive me for " giving them away" just
once, but if they wish to swear to the falsity of the foregoing
charges, I shall attribute the tale to poetry and romance, leaving the god Mercury to bear the brunt of their eccentricities.

*_**

STILSON HUTCHINS, formerly editor of the St. Louis *Times*,
was born among the sterile hills of New England, and imbibed
early in life that spirit of self-reliance and ambition co-exten-
sive with Yankee land.   He came from the humblest walks of
life, and the streets of Boston have often echoed to the sound
of his boyish footsteps in search of work and bread.

The crowded haunts of his native clime were not congenial
to his impulsive nature, and with a bold heart and willing hand
he emigrated to the banks of the Mississippi, and pursued the
uncertain life of a newspaper reporter.   I first saw him in Dubuque, Iowa, in 1865, when engaged on the *Herald* with Den-
nis Mahoney, who had been imprisoned in Fort Lafayette for
alleged treason against the government.   I met Hutchins again
in St. Louis in 1870, as the managing man of the *Times*, and
a free lance in journalism.   He and genial John Hodnett were
the life of the paper, cutting right into the business and circu-
lation of papers that had been established from thirty to sixty
years.·   His race in St. Louis was long and brilliant ; and neither trouble nor misfortune could break his spirit, dull his

ambition, or dim the luster of his editorial genius. In spite of
the most vindictive opposition in his own party, the Democrats
of St. Louis sent him to the Legislature, where he achieved
a reputation for pluck, honesty and legislative daring second
to that of no other member.

As Chairman of the Ways and Means Committee, he became
the leader of the House, and actually dictated many of the laws
that now adorn the statute books of Missouri.

He divines at once the motives of men, possessing unlimited
audacity, combined with faithfulness and remarkable secretive
powers, fights inside the circle and never betrays his fellows to
the cold sneer of the rabble world. Nature and art he twists
to his own uses; and while generous to a fault, he never neg-
lects to take particular care of number one.

In this respect he is only following out the unalterable laws
of self-preservation, and protecting his material interests against
the sharks that lie in wait to entrap the unwary.

The social cheer of Hutchins is unbounded, and when the
cares of daily life are ended, he rollicks away with his companions as free as a boy let loose from school. As an after-dinner
speaker he is unequaled, as a singer of charming melody he
cannot be easily matched, and as a story-teller he is inimitable.

He possesses a strong healthy frame, a square-cut brow, a
bright, laughing eye, a face like a broad-axe, a heart that throbs
like a steam engine, and a soul that is absolutely irrepressible.
Had he been educated in the school of a soldier, or trained in
the upper walks of military life, the dash of Murat, McPherson
or Sheridan might have characterized his warlike career.

I was intimately acquainted with Hutchins during my official
career in St. Louis, and had ample opportunity to sound his
capacity, generosity and honesty, and never found him wanting in these characteristics, but as true and faithful to a promise once given as the stars to their destined sphere.

In the last few years I have frequently met him at the National Capital as editor and proprietor of the *Post*, and the
same pluck, perseverance and capacity that he brought to his

work in St. Louis has at last guaranteed him a magnificent success in Washington.

*_**

JOSEPH PULITZER, the editor and proprietor of the St. Louis *Evening Post-Dispatch*, and present proprietor of the New York World, is a stalwart son of the Fatherland. Nature fashioned him above many of his companions, and a rugged experience has polished him into a success. He emigrated when a boy to America, and when first he appeared in St. Louis, secured his bread by daily labor. He fought for the Union during the late Rebellion, and afterwards became a newspaper reporter and writer for the Westlich *Post*, one of the best German journals in the nation. In time Pulitzer became part owner of the *Post*, and while see-sawing between the two political parties, occupied several places of honor and profit in city, county and state governments.

When Missouri determined, a few years since, to break loose from the "Drake Constitution," she sent a number of her most prominent citizens to Jefferson City to make a new one, and Mr. Pulitzer was chosen from the city of St. Louis to aid in the manufacture of the present organic law.

He is a bold, intellectual, sarcastic character, taking the world as "mine oyster," throwing the shells to the rabble, while he swallows the succulent bivalve with that grace and dignity conjured out of the precincts of a superior nature.

Had Pulitzer lived in the days of Lessing, Kent and Gœthe, he might have aspired to the literature and philosophy of these renowned Germans, and even now he is capable of writing a solid editorial on any subject his mind attempts to fathom ; while as an orator he shines with force and brilliancy, never failing to impress his audience by the beauty of his words and the intensity of his action.

*_**

Col. WILLIAM M. GROSVENOR is a natural Bohemian, not from a foreign clime, but from the green hills of New England. He is also a natural politician, taking to political intrigue as easily and felicitously as the most renowned diplomat takes to brandy, confidence and lying. As a financial and political writer he has few equals in America, and no superior. He was for many years editor of the St. Louis *Democrat*, and impressed the stamp of his wild genius upon that paper. There is no reason why he should not have been in the Congress of the United States as a representative or senator, for surely he had more practical, active, brilliant brains than Brown, Drake or Schurz. He was for many years the power behind the throne upon which these men sat ; and although William McKee, the proprietor of the *Democrat*, possessed unusual political sagacity, he always deferred to the broad-axe logic of Grosvenor.

I have often, over the wine cup in midnight hours, talked politics, patriotism and financial business with Con. Maguire and Col. Grosvenor in the snuggery of John King, under the Planter's House, and I must say that for fine conversational ability Grosvenor could not be easily matched. On the hustings he was forcible and brilliant ; having that swinging, debonair manner that magnetized an audience, and elicited the loudest applause by his beautiful flights of fancy and the logical periods that fell from his eloquent lips.

**

WILLIAM HYDE, of the *Republican*, is the opposite of Col. Grosvenor in off-hand brilliancy ; but as a solid, staying character, he has no equal among St. Louis journalists. As a partisan, he is conservative ; as a friend, he is true and unflinching, and as a solid, fearless man, he is safe. He is one of the characters that average well, and while many of his compeers grow threadbare with time, he "wears" the whole year round, and his friends find the latch-string to his home and heart hanging just where they left it.

Although Mr. Hyde and myself were of opposite political sentiments, we never let that interfere with our social cheer when John and George Knapp joined us at the fascinating fount of Jaccoby, who dispensed decoctions fit for the most esthetic followers of Bacchus.

George Knapp, the senior proprietor of the *Republican*, was a man of the kindest heart, and one of the oldest and best newspaper men in the nation.   His word was his bond, and his judgment invariably safe.

*_**

J. B. McCULLAGH,   editor of the *Globe-Democrat*, was born in Dublin, Ireland, and like millions of his race, emigrated to America to find fame and fortune as the result of thought and labor.   After arriving in the New World he performed the drudgery of a newspaper office in various places, and was for some years connected with the Cincinnati *Enquirer* and *Commercial* as reporter, correspondent and editorial writer.   During the war he was known as a very enterprising correspondent from the front of battle, and on one occasion was so enterprising in getting news ahead of his compeers, that General Grant ordered him out of the lines.   When Andy Johnson became President, "Little Mack" was writing for the Cincinnati papers, and upon a great issue between the President and Congress in the days of Reconstruction, the irrepressible Celt had a long "interview" with Mr. Johnson, and sent it broadcast through the country.   This was a novel stroke in journalism, being the original "interview" of all the interviews that have taken place since.

During the editorial career of "Mack" he has coined a number of words, among them "skedaddle," "blizzard" and "boom."   The first means the running away of a soldier, the second means a fierce, frosty Texas wind-storm, and the third means a great rise in public opinion, as a flood might rise in the mountains and float millions of saw-logs to the deep waters below.

As an epigrammatic writer he is unequaled.   He can tag a friend or an enemy with a word or phrase that will follow him to his grave.   The most caustic, pinching paragraphs fall from his facile pen, and he grasps with almost unerring knowledge the drift of public opinion.   Naturally he is a Democrat, but through policy and interest, party harness falls upon him very lightly ; and while he may of late years have voted the Republican ticket, yet, on general principles, he votes for the man and not the party.

I have seen McCullagh 'and Hutchins break lances of fun and wit at Southern Hotel banquets, and it was better than a circus to witness the jolly eccentricities of these inimitable wags over the " walnuts and wine" in midnight hours.

I was intimate with "Mack" during most of my official career in St. Louis ; and if Bonnett and Frank Gregory are alive, they may remember how, on Fourth street and in the resort on Pine street, we cracked jokes to the music of champagne artillery. · It was a "cold day" when " Mack" refused a fine bird-supper or a wine-bath, and I must say that his fellow journalists of St. Louis never failed to play " Barkis" to my "Peggoty." They were the most generous fellows I ever knew—with another man's purse—a remarkable weakness of all "good and true" Bohemians.

*_**

Hon. DAVID H. ARMSTRONG was born in Nova Scotia, and came to St. Louis more than forty years ago. He taught school for awhile, and earned a fine reputation in teaching the young idea how to shoot. He engaged in politics soon after his advent to Missouri, and never failed to talk, work and fight for the Democratic party. At one time he was postmaster of St. Louis, and for many years held the position of chairman of the Democratic State Central Committee. During the war he was in constant hot water with the Union soldiers and citizens, for while he may not have believed in the dissolution of the Union, he insisted that everything should be done according to the " constitution of the fathers." He forgot that murderous war wiped out all constitutions, and that bayonets were put above all constitutional provisions.

The war closed in Missouri with seventy thousand men who sympathized and fought for the South, disfranchised by the " Drake Constitution." Through the instrumentality of Col. Armstrong and his trade with Gratz Brown & Co., the Liberal ticket was elected in 1870, and every man in Missouri was as good as his neighbor, and as the Hibernian says, "a great deal better."

When the labor-strikes of 1876 paralyzed the business of the country, as if an electric shock had passed through the body politic, Armstrong was police commissioner of St. Louis; and as the controlling spirit of the board, marched his policemen and militia to the revolutionary rendezvous of the rioters, and dispersed them at the point of the bayonet. He is a very rugged character. Look at him from a surface view, and you behold the lion, who has warred with trouble and bitter experience. But on a closer view, his friends know that the gray and gnarled oak is of sterling worth, a loving friend who will grasp your hand in the vale of adversity, and shed a tear with the sweet pathos of a beautiful woman upon the ruin that misfortune may have wrought. A nobler or kinder heart never beat in man; and when even his bold record as a United States Senator is forgotten, the memory of his blunt but generous deeds will blossom from the dust of Bellefontaine and be remembered by every one who hates hypocrisy and loves liberty.

*_**

Isaac Cook, President of the American Wine Company, is a man of the strongest will, and a citizen of the finest judgment. The memory of living man does not run back to his early boyhood, and it has been quietly suggested by Charley Warner that "Ike" never had a boyhood, but was born when he was a hundred and eighty years old. Some say that he was a sign painter with Michael Angelo, and aided in frescoing the dome of St. Peter. But others have alleged that he and Senator Douglass learned the Cabinet business in Vermont, and made Bureaus for the United States Government in Washington and Chicago.

He knew how to "keep hotel," at any rate; for the American House in Chicago was for many years the resort of "good fellows" and the Democratic party, and the same was presided over by Ike Cook.

Stephen A. Douglass was at one time the bosom friend of Cook; but when the Senator broke away from President Buchanan upon the question of squatter sovereignty, Mr. Cook proposed to remain and run the Chicago post-office in the interest of the Administration.

He made a notable speech on one occasion to "the boys" who assembled with banners, torch-lights and thirst in front of his mansion. In standing by his cause, he wound up with the following peroration: "Boys, 'Truth *squashed* to earth will rise again,' and I'll bet you a thousand dollars on it!"

**

E. O. STANARD is a fine specimen of western manhood. His early life was spent in Iowa, from which state he removed to Illinois, and taught school. He appeared in St. Louis as a stranger, and soon began a successful business career. For many years he carried on the business of milling wheat, and his brand of flour is known all over the world. As a member of the Merchants' Exchange, and as its President, he secured the confidence of all with whom he traded, and his word for a car, train or ship load of grain is as good as gold.

He has been successful in the political field, being elected Lieut.-Governor of Missouri, and afterwards honored with a seat in Congress by his Republican constituents. It is not generally known that while Mr. Stanard was in Congress he did as much as any man in that body for the interest of the navigation of the Mississippi River, and while a member of the commerce committee secured the enactment of the law that gave James B. Eads the privilege of making the jetties a success. I was on the floor of the House the very day the bill was passed, and saw Stanard in constant and earnest argument with the halting and indifferent, urging them to support the claims of the Mississippi Valley, and impressing them with the commercial necessity of a free, unimpeded river to the gulf and ocean.

The jetty system has proved a great success. Where lighters took millions from the pockets of producers and merchants, by transferring freight from ocean vessels over a bar with only nine feet of water, the largest ocean steamer—drawing twenty-five or thirty feet—can now steam up to the wharves at New Orleans and discharge and ship the products of all climes. The action of Eads and Stanard has made bread cheaper, and every citizen of the Union to-day profits by their genius.

*_**

A. W. SLAYBACK, previous to the war, was a lawyer in St. Joseph, Missouri. When the first gun of rebellion sounded, he thought it his duty to go down to the front of battle and fight for the Southern Confederacy. Thought and action go hand in hand with such dashing characters, and leaving relatives and friends behind, he fought over three years for the "stars and bars" and the "lone star of Texas."

When the "Lost Cause" furled its banner forever, Slayback took a trip to Mexico with a colony of defeated Confederates, intending, no doubt, to deprive the United States of his brains and genius; but a longing for the rolling hills of Missouri took possesion of his mind in the gloomy vales of exile, and hearing that a parental government was not going to cut his head off, as had often been the case in other lands where rebellion suffered defeat, he quietly came back to that state, and found the world going on just as naturally as if he and his self-exiled party had not spurned the embrace of Uncle Sam. He settled in St. Louis, and at once took position as a talented and pugnacious lawyer—one whose whole hand and heart went together with the untiring force of a steam engine.

As a fiery and brilliant orator, Slayback had few equals; and the very intensity of his periods and gestures forced conviction on the mind of the listener. His address upon the occasion of the decoration of soldiers' graves by the "blue" and the "gray," in May, 1872, was a fine production. His reasons for the surrender of the Southern soldiers were criticized by his own comrades; and as there is a great deal of philosophy and good sense in his remarks, I give herewith the reasons as he stated them:

"I will tell you why the Southern soldiers grew weary of the contest and surrendered their arms. It was because, after all their privations and losses, and cruel grief over the bloody graves of their fallen comrades, they began to look to the future, and to say: 'Well, what then?' Made wiser by the stern education of war, their love of constitutional liberty made them tremble for the consequence of final success. They saw that the end of the war in that way would be the beginning of others. They cast their eyes upon the government at Richmond, and its constitution recognizing the right of any state, in certain contingencies, to set up a certain nationality .or itself, with its little president and little senate, its little supreme court and its little navy, with its Palmetto, its Pelican, or its Lone Star for its flag ; and the soldier began to ask himself, 'For what am I fighting?' Will my children be better off when the wrongs I am redressing shall have been succeeded by others of greater magnitude ? Will my constitutional rights that will remain to me in any event be as safe under the new nationality as under the old ? And what can posterity gain by exchanging for still another experiment the illustrious fabric that Washington, Hamilton, Jefferson, Adams and the brave, wise and good men who shared their counsels and dangers established and bought with the blood of my ancestry of the Revolution of 1776 ? ' It was this appalling logic which fastened upon the minds of the Southern soldiers,

> "Like a phantasmia or hideous dream,"

and then and not until then did their hearts begin to fail them. Hence it was that when they furled their flag, they furled it forever. Hence it was that when they laid down their arms, they did so with the full expectation, wish and understanding that the flag they had fought should become the emblem of their chosen nationality, and that henceforth and forever these states should be in fact, as in name, the United States of America!"

The logic of this speech, to my mind, is irresistible ; and while many insist that the ex-Confederates laid down their arms because they were overpowered by brute force, I still believe that thousands were inspired with the reason thus given by Col. Slayback, and could truthfully exclaim with the divine bard, that it is far better to

> " Bear those ills we have,
> Than fly to others that we know not of!"

The killing of Slayback, in self-defense, by John A. Cocke-
rill, is too recent for me to comment upon ; the public being
thoroughlyconversant with the sad affair.

*_**

Captain JAMES B. EADS is a man of remarkable perseverance
and of extraordinary genius. His perceptive faculties are largely
developed, and his head might serve as a companion piece to
that of Bismarck or Humboldt.

Sir Christopher Wren and John A. Robeling were never inspired by a larger scope of ambition in the profession of engineering and architectural skill than Eads.   He is equal to any
emergency.   When the United States Government wanted iron-
clad boats to ply up and down the waters of the Mississippi
Valley during the late war, Captain Eads jumped into the
arena, and fitted out a number of iron-clads to guard the commerce of the West.

When St. Louis stood halting for many years as to connec-
tions with the East, with small ferries and a river of ice at its
front door, it was Eads that came forward, and threw across
the Mississippi one of the finest and strongest steel bridges in
the world, resting on piers and abutments that take hold of
the "rock of ages."

When the mouth of the Father of Waters became filled and
choked with the sands of centuries brought down from the
golden ribs of the Rocky Mountains, it was Eads who planned
and executed the herculean task of a national dentist, and tore
away its snaggled teeth and lumpy roots, giving to the nation
a free river to the bounding billows of the ocean.

Foolish people talk over and haggle about the cost of iron-
clads, bridge and jetty, but if they cost a hundred fold more,
the state and nation would be the winner ; and when the buzzing May-flies of to-day are forgotten, the great and glorious
engineering feats of James B. Eads will be cherished and remembered by a grateful and prosperous country.   He needs
no monument but his generous deeds, and no glory but the
magnificent works he fashioned and erected ; and when a thous-

and years hence Macaulay's wandering traveler from New Zealand shall rest and contemplate upon the broken arches and toppling piers of the St. Louis bridge, the name of Eads will shine out bright and clear amid the wrecks of tide and time.

*_**

THE OWL CLUB, of St. Louis, was composed of a number of choice spirits. They were mostly newspaper men, who could drink with the ease of a fish, talk wit, and sing in the tones of a mocking-bird. They would have been appreciated around Covent Garden in the literary London of long ago.

Eugene Field was a poetic leader, a rare genius in midnight hours, and a Bohemian of infinite resources. He could sing like a thrush and talk like an orator.

Billy Steiggers is a wiry, impulsive, good-hearted mortal, who brought wit and rare songs to "The Owls," and never refused to bathe his classic form with the imperial vintage of Ike Cook.

Estell McHenry was a Kentuckian, and learned in his college days some sweet darkey melodies. His voice was rich and high, and when he sang the "Pea Vine," and appealed to "Ca'line" to "dance," the boys could not resist the impulse to execute the "grape-vine twist."

George Gilson was a never-failing attendant at the meetings of the "Owl Club." He would miss a meal or fail to attend church rather than absent himself from the vocal conclave.

My songs, "Go Way Old Man," "Lula," "Dearest May," "Karney," "Off to Baltimore," "The Tramp," and "Old Kentucky Home," never failed to secure a rich chorus. Sometimes before church began on summer evenings, the "Owls" would spare a few lingering moments at "Lupe's," "George's" and "Harry Hall's," and give to the crowd waiting at the Post Office "corners" a foretaste of the hymns awaiting them in the solemn aisles of Christian worship. I have known many instances, however, where the congregation assembled to hear the "Owl Club" far exceeded the drowsy listeners to the ministers.   But there is no accounting for taste in this queer world of ours.

Frank Gooley, a faithful mason and true man, was a veteran member of the "Owl Club," but sad, to relate, his loving, social light went out forever in the smoke and fire of the Southern Hotel.

> Peace to his ashes, a tear for his loss;
> Gone to the home of the crown and the cross!

CHAPTER XXVII.

THE WHISKEY TROUBLES.—MY INDICTMENT, TRIAL AND IMPRIS-
ONMENT.—ADDRESSES TO THE COURT AND JURY, ETC.

In the winter of 1874 and 1875, the agitation of the third
term question for President was favorably considered by one
class of citizens, while another class fiercely assailed any one
who dared to indulge in such outrageous opinions.

The Civil Service and Political Reform Association of America were surcharged with the idea that if General Grant should
be nominated and elected President for a third term, the nation would sink into indistinguishable ruin, and liberty itself
take flight into the realms of oblivion.

Something must be done to save the Republic from the
clutches of a tyrant and a usurper, who had once accidentally
conquered a rebellion against the Union ! The stride of the
modern Cæsar to imperial power must be checked at all haz-
zard. What should be done?

A conclave of these patriotic reformers met in New York,
and, imitating the tailors in Tooley street, resolved themselves
into the people of the United States. Some person must be
found who was in a position to knife the administration under
the fifth rib, bring disgrace upon the President and his political friends, scandal to the nation, and disgust for laws only
enforced to minister to the ambition of a man who was flattered by his henchmen into the belief that he would ride in
triumph into the presidential chair on a wave of reform.

Benjamin H. Bristow, of Kentucky, was the Brutus selected
by political conspirators to stab and tumble down from his exalted station the President of the United States. A more willing individual could not be found to deal the blow or stab

the man who lifted him from an obscure country lawyer in a border state, through the successive grades of district attorney and solicitor general, to the Secretaryship of the Treasury.

In every land and clime, where government taxes whiskey as the product of grain, more or less defrauding of the revenue has taken place. In Germany, France, England, Scotland and Ireland the tillers of the soil in their mountain fastnesses have spurned with contempt the proposition to tax the product of their soil, and have evaded payment of revenue whenever possible. In the days of Washington, a good share of the people of Pennsylvania refused to pay taxes, and the great general of our Revolutionary War had to send troops to crush out the famous "Whiskey Rebellion."

In our times certain people of Missouri, Tennessee, Georgia and Kentucky have, in daily defiance of revenue laws, distilled the products of their soil in the gulches of rough hills and on the tops of high mountains. The "Moonshiner" and his family, since the war, have been objects of constant pursuit and prosecution ; yet, even down to this very hour, the government of the United States has not been able to stamp out the small kettle whiskey manufacturers of the mountains Why? There is a natural idea of independence in the breast of the rough farmer and stalwart backwoodsman, that says what nature yields under his laborious hand can be manufactured and sold without a hoard of petty officers hounding his footsteps. There are many of these rude swains who have never seen a revenue law or suffered the black-mail inspection of local tyrants. They never consider that it is the province of government to provide "ways and means" to maintain its own existence in peace and war, and, therefore, regard the taxing of their grain crops as tyrannical.

In the cities of the Union there are larger establishments for the distillation of spirituous liquors, and the parties running these distilleries have a better knowledge of their rights and duties under the laws than the rural citizen who acts on "his own hook" among his native hills.

In the spring of 1875, it was determined by the Secretary of the Treasury, in furtherance of his scheme for the presidency, to make a bold raid upon the distilleries in several of the Western states, where General Grant was considered strong. After agents and political strikers had been investigating for many months, the Secretary, on the tenth of May, 1875, pounced down simultaneously upon distilleries in Ohio, Indiana, Wisconsin, Illinois and Missouri, and seized indiscriminately a large number of liquor establishments. He procured the arrest of distillers, collectors, agents and supervisors. Then the associated press from Washington, New York, Cincinnati, Chicago and St. Louis began an incessant fire of newspaper bullets, making the Secretary the greatest reformer of his time, consigning every man, woman and child in the whiskey business to the hospitable walls of a penitentiary.

Mole-hills of revenue frauds were manufactured by the Civil Service Reformers into mountains of corruption; mountains were exalted to the fiery heights of volcanic ruin, and the Republic was on the down grade to the realms of Pluto!

The rebellion that Grant put down was not a circumstance to the danger arising to the nation from the copper kettle of the fraudulent distiller; and while he may have defrauded the government out of a thousand dollars a year, the newspaper press was certain that at least a million had been stolen by each distiller, rectifier and officer in the country.

During the summer of 1875 the United States Grand Jury was assembled in St. Louis and Jefferson City, and a cloud of witnesses were sent before these "good and true men" for the purpose of indicting every man that would not bow down to Bristow, and raise his hands and voice to the coming Moses of reform.

Detectives were as thick in St. Louis as maggots around a corpse; and the room of the district attorney was the scene of poor, little, cowardly creatures, who always run at the first crack of the rifle, and beg on their trembling knees immunity from the imagined terrors of imprisonment.

After six weeks of detailed threats and secret investigation, a large batch of whiskey men, citizens and officers, were indicted by the Grand Jury ; the majority of the jury being political enemies of President Grant.

Among the rest, I was indicted for an alleged conspiracy to defraud the revenue, the written instrument stating that I had knowledge that fraud was committed by distillers and rectifiers, and did not report the same to my superior officers, as provided in section 5440 of the United States Statutes. I gave bond in the sum of twenty-five thousand dollars for my personal appearance at the next term of court.

The Grand Jury had heard of me so much in their six weeks' investigation, that they concluded to summon me as a witness, just before they adjourned *sine die.* I was surprised when Marshall Newcomb served upon me a paper to appear forthwith before the Grand Jury, feeling outraged that the secret "Star Chamber" that had indicted me should add insult to injury by the official summons.

I walked from the Planter's House down Olive street, to the court-house on Third street, and slowly mounted the gloomy staircase to the dark jury-room in the top corner of the ancient building.

The more I thought of their desire to see me as a curiosity, and humiliate me as a man, the more did my heart shake up its resenting powers ; and I ached for the opportunity to show my disgust for the loyal, rebel, Dolly Varden conclave of Bristow conspirators.

When I entered the room I saw a long table with about twenty men ranged around, gaping at me with a leer of curiosity and imbecility upon their dark faces. · The district attorney and the foreman, with a short-hand reporter, sat at the head of the reputation slaughter-table.

The foreman motioned me to the front, told me to hold up my hand and be sworn. I declined to be sworn at that time, and placing my hand on the back of a chair addressed the jury in about the following language :

Gentlemen of the Jury :

On the eve of your adjournment, after a six weeks' scandal-hunt, and after my indictment by your body, you have deemed it proper to summon me to answer certain questions.

My indictment was secured by perjured testimony, after a promise of immunity by the district attorney to the thieves he manipulates for his official expectations. It is the first shadow of disgrace that has ever fallen across my pathway, and as your body has put this stain and trouble upon me, I shall now, and to the end of these persecutions, give you and the political officers of the government all the defiance I can master. You have acted, not for the enforcement of the revenue laws, but to further the presidential ambition of the Secretary of the Treasury, and this Venetian council are simply his tools.

I decline to be sworn by this jury, and shall not answer except I am compelled by His Honor, Judge Treat. I know my rights, and know full well that your only object is to twist me into saying something that may injure myself or friends, which I do not propose to do. Now, gentlemen, please consider that I have treated you with all the contempt in my power, and I defy you to perform your worst."

After an hour or so, the district attorney fixed up a paper reporting me as an unwilling witness to the court ; and with the foreman I was mustered before the august tribunal of justice, and underwent investigation by Judge Treat. He turned to the statute, and said that I was not compelled to answer any questions that would militate against myself, but it would be best for me to be sworn, and then do in the premises what I thought right.

I consented to comply with the rulings of His Honor, went again to the Grand Jury room, was sworn, and answered a number of questions propounded to me by the district attorney, to the infinite disappointment and disgust of the jury. I was finally released as an unusually stubborn witness, and since I knew nothing of wrong against General O. E. Babcock or

16

President Grant, these political conspirators had no further use for me. The whole prosecution was inaugurated and continued for the purpose of smirching the occupants of the White House.

The same character of indictment was found against me in the Western District of Missouri that had been secured in the Eastern District; the prosecution having determined to make sure of me anyhow, and put me on the legal rack at the *first* court assembled in Jefferson City.

The most outrageous newspaper lies were sent all over the country about me. One day I had sailed to Europe from the port of New York with a hundred thousand dollars in a grip-sack. The next day I had jumped my bail bond, and gone to Mexico. Soon after, I had committed suicide by leaping from the St. Louis bridge, and the next moment my wife had died of a broken heart in consideration of the ruin I had wrought.

All this vacation time I was drinking spring water and other exhilarating fluids near Green Lake, Wisconsin, dancing and singing at the Oakwood Hotel, jesting with beautiful tourists, fishing for bass and pickerel in the green waters of the lake, and in twilight hours wandering in the grove with my wife and her lady friends, rollicking away in love and poetry.

If the newspaper puritans knew how happy I was, and the real indifference I felt at their efforts to put me in prison, a hardware factory would not be sufficient to furnish files for their biting.

Political sycophants and personal cowards had little conception of the determined character they were dealing with ; for if they but knew it, even the scaffold has no more terrors for me than the prison, when my heart and soul are grounded in the right. But the human midgets who pursued me had no thought of what a true man will do when pursued by political frauds. In life they doubt and hate themselves, and in death they are detested and forgotten.

Complications existing between the duplicate indictment at Jefferson City and the one in St. Louis, culminated in my sueing out a writ of *habeas corpus* touching the matter of arrest and bail. The case was heard before the full bench of the United States Court. Justice Miller, of the Supreme Court, Judge Dillon, of the Circuit Court, and Judge Treat, of the District Court, heard the motion for release from arrest. When the hour arrived, Marshal C. A. Newcomb produced me in court with his return to the writ. The court-house was full of anxious and curious spectators. My lawyer was not present to argue the motion, so I concluded to argue the case myself, notwithstanding the old adage that, "A man who acts as his own lawyer has a fool for a client." But I have never been much alarmed at the axioms sharpers set up to control cowards.

The following short speech was made to the bench, with a spirit of satire and earnestness:

"May it please the court, I have to say, in reply to the hasty action of the marshal in returning the writ of *habeas corpus* before the expiration of the three days allowed him by law, that my attorney, Judge Chester H. Krum, is now in Jefferson City, and will not probably return before Saturday. In consideration of this fact, I pray your honor to grant me the five days allowed by law in which to prepare for the defense of my personal liberty.

I am ready and willing to give bail for any charges that are pending against me in Jefferson City, but as I am under bond to appear here from day to day, and not being endowed with the elements of ubiquity, I trust this honorable court will hold me to answer its demands on the principle that the first mortgage takes precedence against all subsequent claims. Like Desdemona, I have a divided duty to perform, and while I shall give to Brabantio all the legal friendship that is asked, I give to Othello that love born of respect and duty.

Notwithstanding the cowardly reports of the newspapers that I had absconded for foreign lands and was a fugitive from justice, I stand here to-day as a voluntary testimonial to their falsehoods. While life lasts, I shall never desert my family, my honor, or the duty I owe my fellow man ; and all I ask, standing here upon the threshold of the courts of my country, is simple, unadulterated justice. ''

Justice Miller said the matter could stand over till Monday next. He also stated that he knew of no reason why the prisoner could not give bail in St. Louis without being required to go to Jefferson City for that purpose.

It was consoling to know that through the spring and summer of 1875, the friends in and out of power, whom I had known for many years, never lost faith in me.

I append hereto an autograph letter, by permission, from General F. E. Spinner, who had been for more than fourteen years the watch dog of the Treasury, but who was finally forced out of office by Bristow, **because** he would not ''Bend the pregnant hinges of the knee, that thrift might follow fawning.''

In the midst of my legal troubles, I called at the headquarters of Gen. W. T. Sherman for the purpose of getting a copy of his Memoirs of the Rebellion. He was located in St. Louis at the time, with most of his staff—gentlemen whom I met in the social walks of life. Col. Audenried, a brave and gallant gentleman, ushered me into the General's room. We greeted each other as soldier acquaintances, and I disclosed my business with the remark that I should be pleased to have him write his name in his Memoirs as a remembrance.

He at once said : ''Joyce, what is this infernal thing I see in the papers about whiskey indictments against yourself and others? ''

I told him it was nothing but a political move of the Secretary of the Treasury, to bring himself into national notice on a very small capital, and, as a reformer, endeavor to clutch the Presidency.

Sherman said : ''You know I am an everlasting friend of a good and brave soldier, and what I want to know from you is this : Are you right, or are you wrong? If wrong, I'm against you ; and if right, I'll stand by you to the last.''

Treasury of the United States,
Washington, April 16th, 1875.

My dear Colonel:

Your very friendly, and exceedingly kind letter, of the 12th instant, was received by yesterday's mail.

While your conjectures as to the cause that prompted my resignation of the office, that I held for more than fourteen years, are true in the main; yet, the President is entirely blameless, of any blame attaches for it any where. — I told him that I needed rest, and I doubt whether today, he knows of any other reason for my retiring from public life. —

The faith, that you speak of, that the People have in my official integrity, I feel conscious, is well placed.

I have never desired to be rich, and thus have not any temptations to come by money dishonestly; and I have never for a moment lost faith in myself, or doubted my power to resist every impulse to do a wrong to any one.

While I have said that I needed rest; yet, I am happy to say to you that I health and power of endurance is better and greater than for many years past.

I shall leave the office without a single regret, on my own account. — But, the fear that harm may come to many of the hundreds of my friends who I leave with a father's love, makes me feel sad and very unhappy. —

As yet, I don't know what disposition I shall make of myself. — But, probably, shall alternate, as the seasons change, between the Valley of the Mohawk, and the banks of the St. John, in Florida; at either of which places I shall cherish the hope that I will be able to often welcome you and yours,

Very sincerely your friend,

E. B. [signature]

John A. Jones, Esq.,
St. Louis, Mo.

I assured him I was right, and that in the coming years he would be convinced of my truth and integrity. Upon the fly-leaf of his book he then placed the following inscription :

"Inscribed to my friend and fellow soldier, Lieut.-Col. John A. Joyce, who bears an honorable wound received at Kenesaw.

With the compliments and best wishes of   W. T. SHERMAN,
Saint Louis,   General.
    June 24, 1875.

Bristow was desperately in earnest in pushing my trial at Jefferson when his henchmen at St. Louis found that I could not be used for his political ambition. Orders had gone out to the District Attorney to push me at once to trial, and force me into measures or prison.

The newspapers kept up a fusillade of buck and ball, shot and shell. Detectives were on the track of every man who dared to sympathize with the indicted parties, and it was worth a citizen's reputation to go upon the bond of any defendant. A long, snaky, sniveling hypocrite wearing the harness of the Department of Justice in St. Louis, did not hesitate to throw odium on some of the best people of Missouri who had the bravery to stand by friends for their personal appearance when the courts demanded their presence. This walking blacksnake even telegraphed to District Att'y Botsford that the bond I had given was a "straw" bond, although the day of the receipt of the dispatch I was present in the court-room of Judge Krekel, who rebuked the superserviceable official toady by stating that if the bond was "straw," the gentleman himself was not.

My case was called up in September before Arnold Krekel, the United States District Judge ; and while I gave twelve sworn reasons for a continuance to the next term of the court, they were brushed aside as chaff, and my case set for absolute trial on the 20th of October, and I began to collect evidence for my defense, during the few days left me before trial.

The four counts in my indictment charged that I conspired with one Feineman, a rectifier, and Sheehan, a distiller, and that I did not report knowledge of fraud to my superior officers.

Inscribed to my Friend
and fellow soldier Lt Col
John A. Joyce, who bears
an honorable wound received
at Kennesaw —

    With the compliments &
best wishes of
        W. T. Sherman
            General.

Saint Louis,
    June 24, 1875=

On the 9th of October, 1875, I called at the Treasury Department in Washington for the purpose of securing an official copy of a report I had previously made in regard to the very parties with whom it was alleged I conspired to defraud the revenue.

I saw Commissioner Pratt and procured the paper I wished, took it to Mr. Bristow, the Secretary of the Treasury, who attached the following official certificate that I desired to use in evidence at my trial :

UNITED STATES OF AMERICA, }
Treasury Department, Oct. 9th, 1875. }

Pursuant to Section 882 of the Revised Statutes, I hereby certify that the annexed are true copies of original papers on file in this Department.

{ Seal. } In Witness Whereof, I have hereunto set my hand, and caused the seal of the Treasury Department to be affixed, on the day and year first above written.

[Signed]   B. H. BRISTOW,
Secretary of the Treasury.

When Bristow signed the above certificate in my presence, and delivered the document into my hands, he threw himself back in his official chair and opened the following plastic conversation :

"Colonel, I'm sorry that you have got into this trouble ; I have heard of you as a gallant soldier from Kentucky, and it pains me to see any man from 'our state,' who fought for the Union, in jeopardy.   All I wish is to make a success of these whiskey prosecutions, and if you will assist me I'll see that you have no trouble."

I replied that I was just as sorry as he was—perhaps more— that these troubles had come upon me ; but how I could assist him in making a success of the prosecution was a mystery, as he knew that I had no knowledge of the whiskey frauds in Missouri.

He said: "Well, Colonel, that's all right; I have no disposition to pursue you to prison, as you were a mere subordinate; but I feel that these parties over the way (pointing to the White House) were the responsible heads of the whole whiskey conspiracy, and I know you are intimate with them.

I said I knew nothing about it, and so far as the White House people were concerned, I had never in the whole course of our political and personal friendship spoken to them about whiskey frauds.

He looked up and smiled with a bland expression, and remarked : "Well, if you want to go to prison for other people, it is none of my business."

I arose from my seat by his official chair, and replied to the cunning bid he had put in for state's evidence : Mr. Secretary, I told you candidly and truthfully that I knew nothing of frauds upon the revenue ; and I regard your efforts to put me in the light of an informer as an insult, and your desire to bring higher officers into disgrace, a piece of injustice.

That speech sent me to prison. I then bowed myself out of his office and have not spoken to him from that day to this.

Promptly on the 20th of October, 1875, I was placed on trial at Jefferson City, upon the following four counts of the indictment :

1. That one John A. Joyce, late of the Western District of Missouri, and a United States Revenue Agent, had, while acting as said Revenue Agent, knowledge and information that B. A. Feineman and F. A. Hasselman, rectifiers and wholesale liquor dealers, neglected to make an entry in their books of 243 original packages of distilled spirits which had been received by them from Edward Sheehan and John P. Sheehan, distillers; that said Joyce, who was a Revenue Agent, failed to report in writing said knowledge and information of said violation of the Revenue laws.

2. That he (Joyce) knew of said B. A. Feineman & Co. having emptied 243 packages of distilled spirits without first having effaced and obliterated the marks, stamps and brands thereon, and the same he failed to report, as required by law.

3. That Sheehan & Son were engaged in and carried on the business of distillers of distilled spirits, at St. Joseph, with intent to defraud the United States Government of the tax on the spirits distilled by them, and that the said John A. Joyce did then and there fail, as such officer, to report, in writing, said knowledge and information of said violation, which was known to him, to his next superior officer.

4. That said John A. Joyce did, on the last day of April, 1874, at St. Joseph, Mo., then and there conspire and collude with Edward Sheehan & Son to distill and sell distilled spirits without paying the taxes due the United States thereon, and to divide between themselves the gains and profits arising therefrom.

Feineman, the rectifier at Kansas City, said in his evidence: "I did not tell Joyce whether the whiskey entered on my books was straight or crooked; he did not ask me; I gave him to understand that all the whiskey on my books was straight."

Dr. Joshua Thorne, a former Assessor of Internal Revenue, and a voluble man, said: "I remember talking with Joyce in May, 1873, in regard to making whiskey, but as I was afraid to talk with him about whiskey, introduced him to Mr. Kingsbury."

Mr. E. W. Kingsbury, a United States Storekeeper, said: "I had a conversation with Joyce in the summer of 1872, about raising some money out of the whiskey business for election purposes. That was the first and only conversation I had with Joyce, and I suppose he had something to do with my removal. I have not had kindly feelings towards him since that time."

Henry Borngesser, the gauger at Sheehan's St. Joseph distillery, said: "Joyce was at our distillery once; he told me not to use such large tacks in putting on stamps. This was all the conversation we had. I knew distilled spirits were manufactured and shipped without payment of tax. I am indicted."

Mr. A. W. Wells, Deputy Collector, said: "I knew of an order changing storekeepers and gaugers in the district; saw Mr. Joyce about the time, and told Mr. Wilkinson that there would have to be a change made in the storekeepers; that Mr. Bittenger would be gauger, and I would be storekeeper."

John P. Sheehan, the son and foreman of Sheehan's distillery, said: "We began shipping illicit spirits in 1873, and ceased about the 15th of April, 1875. We stopped shipment before Joyce came to see us."

Ferdinand Rendleman, the storekeeper at Sheehan's distillery, said : " Joyce was at our distillery with Mr. Bittenger, just before the seizure. He looked over our books, and took some numbers. Sheehan was excited in the presence of Joyce, when he began his examination of the books. I ran away to Texas when the seizure was made, and was brought back to be used as a witness. I am indicted for fraud. I got fifty cents a barrel from Mr. Sheehan tor allowing him to take the crooked whiskey away from the distillery. Borngesser, the gauger, got one dollar a barrel for helping to steal the whiskey. All this time we got our pay from the government."

Col. Wm. H. Parker, Collector of Internal Revenue for Colorado, said : " I talked with Joyce in his room in his hotel at Kansas City, regarding the seizure of several rectified packages shipped from the the 6th district of Missouri. There was an informality in the marks and brands, and a discrepancy in the guaging. I told Mr. Joyce there was a discrepancy of two or three per cent. in proof between the gauge of Hamilton, of Denver, and Marsh, of Kansas City, but this might naturally occur.

Col. Joyce asked me to furnish him with a copy of duplicate numbers, that he might search the rectifiers' and distillers' books. I visited Feineman's establishment with Joyce, staid about an hour, and we left together.

Col. Joyce did not invite Supervisor Hedrick, Revenue Agent Brown or myself to examine the books ; neither did he suggest or intimate that it would be as well not to examine them. We were all officers and could examine the books as well as Joyce.

Frank Hamilton, gauger, said : " I saw Joyce and Parker at the Pacific House. Col. Parker had the memorandum serial numbers of the barrels that had been shipped by Feineman. Joyce did not make any excuse for Feineman. Joyce came from St. Louis to Kansas City to meet us. He did not apologize for Feineman & Co. Joyce took us all over to Feineman's, and left us there to examine what we wished."

George Walker, clerk of Supervisor Meyer, produced an official letter of Joyce, showing that a report had been made of what he found in Kansas City.

E. R. Chapman, clerk, produced an official copy of a letter of Joyce to the Department.

A. M. Crane, Revenue Agent, showed that the serial numbers are only entered once in the books, whereas there may be duplicate numbers in existence. Sheehan's books and Feineman's books coincide exactly as to sales and purchases. Packages may be shipped which are not on the books.

The foregoing is the evidence of the government taken from the official record of the court proceedings. Now, after the lapse of eight years, when a calm view can be taken of those inquisition days, I simply offer to an honest world, and the friends who know me best, the following reports as a clear rebuttal of the evidence advanced by the prosecution.

The reports will give the lie to the counts in the indictment. I honestly reported the figurative theory I found on the rectifiers' and distillers' books in Missouri, but did not report the marks and brands on the barrels in Colorado, because I did not have an opportunity to examine the material facts.

(COPY OF TELEGRAM.)

St. Louis, Missouri, April 23, 1875.

Hon. J. W. DOUGLASS,
    Com'r Int. Rev., Washington, D. C.

    Pursuant with telegram April seventeenth (17), to the Supervisor, have conferred with Collector Parker, of Colorado, relative to detention of spirits from the District. Has Parker reported seizures?

(Signed) JNO. A. JOYCE, Rev. Agent.

(COPY.)

UNITED STATES INTERNAL REVENUE.
Supervisor's Office, Dist. of Missouri, Kansas and Arkansas,
St. Louis, April 26th, 1875.

Sir:

    I have the honor to state that in accordance with instructions, on the 18th inst., I proceeded to Kansas City, Mo., to confer with Collector W. H. Parker in relation to the detention of certain rectified spirits in Colorado that had been shipped from this supervising district.

I met Collector Parker, Gauger Hamilton, Revenue Agent Brown and Supervisor Hedrick, and heard the verbal statement of the Collector touching the causes that induced him to detain the spirits in question.

Several packages have been detained or seized, belonging to H. W. Gillett, of Leavenworth, Kansas; Westheimer Brothers, of St. Joseph; and B. A. Feineman & Co., of Kansas City, Mo.; and two or three lots from liquor men in this city.

Collector Parker placed in my hands a memorandum of serial numbers taken from some thirteen barrels out of the hundred and two rectified packages detained at Granada, Col., which were shipped to Chick, Brown & Co. by B. A. Feineman, of Kansas City.

I traced the serial numbers in question through the books of Feineman to the distillery of Edward Sheehan & Son, and the rectifying house of S. Adler & Co., of St. Joseph, and followed the dumping notices (Form 122) into the office of Collector C. B. Wilkinson, 6th Dist. Mo., and find them properly reported in accordance with law and regulations.

Collector Parker stated to me that the causes which led him to detain the spirits in question were the omission of some portions of the marks and brands on the barrels, and a difference of one or two per cent. below proof-marks, or a difference of one wine gallon to the barrel; all of which causes may be explained by the different mode of gauging by the respective gaugers and the leakage and evaporation that will take place in the course of time and distance of transportation.

In my investigation of this matter I cannot find where the Government has been defrauded out of a dollar; and while some of the exact marks and brands may have been omitted by the gaugers differing themselves respecting the contents of the casks, yet I have been unable to trace any fraudulent transactions by the owners of the spirits.

Very respectfully,

Hon. J. W. Douglass,   (Signed)   John A. Joyce,
    Com'r Internal Revenue,   Revenue Agent.
    Washington, D. C.

After a trial of three days, Judge Krekel charged the jury in the following language and logic:

The first three counts of the indictment charge the same offense, the having knowledge or information of a violation of the revenue law, and failing to report such knowledge or information to his superior officer, as required by law. They differ in this, that the first count charges the violation to have been by Feineman & Co., by not making the entries in their books as required by law; the second count, that Feineman & Co. emptied packages without canceling and obliterating stamps, as required by law; and the third count, that Sheehan & Son distilled spirits with intent to defraud the United States of the tax. By the setting out of the specific knowledge or information, it is intended to advise the defendant with what he is charged, and in your passing upon either of the three counts, you should find that the defendant had the knowledge or information of the offenses specifically set out. You should pass upon each of these counts, and find whether the defendant, Joyce, had knowledge or information thereof and failed to report in writing to his superior officers. You will find upon each count, guilty or not guilty, as in your opinion the evidence may justify.

The fourth count of the indictment charges that defendant Joyce conspired and colluded with Edward Sheehan to distill or sell spirits to defraud the United States of the tax. By conspiring is here meant an understanding between Joyce and Sheehan that they would aid and assist each other in the distilling and selling of spirits without paying the tax. The existence of such a conspiracy you must find from the evidence. Whether you will find such a conspiracy to have existed unless some act in furtherance thereof was done, is for you to determine.

About four o'clock on the afternoon of October 23d, 1875, the jury after an absence of over four hours, brought in a verdict of guilty on the four counts in the indictment. It was Saturday, and they wished to get home to their friends and families in the country. Mr. Cox, of the jury, had a sick wife; Mr. Fullilove had a cramp in his stomach; Mr. Leith wanted to hold out for innocence to the last; but in order to secure a verdict, he finally consented to toss up coppers with Mr. Johnson—heads they win, tails I lose. The toss of the copper settled my case, and these "good and true men" brought me in guilty of conspiracy with Edward Sheehan, with whom not a single overt act was proven, but on the contrary, his own son said that they had ceased illicit distilling before I visited their establishment, and that when I examined the books, the fifty cent thief, Rendleman, said, "Sheehan was very much excited at my presence." Is it reasonable that one conspirator should be "excited" at the presence of another?

In the days of Blackstone and the common law, if a jury should secure a verdict by chance, in casting lots or tossing up a penny, the whole thing would have been pronounced null and void.   But in the days of political ambition and public clamor, with pliant people for jurymen, acknowledged thieves for witnesses and a severe man for judge, the Lord himself would have stood no chance for acquittal, but suffered conviction and crucifixion as of old.

The prosecuting officers now felt sure that this "coon" would come down from his lofty oak and crawl in the dust for immunity from punishment.

My lawyer made a motion for a new trial, pending the determination of the court.

I was given over to the custody of the marshal, but the government officers were so rampant that in a few days the judge, who kept one eye on the law and the other on the newspapers, ordered me to jail, although I was under bonds for twenty-five thousand dollars.   Everybody who knew me felt that I would not run away to satisfy the prosecution, if a million dollars in gold were offered me as an inducement.

I remained in jail until the 13th of November, without the judge giving a single indication of granting me a new trial. Punishment without sentence was being inflicted from day to day, with no surety that months might not march into years, and death from exposure ensue before I began to move through the dark tunnel of regular imprisonment.

Letters, telegrams and officers moved about from Washington to St. Louis and Jefferson City, all looking to the spring trials to come off at St. Louis, against McKee, Avery, and particularly General Babcock.

The government imagined that I was the club to smash Babcock, and they would simply hold me in jail as a prospective witness, and when the time came launch me into St. Louis.

The district attorneys at St. Louis and at Jefferson City, and other officers, had long and secret consultations as to how they could best use me in the interest of the prosecution.

I was secretly advised by "a little bird" of everything that the cabal did, and just as Dyer had fixed his legal papers to transfer me to the "Future Great," I had my attorney, Major

A. M. Lay, go into court and demand an immediate sentence upon the indictment on which I was convicted.

A thunder-clap from a clear sky could not have been more surprising than this unusual action of mine. The district attorney and judges were nonplussed, but could not, in decency or law, decline my invitation for sentence on the withdrawal of the motion for a new trial.

The following letter from my lawyers had its proper weight in determining my action in demanding sentence:

St. Louis, Nov. 11th, 1875.

Col. JOHN A. JOYCE,

Dear Sir: It is manifest that Judge Krekel will suspend action upon your motion for a new trial, so as to enable him to order your removal for trial to this district. Here the indications are all one way—that you are to be brought here if possible. We write understandingly.

There can be but one opinion as to the proper course for you to pursue. Your motion for a new trial ought to be withdrawn, and sentence imposed. This action becomes inevitable in view of the settled purpose to overwhelm you. If you withdraw your motion and demand your sentence, then you will be in a proper position to resist all efforts to subject you to unnecessary trials and more persecution. It does seem to us that you have only one course to pursue. If you resolutely withdraw your motion and demand sentence, you will stand better before the country.

We advise this course candidly, earnestly, and as we conceive for your own best interest. If you conclude to take this course, we earnestly advise you to make no speech before the Court, but simply to take whatever sentence may be imposed resolutely and manfully, as you have met everything thus far. The assurances and indications of clemency from Washington are clear and favorable. You must do nothing to prejudice yourself. But if you do come here notwithstanding the withdrawal of your motion, then the sympathies of the people will be with you as a victim of mere persecution; your prosecution would be unjust. The matter is in your own hands.

Very truly, JEFF. CHANDLER.

KRUM & MADILL

When I found what the officials wanted, I concluded to act the other way.

On the 13th of November, I was taken to the court-house for sentence. It became noised about Jefferson City that I was going to make a speech in my own defense. The court-house was full of curious listeners, a jury was sitting in the box, the judge came on the bench, and all was quiet and solemn as the grave.

When the preliminary speeches of the lawyers were finished, Judge Krekel asked me if I had anything to say before sentence was passed. I arose with a defiant attitude, and delivered the following:

"Before this honorable court passes sentence, I beg leave to state that my conviction was secured by the perjured testimony of self-convicted thieves—Feineman, the rectifier, Borngesser, the guager, and Rendleman, the storekeeper, all lineal descendants of those ancient scoundrels who crucified Christ, came upon the witness stand, and paraded their own infamy by acknowledging that they had stolen whiskey from the government, through a term of years at the rate of from one dollar to fifty cents per barrel. The pencil of Gustave Dore could not do justice to those three wandering Israelites, who seemed ever on the lookout to steal small things when big ones were conveniently at hand. Feineman and Fagin are identical characters, and should be immortalized in living infamy. I dismiss these pillars of fraud and perjury, consigning them to the devouring fury of a rotten conscience.

I was indicted for failure to report in writing certain alleged knowledge and information of certain fraudulent transactions of petrified perjurers. The jury found me guilty on the counts, but as a matter of fact the conclusion was as false as the evidence. I agree that it had the appearance to the jury of failure of duty. We know, however, that things are hot always what they seem. I simply declare, upon my honor as a man and my allegiance as an American citizen. here, in the presence of this honorable Court, to the whole world, and facing my God, that I am absolutely innocent of the charges trumped up against me by pretended friends and viper enemies.

It has not been shown in evidence, or even intimated by anybody, that I ever received a single cent in fraud of the revenue.   Then where is the motive that induced me to withhold the information?   I did make a report in writing to the Supervisor and Commissioner Douglass. The report, it is alleged, was not full.   Neither was the information in my possession full or complete, as the facts were in Colorado, out of my district, and the theory I reported was in Missouri.

The district attorney of the United States, in his concluding speech, introduced my copy-book, showing the transmittal letter to the supervisor as something fraudulent.   My lawyers or myself had no opportunity to explain the letter in evidence, which could have been done to the utmost satisfaction of everybody concerned.

Your Honor, from the beginning of the case to the end, extended consideration and ordinary rulings. For this I thank you in the name of the people and in the name of justice.   I stand here to-day strong and bold in conscious innocence.   My heart is actuated by that noble impulse that nerved Winkelried when he opened a breach for the liberty of his country; or by that lofty courage that inspired Sir Walter Raleigh at the block! Like Raleigh I may have puffed smoke through the window at the execution of some official Essex; but I never trampled upon the royal robes of the virgin queen!

For myself I have no fear of any punishment on earth, yet in behalf of my past good character, this being the first suspicion of guilt that ever darkened my life, and in consideration of the support I owe my wife and children, I ask that magnanimity at this bar of justice that would be reasonably claimed by yourself under like circumstances.

A few short years will sepulchre the living of to-day with the dead of yesterday, and the celestial sunlight of to-morrow will bring us all to the bar of Omnipotence, where the judge, jury, lawyer and client will meet upon the level of eternity and part upon the square of final judgment.   Then all hearts shall be laid bare, and truth will rise in magnificent triumph.   The blood of innocence flows free and unruffled through the channels of this frame, and the artificial terrors that surround the victims of crime, find no lodgment in my heart. When I look back to the field of battle where I fought and bled for my country in its hour of terrible trial, I wonder whether patriotism is but a name, and gratitude of nations a mockery and sham to lure the brave to destruction.

My simple sin is that of omission, and for it I suffer the deepest humiliation, while all the glorious services and recollections of the past are buried in the grave of forgetfulness. Is this right ? Is this just ?

This epidemical era of reform has arisen like the rush of a mighty flood, and speeds on toward the gulf of punishment. The good and the bad suffer alike. The stream is full of driftwood and dead timber, while many young oaks and tall sycamores on the banks are loosed from their firm foundation and dashed into the river of destruction. But the rain falls lightly on the mountains, the sun shines warmly on the plains, and the flood, even now, is settling into its former bed, where the crystal waters shall again reflect the green foliage of the oak and sycamore, and the gentle breeze and the birds of spring shall make merry music in the cathedral aisles of generous nature !

The prison walls that hemmed in Galileo, Columbus, Tasso and Napoleon did not measure the minds of the men. It is true their bodies suffered some torture, but the proud spirit that rose in their hearts leaped the bounds of clay, and soared away into the illimitable region of science, poetry and war, making them monarchs of the hour, and masters of eternity ! Humble as I am in the walks of life my soul is inspired by their illustrious example ; and it shall be my future endeavor to show the world that although I may suffer for a time the penalty of perjured testimony, yet like a mountain crag I shall breast the pelting storm, and lift my head clear and bold to the coming sunshine of truth and redemption ! I have done."

Judge Krekel immediately pronounced upon me a sentence of six months imprisonment on the first count, six on the second, and six on the third ; and on the fourth count, for conspiracy, which he intimated was not proven, imposed the term of two years, making in all a sentence of three years and a half, in addition to a fine of $2,000. And to add insult to injury, the judge who imposed this cumulative, illegal sentence on one indictment, made out the commitment so that the long term, on the fourth and last count, would begin first.

But what cared the political conspirators for personal liberty, so they stopped with the hare and ran with the hounds of public clamor. Montezuma had placed another Aztec on the sacrificial block to glut the thirst for blood ; and as I was the first immolated, the death-dance and glee of the conspirators were unbounded.

The prosecution of Col. A. C. Dawes and Major John L. Bittenger, of St. Joseph, Missouri, was a cruel commentary on justice. The former was a railroad man, and had no more to do with gauger Bittenger in whiskey matters than an unborn child. If. Dawes ever sinned, it was through his generosity, and if Bittenger ever fell into fraud, I never knew it.

The sleuth hounds of the law about St. Joseph were not satisfied with smirching the good name of officers, but, for no reason in the world, drew in the name of Major H. R. Hartwig, an enlightened German, and others. The officers also made some cruel insinuations against Col. G. H. Koch, a prominent banker of St. Joseph, who happened to sign the bonds of certain officers and citizens as a personal accommodation. The cradle, the home, the street and the grave were searched by ravenous officials to secure a conviction at all hazard. Yet, where are the strikers of Bristow to-day ? Dispersed and forgotten for their subservient, heartless ingratitude and cowardice.

IMPRISONMENT.

Just as the sun was sinking behind the western hills and gilding the Missouri River with his golden beams, on the evening of November 15th, 1875, I passed the portals of the prison and shut out the wolves and jackalls that had pursued me for many months. A feeling of quiet and relief pervaded my heart when this goal of misfortune closed its portals upon me.

I felt exhausted, as I had often felt after a day of battle and blood, and that bleak November night, with a quiet conscience, I slept soundly upon the floor of a stone cell. It was certainly a new experience to a sane man, and a strange situation to one who knew himself to be innocent, the victim of a political conspiracy more cruel than any whiskey men could establish.

But my mind had long been made up to the very worst dose the government could administer, and I was prepared to take a bumper of gall or quaff the hemlock with the stoical independence of Socrates.

The officers of the prison treated me with the greatest kindness and consideration. They had heard of me in Missouri for many years as a liberal citizen to those who were under the political harrow; they knew me as a man of education, and believed me to be the victim of a political persecution.

I desired to do something in the prison to relieve the monotony of the lingering hours, and requested work. There were more than thirteen hundred prisoners in the institution.

The "Old Hall" contained about six hundred prisoners, three tiers of cells rising to the roof and terminating against the rough stone walls that shut out the world. A state guard had charge of this building, whose business it was to release the prisoners each morning for breakfast and work, and in the evening to count them in two by two, and lock them up for the night. Capt. W. H. Bradbury was the executive officer of the prison. He had been connected with it about thirty years, and was a terror to evil-doers; but to those who performed their duty silently and uncomplainingly, he was ever considerate and friendly. He asked me if I wished to take charge of the "Old Hall" as a confidential man for the state, saying it would save fifty dollars a month. I took the keys, and superintended the exit and entrance of prisoners morning and evening for more than a year. When my five turnkeys locked and bolted the cells, I in turn locked them up, took the keys to the round-house, and then went to my own room in the hospital outside the walls.

My room was large and comfortable, and was never locked. Two windows looked out on the waters of the Missouri, and two others overlooked the house-tops of Jefferson City, with the dome of the capitol and the hills beyond looming up like sentinels guarding the state. My snug quarters were carpeted, and on a corner table I had a collection of writing material and books to amuse myself with, in lonely hours.

The measured tread of the guard, as he paced his lonely rounds, sounded dull and solemn in the silent night; and when the storms of winter and the howling winds of March shrieked about the high walls and lookout towers, a shiver of nameless dread shot across my soul and awoke in my heart messengers of mournful memories.

Often have I read the long, long night through, with Bacon, Montaigne, Shakspeare, Horace, Plato, Dickens, Goldsmith, Junius and Irving for my companions; and when the cool, gray shadows of morning crept over the eastern hills, I would still be pondering upon the beauty of thought and wisdom of these authors, who brought me the sweetest consolation in the gloomy hours of imprisonment.

When all was as silent as the grave, and I imagined everybody was at rest but the sentinel, Capt. Bradbury, with his severe face and tall form, would sometimes enter my room to bid me good night. "Ah, writing more poetry, are you?" would be his salutation.

I replied, that I was far away from his control, communing with my wife and children, and as the spiritual part of man could not be bound or confined by courts or prisons, he would permit me to muse away into the realms of fancy.

The Captain often sat with me by the hour, and seemed ever interested in my conversation. In my presence his stern look melted into kindness, and his iron hand held out the olive branch of generosity and love. Wardens Sebree, Willis and Bradbury were my friends, and never lost an opportunity to make my situation as pleasant as the strict rules would permit. From the time I entered the halls of punishment to the moment of my retirement, there was not a word said nor an act performed that grated upon my sensibilities as a man.

Travelers from state and nation visited the prison almost daily; and as I had been an object of national notoriety, the people were curious to see a man who defied judge, jury and government. Many came from motives of genuine sympathy, and even when tourists and strangers rushed to see and talk with me, I never denied them the opportunity.

I have never, up to the present moment, realized that I served a single day in prison, and the whole affair seems to me now like the phantasmagoria of a vanished dream, leaving no remembrance behind but the audacity of a soul that the rude blasts of the world could not humiliate or subdue.

My oration before the court was copied and commented upon by all the prominent papers in the United States, and while some of them rebuked me for unheard-of boldness, the large majority wondered at my audacity and complimented my eloquence under the trying ordeal of sentence.

From a large number of complimentary editorial comments, I submit the following leader from the *Daily Inter-Ocean*, of Chicago:

WHISKEY AND RHETORIC.

That the wind is tempered to the shorn lamb and the burden fitted to the back which is designed to carry it, are again demonstrated by the circumstances attending the recent sentence of ex-Revenue Agent Joyce at Jefferson City, Mo., for complicity in whiskey frauds. It is evident that Joyce rather enjoyed the proceeding. It gave him a chance for a stunning speech, which he never could have made otherwise, and presented an opportunity to hand down his name beside the names of Sir Walter Raleigh, Galileo, Napoleon and others, which he embraced with an exultation peculiar to that heroic class with whom he thus became identified. For certainly that speech of Joyce's was no ordinary effort. It was not the disconnected, disjointed, inelegant harangue of your vulgar criminal. It is plain that Joyce has become familiar with noble lives and grand examples. Sentimentally, too, he agreed with them, but when it came to practical test, Joyce was wanting. He put his virtue all into theory, and hadn't enough left to practice with. And yet, as we said, he rather seemed to enjoy his sentence, because of the opportunity it gave him to make a very remarkable speech.

We do not know that his remarks were impromptu; it is rather probable, indeed, that they were not; that they were carefully thought over and prepared purposely for effect. Still, that does not alter the fact that the speech was a singularly able one in spite of its rather grandiloquent tone. For there are times when grandiloquence is not altogether inappropriate, and however carelessly the public were disposed to regard the proceedings of the court at Jefferson City, to the prisoner it was a time of great solemnity and great trial, when figures, metaphors and comparisons which would not have been allowable otherwise were pardonable.

Mr. Joyce's opening denunciation of the witnesses against him reminds us of Daniel O'Connell's allusion to Disraeli, whom he described as "a lineal descendant and heir-at-law to the impenitent thief who died on the cross." Joyce evidently had this paragraph in his mind when he referrec to "Feineman, the rectifier; Bonngeisser, the gauger, and Rendleman, the storekeeper," as all "lineal descendants of those ancient scoundrels who crucified Christ." Said Mr. Joyce:

"The pencil of Gustave Dore' could not do justice to those three wandering Israelites, who seemed ever on the lookout to steal small things when large ones were conveniently at hand. Feineman and Fagin are identical characters, and should be immortalized in living infamy. I dismiss the peddlers of fraud and perjury, consigning them to the devouring fires of a rotten conscience."

Mr. Joyce compared himself to Arnold Winkelreid and Sir Walter Raleigh in the following very neat sentence, which, when disassociated from the charge against him, that makes such comparisons a trifle ridiculous, is very good indeed:

"I stand here to-day strong and bold, conscious of innocence. My heart is actuated by the noble impulse that nerved Winkelreid when he opened a breach for the liberty of his country, or by the lofty courage that inspired Sir Walter Raleigh at the block. Like Raleigh, I may have puffed smoke through the window at the execution of some official Essex, but I never yet trampled upon the royal robes of the Virgin Queen."

The remainder of the address, as we said before, is rather remarkable, and shows the prisoner to be not only a man of education and extensive reading, but one possessed of a fine imagination and no mean rhetorical powers. His speech was a solemn and reiterated denial of his guilt, and the expression of an abiding confidence in the final vindication of his good name.

If the charges are well founded, Mr. Joyce has one talent superior to his eloquence, and that is his unexampled impudence. Whatever may be the truth about his guilt, however, it is certain that the Missouri state's prison contains a scholar and an orator such as its gloomy walls have seldom, if ever, held before.

I received a large number of letters from friends and strangers immediately after my incarceration, all of them breathing a spirit of sympathy and encouragement. My lady friends were particularly kind in their expressions of regard and love, saying that no matter what the world thought, they were of the decided belief that I was a persecuted man, and put forth as a vicarious sacrifice for the sins of other people.

One of the most consoling letters I received was the following, from. Col. J. C. Normile, District Attorney of the county of St. Louis—a man who knew me intimately in days of sunshine, and believed in me during the storms of misfortune:

St. Louis, Jan'y 13th, 1876.

Dear Joyce:

I received your welcome letter of the 1st inst., and would have written an earlier reply but for the combined result of much work and constitutional laziness in the matter of letter-writing. I have nightly resolved to write, and as often suspended my resolution until the following night.

The Supreme Court, the Court of Appeals, the Criminal Court and the Grand Jury are all in session since Jan. 3d, and having to distribute myself among them all, you will readily see that I have little time at present for concentration sufficient even to write to an old friend like yourself.

The crowd of the Southern Hotel often speak of you with pleasant recollections of the past, and with regret for your present condition. No one can sing " Mrs. Kearney" like you, they say, and it is also asserted that nobody can enliven an evening of innocent revelry like that mad wag Joyce. I hear this said frequently by those who knew you in better days, when even a shadow of suspicion had not tarnished the luster of your integrity.

That one so genial, gifted, generous and warm-hearted as you should be found among the Ring, was truly painful to those cherished friends, who were the last to believe it, and the first to defend your fair name whenever assailed.

The papers keep you posted on passing events, and they also keep us acquainted with your business. I see you are engaged in writing a novel and a drama on whiskey-ring troubles. You are imprudent in keeping your mind hot by dwelling so much on these subjects. To forget them, should be your aim. I would suggest to you to perfect yourself in Latin while in prison. You have a good opportunity to become a fine classical scholar. It will be pleasant reading, and in dwelling on the deeds of antiquity your mind will unbend itself from the terrible strain that has been upon it, and which has broken minds as vigorous as yours. Write as little as possible, and publish nothing. Think on new subjects, and cultivate your brilliant intellect in the calm seclusion of your prison, and you will win a victory from defeat.

There has been some talk of removing all those who were convicted here to some other place of confinement, where they may have to do disagreeable labor. Keeping quiet at present, and until that has blown over, is your best plan. I don't know how soon business may take me to Jefferson City, but when it does, I will be sure to call and see you personally, and read poetry with you for an afternoon.

I have your speech on receiving sentence laid away between the leaves of your decoration-day oration, where I will show it to you when you are liberated. You ask if I have forgotten those halcyon days of yore. I have not, and never shall. For no man living had I as warm an attachment as for you in your better days. A friendship, indeed, more disinterested has seldom existed between men. I well remember the Joyce of those happy days, and in charity I will draw a veil over those scenes, which I know you will one day wipe out and restore yourself to the confidence of friends that have mourned your trouble. Your sincere friend,

J. C. NORMILE.

CHAPTER XXVIII.

PRISON REFORM.

During my sojourn in prison, I studied closely the philosophy of confinement and punishment, looking into the details of each representative case with the eye of a man who wishes to separate the false from the true, the good from the bad. I saw the children of hereditary crime, and the gnarled, crusty criminals of poverty and education come and go like shadows on a dial. It was a school of the ripest knowledge to one of a thoughtful nature, and I made a memorandum of various cases, in order that I might some day give my experience and conclusions to the world.

See John Anderson, a poor, pale boy of sixteen, come through the "round gate" with a swing, launched into the prison-yard like a tired bird that had been shot in the wing in a summer flight. He stole a pair of shoes to keep his feet warm, and ran into a baker's shop for a loaf of bread to appease his hunger. The policemen nabbed him, the jury indicted and convicted him, and the district attorney and judge sent him to prison for a term of two years with hard labor. After being shaved, bathed, and a description of his person taken, he was assigned to a cell with a burglar of unenviable age and notoriety. The contractors in the shoe-shop had him detailed to hammer on heels for two years, until he is finally discharged with a poor suit of clothes, and barely enough money to take him to the nearest city, where he enters the ranks of burglars and midnight robbers, to put in practice what he learned of the old reprobate with whom he celled.

There is Billy Rider, a ward politician, who made himself serviceable in the past to Democratic and Republican leaders, by packing caucuses with his rough following.   He is an impulsive, human wreck, dangerous in midnight saloons, and always ready with a knife to "cut the heart" out of any supposed enemy.   He is serving a term of two years for an assault upon the life of his fellow-man, and takes his confinement with the nervous discontent of a caged tiger.   Had Billy been reared under happier skies he might have been a good citizen, for his worst enemy acknowledged that there was something generous and good beneath his rough, impulsive exterior.

Look at Old Jerry Collins coming across the prison yard, bare headed and in his shirt sleeves, winter and summer, offering his ever-present snuff-box to any friend, and exchanging words of kindness with the officers.   He murdered his wife in St. Louis with a meat-ax for some imagined infidelity on her part ; was tried and sentenced to be hung ; but, as the governor had doubts as to the sanity of the old, gray wreck, commuted his sentence to imprisonment for life.   Jerry was never satisfied with his commutation, but made periodical applications to have the original sentence of death carried into effect, saying that if he knowingly murdered his wife, he deserved death, and if the act was that of an insane man, be should not be in prison, but in the wards of a lunatic asylum.   The old fellow had a great deal of common sense.   He took a great fancy to me when he found that I wrote poetry and loved flowers.   The officers, to satisfy his whims, procured for him flower seeds, and allowed him a little spot of ten by twelve to cultivate his favorite friends.   It was a strange sight to see a wife-murderer bending lovingly over budding roses, daisies, violets, morning-glories, and forget-me-nots in the sunny hours of spring, nursing them with a father's care in hot summer days, and covering them up with newspapers when the frosts of fall chilled their life.

There comes Jack Reno ahead of the long line with the lock step.   He moves to the measured tread of twenty years confinement for cracking open a county safe, and taking forty thousand dollars in bonds.

The robbery was planned with the precision a general plans and executes campaigns. Jack came all the way from Indiana on the information of a "pal," and when the country town was wrapped in slumber after midnight, while his confederate held the string on the outside, to warn him against approaching footsteps, the bold burglar with his cunning implements cracked the treasury safe, and stole the bonds. Then a race was made for the banks of the Mississippi, but fate and sleep induced the robbers to stop on the wayside too long; and Jack was captured without the "boodle," tried, convicted and sent to prison to contemplate upon the uncertain to of human success. Jack had some elements of redeeming virtue. He regarded it worse than high treason or murder to betray a friend, and however his moral nature may have been bespotted by a family of natural Indian robbers, he possessed a kind heart for his fellow-prisoners, and would share the last crust with a cell-mate. It was curious and astonishing to hear him tell of wonderful escapes and daring exploits, boasting of his robbery of persons and banks with the proud air of a man who had performed some noble action, and deemed himself worthy of commendation. Pope must have had Jack Reno in his mind when he said:

> " Vice is a monster of so frightful mien,
> As, to be hated, needs but to be seen;
> Yet seen too oft, familiar with her face,
> We first endure, then pity, then embrace!"

There is Fred Biebush, one of the most daring counterfeiters in the United States, and a wholesale shover of the "queer." For thirty years he has been meat for detectives, policemen, courts and prison officers, eluding their grasp on many an occasion, but serving three or four terms in prison. He is a stalwart, nervous, rickety-hitchity man with, all the secret cunning of his class, the economy of his Teutonic race, but the victim of his own crimes and the betrayal of his "pals." Had common honesty inspired his heart, he might have been one of the first citizens in the community, an honor to his family and a prop to the state, for certainly his shrewd intellect is of no ordinary character.

The strange infatuation of crime takes hold of the heart and understanding like a horrible nightmare, and when we attempt to shake it off, pain comes with the waking, and we relapse into the arms of the fiend that governs our soul with a rod of iron.   This is especially the case with counterfeiters.   Once a counterfeiter, always one.

See Dutch Charlie coming through the "round gate" for the ninth term of imprisonment, with a step as light and happy as when he departed a few months ago.   Thirty years in prison for petty theft has made the old man a natural boarder of the establishment, and the officers say he departs every two or four years with sadness, and returns with a smile upon his familiar face.   There is no joy in the outside world for a lone creature from the Fatherland, and when he wanders back through the crooked vista of memory to his mountain cot amid the streams and hills of the Rhine, his heart sinks within him, and he deliberately commits some minor offence, pleads guilty, and rushes with pleasure to the comforting walls of his prison home. Dutch Charlie could well exclaim with the Prisoner of Chillon :

> " My very chains and I grew friends,
> So much a long communion tends
> To make us what we are ;—even I
> Regained my freedom with a sigh !"

Charlie Weston was the loneliest character I ever met.   His father and mother died when he was very young.   A baby sister and himself were the only ones left of a large family.   Kind neighbors took up the orphans, and bound them to an old childless farmer in one of the central counties of Missouri. The children grew apace.

One cold November day, the passionate, crusty farmer attempted to flog the eighteen-year-old boy with a blacksnake whip.   Human nature, in self-defense, leaped into the struggle, and with one blow of a chance club the farmer was felled to the earth, and died almost instantly.   Charlie was terribly alarmed, went to the house, told what had occurred, and was arrested for murder.

The trial came off in due season, with no one to give a smile or a cheering word to the orphan boy but his sixteen-year-old sister. The jury found him guilty of murder, and condemned him to be hung, but a merciful governor commuted the sentence to life imprisonment.

A few days after the boy's entrance into gloomy prison walls, he heard that his little sister had died of a broken heart. The last link of earthly love had been thus severed, and his best friend had gone into the shadows of eternity. Like Jean Val Jean, his heart-strings of love and home were snapped asunder, and whether a fugitive among the homes of the opulent or a prison worker at the oar of a galley slave, the future bore no flowers of hope, and the cruel world possessed no charms to soothe his sinking soul.

Charlie was nearly six feet tall, handsome and manly, with blue eyes and blonde hair. He was duly assigned a cell, put to work in one of the shops, furnished a copy of the prison rules, and there is no record that he ever violated one.

Days and months ripened into years, and still the dead level of prison monotony went on. Spring came with its birds and flowers; summer shone with its ripened grain; autumn with its purple fruit and golden foliage, and winter with its chilling blasts and drifting snows came to pivot up the long, long year.

Daily and nightly Charlie came and went to his silent cell from constant labor, without a word of encouragement or hope to brace up his mournful moments. He saw other prisoners get letters of love and consolation from absent friends, and receive daily calls to cheer their solemn hours, but for the term of twelve years he never got a letter, or saw a mortal who cared whether he lived or died!

The Bible was his constant companion, and out of its rich promises he hoped for peace and forgiveness. He was dead to the world, and might as well be resting in the gloomy grave. Daily and nightly he prayed for relief.

At last the prison officers took notice of his orderly, faithful, honest work and good behavior. Warden Willis, with his generous heart, and Captain Bradbury, with his iron justice, brought the case of Charlie to the notice of the prison board, and to Lieutenant Governor Brockmeyer, who granted pardon on the 4th of July, 1877. The pardon was communicated to Charlie and all the prisoners on our national holiday, and was the gift of a generous executive to the merit of a man who had been voted by the prisoners as an exemplary and deserving candidate for executive clemency.

An innocent man, unconscious of premeditated wrong, with no malice aforethought, was thus released after a silent and solemn imprisonment of twelve weary years. I saw the stalwart man of thirty when he received notice of pardon, and he gazed into vacancy as one in a dream, not believing that any human being had ever taken interest enough in a friendless man to procure him a pardon. Like an oak struck by a withering blast, he broke down, threw himself on his bench at the table, and cried like a child that had been locked up in a closet by his mother, and forgiven with a kiss.

When Weston passed through the "round gate," and emerged into liberty, I saw him look back, heave a long-drawn sigh, and vanish with tears coursing down his pale cheeks; and as he walked out again into the rushing world a free man, I could not help thinking how sad and lonely was his lot.

> "Lone as a solitary cloud,
> Lone as a corpse within a shroud."

Century after century has wheeled away into nameless oblivion, and yet the world has not advanced much in the care and reformation of its criminal classes. The handcuffs, the stocks, the thumbscrews, the rack, starvation, the dungeon chains and the lash are still in existence, but no real reform in the prisoner seems to be attempted or attained. Ignorance, poverty and intemperance are the fruitful parents of crime; and until a cure for these inherited and acquired evils is found, no good to the convict can come of the present system of punishment and pretence of reformation.

After a careful study of the whole subject, looking into the details of prison life, and sounding the springs of human nature, I have come to the conclusion that the state should have entire control of its unruly and unfortunate children, and put forth an honest effort to reclaim its prodigal sons and daugh·ters, and throw out every inducement to make them lead peaceful and honest lives.

The state does not wish to make money out of the sweat and blood of its unfortunate children, like the monopoly contractor who hoards up wealth at the expense of the poor and friendless convict, and turns him out to beg or steal at the expiration of his term. Why should the state and nation delegate its authority to a few cormorant contractors as against all other citizens? Monopoly is not consistent with the genius of a republic.

If each state of this Union will crystallize the following suggestive bill into positive law, society will enter upon a new era, and instead of the convict being turned out poor and desperate to prey again upon society, he will retire from his first punishment with a good amount of money to his credit, and above all have a practical trade, by which he may gain support by honest labor. The prisoner must know that obedience is his first duty, and the keeper or warden his best friend. The officers must be strict, but perfectly just.

A BILL for the Labor, Better Care, and Reformation of Prisoners.

Be it enacted, etc.

SEC. 1. The office of General Superintendent of Prisons is hereby created, whose salary shall be five thousand dollars per annum and reasonable traveling expenses.

SEC. 2. Convict labor by contract is hereby forever abolished, and the system shall no longer exist. Hereafter the state shall take active control of the discipline and labor of prisoners.

SEC. 3. It shall be the duty of the Superintendent of Prisons to purchase all raw material, and he shall sell the manufactured products of prison labor, turning the proceeds thereof into the care of the State Treasurer.

SEC. 4. The Superintendent shall see that a full and complete set of books is kept, giving the detail of every purchase and sale transaction ; and at the end of each fiscal year he shall make a full report to the Executive of the State, who shall transmit the same to the House and Senate with his annual message.

SEC. 5. The Superintendent shall have his office at the Capital, and be empowered to hire such clerks and agents as he needs for the execution of his duties.

SEC. 6. In all the state prisons of the Commonwealth there shall be taught in detail to every able-bodied prisoner one of the following trades, during his or her term of imprisonment : Shoe-making, tailoring, blacksmithing, stone-cutting, wooden and willow-ware, tinning, saddle and harness-making and box-making of all kinds.

SEC. 7. With the commitment of each prisoner the clerk of the court shall transmit to the warden a statement of the total expense of arrest and trial of each convict, to be charged against the prisoner on the books of the warden's office.

SEC. 8. Each convict shall be assigned a separate cell, and from the time he enters prison until he is released shall not be allowed to write or speak to any one without the permission of the officers.

SEC. 9. There shall be erected in connection with each prison a large fire-proof store and warehouse, where the raw and manufactured material shall be placed, until the same is properly distributed and disposed of by the agent of the state.

SEC. 10. An expert, intelligent tradesman or tradeswoman shall be placed at the head of each of the ten trades mentioned herein, who shall receive eighteen hundred dollars per annum for instructing the convicts in the full details of each trade.

SEC. 11. The warden shall assign each convict to any of these trades that is best suited to the strength, capacity and ingenuity of the individual.

SEC. 12. A daily, weekly, monthly and yearly cash account shall be kept with each prisoner, who shall first pay from the proceeds of his labor the expense of trial, and forty cents a day for his clothing, victuals and housing during his term of imprisonment. The actual cost to the state of the raw material and its transportation shall also be deducted. All over these amounts arising from the sale and profit of the manufactured goods shall be credited to the prisoner upon the books of the warden and general superintendent of prisoners, and be paid to

the convict by the treasurer of the state, on the certification of
the warden and superintendent, when the prisoner is released
from confinement and punishment. In case of death, the
money placed to the credit of the prisoner shall be paid to his
legal representative, or to whom he wills it, by the State
Treasurer.

SEC. 13. The superintendent shall not sell the manufactured
goods for a price below those of like character in the commercial world, and shall be very careful not to unnecessarily compete with honest labor.

SEC. 14. The superintendent shall see to it that from high
noon of every Saturday, until seven o'clock the following Monday, no work is done in the prison shops.

SEC. 15. A secular school shall be kept in the prison every
Saturday afternoon for the period of four hours, where reading,
writing, arithmetic and history shall be taught by teachers, citizens or competent prisoners, who shall receive therefor fifteen
dollars per month from the state.

SEC. 16. After breakfast each Sunday there shall be held
Bible classes, spelling matches and Divine Worship where each
prisoner shall attend two hours, unless excused by the doctor
or warden.

SEC. 17. The Board of Inspection, shall furnish at state expense, one thousand or more good books for the prison library,
and each convict shall have the privilege to subscribe for one
good, daily newspaper, periodical or magazine, to be given to
him through the warden's office.

SEC. 18. The superintendent and warden shall see to it that
when a convict begins to learn a trade, he shall continue at it
until he has mastered all its details, and be competent on his
release to work as a journeymen.

SEC. 19. The only punishment that shall be allowed in the
prison for violation of rules, is solitary confinement in a well-
lighted cell, with one pound of bread, every other day, at
noon, with a quart of water. This fare shall be kept up until
the prisoner submits, or until the warden is satisfied with the
amount of punishment, under final supervision of the prison
physician.

SEC. 20. The governor, attorney general and treasurer shall
constitute a Board of Inspection, and control and make such
rules and regulations for the guidance of superintendent, warden, foreman, guards and prisoners as they may deem wise and
prudent in the enforcement of this act.

Sec. 21. One hundred thousand dollars is hereby appropri-
ated, out of any money in the Treasury not otherwise appro-
priated, for the beginning and enforcement of the provisions of
this act.

****

In the spring and summer of 1876, the alleged whiskey conspirators of St. Louis were put on trial before Treat and Dillon, United States judges.

The cases of the Supervisor; William McKee, editor and
proprietor of the *Globe-Democrat*; Con Maguire, Collector of
Internal Revenue; William O. Avery, Chief Clerk of the
United States Treasury Department, and General O. E. Babcock, private and official secretary of President Grant, were the
most prominent; the government leaving no stone unturned
to convict and imprison these men.

A number of deputy collectors, gaugers, storekeepers, distillers and rectifiers, were also indicted, and held over the heads
of the prominent characters as state witnesses. These weak
mortals were plastered all over with indictments.

Subordinates were ready and willing to swear to anything
suggested by the district attorney, and as they all had promises
of immunity from punishment, they were daily drilled in their
role of perjury!

It was laughable, if not serious, to see the little human May-
flies buzzing against the window-panes of official power, hunting for a hole to crawl out and escape the frosty expectations
of tight stone walls. But God had fashioned them in a crooked mould, with trembling hearts, and they could not help beg-
ging like spaniels before the rod of official tyranny.

The Supervisor was tried, convicted and sent to state prison.

Mr. Avery, the Chief Clerk of the Treasury Department, was
forced to trial before his lawyers could prepare for his defense.
He was convicted, and literally railroaded to prison, an innocent man, so far as I knew. It was the most cruel thing committed by Bristow in his raid for the presidency.

Con. Maguire was forced into pleading guilty on a promise
of a light sentence, and as he was a poor man without money,

determined to take the self-convicted course, and get out of trouble as soon as possible.

William McKee, proprietor of the *Globe - Democrat,* was a particular object of Bristow's wrath, because the editor did not advocate his presidential expectations. I believed McKee to be a thoroughly honest man, and while he managed his newspaper to make money, he would not stoop to steal or defraud.

Bristow and his officers now put forth their greatest effort to convict General Babcock, and rummaged every nook and corner of the country for evidence to ruin the President's secretary, and even went so far as to attempt to chip into the outlines of Grant himself. Nothing was too desperate for them to undertake in their effort to sully the name of our greatest General, or bring scandal on the White House.

Detectives, spotters and thieves followed the footsteps of Babcock, his lawyers and friends, wherever they turned, and even the private precincts of home and trunks were searched in the vain effort to find personal letters that might be tortured into evidence of whiskey frauds.

One of Bristow's hired henchmen followed my wife and baby from Ripon, Wis., to St. Louis and Jefferson City, gazing secretly at a tin box that he imagined contained the desired letters that had passed between Babcock and myself. The nurse frequently carried the box under her shawl, and wherever they went, either herself or my wife clung to the precious article with unabated vigilance. Dyer and Botsford were sure they were on the right track for the terrible letters that Babcock had written me in furtherance of some wonderful conspiracy; and these two district attorneys having positive information from the shrewd Washington detective, determined to pounce down on the tin box and trunks.

In due course Botsford sued out a search-warrant in the name of the United States, and "the balance of mankind;" and while my wife was visiting me, the detective and district attorney dashed fearlessly down on the old nurse, the trunks, the balmorals and the baby, and with heroic valor captured and instantly opened the long-sought box, containing a spirit lamp, a can of condensed milk, a sugar-teat and a sucking-bottle !

When all else failed Dyer, he stumbled on a fellow named Everest, who had formerly been a third-class clerk in a second-class shoe-shop, and had been made gauger and plastered with indictments for stealing whiskey at the distilleries of Bevis & Frasier and the establishment of Mr. Ulrici.　When he was first indicted he ran off to Canada and Europe.　Then the services of one McFall, a gauger, who had been indicted and was being coached by Pat Dyer, came into play.　John had been interested with Dyer when the latter was in Congress, in procuring claims; and, of course, they knew each other as pure and unsullied patriots.　McFall proposed to get Everest back, and have him swear to anything in the great and good cause of railroading Babcock into the penitentiary.　John and Everest met in New York after the latter came from Rome, where he had been doing pilgrimage at the shrine of St. Peter.　When the usual promises of immunity were understood, the gauger was ready to go on the witness stand, and swear to anything that might save himself from prison.

Everest did take the witness stand, and swore that on a certain day he saw me place a five hundred dollar bill in a large envelope, seal it up and direct it to General Babcock, and mail it at a street-corner postal-box.　This was a direct way to bring money to Babcock, and convince the jury that he knew of the alleged conspiracy.　The cross-examination rather knocked the bottom out of Everest's testimony.

But, in order that the government should not monopolize all the perjury, Emory Storrs, of Chicago, and Judge Porter, of New York, put up a job to get that five-hundred-dollar envelope out of the street box.　At the Lindell Hotel, where these "Greenleaf" guerillas were wont to congregate, some one suggested that Filley, the postmaster, could fix up one of his carriers to swear that I stood around the letter-box until the carrier came on his collection tour, and took out the letter alleged to have been mailed.　Filley was equal to the emergency. He had a pliant letter-carrier named Magill, who did not belong to the mail route of my office. It took but a short time for the legal tricksters to coach the carrier, who went on the witness-stand, and swore that I asked him to take out an envelope from a postal-box on Pine street, and that he delivered it to me.

The cross-examination by Dyer twisted Magill up even worse than Everest had been twisted. Jury, judges and lawyers believed that the carrier had perjured himself.

I simply say, on my honor as a man, and as I hope for peace beyond the grave, that the testimony of Everest and Magill was an absolute lie, manufactured out of whole cloth, web and woof, by the prosecution and defense in aid of their respective causes. But what cared these people for me or my reputation, so they convicted or acquitted their man over my shoulders. I was laid down over the stream of misfortune like a pontoon bridge in war times, over which infantry, cavalry and artillery passed to victory or defeat.

St Louis Mo June 3/72

Col. J A Joyce
    Phil'.
            Dr Sr, I hand
you my Credentials and request to
Delegation to make you my proxy

        Yours &c
            Chauncey I. Filley

CHAPTER XXIX.

The case of the government against Babcock was breaking down very fast, but as a last spike the celebrated "Sylph" dispatch, in Babcock's hand writing, was introduced as evidence of his guilt.

The dispatch to the supervisor read as follows:

Washington, D. C., December 13, 1874.
I have succeeded. They will not go. I will write you.
Sylph.

The goverment attempted to show that this collusive telegram was an overt act of Babcock in furtherance of the conspiracy, advising the St. Louis officers that he had succeeded in preventing detectives from going out to Missouri to make investigation, and that he would write more fully in regard to his action.

The defense endeavored to show that the dispatch was an innocent one, and did not refer to any frauds on the revenue.

The testimony was finally closed, the lawyers made longwinded speeches, Judge Dillon weighed the evidence, and instructed the jury that Babcock had not committed any overt act of conspiracy, thus virtually ordering them to acquit. They retired to their rooms, and under the instructions of Dillon had nothing else to do but to bring in a verdict of not guilty.

Judge Dillon saw the political animus of the prosecution and the weakness of the case, and was the very man to do his duty in defiance of public clamor. The case against Babcock at St. Louis was far stronger than that against me at Jefferson

City; but I had a judge who paid more attention to newspapers than to evidence or law, and in his anxiety to listen to the howl of the rabble he actually imposed upon me a cumulative sentence that common decency afterwards compelled him to set aside under a writ of *habeas corpus.*

During my official career in Missouri and the West, I was personally and politically acquainted with General O. E. Babcock, the official and private secretary of President Grant. I met him frequently on my trips to Washington, and when he came to St. Louis we conversed on general political topics.

General Babcock has been severely blamed for sending to St. Louis the notorious "Sylph" dispatch. In our personal and political communications we made such off-hand signatures as friends frequently use in transmitting private letters and telegrams.

The origin of the "Sylph" signature was this: In the summer of 1874, I was in Washington and at the White House. One evening after office hours General Babcock invited me to take a ride in his carriage. We went over the city, viewing objects of interest, and finally drew up at the granite base of the Scott statue, on 16th street and Massachusetts Avenue. While examining the great stone, which had been brought from the river on rollers, I chanced to look up the street, and saw a very beautiful young lady dressed in fine style, walking erect, light and airy as a dream. In the off-hand manner of my florid style, I called the General's attention to the silken beauty, and exclaimed :

> Her fairy-like form, moulded in beauty and grace,
> Seems to float like a *sylph* on the light wings of space.

The General laughed, coincided with my enthusiastic compliment, and thought comparing the beauty to a sylph was very appropriate, joking me a good deal about my admiration for the fair sex. The couplet of poetry took hold of his mind, and I repeated it to him several times as I saw he liked the good and beautiful.

In subsequent private letters I often used the word "sylph" in closing my political communications, and he would sign incidental notes and telegrams with the same poetic word.

The "Sylph" telegram came near sending General Babcock to prison, and as neither the courts nor any other sources have ever truthfully explained it, I here give for the first time the actual meaning of the dispatch.

Parties from Kansas and Illinois had been in Washington for some time trying to oust the collector of Kansas, and supervisor of Illinois. Politically speaking, we were very anxious to retain these officers, because of their power and fealty to the administration. I had written several times to General Babcock to assist in keeping the office-seekers out ot the old political districts where we could always count on a Grant delegation to a county, state or national convention. Through the General's influence with the political powers at Washington, the office-seeking patriots did "not go," and Babcock "succeed" in keeping old and faithful officers in their places against the conspiring influence of two hungry reformers.

There never was a more innocent communication, and neither directly nor indirectly did it refer to any frauds on the revenue. It was a simple service performed in the political arena of administrative business, and just such work as is performed every day in the week by every executive officer in all civilized countries.

There was no actual woman that either the General or myself personally knew in the remotest degree representing the "Sylph," save the unknown belle on Massachusetts Avenue, who inspired my poetic exclamation.

Had I been in a position to place my hands on the letter of which a *fac simile* is shown on the following page, and present it at the court, Gen. Babcock would have been acquitted in five minutes; but at that time I was representing "Uncle Sam" in his " Reform" raid, and could not spare an hour from his classic service.

Executive Mansion,

Washington D.C. Dec 14th 1874

Dear General

Sent you a telegram yesterday. The parties tried their best to oust your politicul friends in Kan. & Ill. I succeeded in developing their scheme and breaking the back bone of their combination. They will not go as supervisors Collectors or in any official capacity "if the country knows itself and it thinks it does" Politics like war should be conducted on one principle viz. fidelity to your friends and death to your enemies,

Many thanks for the late Editorial in the Herald. It is good. Kindest regards to all friends in St Louis,

Yours Truly

O E Babcock

In all the years that I knew Gen. Babcock, we never intimated to each other any scheme or word touching any design to conspire to defraud the government of the United States, and I never paid him a dollar to do for me any political service; and, so far as I know, no one else ever paid him a cent in furtherance of the alleged whiskey conspiracy. His prosecution by Bristow was a cruel thing, entailing a certain odium that will last to his grave, and imposing upon himself a cost of forty thousand dollars to show his innocence and keep out of the penitentiary. All this in the interest of Reform!

Bristow played his last trump in the Babcock case, and lost. The effort to trace fraud to the White House and saddle it on Grant proved a total failure, and the political conspirators were desperately disappointed. The drama of The Whiskey Conspiracy had been played to full houses, and the audience became restive, many going out between the acts to refresh their anxiety at the failure of unfulfilled promises and great expectations. The curtain was at last rung down to empty benches, the scene-shifters departed, the actors stole away into the lumber of the green-rooms and out into the dark alley of defeat; the lights burned dim and blue, and all that was left was a score of human beings in prison, and the "property man," who held only a few dilapidated distilleries as the profits of the whiskey prosecution.

Grant at last saw that he had been a victim of Bristow's perfidy, and with that defiant boldness which never failed him in the hour of need, he began to kick out of his administration a lot of impudent frauds who had brought scandal, but no taxes, to the government.

District Att'y Dyer was dismissed; Detective Yaryan was bounced; Commissioner Pratt went to short grass: Solicitor Bluford Wilson was sent back to the Sucker State, and Bristow himself was kicked out unceremoniously after his failure to get the nomination for President, at Cincinnati.

The prosecution of the so-called whiskey conspirators, from the beginning to the end, cost the government one million dollars; and in the loss of taxes from idle distilleries and whiskey houses, it suffered a loss of two million more—making in all a three-million-dollar robbery from the vaults of the treasury by a set of official conspirators who acted, not for the enforcement of the law, but to promote their own personal and political ambition.

After eight years, where are the men who made such loud boasts in the whiskey prosecutions? Many of their victims died of poverty and broken hearts by the wayside, while they are only mentioned as conspirators against an administration that had warmed them into life and power. The chief objects of Bristow's wrath were Joyce, Babcock and Grant. I have lived for the past five years, proud, prosperous and patient, on a hill-top overlooking Washington City and the historic waters of the Potomac—respected by all who know me intimately; and for the opinion of the rabble I care no more than for a whiff of idle wind, because their blame or censure is of no consequence to a man they know not.

Gen. Babcock holds a life place in the engineer corps of the United States army, respected and loved by every one whose opinion is worth consulting.

Gen. Grant's little finger to-day is more potent with the present administration and the nation than all the howling reformers in America; and when their work and memory are lost, and they rest in forgotten graves, he will be remembered, and his form will be chiseled in monumental glory as long as liberty and valor find a home in our Great Republic.

Bristow, late Secretary of the Treasury, moves about New York City with the mark of the deceiver on his brow, and wherever his name is mentioned, his betrayal of Grant rises like Banquo's ghost.

'Thus the whirligig of time brings in its revenge.''

CHAPTER XXX.

PARDON AND OTHER MATTERS.

Days, weeks and months wore away the year 1876, and wheeled in the New Year with its hopes and fears. President Grant had pardoned, in detail, all the victims of Bristow's personal ambition, and although I was the first in the United States to feel the wrath of the government, I remained the last one to suffer. Every self-convicted thief in Wisconsin, Illinois, Indiana and Missouri was released from punishment by the courts, or by a pardon from the President, while I, who persistently asserted my innocence, was permitted to languish alone, even against the loud protests of public opinion.

In the spring of 1877, numerous letters of sympathy began to pour in upon me, and even the newspapers and officers that hounded me into prison pronounced my continued incarceration an outrage on the principles of equal justice.

Wm. J. Florence, the well-known actor, an old-time friend, said: " I suppose you will soon be a free man again. Among the many friends you have to sympathize with you, none are more sincere than Florence. Keep the few hairs of poor Old Abe Lincoln I gave you, and prize them as souvenirs of all that was truly good and noble in man."

Judge John M. Krum, a lawyer and prominent citizen of more than forty years' standing in St. Louis, said: " And first, I wish to say that, although you are at present under a cloud, it has not obscured you in the least from my recollection, or lessened you in any respect from my regard or estimation. ' What though the field be lost, all is not lost.' To-day the storm rages fiercely, but to-morrow comes a peaceful day, and the storm has wasted its power. And so, my friend, a peaceful day will soon come to you. Be of good cheer. Your friends, as of yore, stand by you, and will to the death."

Ex-Senator John B. Henderson, who was employed as the special Attorney General to aid Pat. Dyer in the prosecution of the St. Louis whiskey cases, wrote several kind and friendly letters, from which I make the following extracts :

"I have understood that every one is out of prison except yourself, and that those who had not been tried, and who are unquestionably guilty, have been pardoned before conviction. I cannot appreciate the reasons for your further incarceration. There were various rumors here in regard to the matter, one of which is to the effect that certain parties demanded five thousand dollars from you as a condition of relief, and you, refusing to give it, was informed that you could not be pardoned. I can recommend your pardon on the ground that you deserve pardon equally as well as those who have been pardoned.

Gen. Henderson says, in a letter to Att'y General Devens touching my pardon : "I do not hesitate to place his case as one demanding only equal favor and consideration with others. He is no worse than many others unconditionally pardoned ; and when I say no worse, I put the case in the mildest form of expression. I think he is a better man than many who have received executive clemency in the several districts."

The following exceedingly strong pardon papers were presented to the Att'y General, embracing a letter of recommendation from Judge Krekel, petitions from the Senate and House of the Missouri legislature, and the rare recommendation of the Supreme Court of the state ; also the favorable recommendation of five of the jurymen who convicted me on the 23d of October, 1875, and said in their paper only two days afterward, that "It does not appear from the proof that Col. "Joyce ever received a dollar in fraud of the revenue laws."

District Attorney Botsford also strongly recommended my pardon, as did others whose letters I omit.

Jefferson City, Mo., March 21, 1877.

To the PRESIDENT:

John A. Joyce, now confined in the Missouri State Penitentiary, under sentence for violating his official duty as Revenue Agent, is petitioning to be pardoned, and has asked me to favor his application. Heretofore I have refused to join in his, as in every other, application for pardon in the so-called whiskey-ring cases, for two reasons mainly, that I did not deem it best that the administration under which the violations occurred should pardon the offender, and again because I desired to see adequate punishment inflicted on those who had violated not only the law, but their high trust.

The punishments imposed by other judges in similar cases tried afterwards *were lighter* than my own in the Joyce case. His conduct while confined has been reported to me as good. Considering all the circumstances, I recommend his pardon.

Respectfully,   A. KREKEL.

His Excellency, RUTHERFORD B. HAYES,
   President of the United States.

We, the undersigned, Senators of the 29th General Assembly, would respectfully submit to your earnest consideration that John A. Joyce, of the city of St. Louis, is at the present time, and has been for the past sixteen months, an inmate of the state prison of Missouri, for alleged complicity in the late whiskey conspiracy; that all the participants in said conspiracy in Indiana, Illinois, Wisconsin and Missouri have been relieved either by the Courts, or by a pardon from ex-President Grant; that Colonel Joyce was the first tried in the United States, and has suffered longer imprisonment than any one else, he being the only one still incarcerated; that his application for pardon has laid for months in the Att'y General's office favorably recommended by the District Attorney who tried him; that he has a wife and two children depending on him for support, this being the first offence alleged against the aforesaid prisoner, he having led in the past an honorable life; that as an American citizen, he is entitled to the same treatment accorded others for like offenses, and unless actuated by a desire for personal vengeance, a just Government cannot discriminate against Joyce, who still asserts his innocence..

It is therefore the opinion of your petitioners that the principles of even-handed justice, presuming that a wrong had been committed, is now satisfied; and that every consideration of truth, charity, and mercy demands the immediate release of the prisoner; and that he may be restored to his suffering family, your petitioners humbly pray.

Henry C. Brokmeyer,
Lieut. Governor.
Jno. H. Terry.
E. A. Seay.
Waller Young.
A. H. Benkeholder
T. H. Parrish.
I. S. Parsons.
George K. Biggs,
W. W. Mosby.
E. M. Edwards.
S. S, Henry.
G. T. Ballingal.

Daniel Able,
Sec'y Mo. Senate.
Wm. Q. Paxton.
R. Ake.
M. H. Phalan.
James R. Claiborne.
Lee Wight.
T. J. O. Morrison.
John G. Wear.
Robt. G. Coleman.
R. S. Lukenson.
R. P. Wilson.
W. B. Thompson.

A petition similarly worded was signed by members of the House of Representatives, as follows:

John I. Martin.
S. M. Pickler.
Geo. M. Sutherland.
Chas. A. Pollock.
Robert A. Cameron.
D. H. Connaway.
L. A. Lambert.
S. W. Headen.
J. D. Horn.
Geo. W. Rinker.
R. A. Campbell.
Joseph A. Dacus.
Sam. Byrns.
Geo. W. Easley.
Ashley W. Ewing.
John J. O'Neill.
M. D. Blakey.
Jacob A. Love.
Geo. R. King.
G. B. Atterbury.
W. A. Love.
F. M. Coleman.
Charles L. Ewing.
John Ryan.

Wm. Goff.
E. P. Johnson.
E. A. Donelan.
Theophilus Williams.
Jared E. Smith.
D. Procten.
Wm. Gardner.
Jas Southard.
T. E. Evans.
J. B. Brower.
J. Casey Woodside.
De L. Miller.
E. L. Newsum.
Stephen P. Turn.
H. C. Todd.
W. M. Moore.
W. C. Wells.
Abram Dobbs.
P. C. Stipp.
W. H. H. Russell.
E. Buler.
Jasper N. Burks.
William Harrison.
D. C. Gannawoy.

G. N. Nolan.
T. A. Dryden.
H. J. Deal.
L. F. Medley.
Peyton G. Hurt.
W. E. Brown.

L. J. Dryden.
J. L. Farris.
W. R. Wilhite.
R. W. Jameson.
J. S. Richardson.
John H. McHenry.

State of Missouri—s. s.

I, Michael K. McGrath, Secretary of State, of the State of Missouri, hereby certify that the persons whose names are subscribed to the foregoing petitions are members of the Senate and House of Representatives of the General Assembly of the State of Missouri. In Testimony Whereof, I have hereunto set my hand and affixed my seal of office. Done at office, in the city of Jefferson, this twenty-eighth day of March, A. D. Eighteen Hundred and Seventy-Seven.

{ Seal. }

MICHAEL K. McGRATH,
Secretary of State.

To His Excellency, RUTHERFORD B. HAYES,
President of the United States.

The undersigned, members of the Supreme Court of the State of Missouri, respectfully recommend the pardon of John A. Joyce, in consideration of equal justice.

Jno. W. Henry,
E. H. Norton,
T. A. Sherwood,
J. W. B. Napton.

To His Excellency, U. S. GRANT,
President of the United States,
Washington, D. C.

The undersigned, members of the jury who tried the case of the United States vs. John A. Joyce, in the District Court of the United States for the Western District of Missouri, state that the verdict of guilty on the several counts in the indictment was based upon our belief that the defendant had knowledge and information of fraud and did not report the same to his superior officers.

It did not appear from the proof that Col. Joyce ever received a dollar in fraud of the revenue laws, and in consideration of this fact, coupled with his past good conduct, we would most respectfully recommend him to Executive clemency.

October 25th, 1875.

James Cook,
Robt. N. Leith,
G. W. Oakes,
Ephraim Johnson,
J. L. Fullilove.

The 4th of March, 1877, came and went, and notwithstanding the personal and official recommendations I brought to bear, President Grant went out of office without giving me the clemency he extended to self-convicted thieves.

I have since learned, from the best authority, that my official papers were held back by Alphonzo Taft, Attorney General, and were never presented to the President. I will also state that a trio of licentious Washington blackmailers did attempt to make me pay five thousand dollars for a pardon. I leave Taft and a just government to explain the cruel exception made in my case.

For five months after every one else was out of prison, I was held for no earthly reason imaginable except to satisfy some personal vengeance of the pardon brokers, who could not intimidate, control or blackmail me.

Time with its ceaseless tread brought around July, 1877, and as my attorney and self felt that Judge Krekel had committed a great wrong in giving me four separate punishments on one indictment, determined to apply for a writ of *habeas corpus* before the same man who imposed a *cumulative* sentence. Accordingly ex-Governor Thomas C. Fletcher, my attorney, sued out the proper writ, and brought me before Krekel, who made some preliminary remarks, and temporarily released me until he could consider all the legal points involved.

For several weeks I remained at the Madison House in a state of suspended animation, waiting for the decision of the judge.

Finally, after corresponding with Judge John F. Dillon, of the Circuit Court, and scanning the daily papers with the eye

of a politician, Arnold Krekel "went back" on himself in the
following language:

"Ex parte John A. Joyce:
Petitioner is before me on a writ of *habeas corpus*, seeking
to be discharged from imprisonment on judgment of this court
in one of the whiskey cases.   This indictment under which the
conviction is had is drawn under the fourth and ninth subdivis-
ions of section 3169 of the Revised Statutes of the United
States.   The pleader saw cause to reverse the order of the statute, and in the three first counts of the indictment, under the
ninth subdivision of the section cited, charges that defendant
Joyce had knowledge of Feineman and of Sheehan violating
the revenue law, and failing to report such knowledge as required.   The fourth count charges that Joyce conspired and
colluded with Sheehan to defraud the United States, an offense
under the fourth subdivision of the section cited.   On trial the
defendant was found guilty on each count in the indictment,
and after filing a motion for a new trial, he withdrew the same
before hearing, and demanded judgment, which was entered,
and is in the following form: 'That the said John A. Joyce,
defendant, be imprisoned and confined for the term of two
years in the Missouri Penitentiary under the fourth count of the
indictment, the first term to commence on this 13th day of
November, 1875, and that under such count he pay a fine of
$1,000, and he be further imprisoned and confined in such
penitentiary for the term of eighteen months under the first,
second and third counts of the indictment, and that under such
counts he pay a fine of $1,000, the second term of eighteen
months to commence on the expiration of the first term of two
years, and said two terms to constitute a continuous imprisonment of three years and six months.'
Joyce in his petition for the writ of *habeas corpus* claims
that the four counts of the indictment charge but one offense,
and that when the court entered judgment on one count it exhausted its power, and that Joyce having served his sentence

of two years, after allowing due credit for good behavior, he i,
entitled to a discharge, thus virtually claiming that the conspiring and colluding to defraud the United States under the
fourth division of section 3169, and under the ninth division,
the having knowledge of the commission of offenses against the
revenue law, and failing to report, are one and the same offense. There is no doubt that two offenses—the conspiring
and colluding to defraud, and the having knowledge of the
violation of the revenue law without reporting, may be committed, for they have no necessary connection; at least, a
knowledge of the violation of the revenue law by others may
be had without the person having such knowledge being in collusion to defraud. The various counts of the indictment under
consideration so charge the offenses as to connect them with
the conspiracy to defraud entered into between Joyce, the revenue agent, and Sheehan, the distiller.

Joyce, the revenue agent, ought to have known that others
besides the distiller must violate the revenue law in order to
carry out the design of the conspiracy to defraud, for without
such violation it could not have been carried out and made ef-
fective. Feineman, the rectifier, was made the willing instrument in the conspiracy; the gauger and warehouse-keeper
became the paid tools.

The evidence on the trial was all directed to the establishing of the conspiracy to defraud, for while the prosecution
might have fallen short of a conviction in this particular, it
could still have succeeded in showing that Joyce knew of violations of the revenue law without having reported them.

The proper judgment upon the verdict rendered was for this
conspiracy count. The present inquiry is, Did the court ex-
ceed its power in rendering the judgment it did? There is
no doubt upon my mind that the judgment of the court
should have been but for one offense, and had the motion for
a new trial not been withdrawn, but considered, it is probable
that on consideration the conclusion now reached would then
have been arrived at. This happened to be the *first* of the

long line of whiskey fraud cases, afterwards tried here and in other courts, and well do I remember my deep anxiety to bring offenders to justice on the one side, and not to be unjust to the defendants upon whom outraged public opinion was about to descend. The question of law, it must be admitted, is a grave one, as to how far the court under *habeas corpus* proceedings can review its former judgment; for it amounts to nothing less than this. Upon the point of pronouncing on the judgment only, upon the various counts of the indictments, I have the full support of decisions rendered in the Tweed case. Upon the extent of the power of a court to review its former judgment in order to see whether it had power to pass the judgment it did, the Supreme Court of the United States, in Ex parte Large, 18th Wallace, has passed. But above all I feel relieved, because the judgment about to be entered can be reviewed, and the various questions involved authoritatively settled on appeal. *The conclusions arrived at are that the indictment under consideration in its various counts charges but one offense; that when the court entered its judgment on the conspiracy count it exhausted its power, and that the rest of the judgment is void;* that Joyce, having served the full term of his sentence of two years, after allowing due credit for good behavior, is entitled to a discharge, which is granted him.''

After my release, the United States District Attorney took an appeal to the Circuit Court, holding over me a tacit threat and weighing me down with the lingering chains of modern political, policy law.

I was still, like Mahomet's coffin, suspended between earth and sky, and felt that

The young and the old
This truth may unfold,
That things cannot always go right.
Sometimes you'll be sure
Your friend is as pure
As streaks of the sun's brightest light.

> But as clouds may arise,
> To darken the skies,
> And the bright light of noon may grow dimmer,
> In the first flush of youth,
> You may learn this sad truth :
> "There's a great many holes in a skimmer !"

In order to knock the whole bottom out of the Government "skimmer," I concluded that a full and unconditional pardon would be the best thing to foil the blackmailers and pardon-brokers, and immediately went to work to obtain presidential clemency.

On my way to Washington, in August, I stopped for a day at the Palmer House, in Chicago, and was interviewed by representatives of the *Times* and *Tribune*, whom I had known in the days of my political power. They spoke of me in the most charming and complimentary manner, and even the editorial comments were flattering.

Col. Jack Hinman, of the *Times*, one of the best newspaper men in the United States, interviewed me for his journal, and afterwards introduced me to Mr. Storey, the sage proprietor, who treated me with kindness, and talked upon the philosophy of the whiskey prosecution, saying that it was all "great cry and no wool !" I also talked with the late Sam. Medill, of the *Tribune*, a gentleman of fine intellect and sterling integrity.

When I reached Washington, and retired to my home on the heights of Georgetown, the *National Republican* sent a very intelligent young man to interview me on the general policy of the whiskey prosecution. Speaking of my home and self, the reporter said :

" The walls were covered with paintings, but the most striking picture was one in the centre of the room—a full-length, well-executed crayon portrait of a handsome man with dark hair and a moustache, flashing eyes, and of rather spare figure, though finely formed. It was a portrait of Joyce before he entered prison. He soon came down stairs in his shirt-sleeves.

It was the same face that could be seen in the picture, but the thick hair had turned prematurely gray.   The eyes still sparkled.   The figure was fuller.   Before Joyce's imprisonment he weighed 150 pounds, now he weighs 175.   Evidently he did not worry much over his bad luck.   Col. Joyce has all the appearance of an educated Irishman.   His features are regular and handsome.   His head is shaped well, and his forehead, encircled by iron-gray locks, is high and intellectual.   He has a sort of half-military air, which is more noticeable when he wears his hat—a black felt of the military pattern.   Though no one would detect the least "brogue" when he talks, his voice is Irish in its richness and fulness.   Like an educated Irishman, he is a ready and voluble talker, and forms good round sentences as fast as his tongue can trip through them."

On the morning of the 18th of December, 1877, I was introduced to President R. B. Hayes by Senator William B. Allison, in order that I might make a statement touching the justice of granting me a pardon.   Other good friends, like Hon. W. W. Curtis, of Georgetown, interceded in my behalf, and gave testimony to my general character for truth, faith and honesty.   My interview with the President lasted about half an hour, when I rounded off my argument with the remark that if I could not be granted a full and unconditional pardon on the simple ground of equal and exact justice, I did not want it.

My enthusiastic statements brought smiles and interest to the President, and as an evidence of his earnestness I found lately that he wrote, that very day, the following letter to his Attorney General:

Executive Mansion, Washington, D. C.,
December 18th, 1877.

DEAR GENERAL:

I understand that John A. Joyce has served out his time, and that application is now made to relieve him from the legal disabilities consequent upon his conviction.

If the grounds as presented are sufficient to warrant that action, I shall be glad to have it done.

I will call in the morning, and talk with you about it.

Very truly,
R. B. HAYES.

GEN. DEVENS,
Attorney General.

Dec. 18, 1877.

Dear General:

I understand that John A. Joyce has served out his time, and that application is now made to relieve him from the legal disabilities consequent upon his conviction. If the grounds as presented are sufficient to warrant that action, I shall be glad to have it done. I will call in the morning and talk with you about it —

It is very seldom that the President of the United States takes such personal interest in matters of pardon. But Mr. Hayes felt and knew that I had been the victim of an unholy vengeance, run off into the forest of misfortune as a scape-goat for the sins of the Jubilee conclave—a first-class vicarious sacrifice. The next day after my interview with the President, I called at the State Department, and Mr. Sevellon Brown, the gentlemanly and intelligent chief clerk, handed me a full and unconditional pardon. Thus, after a fight of more than two years with the United States Government, it bluntly stultified its own action by a successful writ of *habeas corpus* and pardon, restoring me to every right I possessed before Bristow's Presidential bee began to buzz in his bonnet.

What a commentary on human justice ! What a burlesque, trial by jury ! What a model, the Judge who imposes sentence on the rise and fall of public opinon ! The punishment for conspiracy should be sharp, short and decisive. The small and the great should be dealt with according to their responsibility, and no special privileges should be granted to any one.

Pardon should be granted to the innocent, but to others only under extraordinary circumstances ; yet, sad to say, there is no privilege this side of the grave that cannot be purchased by money and political influence.

The duplicate cases standing against me in St. Louis were so weak that Wm. H. Bliss, Dristrict Attorney, did not wish to try them. The perjured witnesses that had been used in the hot days of 1876 had not the inducement to lie, since the terrors of imprisonment were passed. My attoney, ex-Governor Fletcher, called up the cases and they passed off on a plea in bar and demurrer, by the rulings of Judge Treat, judgment being entered in my behalf. Thus the last shot in the blunderbuss of Bristow was exhausted, and the great reform boom that went up like a rocket came down like the stick.

The celebrated apostrophe of Madam Roland to the statue of Liberty, on her way to the scaffold, might well have this modern rendition : "Oh ! Reform, Reform, how many crimes are committed in thy name ! "

CONCLUSION.

The reader who has followed me over the mountains, valleys and streams of this "checkered life" deserves commendation and thanks; and while he or she may have thought that some things were said and done that might have been avoided, yet in the usual course of human affairs it was natural to do and act just as the brain and heart dictated.

I am candid to acknowledg that I have had sins of omission and commission. Who has not? I have warmed friends to my generous bosom, and have been betrayed. Who has not? I have seen the man and woman I supported walk on the other side of the street, fearing to look at the man who had saved them. Who has not? I have seen human lizards sun themselves on the flowery banks of prosperity, and fly under the stones at the first thunder-clap of adversity. Who has not? I have seen the bad and corrupt go down to the grave of respectability, while the impulsive, good, and true received the shocks of misfortune, and died in disgrace and poverty. Who has not? I have seen many varied peculiarities of life, but I never yet saw a man finally forsaken who had the self-reliant power to stand by himself and defy the onslaught of a rabble world.

For the little May-flies of fashionable opinion I care no more than for the idle wind that wanders o'er the lea; but for those true hearts that can separate the false from the true, and distinguish right from wrong, my most sincere respect is enlisted. Let us all live and act for the honest opinion of those who know us best, and leave the rest to God.

POETIC WAIFS.

JOHN A. JOYCE.

" To clothe the fiery
thought
In simple words suc-
ceeds,
For still the craft of
genius is
To mask a king in
weeds."
"Curst be the verse,
how well soe'er it flow,
That tends to make one
honest man my foe."

KISS WHILE YOU CAN.

KISS while you can; wait not for to-morrow;
The form that you love may wither in sorrow;
The lips that you press in passion to-day
May fade in a moment, and vanish away.

The dark raven locks that glisten to-day
Soon are supplanted by silvery gray;
The fire in the eye and bloom on the cheek
Will vanish in air, then others we seek.

Cherish the heart, and the brave, hoary head—
True in old age as when first they wed;
Lavish sweet love on each other to-day;
Remember, my darling, we're passing away.

Time, in his flight, will not stop to debate;
Richest inducements will not make him wait;
Then while he is here, let's brighten his hours,
And sparkle and shine like dew on the flowers.

Sigh not and brood not o'er gems that are lost;
Year after year buds are killed by the frost;
Tears will not bring back the lips that are fled—
The kisses we gave are gone to the dead.

KATIE AND I.

KATIE and I sat singing, singing,
  As the moon went down;
While bells were loudly ringing, ringing,
  In the far-off town.

Katie and I sat thinking, thinking,
  Of the long ago;
Sweet baby fingers lightly linking
  Memories under snow.

Katie and I soon sleeping, sleeping,
  'Neath the silent sod;
Our spirits fondly greeting, greeting
  Children, rest and God.

MY BABY'S EYES.

MY baby's eyes, in melting blue,
  Are beaming bright as morning dew
And from the sky light take a hue,
Or like the starlight, clear and true.

My baby's eyes, in liquid roll,
Enhance my world from pole to pole,
And love sits smiling in that goal,
Forever speaking to my soul.

My baby's eyes, in other years,
May fill with many scalding tears;
And yet, through cruel taunts and jeers
A mother's love will banish fears.

My baby's eyes, in blight or bloom,
Those glorious orbs, in grief or gloom,
Shall be to me, in dearth or doom,
The dearest diamonds, to the tomb.

TWENTY YEARS.

A MEMORY OF MT. STERLING, KY.

TWENTY years are gone to-morrow
  Since these streams and hills I knew;
'Twenty years of joy and sorrow
  Brings me back, dear hills, to you.

Many friends I loved are sleeping
  On the crest of yonder hill;
'Neath the willows gently weeping,
  Near the sound of Perry's mill.

Beaux and beauties that I cherished
  Left me in their early bloom,
Yet their memory never perished
  With the blight that blurs the tomb.

Raven locks no more are shining;
  Lost and gone the flowers of May;
Yet how vain is all repining
  In my crown of silver gray.

Vanished voices in the twilight
  Float above the hill and plain;
Call me fondly to the skylight,
  Thrill my heart with love again.

DREAMING.

DREAMING, dreaming, only seeming
  That I loved you long ago;
Weeping, weeping, fondly keeping
  Secrets from both friend and foe.

Thinking, thinking, lightly linking
  All the hopes that filled the past;
Peering, fearing, gently nearing
  To our promised joys at last.

THE SUNBEAM.

A BEAUTIFUL beam came into my cell,
   Fresh from the eye of Jehovah, to tell
That bolts and bars cannot keep out the light
Of truth and justice, of mercy and right.
It checkered the flags through the iron door,
And danced in the shadows that kissed the floor,
And loitered about in a friendly way,
Until beckoned home at the close of day;
When out from the window it flew on high,
And hastened back to its home in the sky.
I followed the beautiful beam, at rest,
To a sea of light in the golden west;
It dropped to sleep on the dark blue sea,
And left me the sweetest memory.
I turned to my soul for calm relief,
Balm to my wound, a check to my grief—
When visions of glory shone from above,
Where the light is God, and God is love.

A TOAST.

HERE'S to the girl of gladness and beauty,
   Who's always alive to hope, love or duty;
Who fills up the cup and empties the bowl
To the choice of her heart, the pride of her soul.
Who's merry and happy with love, song and
        dance,
Pleased with the pleasure of life in a trance—
Sunshine and flowers make up her romance.

Here's a toast to the lass so kind, true and free,
Who quaffs off a cup to memory and me,
And wafts o'er the billow her sighs of regret
For hours that are gone and suns that are set.
One changeless as fate, who loves to the close
Her wandering hero, through strife and repose,
Fresh in her beauty as dew on the rose.

GOD IS NEAR.

GOD is near upon the ocean,
  God is near upon the land;
He is All, both rest and motion—
  We are only grains of sand.
Little mites upon life's billow,
  May-flies buzzing out the hour,
Dreams upon a fevered pillow,
  Dew-drops on a withered flower.
Only waiting for to-morrow,
  That has never come to man,
Here we live, in joy and sorrow,
  Chasing phantoms as we can.
Chasing pleasure, chasing greatness,
  Over tangled walks and waves,
But we learn the bitter lateness
  Just before we find our graves.
Hope is nigh, with fairy fingers,
  Tracing sunbeams on the way;
Magic memory ever lingers,
  Busy with the by-gone day.
Life and death are but the portals
  To a realm of endless rest;
God is working through his mortals;
  All in some way shall be blessed.

———⸎———

FORGETTING.

THE friends that I loved in December,
  And cherished so fondly in May,
Have long since forgot to remember,
  And vanished like dew-drops away.
In sunshine and power I was toasted
  And feasted by courtiers so kind;
And, oh! how the parasites boasted
  Of the wonderful traits of my mind!
But when the dark hour of my trouble
  Arose like a storm in the sky,
The vipers began to play double,
  And forgot the bright glance of my eye.

WAITING.

HOW well I remember, darling,
  In the beautiful long ago,
When we pledged our love with kisses,
  Down by the brooklet's flow,
  Where the shadows come and go.

Now I am broken-hearted;
  The light of my soul hath fled;
A weary pilgrim, waiting
  To join the ranks of the dead,
  And lay down my weary head.

Alone in the moonlight, watching
  At her grave, I lay me low,
While the winds go whistling by me,
  And my darling under the snow,
  Buried forever, joy with woe.

MATTIEVAN.

I'M dreaming of my darling, night and day;
  My life with her is one sweet, perfect plan;
Her bright eyes, like the sunshine of the May,
  Sparkle love, and whisper: " Mattievan."

Her voice comes in the midnight lone,
  And lingers at my pillow, but to scan
A heart that beats for one sweet girl—my own,
  My darling little sweetheart—Mattievan.

Just see her in the waltz, so light and free!
  A jewel on the breast of any man.
She may flirt with all the world but me—
  My own dear, little sweetheart—Mattievan.

MAZY.

SHE sleeps on the hill, near the crumbling mill,
  And my mind is nearly crazy
When I note the hours and the faded flowers
  Gone with the sun and the daisy.

Through the orchard, wild as a loving child,
  She sported long in the clover,
And the blossoms free, from the apple tree,
  She heaped on her pet dog, Rover.

The bees she chased, in her laughing haste,
  In the fields and nooks so sunny;
With roses red she decked her head,
  And life was sweet as honey.

How cruel years, with hopes and fears,
  Have furrowed my heart and features!
With autumn's blow and winter's snow
  Comes trouble to earthly creatures.

A few more years, and a few more tears,
  Will waft me away to Mazy,
And I shall sleep where the willows weep,
  On the hill, by the mill, 'neath the daisy.

THE FIRST KISS.

IN the month of November, the day I remember,
  Now gazing o'er mountain and plain,
My heart travels back to that flowery track,
  And lives in the light of her eyes once again.

How glorious and bright were the stars of the night
  With the whip-poor-will tuning his song,
When our hearts were so true, and I lov'd only you
  In that multitude rushing along.

The day never comes, and the night never goes,
　But I sigh for the woodland and stream
Where we sat in the moonlight, living in love
　In that bright, sunny land, like a dream.

Many years have gone by, still I sadden and sigh
　For the musical strains of the past;
My heart fondly turns to incense, and burns
　On the altar of love to the last.

One by one we step out to that land full of doubt,
　Where hope only leads up the way
To a realm of bliss, where an angelic kiss
　Bids us welcome to eternal day.

The lips of an angel can never impart
　A pleasure so pure and so true
As I felt in my soul and my fluttering heart,
　In the moonlight, when first I kissed you.

MY LITTLE ROBINS.

THE twilight deepens in the rosy west,
　My truant robins seek their downy nest;
All day long their little feet have wandered,
And I upon their sport have fondly pondered,
And set my soul upon the years in view
When baby robins shall their love renew;
When little darlings from the parent home
Will spread their wings in other climes to roam,
And leave me in the twilight sad and lone,
To muse upon the beauties once mine own.
Will all the birdies that I nursed and dandled
Think of mother dear who fondly handled
The little wings and tired, tiny feet
That snuggled at my breast, so pure and sweet?
And will the winter, with its chilling snow,
Bring back no sunbeams to my clouded woe?
Or must I look beyond the grass-grown tomb,
To see my sweet ones in celestial bloom?

MASONIC BRIGHT LIGHT.

H ERE'S the Templar Knights from the East and the West,
   Children, children, won't you follow me?
From the North and the South we all march abreast,
   Halle, halle, halle, hallelujah!
No more do we march as the Gray or the Blue,
   Children, children, won't you follow me?
But our plumes are white, and our hearts are true,
   Halle, halle, halle, hallelujah!

CHORUS.

In the morning, in the morning, by the bright light,
When Gabriel blows his trumpet in the morning.

As a warrior band we march to the fight,
   Children, children, won't you follow me?
Our swords shall flash in the cause of the right,
   Halle, halle, halle, hallelujah!
The poor and the weak we are pledged to protect,
   Children, children, won't you follow me?
We are Christian men, without any sect,
   Halle, halle, halle, hallelujah!

CHORUS.

Then up with the Cross, and a cheer for the Crown!
   Children, children, won't you follow me?
The Crescent of the Pagan is almost down,
   Halle, halle, halle, hallelujah!
Then hurrah for the girl we all love best!
   Children, children, won't you follow me?
From the North, the South, the East and the West,
   Halle, halle, halle, hallelujah!

CHORUS.

TOLL THE BELL.

TOLL the bell slowly, meekly and lowly,
  There comes an inanimate clod,
Sleeping forever beyond the dark river—
  A mortal has gone to his God.

Toll the bell faintly; echoes so saintly
  Are sounding o'er river and lea,
Telling the living all need forgiving
  Before God and eternity.

Toll the bell lightly, daily and nightly,
  A spirit is watching for thee;
One that has loved us, one that has proved us—
  Some fond soul who loved you and me.

Toll the bell sadly; heart-broken, madly,
  We kiss the cold lips of the dead;
With hope, love and tears, run back o'er the years,
  To pluck out some cruel word said.

MY WAR-HORSE, "BOB."

IN MEMORY OF COL. CHAS. D. PENNYBACKER'S PET.

FAREWELL, farewell. my beautiful bay!
  Sadly I sigh for your loss to-day;
My thoughts go back to the long ago,
Where we tramped and fought with the deadly foe

Of all the friends that I ever knew,
None served me so kind, so brave and true.
Ah! how shall I tune this nameless lay
In memory of my dear old bay?

No bugle note shall ever again
Call thee to muster on hill or plain;
Where passion and pelf cause men to bleed,
No more shall I ride my gallant steed.

In the days of war, when blood flowed free,
We campaigned together, you and me;
Now who can blame me to grieve and sob
For losing my friend, my war-horse, " Bob."

Brave comrades have fallen by my side;
In the battle ranks they fought and died;
Yet, even these heroes, young or gray,
Were not more prized than my noble bay.

OCEAN MEMORIES.

YEARS have gone by since we met at the sea,
The kiss that you gave, love, lingers with me;
Thrills in my heart like an angelic tune,
Perfume distilled from the roses of June,
Silvery light from the face of the moon.

Lulled to repose by moan of the ocean,
Clasped in a thrill of blissful emotion,
Sunlight and starlight we catch but a gleam;
The world is afloat, we live in a dream,
And things are not, surely, all that they seem.

Your secret and gem I still fondly keep
So close to my heart, awake or asleep;
The world has no treasure dearer to me;
Unpurchased, unsought, love without fee,
Was that soul-thrilling gift down by the sea.

Absent and lonely, my soul flies to thee,
Back to the shore of that sweet summer sea—
A land where the vine and the orange both bloom,
And silver and gold its mountains entomb—
A paradise planted, rich with perfume.

Sadly I sigh for your living embrace,
Fancy awakens the light of your face;
Out through the mists of yon echoless shore
Angels are calling my lost, loved Lacore;
Sighing, I pine for your love evermore.

WHEN I AM DEAD.

WHEN I am dead, let no vain pomp display
A surface sorrow o'er my pulseless clay;
But all the dear old friends I loved in life
Can shed a tear, console my child and wife.

When I am dead, let strangers pass me by,
Nor ask a reason for the how or why
That brought my wandering life to praise or shame,
Or marked me for the fading flowers of fame.

When I am dead, the vile assassin tongue
Will try and banish all the lies it flung,
And make amends for all its cruel wrong,
In fulsome prose and eulogistic song.

When I am gone, some sage for self-renown
May urn my ashes in his native town;
And give, when I am cold and lost and dead,
A marble slab where once I needed bread.

When I am dead, what matters to the crowd?
The world will rattle on as long and loud,
And each one in the game of life will plod
The field to glory and the way to God.

THE DAYS ARE GROWING SHORTER.

THE days are growing shorter every hour,
And all the sweets of life are turning sour
The morning dawns to me without a plan,
And everything seems happy but frail man.

The friends I knew and loved in former years
Have vanished like the sunshine through my tears :
They fill my soul with thoughts of long ago,
And memory brings me only bitter woe.

Sweet beauties that I cherished in their bloom
Went quickly to the cold and silent tomb,
And friends that were the dearest unto me
Are lost beneath the moaning weary sea.

The evening star is beaming soft and lone,
The forest trees are bending with a groan,
And in my heart there springs a nameless grief;
The grave alone must bring its sure relief.

The midnight hour approaches, sad and still,
Wild phantoms come and go against my will;
Yet, through the fearful gloom methinks I see
A vista reaching to eternity.

OAK HILL.

GRAND home of the dead! I mourn as I tread
  Near the forms that crumble below;
How sad and how still the graves at Oak Hill,
  In the quiet evening glow.

Here's an old, old stone, moss-grown and alone,
  Where Time has left not a trace
Of the name it bore in the days of yore,
  When the body ceased its race.

Vain, vain is the thought; no man ever bought
  Exemption from final decay;
To live and to rot, and then be forgot—
  The fate of the quick of to-day.

THE ATTORNEY-AT-LAW.

AN attorney-at-law lately put up his shingle,
And had scarcely enough of the specie to jingle;
He said to himself: " I shall work long and late
To find a rich will or a bankrupt estate.

So he sat in his office and puffed, day by day,
Forming rings of blue smoke, that floated away,
While with Parsons and Kent, and Blackstone and Chitty,
He appeared to his neighbors so wise and so witty.

At length a rich miller, by name Calvin Brown,
In search of a lawyer, came into the town,
And spying a smoker, he thought he would pin him,
And marched up the stairs to the office of Skin'em.

"Good morning," said Brown, to the lord of the laws;
" I 've come to consult for the good of my cause."
" Be seated," said Skin'em; " I know you'll be gainer,
But first, I require, now, a thousand retainer."

Brown stared in surprise at this heavy demand,
And said it was more than he felt he could stand;
But the " limb of the law" a glance at him flings,
He puffed his cigar, and went on making rings.

The miller, at last, like the fly in the fable,
Was caught in the web; where, entirely unable
To cope with the spider that bled him so neatly,
He gave up the ghost, and passed off completetly.
*   *   *   *   *   *
Skin'em is now the sole administrator;
And you may be sure that, sooner or later,
The widow and orphans of one Calvin Brown
Are bereft of a home, and put on the town.

Then Skin'em will shine as a brave lady-killer
On plunder he filched from the honest old miller,
And the people will gaze on his rich turn-out,
And say to themselves: " How did this come about?"

Poor dupes! you are fooled by the gauze and the glitter;
You begin with the sweet, and end with the bitter;
And fellows like Skin'em lay ever in wait
To pounce on the bones of a crumbling estate.

Thus the law, you must know, is made for the rich,
And the poor, as of old, are left in the ditch;
No matter what rights you may have to maintain,
You'll lose in the end, should you dare to "retain."

Now take my advice, and keep out of the law;
For once in the toils of its ravenous maw,
You are sure to be plucked, without mercy or grace,
And come out the last at the end of the race.

UNKNOWN.

I GAZED on the babe at its mother's breast,
And asked for the secret of life and rest;
It turned with a smile that was sad and lone,
And murmured in dreaming: "Unknown, unknown."

I challenged the youth so bold and so brave,
To tell me the tale of the lonely grave;
But he sung of pleasure, in musical tone,
And his echoing voice replied "Unknown, unknown."

Then I questioned the gray-haired man of years,
Whose face was furrowed with thought and tears;
And he paused in his race, to simply groan,
The soul-chilling words: "Unknown, unknown."

I asked the lover, the poet, and sage—
In every clime and every age—
To tell me the truth, and candidly own
If, after death, it's all unknown, unknown.

I soared like the lark to the boundless sky,
Sighed in my soul for the how and the why;

The angels were singing, and just had flown ;
I heard but the echo : " Unknown, unknown."

I read in the hills, and saw in the rocks,
A lesson that told of the earthquake shocks ;
I gazed at the stars, from a mountain cone, ·
But they only answered : " Unknown, unknown."

Thus am I tortured by fear and by doubts
In tracing the way, where so many routes
Are ever in view, but quickly are flown,
And all that I know is : " Unknown, unknown."

At last I determined to surely find
All hope and all bliss in my mystic mind ;
But just as sweet peace came to soothe me alone,
The wild witch of doubt shrieked : " Unknown ! unknown !

The sun and the moon, the winds and the wave,
May perish in time, and sink to the grave ;
The temples of earth shall fade, stone by stone,
And mortals still wail out : " Unknown, unknown."

The millions of earth that battle to-day
Are but a handful to those passed away ;
The future is countless ; men from each zone
Shall flourish and die in the far-off Unknown.

We come like the dew-drops, and go like the mist,
As frail as a leaf by autumn winds kissed ;
Fading away like the roses of June,
Wishing and waiting to meet the Unknown.

Nature, oh ! Nature, thy God I adore ;
There's light in thy realm—I ask for no more ,
From the seed to the fruit all things are grown,·
Yet, while we know this, the cause is unknown.

When matter and mind are perished and lost,
And all that we see into chaos is tossed,
From nothing to nothing we pass out alone,
Like a flash, or an echo—" Unknown, unknown."

www.ingramcontent.com/pod-product-compliance
Lightning Source LLC
Chambersburg PA
CBHW031039120726

47905CB00007B/2244

9 783337 055134